# ONLY PROTECTOR ALPHAS

## REBEL WEREWOLVES BOOK THREE

## ROSEMARY A. JOHNS

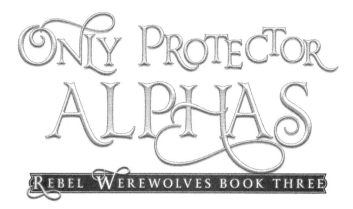

# ONLY PROTECTOR ALPHAS

## REBEL WEREWOLVES BOOK THREE

USA TODAY BESTSELLING AUTHOR

# ROSEMARY A JOHNS

ONLY PROTECTOR ALPHAS

REBEL WEREWOLVES BOOK THREE

**I was gifted three wickedly handsome wolf princes…**

…but now I'm the wolves' prisoner.

I'm Crimson Tide. For centuries, witches have been at war with werewolves. As a kid, mom coached me that I was a Charmer with the badass magical power to control the scorching hot shifters.

Except, what if controlling them makes me the bad guy? How do I save my own witchy ass, as well as Wolf Kingdom, when I'm trapped in a wild land of fanatics and secrets?

To survive in the Kingdom of the Alphas, I must:

**Rule #1 Never be tempted by the cursed protection of an Alpha**

My pack hold dark and dangerous pasts, but I'm still driven to protect the gorgeous shifters, angels, mages, and gods who are mine.

Am I right to trust that they'll protect me back? Or will loving the wolves get me killed?

Either way, I'll fight for the wolves' freedom and create a new legacy for the name Crimson Tide…

…or like the Charmers before me, I'll become my princes' worst nightmare.

ONLY PROTECTOR ALPHAS: REBEL WEREWOLVES BOOK
THREE © copyright 2020 Rosemary A Johns
www.rosemaryajohns.com

Fantasy Rebel Limited

# CONTENTS

## REBEL ANGELS - COMPLETE SERIES

**COMPLETE SERIES BOX SET: BOOKS 1-5**
**VAMPIRE HUNTRESS**
**VAMPIRE PRINCESS**
**VAMPIRE DEVIL**
**VAMPIRE MAGE**
**VAMPIRE GOD**
**VAMPIRE SECRET: REBELS AND RENEGADES**

## REBEL VAMPIRES - COMPLETE SERIES

**COMPLETE SERIES BOX SET BOOKS 1-3**
**BLOOD DRAGONS**
**BLOOD SHACKLES**
**BLOOD RENEGADES**

**STANDALONE NOVELLA - BLOOD GODS**

**REBEL WEREWOLVES - COMPLETE SERIES**

**ONLY PERFECT OMEGAS**
**ONLY PRETTY BETAS**
**ONLY PROTECTOR ALPHAS**

**REBEL ACADEMY**

**CRAVE**

**REBEL: HOUSE OF FAE - COMPLETE**

***AUDIO BOOKS***

## CHAPTER 1

B ehind the moonshine speared alcove that divided guests from guards, prowled beasts with beautiful faces.

*Only Protector Alphas*, promised the neon sign.

If I hadn't known better, I'd have thought that I was shifting on my knees on a satin cushion at a midnight feast in a barracks, except for the fact that it was an all-female army of werewolves, and as a witch, I was the enemy.

*Plus, boy did I know better.*

My nose wrinkled against the earthy scent, even as I turned my face up to catch the breeze from the open roof of the Crescent Base. The moon shone down on the crescent-shaped table with its bank of computers that monitored the Omegas, mountain of ice-cream and sprinkles, and war plans that had become mixed together, as the Alphas partied.

How in the witching heavens had it only been a day since I'd been trapped underground in the Kingdom of the Gods? When shifters fed from moonlight, how did they bear to be buried in the kingdom below?

The Alpha warriors gleamed; the moonbeams danced across their skin. The light lit up the ivory walls like bared fangs and the glass wall that showed out to the murk of the River Thames, which was the same river my great-grandmother — *the Crimson Terror* — like a twisted Pied Piper had drowned the wolves' ancestors in, after the witches had won the Wolf War.

*Hey, that didn't make me squirm with guilt at all.*

My red shadows twitched, caressing each other in comfort, but they'd been subdued since Princess Vala had Wolf Bitten me. She'd threatened that a *crimson tide of blood* was coming, then she'd started the slaughter with my throat.

My parents had been devoured by werewolves. *Was being bitten and allowed to live even worse?*

I reached up to the bite, wincing as I traced it. Unlike Moon, I didn't get happy tingles at the touch, only a searing pain that shuddered through my shadows.

Vala had messed with my wolf side, and even if the covens would hex me for admitting it, I'd found myself growling enough times to know that a Wolf Charmer was connected to her wolf Charms in a complex way.

Honestly, that freaked me out because becoming a wolf had been one of my greatest fears since Aquilo's bullying twin sister, Lux, had pretended to transform me into one as a kid.

*But that had only been a trick, right?*

First, an Alpha had bitten me, and then I'd been left kneeling in the Crescent Base in the corner (the one that Vala had told me was reserved for badly behaved Omegas), whilst the Crescent gang of assholes danced and screwed.

Although, the Alphas had also petted and cooed over me like I was on my Honeymoon. I shuddered because the only thought worse than playing the bride to Vala was any of my Charms playing the husband. My shadows quivered in distress that I'd been separated from my pack of wolves, angels, and gods.

*Was it weird if I missed the days when I could just stuff them into something and at least know where they were?*

Then I groaned, as a rubber hit me between the eyes, bouncing into my lap.

*Hey, now I was even being attacked by falling condoms.*

Unless, you know, it was a divine sign that I'd get sexy times today…?

I *eeped*, as all of a sudden, the rubber jumped off my lap, spinning into the air with the grace of a ballet dancer, before hopping with a cheeky wriggle of its latex tail into the hand of a cute man with a mop of dark hair, a scarred eyebrow, and soft eyes.

*He was a mage?*

Rubber Mage shot me a sheepish grin. "Sorry, Omega Witch. My magic becomes volatile when I'm…" He gestured at the hard length tenting his pearly white trousers.

I flushed. "Firstly, I'm not an Omega Witch, whatever on a mage's blue balls that truly is, and secondly, that's overshare."

Rubber Mage chuckled. "Whatever you say, *Omega Witch,* and I won't have blue balls for long."

I gritted my teeth, as my shadows thrashed. Then Rubber Mage wandered back to his Alpha, who sprawled on an armchair in front of the table. He straddled her lap, dipping to kiss at her neck. He didn't look like a prisoner, even though as a mage he must've been *thrown to the wolves* by his own witch family for being a male with magic. Yet as the Alpha quivered underneath him, there was no doubt that he was seriously taking charge…*and willing.*

Then gentle hands clasped around my waist, pulling me around tentatively, as if expecting to be rejected.

Aquilo's cool gaze met mine. "What if I tell you that *my* magic becomes volatile, when you stare at some other mage's—"

"Monster dick?" I smirked, curling closer to Aquilo and sniffing his reassuring scent of fresh linen.

Aquilo was pale and beautiful beneath the moonlight. His black shirt hung open, and I was desperate to touch the dip of his collarbones, but I hadn't saved him from his family and Vala to *use* him as well.

I loved him, but I'd never rush him.

Aquilo appeared to catch my thought, and his gaze became steely. "Do you believe me to be breakable?"

His hold firmed on my waist, as he rested his forehead against mine. He'd been left in the corner with me, since we both belonged to the princess now.

*And how much did that thought freak me out?*

Aquilo's eyes froze to crushed ice, and heat shot through me at the danger. His magic wound around me in a whirlwind that whipped my red-and-black ballgown into waves. When my fingertips pressed over the hollow of his throat, where the blood pendant had once rested and seared his skin to bind his magic, his gaze became fragile.

"I asked you to marry me," I whispered; my lips touched his on each word. "I seriously don't want any other mage."

"As a male within a witch's household, I learned to *play* broken, until I could show my teeth." I startled, remembering the way that Aquilo had led the vampire army to win the battle against Stella and the witches. *How long had he known the vampire Duke Dual?* "Hide your fangs now, so that when you bare them, you may savage kingdoms."

My pulse pounded, as my shadows rose up, shadowing the room into a crimson sea.

Mischief — Archduke, Seraphim god, and *mage* — would love Aquilo. Were all mages snarky, snooty, and wickedly hot when they got with the whole *savaging kingdom* talk?

"Someone put on their godly pants today." I smiled. "Mischief is a royal prick but his glittery ass said the same thing. Trust me, you'll like him."

"Do you wish to talk of royal pricks, or allow me to kiss you now?" Aquilo drawled.

My skin was suddenly too hot. I wet my lips. "Honestly, that's not even a choice. Willing and seriously enthusiastic for all kissing action."

Aquilo's white-blond hair fell across my eyes, as he feathered a kiss to my lips, jaw, and then down my neck. He glanced up at me questioningly, and I nodded. Then he licked across Vala's bite.

*Finally those happy tingles showed up.*

I grasped Aquilo's wrist with the blood bracelet that connected us, licking across its throbbing edges to match his licks across my own bite. Aquilo keened; his dick in his jeans hardened against my leg.

I rested my teeth against his wrist. *I craved to bite...*

Aquilo's eyes narrowed in confusion. Then he swallowed, before pressing his wrist harder against my teeth like he could break his own skin in sacrifice.

"Savage, remember?" He met my gaze like it was a

challenge. "Or do you wish to sever our engagement, as my mother claimed when she held me apart from you, but merely fear causing my death…?"

I bit through the blood bracelet like I could take away its control and instead, protect Aquilo and all my pack. I marked him to erase his mom's hateful words that made him feel like nothing but unwanted property.

I *wanted* him, and he was mine.

I'd never thought myself a possessive dickhead before I'd returned to England, but becoming a Wolf Charmer and Wolf Witch turned you into one, who knew?

The tangy blood thrummed through me.

*Hey, it looked like I did have a biting kink.*

Aquilo howled and arched. His eyelashes fluttered, whilst his fingers straightened, before curling into fists. Then his eyes rolled back, and he collapsed as he came in his pants.

I blushed, and the Alphas cheered. Rubber Mage winked like I'd passed the initiation into their pack.

Why were there so many mages here with the Crescents? Had they all been thrown to the wolves? Yet they weren't cowering in terror. Unless, you know, scoffing ice-cream, transforming cups by magic into dancing unicorns for kicks, and cuddling Alphas were signs of fear that I'd never been taught by my non-magical uncle.

The mages appeared to be more like lovers than prisoners or slaves.

I brushed the hair off Aquilo's forehead; he'd always been a pretty, elitist asshole but now he was *my* pretty, elitist asshole. He was also a virgin. Vala had attempted to steal his first experiences, but I'd create new ones for him.

Vala and these Alphas thought that they were protecting the Omegas and Wolf Kingdom, and honestly, with their moonlight, screwing, and orgy of ice-cream, they were more alive than Queen Banan with her shrines and stuffed Omegas in the Museum of Death.

Vala hadn't been dicking around, however, with her warning about the *crimson tide of blood*. If I had to play the Omega to these Alphas to stop that happening, save both witches and wolves, and atone for my ancestors' genocide then I would, even if my shadows seethed at the thought.

All I craved was my art gallery back in America, along with a honey lavender latte (like drinking summer), and a glazed donut. But failing that, I'd take a blissed out Aquilo. I sighed, chasing after the last taste of him on my tongue.

Brain, stop the naughty images about how *that* sounded.

Aquilo blinked awake. His pale blue eyes were

unusually soft and fuzzy, as he stared up at me like *I* was the moon.

"Hey, Mr Just Had the Best Orgasm of His Life." I stroked down his cheek.

"Hey, Miss Bighead…although not entirely inaccurate. Did you have to make me sticky?"

"Dude, ungrateful," I pouted.

Aquilo raised his wrist, and I couldn't find it in me to even wince at the imprints of my teeth marking the blood bracelet. When I turned my head and caught the bite with a gentle kiss, he gasped. "Perhaps, I should say: Miss Bitey."

I snorted. "*Mrs* Bitey." My heart thudded hard in my chest, as I leaned in to catch his lush lips with mine.

Then my stomach growled, and I pinked.

How could I be romantic when I hadn't eaten since… *How long had it been now?*

Aquilo shot me a haughty grin. Then his stomach rumbled even louder than mine had. He cringed, whilst my shadows burst out at my snicker, tickling Aquilo's ribs. He spluttered with laugher, wriggling away from me towards the edge of the alcove like a squirming kitten.

"Mrs Bitey," he hissed between giggles, "I said *savage*, not *tickle*."

"*Aw*, do you want me to kiss it better?" I dived over him, kissing down his neck, whilst my shadows wrapped around him in tickling waves.

I'd never seen Aquilo like this before: free and unreserved. *Was he like this with anyone else?*

Aquilo and I had both been raised as magical kids, who'd had to hide who we truly were. If he hadn't been forced by his sister to bully me, could we have been friends?

*Had Aquilo been what I'd spent my life missing, as much as my Charms?*

I squeaked, as Aquilo sent a ripple of wind in retaliation across my skin. I shivered. His magic caressed me, blowing my hair into the air behind me, which should've made me want to kick his ass for frizzing my curls, yet the touch was intimate and loving like he was sharing his true self and magic with me.

*It was freaking beautiful.*

Was this the first time that he'd ever dared play with his magic like this?

Aquilo's smile was gentle, as his breeze curled around my shadows, hugging me closer.

"I'd say that I was sorry to interrupt your sexy times, but as the Prince of the Alphas, I hold to this quaint tradition of not lying." Emperor leaned over the alcove, peering at Aquilo and me with an amused twitch of his lips.

I startled, gazing up at the third of my Charms, who rested with casual elegance scrutinizing me, as if he didn't belong in my Omega naughty corner.

In his golden suit and robes, Emperor was a

gorgeous butterfly in the midst of this Alpha party. Even though he was from a rival wolf kingdom, he'd never looked so regal or undaunted.

"Screw tradition." I launched myself up, snatching Emperor by his silky collar and hauling him into the alcove.

When I pulled him down amongst the cushions, hugging him as tightly as I would've done Moon who was the King of Cuddles, Emperor held onto me with equal desperation.

I hated being separated from my Charms, who I'd Claimed and Wolf Bitten. They were mine, just as I was theirs. I hadn't understood pack before, but now I knew that it meant to *protect*. Not knowing what'd happened to them was a torture worse than radio show banter or some asshole scrolling through your phone's photos without asking.

I stroked over Emperor's muscled back; his strength was reassuring. "How's my *good* wolf?" I whispered.

Emperor shuddered. "Damning you on hide and fangs for making me hard in these tight pants again."

I snickered. "You're lucky that I'm only making you hard."

Emperor raised his eyebrow, whilst pink spread down Aquilo's cheeks and neck. I didn't miss how Emperor clasped Aquilo's hand, and Aquilo squeezed his fingers.

"She tried the same trick on me, but I had to

consider that my suit is dry clean only." His gaze swept over Aquilo's pants. "It appears that you have no such worries."

I rapped his shoulder. "I take it that you didn't drop by just to comment on how practical our clothes are to launder…?"

"Vala's charming gang, the Crescents, decided that I would be of use to them as an entertainer." Emperor tossed his golden hair, before sighing. "It appears that my reputation precedes me."

I couldn't stop the growl. "No one's using you like a party favor again. You have a choice now, and I thought that I'd kind of made it clear that I'm big on consent." My gaze swung to Aquilo, who cringed. "That means you too, Gandalf the early years."

"You're not much of an Oxford witch, Sabrina," Aquilo drawled. "Where's the putting us in our place? Why would you give up your control?"

Suddenly, both their gazes were too intense and searching; I shifted.

Moon had only survived as the magical Moon Child because I'd been able to make our bond one of equals, and I craved for my pack to have equality, even if I was the leader. Maybe it was because I'd been raised amongst the non-magical in America, or perhaps, I'd always have been a rebel.

"Because I love you," I replied, softly.

*Aquilo's gasp was worth it. Emperor simply smirked.*

Then Emperor pressed his lips to the top of my head. I closed my eyes, losing myself in his scent of honey dripping over liquorice. Yet the sharpness of the liquorice was much stronger than it'd been before.

*Was he losing control of his Alpha side?* What would happen if the truth of Emperor's nature was discovered in this Kingdom of Gods? Would he be executed?

My eyes snapped open in alarm.

"The Alphas merely wish me to play the piano for them," Emperor's mouth curved against my head on each laughing word.

*Thank Hecate…*

I already knew that my second Charm, Amadeus, was being punished in the Isolation Room. But what about my first Charm, the Prince of the Wilds?

"Moon's with you, right?" I struggled to stand, but Emperor yanked me down.

"He's in the Pleasure Pool." Emperor grimaced. "I don't imagine that it refers to Jacuzzis and fun water slides. I wish that I could rescue him from the appalling name alone."

Okay, so it was a name plucked out of an incubus' dream, but *I* still desired the pleasure of Moon's angelic eyes and sinful body. I couldn't imagine a better named pool for him, unless it was the Lake of Defiant Rebels or The Snuggling Tree.

Emperor's eyes narrowed like he'd caught my

thought. In turn, I widened my own eyes in pretend innocence.

"I don't trust the Alphas here," Emperor explained. *Hey, I never said that I could pull off the innocent act.* "The danger is greater than I'd imagined. Some of the Alphas in my own kingdom, who I grew up with, at least strive to treat Omegas as more than objects to hide in shrines. These ones, however, are *broken*."

I glanced out at the shimmering sea of Alphas with their mage lovers. "Huh, so you truly can screw too much…?"

Emperor traced over the bite on my neck, and I winced. "How sweet that you believe them *safe*. They train to protect their Omegas but they never can because of witches—"

"Like me…?" My voice hardened. "Harsh."

Emperor arched his brow. "But entirely fair. Training but failing to protect the Omegas…for decades…has damaged these Alphas." He glanced between Aquilo and me before hissing, "Can't you see that this room is set up for war?"

I scanned the computer screens and table, which although it was littered with ice-cream and chocolate sauce, also had what looked like one badass chess game going on. Yet it could just as easily be…*a war plan.*

Emperor had been trained as a diplomat, and my aunt had called wolves *princes in diplomacy.* I needed Emperor for his skills now.

Aquilo settled back into the cushions, unraveling an ivory thread. "Who do they believe that they're fighting and how could they win?"

Emperor studied Aquilo with such tenderness that it made my heart ache. I loved that my Charms had accepted my fiancé as pack, even though he was a mage from the House of Blood. Unlike these assholes in the Kingdom of the Gods who blamed Aquilo for his family's crimes, my wolves accepted him for who he was, just like they accepted *me*.

"War with fanatics is rarely about winning as you or I would consider it. They believe themselves already to be *dead*. What would someone be prepared to do who believed themselves no longer alive?" When I shuddered, Emperor rubbed his nose against mine. "A trick that I learned in my days as my mother's entertainer: everybody talks in front of you. The Alphas bringing me here spoke of a delegation from all three kingdoms in two days to discuss the events in the covens and *you…*"

*Two days…?*

My shadows rose and fell in uneasy waves. How was I meant to stop what'd been planned maybe since the end of the Wolf War itself a hundred years ago…?

The one thing I knew was that as a Wolf Witch I was stronger with my pack around me. Was that why Vala had turned me into a Bitten and separated me from them?

I wet my dry lips. "Don't I feel special."

Emperor's teeth lengthened, as his claws bit into my shoulders. "As *special* as a reason to start a war. If we don't discover what's awaiting my kingdom and Moon's within two days—"

"Enough gossiping, Omega." Rubber Mage gazed down at me, raising his scarred eyebrow, and I stiffened. He crooked his finger at Emperor, and Emperor stiffly rose to his feet, brushing off his suit and straightening his robes. "We want a sing-along."

Emperor ducked his head, but winked at me. Then he strode to the piano in the far corner of the room. He sat on the stool with a flourish, before pounding on the keys in a wild rendition of "Sweet Transvestite" from the *Rocky Horror Show*.

I blinked. *Okay, I hadn't been expecting that.*

Aquilo chuckled as he crawled closer. "Hidden depths in that wolf, I believe."

"Trust me, he's not hiding." I studied Emperor; he was a ray of sunlight in the night.

The Alphas laughed and joked, jostling around Emperor like he was already their favorite Omega. When they joined in the chorus, Emperor was as comfortable with them as old friends. Perhaps, he truly had spent time around Alphas in his own kingdom, and not ones who'd wanted to step on him like the Alphas in Moon's Kingdom of the Wilds.

I'd imagined that the Kingdom of the Alphas would be filled with *psychopathic elitists* like Stella had told me, but maybe they also dressed up in top hats and suspenders, whilst dancing to "The Time Warp".

My cousins had held "Rocky Horror Picture Show" parties that'd been legendary in East Hampton. Mainly because that wasn't the kind of thing that the billionaire yachting set attended. Unless, you know, they *did*, as long as they wore masks.

Vala's Crescents were no older than my Charms. *Did they hate their role as much as the princes hated theirs?*

Seizing the distraction, I nudged Aquilo's shoulder, before edging out of the alcove on my hands and knees. Aquilo followed at my heels. Who'd notice the two bad Omegas, when they had the star of the show performing?

If I only had two days to discover Vala's plans for war, then I needed the power of my Charms united. *I had to rescue Moon.* I crawled towards the door because if the Alphas were in here and *entertained*, then I had the best chance to reach the Pleasure Pool.

*Crack* — I yelped as my head smacked into something bony.

I reached out to slide my hands up the surprisingly smooth column, which was blocking my escape.

"Look up," Aquilo hissed.

*When did anything good come of following that order?*

When I raised my gaze, I met Vala's stormy eyes. Her hair was twisted in two coils on her head like twin moons, and her thick eyeliner was surrounded by glitter: an asshole playing at siren. My hands were clamped around her thighs through the slit in her dress.

Huh, so it was possible to feel embarrassed, even after being forcibly Wolf Bitten.

I stared at my hands, and so did Vala. I pulled them away like a retreating army. Then I gasped, as the bite on my neck seared at her displeasure. I doubled over, clasping my fingers over it, as if I could pretend that I wasn't kneeling at the feet of my enemy, whilst she burned her hatred through her bite.

My great-grandmother had murdered wolves, just as wolves had murdered my parents. Now I was at the mercy of the first werewolf princess to dare transform a Wolf Charmer into a Bitten, and the only one holding back the crimson shadows from crashing out of me in a deadly tidal wave to seek vengeance on the other Alphas was *me*.

It took strength to submit, as much as to conquer.

Yet what if Vala didn't crave submission. Instead, she sought to spark *my* powers and the *crimson tide* of blood.

## CHAPTER 2

The moon bled through the open roof of the Crescent Base across walls that were lit in neon with the gang's propaganda: **We Are the Dead**, looped with, **Only Protector Alphas**.

I scrunched my nose against the fat droplets of summer rain that drizzled down my neck, cooling the burning bite. My shadows seethed. When I pulled my hand away from my throat, Aquilo traced down the edges of the bite, and the pain transformed to pleasure. I leaned back against him, and his hair feathered across my cheek, as he leaned forward, clasping me to his chest.

Slowly, my shadows calmed, whispering around Aquilo in teasing kisses.

I wasn't a total witchy dick: I knew that I wasn't

safe. *But cauldron's and broomsticks, it was easy to pretend when I was caught in Aquilo's arms.*

Vala tapped her shoe. "Wow, on my fangs, I won the bet. You've already attempted to escape from the Omega Corner. What…? Did I not supply enough cushions for the brat witch? Do you prefer wolf pelts to satin?"

*Don't think of the white wolf fur on mom's bed… It's gone now…the whole House of Silver…gone…*

My shoulders hunched. *Yep, that was me wrecked in a single shot.*

Still, my uncle had always taught that you should never show weakness to competitors.

I clenched my jaw. "We're just out for a walk, right?"

Vala snorted. "I'm not loving the witching *lies*. Naughty, naughty, Omega."

I winced. If Vala wanted to seriously treat me like a wolf, then she'd get the wolf method of distraction.

I sank my teeth into her ankle.

Vala howled, shaking her leg to try and dislodge me. I gagged on the taste of her blood, which was as foul as Aquilo's had been delicious. My red sizzled in equal disgust at her taste; the bond itself burned.

Yet Vala didn't swipe me with her claws or savage me back. Was it because she'd bitten me? Had she ended up biting herself in the ass by making me untouchable?

Did she now have the duty to protect her own enemy?

*That was what I called karma.*

"By the light of the moon," Vala chanted through gritted teeth, "I am dead, we are dead, and shall remain now and always dead."

Instantly, the piano and singing cut off.

"We are the dead," the Alphas sang back in disturbing monotone.

*Honestly, I'd preferred their version of "Sweet Transvestite."*

"Unhand me," Emperor snarled.

When I heard a scuffle and *bang*, I immediately pulled my teeth out of Vala's ankle with a satisfying final twist, before leaping up along with Aquilo.

Emperor had been pulled away from the piano. The stool had been knocked over, whilst Emperor was now bent over the crescent-shaped table with his arms pulled behind his back by Rubber Mage. Yet I could tell that it wasn't being done with the same roughness that I'd once witnessed an Alpha treat Emperor in Wild Hall.

Bullies I understood, and Vala was the wannabe war leader with her gang.

The charity case from England, I'd been bullied throughout High School, and I'd fantasized about how I'd take down the leaders of the snobby gangs. If you could make their followers laugh at them, it took away their mystery and power.

I hadn't been able to do it in America, of course. *I'd* have been the one laughed at or gutted if I'd tried. But now I had powers, pack, and the drive to protect *all* the wolves and not simply survive.

*On a witch's tit, I hoped that it was enough.*

When Rubber Mage slammed Emperor against the table again as if for emphasis and the unusual looking chess pieces trembled, Vala growled.

"On fear of silver, be careful!" Vala slunk to the table, steadying the pieces.

When Aquilo caught my eye with a grin, I knew that he understood the game of Take Down Vala.

Okay, so I wouldn't use my shadows to control and conquer but that was *my choice*, and I still had other skills. It didn't mean that I had to take the wolves' brutality.

My shadows thrummed with joy, as Aquilo and I strolled either side of Vala.

Wind *whooshed* around Aquilo like he was the eye of the storm. His hair whipped across his ice-blue eyes.

I cocked my head, studying the board. This wasn't chess or a fantasy war game: *it was battle plans.* Who was Vala intending to conquer?

"A black hat to represent a witch, seriously?" I *tutted.* "I resent the witchaphobia."

Vala clacked her golden claws against the table. "What's that? Fear of witches?"

Aquilo leaned over the board. "Then what's fear of mages?"

A breeze shot from the tips of his fingers, sweeping the pieces flying like the wolves who my great-grand-mother had controlled in the Wolf War. The mages gaped at him in admiration.

Rubber Mage let go of Emperor as he smothered his laugh in his palm.

"*Oops*." Aquilo ran his hand through his hair with affected boredom, "My mother always did say that I was deplorably clumsy."

Vala yowled in outrage, raising her claws to swipe across Aquilo's cheek. My pulse pounded at the danger to my brave fiancé (and boy, did it make me hot to see him standing up to the Alpha who'd humiliated him in the Museum of Death). I blocked her, snatching a bottle off the table and squeezing.

Chocolate sauce squirted over Vala's shocked face. It dripped down her cheeks and tangled in her hair, transforming her into a chocolate monster.

It was almost as satisfying as squirting the sauce onto Moon would've been. If it'd been Moon, however, I'd have been able to fulfill my fantasy of licking it off…

I flushed, whilst warmth curled through me, until I shrieked at the sudden cold, as Vala slammed a bowl of melting chocolate ice-cream into my face.

Aquilo burst into giggles, which was a sound that I

hoped to hear again when I wasn't gasping and struggling to wipe candy sprinkles out of my eyes.

When I glanced through eyelashes that were matted with ice-cream across the table at the Alphas and mages, I realized that they were desperately holding back their laughter. Then I caught Rubber Mage's eye, and something sparked.

*Wait, did he understand what I was trying to do…?*

He inclined his head, before his scarred eyebrow rose, and he hollered, "Food fight!"

Emperor shoved himself off the table, ducking behind it because there was no way that he was risking his suit or hair. Well, that was what I got for Claiming a haughty prince as my Charm. I must be in love with Emperor because all that thought did was make me smile fondly, as if it was a cute eccentricity like making up names for your feet — *don't judge me.*

The other mages, however, snatched up the remains of the feast and eyed Vala and me with delight.

Vala backed away, raising her hands. "I am the dead," she started but it sounded more like a plea.

The mages launched the food, which splattered across the Crescent Base like a sticky rainbow.

Vala might be dead, but she was just discovering that there were others in her kingdom who still clung to life.

I squealed as I gripped Vala by the shoulders and

brought her tumbling onto her ass next to me in the sludge. She shrieked, pinning me under her.

Maybe enraging the Alpha princess wasn't the best plan but boy, was it fun...*and ripped down her propaganda better than any words.*

I reached for my shadows, but they ached, held inside by the forced and false bond of wolf royalty onto a Wolf Charmer. Yet Emperor had told me that I was more than a Charmer or a Witch. I was Crimson and I could take down a wolf with...

*A cucumber...?*

My fingers slipped in the puddle of strawberry sauce around the cucumber. *What kind of health freak had a salad at a midnight feast?* I grasped the vegetable, whacking Vala across the forehead.

Vala's claws retracted, and she sat back on her ass. Then she blinked at me. "Fur and fangs, a Charmer would fight me with a...?"

I opened my mouth to answer, before finally glancing down at my hand...and the neon pink dildo.

So, it was possible to be even more embarrassed.

I reddened. "*Duh*, that's why I'm a rebel."

Emperor strolled to one side of me, and Aquilo to the other, before they helped me up.

Vala slunk to her feet with a sexy wriggle like she wasn't covered in chocolate sauce and hadn't just been hit over the head with a strawberry flavored dildo.

Although, that did sound like one kinky porn movie

"This is what happens when you treat witches, Omegas, or mages as equals," Vala sneered. The mages stilled. "Naughty and now dirty. You'll clean off in the Pleasure Pool. My mother wishes to see you," her mouth twisted, "and I promise that you shan't want to be seen in this disgraceful state. If I were you, I wouldn't want to be seen by her at all." Then she gripped my arm, whispering into my ear, "She still believes you a god." Her gaze dropped to the dildo that I was clutching like an unwanted Christmas gift. *Would it draw more attention if it clattered to the floor now...?* "Yeah, Goddess of Vibrators."

"Oh," I lifted my eyebrow, "does it vibrate too?"

Emperor reached around like an encouraging lover with a practiced move that showed he had way more experience than me and switched it on.

Into the silence of the Crescent Base, the vibrator buzzed to life, twisting like an eager snake.

"Thanks for the help," I gritted out.

"Any time." Emperor waved his hand with a smirk.

Vala licked the chocolate from her lips, as her fangs extended. "*I see you*, and I'll protect you from yourself."

I startled, when she lay the back of her hand against my check. I fought not to flinch.

*Jesus, what was with the deep and meaningful moment from the chocolate monster?*

Vala reached out, squeezing the head of the vibrator,

until it squeaked to a slow death. Emperor and Aquilo winced, protectively cupping their hands over their dicks through their pants.

My heart pounded, as Vala leaned closer to her bite on my throat.

*Breathe, Crimson… She can't bite you twice…can she…?*

When Vala traced over the bite, it stung; my magic rejected her and the bond. "I *know* you, Charmer. Your pack are now *my* pack. Don't you wish to discover if they're even alive?"

I stiffened; my eyes widened, and I forgot to breathe.

Then the dildo did clatter from my hand because this was worse than being bitten. *What if Moon and his brother, Amadeus, and the angels were dead?*

Vala's claw dug into the bite. "Don't you see the blood rising? This is *my* kingdom. Soon, you'll be a ghost as well, trapped here amongst the ranks of the dead."

## CHAPTER 3

When the Crescents shoved me through the iron doors into the Pleasure Pool with Aquilo clasping one of my hands and Emperor the other, a sweet lemony scent blasted over me like a breath of life. I shivered both at its cool and the terror that I'd discover Moon drowned in the waters like his ancestors had once been by my own.

*Holy hell, don't let this be the kind of neat cycles of history that Stella had once woven into Fate.*

Yet there was nothing neat about the fact that it was a mage and a werewolf who squeezed my witchy hands in reassurance. Stella would never have woven the way that we were united in both love and fear unless, you know, Emperor had been on his knees in panties.

Although, I could get behind that if Emperor was *willing*.

Ahead, gray gauze screens hung from the ceiling and overlapped. I squinted, desperate to see through them, but the world was blurred to spooks, which whispered with the gush of water beyond.

*Not dead...not dead...please, please, please...*

Where was Moon? *Where in the witching heavens was he?*

Yanking my guys after me, I shoved through the screens, and they *thwapped*, stinging across my cheeks.

"Moon! Your big, bad wolfie ass had better be here because if you're not..." My voice cracked, and I bit my lip hard, before licking at the ice-cream that'd dried there.

Moon was my first Omega Charm and the Prince of the Wilds. He was also the magical Moon Child, and my red foamed with the need to be bonded to his magic again. I'd Claimed Moon in the most primal way, but I was also his: we were equals. I now knew what it felt like to be Bitten by an Alpha who didn't treat you like one, and hey, was that not a cuddle fest of fun.

*I loved Moon.*

Huh, that was no longer hard to think, and it'd only taken fear of losing him — *again* — to make that as clear as the screens were cloudy.

With a growl, I pulled away from Aquilo and Emperor, tearing at the screens that kept me from my Charm.

Aquilo blinked. "Food, vibrator, and now curtain

fights. Have you considered that the princess' bite might've driven you crazy?"

Emperor dragged Aquilo to him by his waist.

*Wow, Emperor was way taller than my mage fiancé and had seriously discovered an outlet for his Alpha vibes.*

"Have you considered, mage, that you owe respect to the Chief Alpha?" Emperor arched his brow imperiously.

Emperor might as well have added *and me* because it was all there in the way that his fingers bit into Aquilo's waist, at the same time as his thumbs massaged away the hurt.

*Should I've found it so hot to see them together like this?* I'd wondered what it'd look like when my two snooty guys faced off...and yeah, it was scorching hot.

To my surprise, Aquilo rested his forehead against Emperor's. His hair fell into his eyes, as he relaxed into Emperor's hold.

"She already has my respect." Aquilo's gaze darted to mine, and my heart stuttered at the warmth in the usually icy blue of his eyes. "Along with my love."

Emperor pressed his lips to Aquilo's. "Well, now I know that you're pack because you love our dirty little witch."

My breath hitched, and I struggled in the gauze like a fly in a moon web. I'd just discovered something even more hot than seeing Aquilo in Emperor's arms and that was hearing them both affirm their *love* for me in their special ways.

Emperor smiled fondly at me like *dirty little witch* was a Shakespearean sonnet. Perhaps, in the shifter world it was, and there was no complaining from this Charmer because I'd happily wake up to the love of my pack each day along with my shot of espresso.

*Boy, would I love an espresso right now…*

Emperor swung Aquilo around to me, and his claws extended. "Since we have no dildos to battle, how about we pull down these charming drapes?"

I scuffed my foot along the twisted material. *How long before they stopped kicking my ass over that?*

When Emperor tore savagely through the drapes with his claws, I winced at the *rip*. Then he hooked his hands under my arms and pulled me out of the web, clasping me to his chest; his heart beat faster than I'd expected against my own.

*Was he as frightened for Moon as I was?*

Aquilo spun whirlwinds around him with a power that stole my breath. He'd hidden his magic for so long, it was both spellbinding and sexy as sorcerer's hell, to see him now controlling the elements with such *joy*.

*Did I look like that with my shadows? Or did I sport the predatory darkness of my great-grandmother?*

Aquilo caught the tatters in his whirlwinds, wrenching them away from the ceiling and flinging them against the far wall.

When the breeze died down, I stared across the Pleasure Pool, which had been revealed.

The circular marble pool itself was vast, murky, and still. Exotic blue waterlilies floated on top like crocodiles, whilst their stone companions spurted water into the pool from the sides. Above, antique lanterns cast a warm glow through a veil of yet more gauze.

Omegas cowered away from us in alcoves behind the pool. At least that meant the Omegas gave up the living statue gig when they were threatened by spinning sheets, which meant that they couldn't be totally brainwashed, right?

Then I let out a soft gasp as I became unexpectedly breathless. Waves of sweet citrus aroma hit me, wafting from the waterlilies on the pool; my skin tingled and my vision blurred.

I pulled out of Emperor's hold, taking several unsteady steps, *clacking* over the marble in the silence.

"*Moon*," I whispered.

Moon lay stretched out — *naked* — on a raised outcrop, which glimmered and shifted as if alive. His long pale limbs were as sinfully beautiful as the witches had always taught under the lanterns' light. Beside the water, he looked like a curly haired merman, if merman had been startled into growing fangs and claws.

A *merwolf* would be an epic combination. Although, if Amadeus could be a wolf *and* an incubus, for all I knew there could be a wolf *and* a merman.

*Why did those kinds of thoughts feel natural now?*

Then Moon's gaze met mine with a vulnerability like he was lost, and it made my guts clench.

*What had happened to him?*

"In the furless heavens, are you another dream?" Moon murmured.

"If we were, would I be able to do this?" Emperor pinched Aquilo's ass.

Aquilo yelped, rubbing his ass with affronted haughtiness. "Gorgeous but dumb, I see. It only works if you pinch the one who believes themselves to be sleeping."

Emperor winked at me. "Everybody always notices the gorgeous."

Moon snorted. "Aye, this is real." Then his breath hitched. "*This is real.*"

When he struggled to stand, the outcrop sucked at him, as if it was attempting to hold him in place…*and apart from me*.

My shadows shot out, at the same time as Moon's silver magic. As they entangled, I moaned, electrified.

*Moon was alive…and Vala was in for a serious ass kicking.*

Together and united, Moon's magic and mine pulled together, freeing Moon from the pool.

Moon dashed towards me (I'd forgotten how fast he could run), grasping me around the waist and twirling me around. Our magics spun with us, caressing and cocooning, until every nerve lit up, and my skin prickled with sensation.

At last, Moon placed me down, allowing his own magic to retreat. He studied me like in the short time that we'd been separated, he could've forgotten what I looked like. His dark lashes were matted with tears, and I'd never seen such intensity in his amber eyes.

"Don't scare me like that again, Charmer." He licked down my cheek and then scrunched up his nose. "Are single skins always such messy eaters?"

Emperor chuckled.

I shrugged. "You should see the princess."

"I'd rather be flayed." When I winced (because there was such a thing as *too soon*, when Moon had almost been flayed at Ivy's hand), Moon licked down the corner of my mouth in apology. "At least it's my favorite flavor of ice-cream."

*A lick was almost a kiss, right? I mean, to the wolves it was probably first base...*

Yeah, that was what was known as a Self-Bullshitting Spell.

*I needed Moon's soft lips to kiss me...*

Instead, Moon nuzzled into his favorite spot on my neck. At least, I now had an armful of warm snuggling wolf: Moon gave the most epic cuddles.

*How had I ever lived without my pack?*

Except, then Moon sniffed at my neck, and his growl rumbled, vibrating through me.

"By my fangs, the bastard princess dared Wolf Bite you…?" Moon's breath gusted across the fading bruise on my neck.

I stroked across his curls, which now smelled lemony and fresh, to calm my brave wolf. Moon had ripped out the throat of the last bitch to force a Wolf Bite. Vala should be more frightened of this Omega than of me. "*The bite* is all for show. Trust me, I hate it too, but it's a political move, rather than a proposal. The asshole did it to control me, but it's kicked her own ass because now her Crescents won't fight me. They call me *Omega Witch* and kind of don't even monitor me."

"Goddess Moon! I couldn't stop her—"

I hushed him, placing my finger over his lips.

It was hard to stop thinking about those lips when my finger was just there and Moon's tongue swiped out to draw my finger into his wickedly nibbling mouth.

I massaged the satiny skin of Moon's hip in soothing circles. "Chill out. Do you honestly think that I'm the kind of jerk who'd be ashamed to be called an *Omega*?"

Moon closed his eyes, drawing back to rub his head against my throat. "Only you could say that." His voice was tight and unexpectedly raspy with emotion. My shadows flowed around him in comfort. He opened his eyes again, staring up at me with the type of awe that I'd only seen directed at Mischief before. "I've longed for someone who truly *saw* Omegas."

I flushed, shifting from foot to foot. When I looked

up, Emperor's eyes gleamed; his look was hard like he wished *he* was the one holding Moon and being loved.

*Or that he should've been.*

I hurriedly swung to study the Omegas, who were standing in the alcoves. Like the Omegas in the Lunar Shrine, they were the wolves who'd been saved from the Training Centers but still couldn't be loved as anything more than Queen Banan's surrogate children. They were watching Moon and me with a longing that twisted my insides.

Yet had they been placed in here to guard Moon or spy for the queen or princess?

I'd learned from my uncle that there were different factions within organizations and knowing what motivated them, so that you could work with all of them (okay, he'd used the word *manipulate*), was Business Like a Billionaire 101.

*What was the bet that working the different factions in the Gods would also be Wolf Witch 101?*

Yet Moon and I had sworn that we'd save all the Omegas. I now knew that it was more complex than that: we had to find a way to save Wolf Kingdom itself.

*But hocus pocus, I couldn't leave the Omegas to suffer much longer.*

When Moon's dick twitched, at the same time as his lips curled against my neck, I pinked with a heat that flooded through me. The scent of the lilies became overwhelming, as they floated towards us in the pool.

*Were we being drugged?*

I blinked at the sudden explosion of the band Franz Ferdinand's "Darts of Pleasure" from the gauze of the ceiling, which swayed like ghostly dancers to the dark and dangerous passion of the song.

The tips of Moon's ears turned red; *now that was an adorable look.* "The pleasure pool reads your mind...or your pleasure," he muttered.

*It was an incubus pool, freaking fabulous.*

The waterlilies twirled in a dance of their own. Their huge petals pulsed open and closed in a way that made me clamp my own legs shut.

*Okay, I got the point, pleasure flowers...*

"Franz Ferdinand for my Aries rebel." I grinned. "Dude, they sent you on a spa day."

Moon huffed. "Aye, right. It's torture to be trapped in your dreams, yet to be alone."

All this stuff about the Wolf Witch must be right because my red howled through me that *pack wasn't alone.*

"I believe that Amadeus, you, and I have already experienced too many centuries of that." Emperor strode to Moon, snatching him from me to hold him to his chest. Moon whined, but didn't pull away. Instead, he allowed himself to snuggle closer, and I hated that something had separated the three princes for so long. *What on earth had stopped them being friends?* "Do you know how often I dreamed of you and our sexy incubus prince? *Every day that we were apart.*" Moon drew back, blinking. "We feared you dead," Emperor added, stiffly.

When Moon gasped, Aquilo slipped his hand reassuringly onto Moon's shoulder, and Moon leaned into his touch.

Aquilo ran his fingers down the hollow of Moon's back. "We're rather glad that you're not."

Moon licked Aquilo's cheek in thanks. Aquilo grimaced, although I noticed that his dick hardened in his pants.

Then Aquilo exchanged a sly glance with Moon, before cocking his head at Emperor. "Oh no, what a terrible shame. Is that a smudge of chocolate down the back of your robes?"

Emperor's mouth gaped in horror, before he twisted around as if checking out his ass. When Moon snickered, Emperor's shoulders stiffened, and he spun to Aquilo and Moon like a professor on two naughty school kids caught out on a prank.

"Why, mage, is that a smudge of chocolate on your *behind*?" Emperor's voice was smooth and hard as steel.

Aquilo *eeped*, clutching onto Moon.

Moon laughed. "Let the big bag Omega protect you from the mean prince."

When Stella had gifted me a wolf as a birthday gift and then told me to take the other princes as Tributes, I hadn't known that the bonds between us would be *real,* and that I'd discover *love* for a mage, angel, and god, as well as these wolves.

*Or that they'd love each other just as fiercely.*

Yet although I'd found Moon, what about the rest of my pack? My heart clenched at the threat Vala had made against them. What if they'd been hurt…? What if Vala had meant that she'd *killed* them…? Hexes and curses, how would I be able to control my shadows then? Or had her threat been to frighten and test me?

"Do you know where Ramiel is?" I demanded.

Moon burst out at the same time, "What about Amadeus and Mischief?"

"Consider that we're not alone," Emperor said, sharply.

Emperor knew more about diplomacy and these kingdoms than me. I hugged my arms across myself as I shot another glance at the Omegas.

*So, they were cute spies.*

"I take it that the pool's magic?" I sniffed, as once again the sweet scent wound around me, tempting me towards the water. I took an unsteady step closer, even as my shadows whispered warnings. "This isn't like some ploy to drown me because Mischief would resurrect me just to kick my ass if I fell for it."

Moon's lips quirked. "On my hide, we couldn't have my Moon God kicking your behind." His magic brushed across mine, and this time I arched into it with a moan. I blushed. Moon tried for smug, but then my shadows swept across his nipples in feather light touches, and he raised onto tiptoes in their wake. Now it was my turn to raise *my* eyebrow. "This pool's a special treat for the Bitten. Its properties are protective, but the sensation…"

"*Woah*, my uncle could've made himself richer than Bill Gates on this."

"Mood killer," Moon grumbled. "Will you leave off fussing, Charmer?"

*When had I started dragging at the lacing of my own dress, whilst squirming around like the star in my own porno?*

"The Omegas here told me as much as they could. The drug is an incubus aphrodisiac." Moon dragged me by the hand to the pool's edge and crouched down. The scent was even stronger here; it made me dizzy with desire. Moon shuddered, skimming his hand just above the water. I didn't blame him, after he'd been traumatized by the Alphas in the Wilds with baths. *Could I help him to accept pleasure in water, rather than pain?* "It's in the air and even more potent in the water. Don't you want to get clean before you get dirty again?"

*Hold up, one of my tits hadn't been hanging out of my dress a moment ago, had it…?*

Kudos to me though on the speed undressing.

Moon grinned, sprawling by the side of the pool. His pupils were blown, and his skin gleamed. I craved to lean forward and taste the salty bead of sweat as it trailed a path down his stomach and towards his dick that pulsed against his stomach.

*Hot skin…hot, hot, hot…*

I shook my head to clear it. Then I glanced back at Emperor and Aquilo.

Aquilo undressed Emperor, who in turn slipped the black velvet shirt from Aquilo's shoulders. It was so different to the way that Vala had shamed Aquilo that it made my witchy ass realize one thing: *Alphas weren't assholes*. But the system that put the Alphas in charge was an asshole system.

A system was harder than an individual to rebel against, but at least I knew what I was fighting.

When Aquilo undid the buttons on Emperor's waist-coat, Emperor stilled his hand.

"Be careful, this is my favorite suit." Emperor stroked over Aquilo's hand as if to reduce the sting of his order.

Yet Aquilo only snorted. "Have I not been dressed in finery my entire life like a doll? Was I not expected to keep it perfect or face a whipping? I shan't damage your plumage."

Moon laughed. "I like this mage."

"Do you also like…" I was about to insert a sexy line about my ass, whilst wriggling out of my dress and panties, when I caught the eye of one of the blushing Omegas in the alcove.

"Turn around wolfie chaste dudes," I hollered.

The Omegas startled, darting doubtful glances at each other, before turning to face the wall.

Guilt squirmed in my guts because making Omegas stand like naughty schoolboys so that I could get my kicks didn't feel right, but since I couldn't send them out of the room it was better than expecting them to watch.

And as they weren't allowed to screw themselves, that would be a dick move.

I wrestled off the dress, which caught on my shoes, before I kicked them skidding across the floor, in more comedy routine than striptease.

The air was hazy with the scent, heat, and drug.

*Witches dancing on a pin, was this aphrodisiac forcing us to desire scorching hot sexy times? Was it playing scenes of Emperor and Aquilo in a sandwich with Moon as the tasty sauce into my brain? Could any of us even consent to this?*

"Don't touch the water—" I hissed.

"Mageball!" Aquilo yelled with more simple happiness than I'd ever heard in his voice, before flinging his now naked ass (and the rest of his fine naked self) into the pool.

*Splash* — Aquilo had tucked his knees up to his chest and his chin under as he cannonballed into the water.

I squawked as a warm wave crashed over me,

shooting my shadows to cover the room in rippling crimson.

Tears dripped off my lashes, as Moon swiped a lick of the pool water off my cheeks.

So much for the *no touching the drugged water, guys…*

Emperor stalked to the pool after Aquilo, before diving in gracefully and emerging beside Aquilo with a shake of his golden tresses like a lion. Aquilo swam on his back towards me as if to escape him, but Emperor growled, diving in pursuit and capturing him. He pinned him against the side.

Aquilo glanced at me pleadingly.

"Don't look at me to save you from the wicked…" At Emperor's pout, I sighed, "but *good* wolf. I'm the poor asshole you showered in drugged water."

Aquilo ducked his head but couldn't hide the smile still dancing in his eyes. "Perhaps, I've always wished to feel what it'd be like to jump into a pool that way."

My gaze softened. "Epic, *hmm*?"

Aquilo squirmed. "I'd suggest that naked was not advisable. Other parts of me are as red as my face right now."

"No fair, I can't see those other parts," Moon murmured. Then his gaze became serious as it met mine. "There's no forcing, if that's what's giving you that pinched earnest Charmer look."

"Hey, I don't have—"

Emperor nodded. "Oh yes, she certainly has it."

Two against one wasn't fair odds, especially when my nipples were peaked and throbbing and images played across my mind of first one and then the other taking each in their mouth and sucking...

Aquilo lifted his eyebrow. "There, I saw it." He glanced down at my aching nubs, before meeting my gaze again. "Although, are you thinking of anything else as well...?"

Except, if I was fantasizing right now, then so were each of my guys.

*What were they seeing?*

Maybe, for once, it was time to show with actions over words, that I meant they had an equal place in this relationship. If Aquilo had been taught all his life that he was nothing more than breeding stock, it'd take experience to show him that he was the same as any guy that I'd have dated in America.

But then, I'd never swum naked with three guys in America.

*Woah, had I been missing out.*

My heart hammered against my ribcage, as I slipped into the pool. The lilies circled closer, and I sank into the syrupy embrace of the water up to my tits. Moon hung his feet over the edge, but when I held my hands out for him to join me, he shook his head.

When The Streets' "Who's Got the Funk" burst out in urban hip hop glory, I twirled around excitedly. *Had*

*Okami's prankster ass set me up?* Then I caught Aquilo's frosty gaze.

"What? The pool's reading me, it appears. Did you imagine that I waltzed, stuck in the House of Blood, to Mozart like a snooty prince?" He drawled.

I choked, glancing at Emperor.

"By my hide, you're all *geezer*, aren't you?" Emperor's teeth extended, before he nipped Aquilo's nose. "And you certainly like risks."

Aquilo's eyes shone, as his hands clutched onto the side of the pool, until his knuckles whitened. "I love to be *free* to take them."

When Emperor kissed Aquilo it was with a savagery and passion that I recognized and ached for. Aquilo arched beneath him, raising his hands up around Emperor's neck and pulling on his hair like he needed the anchor.

When I glanced at Moon, I realized that he was watching with a deep desperation. Was it the kiss that he needed? *Or Emperor?*

I traced over Moon's foot that dangled just above the water, and Moon hissed in a breath. Then I licked up his calf, and his attention was no longer on anyone but me. I peppered kisses up his thigh, as he quivered, switching sides, whilst he struggled to hold himself still. Maybe he wouldn't or *couldn't* kiss on the mouth, but there were other places that he *could* be kissed.

I lifted Moon's leg, kissing the delicate skin behind

his knee and his wide eyes met mine. I nuzzled, sucking a hickey on his inner thigh, desperate to mark him after our time apart. Moon howled, lying back on his elbows to watch me.

When I drew away, I felt the sweep of Emperor's fingers across my shoulder.

"Look what we found inside the sinister waterlilies." Emperor thrust his cupped palm underneath my nose, which was filled with a pearl-like puddle. I wrinkled my nose against the overpowering lemony aroma that made my mind feel full of cotton wool. "Shampoo and cleaning gel of some sort, I'd wager. Allow us to tend to your needs."

I shivered; my skin tingled. Boy, did I wish for him to tend to me, but only if it was what Aquilo and he desired.

*I wanted to be their fantasy.*

I twisted to glance at him over my shoulder, catching Aquilo's eye as well. "I trust you. You don't have to serve me, unless, you know, that's what gets you off. This can be *your* fantasy."

So, that had come out cornier than I'd intended, but it was worth it for the smile now curling Aquilo's mouth, when before there'd been a hesitant shyness. All this was new to him, let alone add in aphrodisiacs and sexy wolves as well.

Then Emperor's breath was hot against my neck, as his fingers carded through my hair, massaging my scalp with the shampoo, and I relaxed back into his arms because boy, this must've been one of the skills that he'd been taught. I'd never felt as relaxed, even as he stoked the warmth that was building inside me.

Aquilo's hands softly cupped my tits, and I gasped, caught between the two men. He washed them, circling the nubs in rhythm with Emperor's circling of my scalp, and I'd have given anything to be able to purr like Ramiel. When I gazed up at Moon, I saw the sadness and yearning in Moon's eyes.

*There was no way that Moon would ever be alone again.*

I stroked over the hickey that I'd sucked on Moon's thigh, and he jumped. Moon's eyes widened in surprise, then Emperor edged me closer to him.

At last, Moon allowed his feet to skim the pool. I smiled with pride because I knew how hard it was to face such fears, before Moon glanced down at his lap and his throbbing dick. Moon was almost as much a virgin as Aquilo, but he knew what it was to be kissed *there*.

Amadeus had touched me with his bare skin, and the feel of this pool was like being submerged in Amadeus' power: every sensation was heightened, until I was drowning in it.

*Had the gel from the lilies been even more powerful?*

My shadows wavered, sensuous.

*We were alive…together…alive…*

Red, bled with silver and blue. Moon's eyes were large and amber…I was lost in them.

Surely no one should feel this intensely? *The stimulation was too much. What was the water doing to me?*

Aquilo brushed his thumb across my nipple, Emperor kissed the back of my neck, and I clutched Moon's thighs because otherwise I'd sink to the bottom of the pool and the pleasure would drown me.

## CHAPTER 4

I was lost in the sensations of the Pleasure Pool and the touch of the three men who I loved. I struggled to surface from the sensual waves but I was caught in a trap of need and desire.

Had Vala sent my guys and me here in order to tame us with pleasure? If she had, I could honestly say that it was working.

Emperor's kisses tingled across the back of my neck, Aquilo circled my nipples with a maddening caress, and Moon held me by the hair, as if *he'd* be lost if he let go.

*How dangerous was the aphrodisiac?*

The light from the lanterns dimmed, and the citrus scent was intoxicating. Had the gauze ceiling always hung so low?

I was burning up… *Black cats and cauldrons, this wasn't a drowning, it was a witch bonfire.*

*Hot, hot, hot…*

Moon's dick looked like a cool Popsicle to my hazy mind. His thighs quivered under my fingertips, as I edged them higher, gently pushing his long legs wider. His pupils were blown, and he licked his lips.

If Moon wouldn't kiss me, then *I'd* kiss *him.*

When Moon arched his hips towards me in encouragement, I bent over, kissing the head of his dick. Then just like I'd craved, I licked down his dick's satiny length.

"Don't move," Emperor commanded, and Moon struggled not to buck. My red coiled around Moon's collar like it could replace it, leashing Moon to me instead, holding him still. Moon whined. Emperor wrapped his arms around my waist like he hungered to protect me, and his wet hair swept across my neck. Then he whispered into my ear, "That goes for either of you."

I shivered as I sucked on Moon's throbbing dick, whilst his silver magic spun out to caress me, just as my red lapped across his nipples. It mimicked every swirl of my tongue, until Moon was whining and biting his lip as he struggled to obey Emperor, despite the tug of my shadows at his neck.

When Emperor's hard dick slid between my thighs as both a tease and a question, the aphrodisiac exploded through me once again.

The waterlilies circled closer.

"Do you wish for this?" Aquilo stroked my ass, bending over to ghost kisses down my spine in veneration. "That we belong together in such a way?"

I reached my hand back to fondle his balls because with a mouthful of dick, you had to get creative with ways to answer, go figure.

*Yet was this my fantasy or theirs?*

I hoped that it was theirs. I'd promised to show them that we all had a choice, and hey, I was seriously into this.

Moon had never looked so beautiful as when he raised his gaze — stripped back and shuddering in passion — to meet not mine but Emperor's over my shoulder, and then watched him with an expression of flushed adoration, as Emperor thrust and sank into me. I moaned around Moon's dick, sending vibrations through him, so that he moaned as well.

Aquilo chuckled against my back; his breath tickled me. "Do that again. Witch and Wolf sound so prettily perfect together."

Emperor rocked into me harder, and every time that I moaned, spiraling towards my peak, so did Moon.

Yet something was missing, even as I prickled with heat. My crimson writhed, stronger than ever before, but unlike in the House of Silver where I'd been joined in my passion with all of my guys, here I only had two of my Charms: *Amadeus was missing*.

Amadeus was the second of my Charms, the Prince of the Gods, and without all three of us being united, my red couldn't be at its most powerful.

*How could I lose myself to true joy without him?*

It was kind of freaky how much I now understood the Wolf Witch side to the Wolf Charmer. I craved all three of my Charms. If I was honest, I craved my two *angel* lovers as well. Even under the influence of the aphrodisiac, I couldn't be forced to forget or become trapped in pleasure because my pack needed me.

*And hocus pocus, I needed Amadeus.*

Suddenly, the waterlilies pulsed open, and Aquilo shielded me, at the same time as Emperor's rhythm stuttered. Clouds of aroma puffed out but now it was *chocolate* scented...just like *Amadeus*.

Emperor gasped, and when I peeked up through my eyelashes, Moon's eyes shone as he trembled.

Was Amadeus being here with us my wolves' fantasy as well?

Now, when Aquilo drew his hand through the water and across my skin, everywhere that he touched warmed and tingled, lighting my nerves like a hundred kisses.

I was nothing but sensation and I'd never been so free.

As Aquilo captured my nipple between his fingers under the water and teased, it felt like it was Amadeus' mouth.

"If he was here," Emperor murmured into my ear, "I'd screw Amadeus, as he screwed you."

My body clenched at the intense intimacy of the image (and holy hell, was that hot), before waves of pleasure crested through me. As I spasmed, Emperor came as well.

Aquilo rested his hand on Moon's thigh and squeezed. "After that, *you* could choose which of us to screw, prince."

Moon groaned, before he came.

*Woah, the Pleasure Pool could even change wolfie semen to chocolate…?* I was so booking this place for my next birthday party, as long as I wasn't, you know, being kept here as a prisoner.

Wait…*prisoner?* Wasn't there something that I should be remembering and, you know, *doing* right now…like rescuing the sexy incubus who I could taste sweet on my tongue?

I swallowed, before licking my lips.

Moon lifted his brow. "Respect. Am I truly that delicious?" I didn't miss the insecurity.

"Dude, I just need waffles as a side-order and I could drink your dick all day."

Moon blinked. "Kinkier than I'd been expecting."

Emperor swam around me, before tilting my chin and pressing his lips to the corner of my mouth. "Thank you. I never thought that I'd be allowed such control."

His small, contented smile warmed me more than

anything could have. His hidden Alpha nature had been satisfied in a way that he hadn't been able to risk before, and it was *epic*. There was no way on earth I'd repress that side of him again, unless, you know, it was to keep his secret.

*Because the asshole Alphas murdered male Alphas.*

Aquilo crossed his arms over his chest, looking away, as pink spread down his chest. Now that the sexy times were over, he was shy again.

Moon stroked Aquilo's cheek, startling him into looking up. "By my fur, I would wish to make love to *you*." He glanced at me. "You're my Charmer's intended, courageous, and noble. I swear on Goddess Moon, you're my pack."

Aquilo uncrossed his arms, licking Moon's palm like he was a wolf himself or like a kind-hearted boy who'd grown up in the House of Blood around enough wolves to communicate with them…to *love them* as he had the Ambassador.

I stiffened, as the haze faded.

The Ambassador, who was Banan's son, had died to save Aquilo, but Banan didn't even know it yet.

*What on earth would she do to Aquilo when she discovered the truth?*

Emperor lounged against the edge of the pool. Water teared down his muscled chest.

"Well, that was stimulating." Emperor flashed a cocky grin. "But although the Omegas might've been unable to witness our *hot enough to melt their chaste little minds* display, they certainly couldn't have missed our *moan*athon."

When Emperor nudged my thigh, Moon caught my eye.

"Aye, we sound good together, and you'd have been *whimpering* if you had the Charmer's sweet lips wrapped around your dick," Moon boasted.

Emperor swept his hair back, molding it into place. "I believe that I had another equally delectable part of her wrapped around me and I wasn't the one whimpering."

"Hey, enough of the Moaning Contests." I flushed like that'd stop the way both their amber gazes swung to me, as if our sexy times had become just another part of their banter. *Was that a wolf or a prince thing?* "What have the Omegas got to do with it?"

Emperor shrugged. "Nothing now that we've scared them away."

*The sneaky…clever…asshole.*

When I slipped my hand across Emperor's butterfly tattoo, and my crimson battled the stinging dark magic to trace its outline, his breath hitched at the tenderness and promise of the gesture, knocking the cocky out of him.

"Watch yourself," Moon murmured, "there are still cameras in the ceiling."

I darted a glance up at the gauze, which hovered above the pool, even lower than before.

"I imagine that the cameras are in those disquieting waterlilies." Aquilo kept his gaze carefully downcast as he stroked Moon's thigh, yet his jaw was tight. I shuddered, whilst the lilies twitched closer. *I'd known that I'd hated those freaking things.* "Do you think me as dumb as the witches believe all males, whether nonmagical or mages? I noticed the computer screens in the Crescent Base, which showed not simply the collars for the Omegas but the rooms across this underground kingdom. The princess rules with some of the same tricks as my sister. The queen worships and spies, but the princess runs a modern police state."

I smarted at Aquilo's pain. "Trust me, I know that you're smart. I'm not your mom or sister. You don't need to earn your love or place, so just chill, right?" Aquilo huffed, but allowed Moon's arm to curl him against his leg, which for Aquilo was seriously *chilling.* "And you're right about both sides in this kingdom. You and I are the only two here not tracked by our collars." When Emperor's eyes narrowed, I held up my finger to hush his Alpha style posturing. "Amadeus is in the Isolation Room to be punished, Mischief is still Moon Leashed, and we don't even know where Ramiel is. And the worst thing…?" When I ducked my head, my hair swung into my face. I hoped that it'd hide the gleam of tears in my eyes from the cameras. "I kind of just assumed that Okami would be here with your princely ass."

Moon jolted, meeting my anguished gaze.

Okami was my magic wolf, who I'd created in America out of a length of silk, and had been my first wolf, before I'd come back to England and Claimed my Charms. My uncle had seen him as a type of *witch therapy* to help me cope with my parents' deaths because he could flatten and be carried in my pocket to comfort me. Yet even though Okami had started as a piece of magical tech, he'd become a member of my pack who was loved as much as any of my guys.

Okami had been with Moon, when Moon had been taken out of the Lunar Shrine, and I'd hoped that they'd keep each other safe.

*Why wasn't Okami here?*

If Vala had hurt Okami's fluffy ass, maybe the *crimson tide* would drown us all once more. At the thought of Okami's pain, my shadows whipped out in tentacles that thrashed across the walls of the Pleasure Pool. My pack shrank back.

"Fur and fangs, enough with the giant squid impression. You know I'm not keen on the whole Tentacle Porn thing." Moon prowled to his feet, holding out his hand to me.

I stared at it. How many witches had been offered a hand in genuine friendship or support by a wolf over the last one hundred years? I hadn't fully understood just how rogue a witch I'd become or how rebel my princes until that moment. When I stared up at Moon, his gaze was soft like he felt it too, and he smiled with such radiance that I ached.

Who was I kidding? *I* was the addict for these princes now.

I clasped Moon's hand, allowing him to help me out of the pool.

When Moon crouched next to the outcrop, however, my brow furrowed.

"Now, don't go waving around those tentacles again," Moon warned.

I tapped my foot against the floor. "Dick way to start a sentence if this is going anywhere good."

Moon clenched his jaw. "No fair, I didn't say this was *good.* The queen sneered that Okami was nothing but *shameful witch magic* and that he *wasn't even real.*" I clenched my fists. Why was I surprised by such dickishness from a fanatical queen who'd bound both my magic and Mischief's, before trapping us in the Lunar Shrine? "Then she ordered Okami *flushed away.*"

I whined, dropping to my knees next to Moon who nuzzled at my neck. I petted his curls, although tears burned my eyes.

The waterlilies floated closer, greedy for my grief. I swallowed; my throat was tight. *But I wouldn't let Vala feast on my tears.*

"Yet on my hide, I begged the Omegas to flush him in here, instead," Moon whispered against my neck.

I held Moon closer, needing the feel of his breath against my skin.

"Flush like a dead goldfish?" Aquilo cocked his head.

Moon reddened. "Are you mocking me, boy? Nay, like the Charmer stuffed me in the wardrobe once. It was the only way to keep him safe."

*Okami was still alive…?*

I sat up straighter, catching Moon's guilty gaze, as I remembered how he'd been sprawled on this outcrop like a merwolf. "Your wolfie ass was *sitting* on him…?"

"I was *guarding* him."

When Moon thrust his arm into the shimmering rock, it was sucked in, as if it'd been sliced off at the elbow. I hollered, and Emperor leaped out of the pool faster than I'd ever seen anyone move, hauling Moon free again.

When Moon's hand slurped out of the outcrop, it was clutching a wet rag…

My eyes widened.

*Shove a broomstick up my ass, what on earth had they done…?*

"Okami, fly to me my silky friend," I whispered.

Okami sneezed and shook himself, forming into a bedraggled wolf who looked like he'd spent our time apart being tortured with repeated swirlies. He sniffled, before defiantly fluffing up his fur and flying into my outstretched palms like I wouldn't notice the way that he swayed.

*The queen was in for a royal ass kicking.*

So, I had to control the seething of my shadows, resist the return of the Crimson Terror, and play a perfect Omega, until I could discover Vala's sneaky assed plans against the other kingdoms' delegates. But none of that meant anything against Okami's pained whimper, as he nudged his nose against my thumb, and his legs quivered with the strain of standing.

My crimson held Okami, stroking him between his fluffy ears. He sighed in pleasure. I bled my magic into him, strengthening and healing, before standing, as he howled like he could take on every Alpha in the Kingdom of the Gods. He darted around my head, until I giggled with dizziness.

Yet if the queen could be such an asshole to Okami (okay, he was made of silk but he was still a wolf), then what was she capable of doing to an angel like Ramiel or to punish their own prince whose back was already a map of scarred pain?

It burned that Vala had claimed my pack and threatened it with the same breath. I had to know that they were all safe.

"I'm sorry to break up the... Is Okami your new hat?" Emperor blinked at the way that Okami had flattened himself into a silver headscarf on top of my head.

Seriously, there was no way that I was escaping Hermione hair now.

"*Hmm*, looks like I'm all out of pockets for him to sleep in, so he's improvised…" I patted my bare ass.

Emperor arched his brow. "Unfortunately, our gorgeous nakedness is rather the point. Those Omega brats stole our clothes." His eyes flashed, his fangs grew, and his nails extended. I shivered at the same time as Moon. *Woah, I never wanted that much Alpha fury directed at me.* "My robes, waistcoat, and suit. Oh, your belongings as well, of course."

"What happened to respecting the Chief Alpha? Put the teeth and fangs away. We'll just have to look at each other's dicks and tits a bit longer. I can seriously cope with that. What's the problem?"

"That we're trapped naked in a Pleasure Pool that can drug, intoxicate, and make us forget our pack, loved ones, and desperate need to save our kingdoms…?" Moon sighed.

"Huh, put like that, we're screwed. What do we do?" I lifted my chin.

Compared to my treatment in the Wilds, I was pampered here but still caged. This was a *fantasy*. I knew that real life hurt but I didn't want to escape it anymore.

Emperor growled (and boy, was he hot when he came over with a fit of the Dom), although he clenched his jaw hard not to say anything else. Then he snatched a gauze screen and ripped through it with his claw. He tossed a length to me and another to Moon.

Aquilo pulled himself out of the pool; he was all elegant pale limbs. His hair dripped into his eyes. When his gaze met mine, I didn't know how I'd missed the love beneath the frosty blue cold. Aquilo shivered, and Emperor tossed him a length of gauze as well.

Aquilo held up the material with a tilt of his head. "Shall I use this as a luxury towel?"

When Emperor marched to Aquilo, I'd expected Emperor to manhandle him. Instead, he gently wound the gauze around Aquilo like a toga.

"How charming." Emperor grinned, tying the final knot to the gown. "Shall we hold a toga party? They can be debauched, and I've often wondered what they'd be like if I wasn't the entertainment."

Moon slipped the gauze around himself, copying Emperor, before wrapping a length around me. The material clung to my wet tits, and I gasped. I could still feel the aphrodisiac, and my skin tingled like Amadeus was ghost kissing me, every time that the gauze rubbed across my aching nubs.

When Moon nuzzled my neck, I lost myself in his touch, clutching onto his curls.

"We'll escape and find the rest of our pack," he promised. "You're the Wolf Witch and our liberator."

I jolted. *What the ever-living witch did that mean?*

Then the iron doors to the Pleasure Pool clanked open, shattering the dreamy fantasy that'd gripped me.

Moon growled, and the water bubbled around the lilies in agitation. Then popcorn scented magic seeped through the room, battling the lemon infused drug, and as the haze cleared, finally so did my mind.

*It was like waking from a dream.*

Now I knew what it'd feel like to be caught in Moon's mind control.

When Mischief flew through the doors with the arrogance of an archduke angel and god who'd been trapped too long with his powers bound, I didn't even try to hide my grin.

"Oh, goodie, a toga party. Shall I assume that my invite was simply lost in the post?" Mischief's violet wings sparked as brightly as his violet eyes. "And by the way, I blinded the cameras. I've been working on that party trick."

Mischief's long silver hair hung down his shoulders, making him still the prettiest guy that I'd ever seen...the prettiest guy with a *silver cuff* around his ankle, which moon leashed him to the Lunar Shrine, trapping him in the Kingdom of the Gods as long as Banan lived.

It was a cuff that was now attached to a chain. Who was taking Mischief out for a walk like a prized poodle? Mischief attempted to swoop towards me, but the leash yanked him tumbling onto his ass.

He glared over his shoulder. "My, what an astoundingly dignified entrance you granted me. Keep up, cub."

Moth shot an apologetic glance at Mischief as he sidled into the room.

Moon's eyes widened at the sight of his teenage brother, before he launched himself through the shattered remains of the screens at Moth and clutched him to his chest. "By my hide, I'll bite your behind if you disappear again."

Moth stroked his brother's back in comfort. "Will you leave off fussing. I'm here now, and it was *you* who disappeared on me in the Training Center and every time that you try and get yourself killed." His gaze flicked to me. "For *her*."

Moon stiffened. "I'm sorry."

"My teeth are small but as sharp as yours." Moth licked his brother's cheek. "They can bite your behind too, brother."

Moon *twanged* the chain that Moth was clasping. "Fur and fangs, if you're already leading gods…"

Mischief looked up from his tangle of feathers on the floor, before trying to readjust himself into an indolent sprawl like he'd intended to land like that. "Tiny creatures, do you not perceive that I allow myself to be led?"

"This is the *royal prick* who you told me about?" Aquilo studied Mischief frostily. "He looks different when he's not fighting or hanging in a shrine. I thought that he'd be—"

"Taller?" Emperor offered.

"Special." Aquilo's lip curled.

*Was he jealous because Mischief was a mage as well and I loved him?*

When Mischief's shoulders slumped and his wings drooped, I dived across the Pleasure Pool with as much enthusiasm as Moon had done for his brother, before dropping to my knees next to him. It'd ached to be apart from Mischief as much as any of my Charms. His magic called to my own.

Mischief wasn't simply special. He was *everything*.

I gripped Mischief's chin, lifting his head, but he wouldn't meet my eye. His wings still enfolded me in their warm popcorn scent like he couldn't resist the feel of me, and boy, did it feel right to be held once more in the wings of an angel.

"Are we done with the schmaltz?" Mischief muttered. "I believe that I've self-assassinated most of my godly credibility but allow me to retain some at least."

Moon snorted. "Aye, right."

When Mischief spluttered in outrage, I tucked a strand of hair behind his ear and caught his lips with mine, startling him to silence.

"Hey, here's an idea: how about you stop hiding?" I murmured against his mouth, between kisses that lit up my nerves like I was still submerged in the pool, but this time I knew that it was about Mischief and not the aphrodisiac. "If you want love and to be as fully part of this pack as the rest of us, *then you are.*"

*Was that the gleam of tears in his eyes?*

Yet Mischief still arched an imperious eyebrow. "Perhaps, I shall accept a little taste of this schmaltz."

Now it was Mischief's turn to kiss me: it was passionate, desperate, and dark. His magic crackled through me, whilst my red crashed over him.

"No fair, where's my little taste?" Moon grinned, as he pulled Moth down with him on one side of me, snuggling closer.

Emperor strode to Mischief, sprawling next to him on the other side. "Nothing is little when it comes to wolves, pun intended."

Emperor stroked through Mischief's feathers, before licking across the throbbing violet wingtip. When Mischief purred, I knew that nothing could be sexier than that sound wrung from an angel.

Aquilo stood awkwardly watching us. My god was powerful but more fragile than I suspected the rest of us were put together, and Aquilo had hurt him. He could stay on the self-imposed naughty step for a little longer.

I tapped Mischief's nose. "I take it that this is better than being tortured by Vala in the Lunar Shrine with 1970s rock music?"

Mischief grimaced, even though he didn't stop purring. "She moved on to German trance music."

Aquilo gasped. "The villain." Then he peeked at Mischief like he feared he wouldn't be welcome (and hey, I wasn't calling it), before sitting cross-legged in front of him. He tentatively touched Mischief's ankle. "How did you escape?"

I could tell that Aquilo was trying to make up for his earlier dickishness.

Mischief smiled, softly. "Your magic is extraordinary. I can sense it from here, mage. Even if you believe *me* nothing special, I hope that you know at least that *you* are."

Aquilo's eyes widened, before he flushed. He wrapped his shaking arms around himself.

Aquilo had spent his life being told that he was *nothing*, *worthless*, or *invisible*. I figured that it took another mage who'd suffered the same to understand how much he'd needed to hear those words.

My red cocooned out to hold every one of my guys like I longed to at once. Aquilo's cheek rubbed against it, and I knew that was his way of apologizing as well.

"We escaped because I'm the queen's kryptonite!" Moth bounced on his knees with pride. Huh, so they *did* have TV in the Training Centers, or comics at least. "She trusts me like I'm her…well…*son*."

"Goddess Moon! You can't be taking risks with a rotten bastard like the queen," Moon snarled. "And why would she think a Wild her *son*? We have a ma, even if I wished that we didn't."

Moth twisted his shirt in his lap. "It's not my fault—"

Moon huffed. "When were you ever innocent, when you started a sentence like that?"

"She adopted me," Moth whispered. "She misses the true prince, her son."

"She can't have you," Moon spat.

"But for now," Emperor soothed, "it rather works to our advantage." He cocked his head, scrutinizing Moth. I forgot sometimes how epic at scheming Emperor was, but also how serious the stakes were. Emperor had been playing a long game here for all the kingdoms over centuries. I had a feeling that he'd *risk* more than the rest of us. *Could I trust him to protect me over Wolf Kingdom?* Was I willing to sacrifice just as much? "She'll want you by her side, and you should—"

"Don't talk to him like he's a spy. Don't *use* him." Moon's eyes glowed, as he glared at Emperor. "On my fangs, what happens if he gets caught, would you protect him or just abandon him like you did me?"

My breath caught in my throat. Was that why Moon had hated Emperor when he'd first seen him again in Wild Hall?

Yet I knew that they'd loved each other as kids, and Emperor had sworn to protect both Moon and Amadeus. Why would Emperor have hurt Moon like that?

Emperor looked stricken. "I'm trying to save the kingdoms and make up for not protecting you…to change it for everybody. I'd rather die than hurt your cub brother—"

"I'm not a *cub*," Moth insisted. "I can play the queen's son. It's safer for me that way. It's your daft behind that I worry for."

Moon brushed his brother's curls out of his eyes. "That's my job: to worry for you."

"Let me for a change." At Moon's soft growl, he giggled. "It's harder than it looks, right?"

"Okay, so everyone's worrying for everyone." I pointed at each of my guys in turn. "We have rescue missions to plan, and I want to know how you escaped from the trance hell of the shrine."

"I told the queen that I'd never been allowed a pet. A *godly* pet, I said, would be brilliant." Moth puffed up his chest with pride. "Every pet has to go for walkies."

Aquilo hid his snickers against Mischief's ankle.

Mischief rolled his eyes. "Oh, how I did ROFL. Wait, no I didn't, because the queen's madness may have me treated as an amusing pet now but do not underestimate it, or we shall all be slaughtered. She mourns the stealing of her son by witches, yet what will she do when she learns that he is in fact *dead*?"

I winced. Mischief was right, no matter how I wished that he wasn't.

Emperor nodded. "She's renowned for *hating* the

other kingdoms, and loving nothing but her own Omegas."

"*Woah*, are you saying..." I glanced between my pack. "...that *Vala* is less dangerous than her mother?"

Mischief sniffed. "I wouldn't go that far. I think they can claim equal psycho honors. It was Vala who sent us here to tell you that she's returning for you at dawn. She passed us in my...walk...and I believe she assumed that I would be humiliated to be seen like this, just as you'd be humiliated to be seen..." He traced over the Wolf Bite on my neck. When I flinched away, Mischief's gaze darkened. "She was wrong on both counts, was she not?"

My chin tilted. If Mischief refused to allow himself to be humiliated, then I refused it too. "How long until dawn?"

"Let me just check my watch... Oh yes, I don't have one." Mischief's eyes narrowed.

"A few hours, I'd guess...maybe?" Emperor offered.

I took a deep breath. "Then you and I, snarky god, will have to get our asses in gear because we're rescuing Amadeus." Moon and Emperor both grabbed my shoulders at the same time, but I held up a finger before they could speak. "You can be tracked with your collars, and I'm not risking Aquilo when I don't need to."

"But you'd risk me...?" Mischief wouldn't meet my gaze, but his expression was vulnerable and raw.

"Since we're rescuing Ramiel as well..." I smiled.

Mischief surged up, yanking me after him and tumbling the others sprawling in a move that was both a mix of hot and royal prick asshole that I'd come to love. "Oh, here's an idea, let's start this mission. Simply be aware that if we're caught (I as a god pet without his owner and you as a stray Omega Witch), then we shall be more than put in the naughty corner."

I swallowed. "Trust me, I know."

His grin was feral. "Then let us show them that no one shall leash a god or bite a Charmer."

"Technically, they already have."

Mischief's wings swept around me. "Technically, no one touches you unless you allow them to in here." He tapped my forehead and then his own. "And I shan't allow them to touch any of my pack."

Yet I only had until dawn to rescue Amadeus and Ramiel, and I didn't even know how long that was.

When I ventured into the unknown dangers of the Kingdom of the Gods with Mischief, I could be leading us both to our deaths.

## CHAPTER 5

I hunched my shoulders, as my throat burned at the dank scent of the Isolation Room, which was nothing but a cave burrowed out of the damp earth beside the Thames. Glowing moons had circled the sign at the entrance like it was a club and not a torture chamber for incubi. Honestly, I'd been half expecting Amadeus to be lit up under a glitter ball, slinking his hips, and singing a sultry rendition of Marvin Gaye's "Let's Get It On."

Instead, there'd been silence, darkness, *and Amadeus suspended in spinning wisps of moonlight.*

I gasped, stumbling forward, but Mischief caught my elbow, holding me back. I struggled, desperate to reach Amadeus, whose head hung down.

Amadeus' hair covered his face like a black shroud, and he was naked apart from the gleam of his collar. He was stretched out with his hands held in the moonlight above his head like chains and palely beautiful even in the shadows. His toes didn't touch the floor.

The back of my neck prickled, and my crimson cringed at how much it reminded me of the crystallized moons that had held Mischief and me captive in the Lunar Shrine.

Why wasn't Amadeus moving? Why couldn't I hear…*anything* from him? *Frogs' toes, was he even breathing?*

My own breath stuttered, as my eyes smarted with tears.

*Don't you dare think it, Crimson.*

*Dead, dead, dead…*

I slapped my own forehead, furious at my traitorous brain, wiping at the tears that'd already slipped down my cheeks. Okami squirmed on his perch on my head, whining mournfully.

Had Vala been angry enough with her own adopted brother for betraying her and falling in love with me to *kill* him? Was this room a grave?

Dizzy, I leaned against Mischief, who wrapped his quivering wings around me. How could I tell the other princes that something had happened to Amadeus? How could I ever leave this tomb myself if…?

*Please, please let my brave second Charm be alive.* I'd give up… *Hey Hecate*, I'd give up my shadows, to bring him to life.

Why hadn't I realized it before? I *loved* Amadeus, and he'd risked breaking the Moon Oath to his sister to save Moon and her displeasure by choosing *Crimson's pack* over his own kingdom and princess. Displeasure for an incubus meant pain, and that made him as courageous as my other Charms. It didn't matter whether they were Omegas, Betas, or Alphas...my princes were as brave as the *female* Alphas who I'd met.

*Bubbling cauldrons, please don't let that have meant Amadeus' death.*

When Mischief had first led me down the corridors to the Isolation Room like he'd been following a hidden trail of breadcrumbs, I'd raised my eyebrow.

"How'd you know the way?" I'd asked.

Mischief had smartly clasped his hands behind his back. "Nothing is truly hidden to an Archduke of the Realm of the Seraphim," he'd intoned.

I'd nodded. "Dude, that's impressive. Do you know what number I'm thinking of?"

Mischief had rolled his eyes. "I apologize, I'd forgotten that you were an *American*. What, am I psychic now? I assure you that I only knew where this despicable room is because I passed it on my *walkies*." He'd pouted. "If I was all-knowing, would I've allowed myself to be caught by Zetta and become trapped in this witchy nightmare?"

And there was the sassy Glitter God that I hadn't... okay, *had*...missed.

"Enough with the American *and* witch bashing. You know that you love both."

Mischief had sniffed. "Perhaps, in small quantities." When I'd reached out to stroke his cheek, he'd turned to catch my palm with a kiss. "Or Crimson-sized ones."

I'd flushed, caught in the intensity of his dark gaze. He was a royal prick who had no idea how to show his emotions but he was also *mine* and he wasn't hiding that.

I'd traced my thumb across his lips, before studying the iron door, which had looked like the one in the Re-education Center: a magic trap to keep everyone out.

I'd booted the door with a *clang*. "How do we get through?"

Mischief had sighed. "First a psychic and then…" His face had scrunched in thought, "…a search engine. This world is as new to me as it is to you, but I'd suggest that your shadows need to stretch their…tentacles…as much as my magic."

I'd grinned. I'd been restraining my crimson for days to honor my promise not to become like my ancestors, but hey, it couldn't hurt to kick a door's ass, right?

When our red and silver magic had exploded out, entwining and blasting into the iron, which had groaned at the force, Mischief had laughed and then I'd been laughing too. Warmth had coiled through me as satisfying as when I'd been screwing in the Pleasure Pool because my shadows had been free and playing with a god's magic.

*Holy hell, what would it've been like if Moon's magic had been joined with ours as well?*

Then the door had finally given way, splattering into thick globules that'd sprayed over us. I'd shrieked, but it'd been worth it to see Mischief's stunned expression, as his hair had been plastered with a tide of iron.

Okami had snickered, wagging his fluffy tail across my face and then Mischief's grimacing one to clean them, before settling back onto my head.

Yet when we'd rushed into the Isolation Room, we'd discovered Amadeus motionless.

I struggled again, before twisting to look at Mischief. His face was pale, as he studied Amadeus.

The room was empty apart from a neat pile of Amadeus' clothes. His gloves were folded on the top. I hated that he'd marched himself into this room at his adopted sister's command and stripped, placing his clothes in that way as if this was a familiar routine or *training*.

"Tell me," Mischief whispered, and I realized that it was the same magic that still leashed him around his ankle and that held Amadeus in a silent moon now, which was freaking him out, "did you enjoy being held as an idol in the Lunar Shrine?"

My jaw clenched. "Jesus, what kind of a son of a bitch do you think I am? I'm not leaving him like that."

Mischief's smile was fond. "Glorious fool, of course not, but how about we strive to keep our *leader* free, whilst those of us who are less loved sacrifice."

My eyes widened. "I said that we were equal and I meant it."

Mischief looked suddenly younger and hopeful but then he scowled. "Childishness."

He twirled, shoving me onto my ass, before stalking to Amadeus.

I hissed, battling to stand.

"You do not have permission to be dead, Amadeus," Mischief's words were commanding, but his voice was softer than I'd ever heard it. "You're needed here…*loved*…I demand that you answer." He coughed to cover the way that his voice cracked.

I pushed myself to my feet, edging closer to Amadeus.

*Please, please, say something.*

Amadeus remained hanging in the smoky moon, silent and motionless.

"Is he…?" All the hexes and curses in the witching world couldn't get me to say *dead* out loud.

When Mischief shook his head, I could've caught Mischief in the waves of joyful shadows that burst from me, flooding the Isolation Room blood-red. Instead, I smiled until my mouth ached. Then I noticed that Mischief wasn't smiling.

"That would be the good news, right?" I ventured.

"Pray, do you not believe that in life there are tortures worse than death?" Mischief demanded.

I tilted my head. "Seriously, I have a whole list: listening to people literally misuse the word *literally*, the way that the hairs around my ankle never seem to shave, and clowns. Trust me though, whatever's happening to Amadeus, he's alive and that's so freaking fabulous I'd *literally* dress as a clown with unshaved legs in celebration."

Mischief's nose wrinkled. "I shall never rid my mind of such a disturbing image."

I smirked. "You're welcome."

"Insufferable witch, your incubus endures the worst torment for his kind," Mischief huffed. His wings spread wide; popcorn scented magic crackled along their feathers and sparked across the moonbeams trapping Amadeus as if testing them for weaknesses. "*Isolation* means no touch. My, what clever wolves they are in this Kingdom of Gods to wreck their prince with his own nature or should I rather call it training...? The magic has stopped him hearing, seeing, smelling, or talking. Such sensory deprivation would starve an incubus." Mischief's eyes became hazy, as he swallowed. *On a witch's tit, was Mischief remembering suffering a similar punishment as well?* My shadows swirled around me, as agitated as I was to kick the ass of whoever had hurt Mischief. I didn't have to be Freud to see that Mischief had suffered one screwed-up childhood. "When I pull the incubus from his isolation," he whispered, "it shall feel like being brought to life."

My eyes widened. "You can save him?"

Mischief gave a wicked grin. My skin tingled, and my pulse beat loudly in my ears.

*Boy, was Mischief hot when he played the masterful card.*

Then Mischief's silver sizzled against the beams, dragging them away from Amadeus.

When I thrust my shadows towards Mischief to help, however, he held his hand up to stop me.

"Desist. I shall accomplish this myself," he rasped.

There was something about the feverish way that he watched Amadeus, which told me he *needed* to be the one to rescue him. When Zetta had trapped Mischief in the House of Silver, he'd been helpless and dying. He'd been unable to save Moon. The asshole witches had reduced a god to a slave, just like Banan now Moon Leashed him.

Honestly, it was my fault too because I hadn't understood that Mischief needed to feel that he had as much a place in my pack as my Charms and Aquilo. Words meant nothing to my mage god, only actions. And he had to prove himself with Amadeus.

I wish I knew how to prove to Mischief that I loved him as well…*because I did.*

When I met Mischief's gaze, I nodded, even though it was agony to haul my shadows back inside, rather than allow them to fight alongside him. Okami nibbled at my hair, yanking on it in retaliation, but I only stroked his head.

*Mischief did know what he was doing, right?*

Mischief gritted his teeth, as his skin became clammy. He wrenched on his own magic, where it'd entwined with the trap, tugging it away from Amadeus. To my shock, it wound around Mischief's chest like glimmering ivy, and Mischief's breathing became ragged.

*Was I about to bring to life one of my pack by sacrificing another?*

I trusted Mischief, but this wasn't the Realm of the Seraphim or some dickish Angel World. I protected my guys, and their gorgeous asses would have to deal with it.

I darted forward to catch Mischief's shoulders, as he swayed, but the magic had already slithered down to his waist and then around his legs like boa constrictors. Mischief's eyes were glassy with panic. So, he had a *thing* about snakes, just like Emperor freaked out over spiders.

Could the trap somehow tell Mischief's fear and use it against him?

Okami flew around Mischief, barking and rubbing his fluffy head across Mischief's cheeks to distract him, just as I licked down his neck and caressed across his peaked nipples. Slowly, Mischief calmed from the panic, turning his head to capture my lips with his in a tender kiss.

"Thank you," he breathed, before his magic surged.

The entwined moonbeams fizzed like they were in agony, pulled against their will towards Mischief's ankle.

I clasped around Mischief's neck. "What on earth are you…?"

"I'm merely trapping the room's magic within the cuff. Please admire the irony," Mischief panted. "The magic, meanwhile, is merely trapping me more firmly within the binding."

*Woah, that would be a hold up one witchy minute…*

"There's no *merely* about it," I insisted.

"Oh, dear. It's done." With a final heave, the magic slithered into the cuff, and Mischief collapsed to the floor.

I tumbled down with him, at the same time as Amadeus fell in a tangle of limbs on top of us both. I yelped, as Amadeus' elbow caught my stomach, and Mischief groaned.

"Don't mind me," Mischief grumbled, squashed underneath Amadeus, "I'm only the hero here."

I snickered, then I brushed Amadeus' hair away from his face. *Wait, why weren't his eyes opening?*

*Come on…come on…just a little flash of those sinful eyes…*

Okami whined, before flying around Amadeus and

munching hard on his ass. I winced. *Huh, Sleeping Beauty Okami style.*

Amadeus' eyes snapped open. I'd never been so relieved to see the way that they glittered. Except, they also gleamed with tears like he was still in agony, and instead of speaking, he whined, high and desperate. Shivers wracked him, and he flinched every time that Mischief shifted beneath him.

Mischief and I exchanged a concerned glance, before Amadeus' gaze settled on me as if believing for the first that I was there.

"You still want me," Amadeus breathed like a prayer.

It was freaking fabulous to hear the beautiful lilt of his voice. But at the same time, my breath hitched, and my chest ached. Had he been trapped here thinking that because of his role in betraying us to his sister and Vala's treatment, he no longer had a place in my pack?

Perhaps, that would be worse than dying to an incubus wolf.

I licked across the seam of Amadeus' lips, sighing at their familiar tantalizing taste of chocolate. "*Always,* remember?"

Mischief wriggled underneath him. "I'm certain that these pants are tight enough for you to be assured that we *both* want you." A ghost of a smile hovered on Amadeus' lips; I hadn't realized how precious his easy laughter had been until Vala had taken it away. "Pray, do you need it branded on your cute behind, alongside the Charmer's Claim, that your entire pack love you?" His gaze softened. "Indeed, *I* love you."

*Hocus pocus, had Mischief always craved the same thing to be said to him?*

Mischief's wings cradled Amadeus, whilst I stroked his hair. Each caress fed him, just like every word of love and desire.

Amadeus darted a glance between us. "Would it please you to go skin to skin?" He murmured. "You give me so much, see, and I've never asked anyone before but…let me show you how much I love you."

Mischief nodded, lifting his hand towards Amadeus'.

I remembered the sensation in Wild Hall, when Amadeus' finger had touched mine through his torn glove. Touching an incubus' hand gave them power: Amadeus had been able to read all my desires, and I'd sensed his. If he was free to use his power, rather than hiding behind his gloves, I had a feeling that he'd be the deadliest of my charms.

What Amadeus was asking for was more intimate than a screw or anything that I'd done with my other princes. Yet Mischief hadn't hesitated.

How could I expect my pack to be honest with me, if I still tried to hide behind masks because hey, being flayed was scary.

I resolutely held up my palm like I was about to go to war.

When Amadeus' lips twitched, it was worth it. He touched the tips of his fingers on each hand to mine and Mischief's at the same time. I heard Mischief sigh as he arched, but I was lost myself by then, spiraling into Amadeus' pulsing needs and darkest desires. I jolted, moaning at the sensation of Amadeus, as I was flooded with his pleasure, which coursed through him and his throbbing dick, and every tingling moment of it to *please me because he loved me...and Mischief.*

At the same time, my own needs, desires, and pleasures spiraled, caught together with Mischief's, until I gasped, peaking on the intimate connection as Amadeus read every fantasy, as well as truth. Like endless mirrors, I saw my love reflected, alongside Amadeus' and Mischief's. I shuddered because our needs matched in a way that wrecked me: we didn't simply love, we *needed* to be loved because we'd lost.

Shocked, I wrenched back from Amadeus at the same time as Mischief did. Then we lay in silence, blinking at each other. I felt like I'd had a mind-blowing screw with both of them and at the same time had just confessed my entire past over tequila.

A headache thumped behind my temples.

Mischief eased himself up, but Amadeus wouldn't let go of him, clinging around his neck, whilst clasping his own hands together, as if to resist the temptation of touching Mischief again with them.

Mischief sighed, sitting Amadeus on his lap. Amadeus snuggled down with a sexy wriggle.

*And that wasn't hot at all...*

But I got it because *skin to skin* brought you closer than screwing, Claiming, or Wolf Biting, and only a couple of weeks ago, I'd been the queen at avoiding second dates.

Okami yapped, before swooping to snatch Amadeus' glove off the top of his pile of clothes and wrapping it around his head, as if he was performing a sensuous dance. Amadeus took the glove and slipped it on like it was another prison. Okami's tail drooped, but Amadeus patted him on the head.

"If it pleases you," Amadeus waggled the fingers on his other hand, "these bad boys need to go back in their holster."

Okami snapped his fangs into the final glove and pulled it onto Amadeus' hand like this service was his way of showing *his* love.

"I take it that you experienced the same as me?" I asked.

Amadeus and Mischief nodded.

When I shuffled closer, Mischief wrapped his wing around me; his feathers were warm and safer than home ever had been. "So, who'd you lose?"

Mischief stiffened. "My magic is terrible." He

avoided my eye. "I had little control over it when I was young, and my father…" He bit his lip. "I was punished for his death; I deserved to be. I assure you, I understand about the need to control power."

He ducked his head like he expected me to reject him even now.

My eyes burned with tears, as I rested my head on his shoulder, and Amadeus pressed his lips to Mischief's in comfort.

Mischief raised his gaze with painful hope.

"Whatever those dickheads did to you, I bet my witchy ass that you didn't deserve it," I replied. "And I'm sorry, you know, about your dad. I'd have loved to have met him."

Mischief's laugh was choked with tears. "I do believe that you're the first person to say that to me."

"By the moon, let me be the second." Amadeus' large eyes shone in the dark. "I'm sorry, see, because my dad was killed when I was…" He broke off, shaking, and Mischief hushed him, clasping his arms tighter around his waist. "My mum fancied a shag with an incubus. My dad was a famous pianist." Amadeus smile was gentle. "He was called to the court by the queen herself for a performance, but when he was there…" How much didn't I want to imagine what had happened to him trapped amongst the wolves? *Entertainer* appeared to have a different meaning than simply playing the piano, as Emperor had shown me. "Mum never meant to have me, of course. Although, I often wondered whether that was the lie, and the queen did want an incubus mongrel." I flinched at the rawness of his pain. "Dad would often tell me the story of how he snatched me back once I was born. I hadn't been given a name, and dad's favorite musician was Mozart, so he named me Amadeus, see? It pleased me to dance, whilst dad played. If we hadn't been in hiding, we'd have been famous, well, dad would tell me that each time that I danced." He fiddled with Mischief's hair like it could somehow protect him from what happened next, and no matter how much I wished that they'd had a fairy tale ending on Broadway, I'd sensed enough when we'd been skin to skin to know that this would be no *Billy Elliot*. "Fur and fangs, when mum and the Crescents found us…"

When Amadeus broke off with a sob, Okami howled and wound around his neck.

*Holy freaking hell…*

"Then I'm sorry too." A tear trickled down Mischief's cheek. "I shall find this foul fiend who is no better than the most brutal of Glories and—"

Mischief's face became lit with a predatory light, which reminded me just how dangerous he could be. "There's no need, see. Mum died in mysterious circumstances. They never could find out how."

Mischief snorted. "You're one terrifyingly pretty Beta."

Amadeus smirked. "I know."

Both my guys had been responsible for a parent's deaths and yet, I didn't care. I'd known that they had secrets and dark pasts but also that they'd risked and sacrificed far more than most dicks who'd have judged them as wicked, savage, or beasts.

All I knew was that they were mine and *I'd* die to protect them. Perhaps, I'd have to give up the title of the First Date Queen...?

Suddenly, Amadeus squirmed around in Mischief's lap, until Mischief's wingtips pulsed with pleasure at the friction across his leather encased dick. Amadeus grasped my hair, yanking me closer.

"*Ow*, enough with the hair pulling, unless, you know, everything's in kinky fun." I batted him away, but he only smelled my neck. "I that the wolf way of telling a witch that she smells?"

"Do you wish to stink of waterlilies? Because you've been poisoned by an incubus." Amadeus had become ashen.

I sniffed at my frizzy curls. "*Hmm*, lemony fresh. Chill out, I was just in the Pleasure Pool..."

"Goddess moon! That's one of the most dangerous rooms in this kingdom," Amadeus hissed; his gaze hardened. Why did I keep forgetting that he was as much an assassin as a sexy dancer? How much of *Flame* — the seducer trained ever since he'd been adopted as prince to draw me in to love him, so that he could burn me — lurked within the Prince of the Gods and how much of the true Amadeus remained beneath the conditioning? "Do you believe that I imagined these s-scars on my back or the s-slaughter of my d-dad? Please, my adopted sister and mum are deadlier than the royals of the Wilds, they just hide their cruelties better."

I took a final sniff of my curl. "And do they just mix into the pool your magic...blood...or pheromones...? Help me out here."

Amadeus curled his tongue behind his teeth, and his smile was suddenly teasing.

*Don't say it...*

"Semen." Amadeus licked his lips, before glancing at my slyly. "It'll be good for your complexion and make your hair shiny." Then he blushed. "Have I shamed you?"

I caught Amadeus' lower lip between mine, sucking and then biting. When he melted against me, I loved that he no longer flinched from my touch. "Hey, there was I thinking that you hadn't personally come on my head."

Mischief spluttered with laughter. "How delightfully romantic."

Amadeus blinked. "Do you wish me to?"

I reddened as much as Amadeus. "That wasn't an offer, come happy. Now we need to get back to that sperm pool because your sister is returning at dawn and if she finds us gone—"

"You didn't have permission to free me?" Amadeus' eyes widened, before he scrambled off Mischief's knee.

Amadeus' chest rose and fell too rapidly, as he spun around like he was looking for the trap to put himself back inside the torture again.

Mischief sprawled back on his elbows. "I assure you that I have begged to be returned to my *discipline* many times, but the woman who first loved me," holy hell, it hurt to hear that but at the same time, I could never hate that someone else had loved Mischief and given him what he needed, as well as a family, "taught me that I deserved to be saved the same as anyone else. It's *our* choice to risk your rescue. It's *your* choice as prince whether you'll attempt the rescue of your kingdom."

Amadeus' laugh was dark and bitter. "You've no idea what I've attempted for this kingdom. But I'm no prince. I was picked to play the part." My shadows seethed. If I couldn't convince Amadeus that he deserved respect, love, and to rule, then how could I save either him or his kingdom? "I'm nothing but a pretty mongrel."

Mischief rose up on beating wings that crackled with magic. "What did I say about daring to call yourself *mongrel*?"

When Amadeus squared his shoulders (powerful now that he'd fed on pleasure), I shuddered that my two guys would be fighting. Yet there was something in the way that Amadeus tilted his chin, as if he didn't understand Mischief's fury, but wouldn't back down anyway.

*Huh, it was almost as if...*

"Hold up on the ass whipping, mongrel isn't simply an insult here, right? Instead, it's like there's more than one of you...more than one mongrel...?" When I glanced between them, I didn't miss the way that both of their shoulders relaxed with relief that they wouldn't have to fight either.

Perhaps, I'd have to be the one to make sure that if there was any fighting, it'd only include wrestling, chocolate sauce, and dollops of nakedness.

Amadeus wrapped his arms around his middle. "*Mongrels* are the same to me, as Omegas are to Moon. They're the reason I lied to you. I would never have... despite everything Vala threatened...betrayed you, if it wasn't for..." He broke off, anguished. "Let me show you, please. The Kingdom of the Gods is riddled with secret tunnels, which the Alphas don't know about. I can take you to the mongrels."

My heart pounded in my chest, and the back of my neck prickled. I was having a nasty case of Betrayal and Lies Tummy Ache again. I had to control the crimson tide of my shadows, and Mischief had just bound his magic even more closely to the Lunar Shrine. I needed Amadeus to survive here, as well as to work out how to stop Vala's plans with the delegates.

Yet did I trust Amadeus to lead me into secret tunnels this close to dawn?

*Yeah, I witching did.*

When I'd touched skin to skin, I'd sensed Amadeus' darkest desire. It'd been to be *loved*…and for a dad who he'd lost to the wolves.

What did it matter that I was a witch? Amadeus and I had both witnessed our parents' murders, and I'd figured that I'd spend my life alone with that grief. Yet now, I'd never be alone again.

Yet that didn't stop my pulse racing because I was about to discover who the *mongrels* were in this underground kingdom, which was as savage as the Wilds, as much a prison as the dome itself, and as claustrophobic as the wardrobe that I'd huddled in on the night of my parents' slaughter.

## CHAPTER 6

E ven with the tight ass of an incubus to watch swaying in front of me down the narrow secret tunnel and the nibbled kisses of a god on *my* ass to distract me, I couldn't stop the panic building.

The trauma of listening to wolves prowl *clacking* around the wardrobe, whilst *I'd* huddled inside and *they'd* devoured my parents, had turned me into a claustrophobic, go figure.

Just for a moment, I froze, and Mischief's nose jabbed me in an intimate place that had my toes curling. Mischief let out a muffled yelp.

*Clack — clack — clack.*

My heart beat so hard in my chest that it ached, and sweat trickled down my neck and between my tits. The earthy walls of the tunnel stank of death and decay: they were closing in. I struggled to draw in deep breaths through my nostrils, as my hands clenched against the clay-like floor.

*Get a grip, Crimson, you're the one clambering through the walls of the Kingdom of the Gods and not the werewolves of your nightmares.*

It wasn't the full moon. The Alphas couldn't shift now, right?

I still glanced over my shoulder like I'd see a pack of wolves hunting me. Instead, there was only darkness.

Yet I'd face even the nightmare of these tunnels and spook wolves, if it meant that I finally understood what dickhead had made Amadeus feel that he wasn't worthy enough to be a prince, simply because he was a *mongrel*, whatever the witching hell *that* was. My shadows hungered to wrap themselves around every wolf who'd bullied him because of his incubus blood and shake the prejudice out of them. But boy, had my time in High School and with the witches shown me that changing people's views wasn't as easy as that.

*Still, surely a little shake never hurt…?*

Then the jab of Mischief's nose sharp between my thighs (was it like a godly power to even have a sexy nose?), made *me* yelp.

"Don't mind me," Mischief circled his nose, and my eyes fluttered shut, "why, I ask, would I mind having my face used as a handy sex aid, whilst we have to return before dawn or risk the princess' wrath. Ah yes, and discover the truth of why your Charm appears addicted to infernal betrayal."

I winced, opening my eyes, as I shuffled forward. "Don't get all preachy Archduke Asshole. Aren't you always the one who rants about the responsibilities of royalty? He promised to show us these mongrels. Let's give him a chance."

I knew that Amadeus was listening. He'd hunched his shoulders, but hadn't stopped crawling, and I hurriedly followed him, until the tunnel widened enough for us to shuffle around to face each other.

Okami wagged his tail, settling onto Amadeus' shoulder with a determined pout, as if to show his solidarity.

Okami had turned wild, but I'd been wrong to ever want him tamed.

Amadeus' face was ashen, and his nail scored across the back of his hand, beading it with blood, until Mischief trapped his hand with his own to stop him.

"It's like this," Amadeus whispered, "I'm not simply Prince of the Gods or even Betas. I'm Prince of the *Mongrels* too because if I wasn't, then they'd have no one to care for them." Finally, Amadeus looked up, glancing between both Mischief and me. "A mongrel is a bastard: *I'm Prince of Bastards.*"

Then he held his breath like he expected us to start ragging on him.

*What kind of dickhead did he think that I was?*

Mischief only snorted. "Oh, I'm already *God* of Bastards, and bastards are glorious."

I grinned. "Then you're *my* bastard."

Amadeus took a shuddering breath. "I still please you?"

His desperate hope flayed me.

"It's interesting that you ask for reassurance *before* your explanation," Mischief said with a steel threading his softness that even had me stiffening. "Do tell us why you've dragged us into the dark? What do you risk so much to show us?"

My red stung me in its fury that I hadn't comforted my Charm, promising that he brought me nothing but pleasure. Yet Mischief was right, and if I was going to be a Chief Alpha, sometimes I had to be a hardass.

*Being a hardass sucked.*

Amadeus whined. Then he gazed at me with his large eyes, which glowed in the black. "Mongrel means non-pure wolf shifter. Do you remember how close I told you my kingdom was before the Wolf Wars tore us apart?"

I nodded, remembering the feel of Amadeus, and his breath gusting against my tingling skin.

"Fae, Fallen, elves, mages, and incubi… The Alphas lure them to their kingdom or else they're thrown to them by the witches. Then they keep their bastards… like me." Amadeus' fingers tightened around Mischief's like somehow, he could be protected from his own truth.

*Son of a bitch…*

I recoiled, swallowing hard, as my red bled down the corridor lighting it in an alien dawn.

How dare these jerks piously pray to their Moon Goddess with their shrines and chaste Omegas sunk in their own grief for their missing and dead, whilst at the same time, they stole the kids of other supernaturals and passed on the pain to them.

Crack my cauldron, I'd hoped that Moth had been the only cub substitute in this kingdom. Was the queen running a whole *adoption* scheme?

Amadeus swiped his tongue across his lips, before admitting, "The cubs are kept in the Mongrel Pit. Then the Alphas choose a cub on their eighteenth birthday like Vala chose to raise me. Except, in my case," he glanced at me with the same anxious hope, "she was training me to sacrifice to the Charmer."

Mischief's expression was dark and cold in a way that reminded me that he was ancient and seriously powerful. Right now, I shivered because it looked like it was *my* witchy ass that he was imagining hurling his silver disks at. "Interesting that you also *chose* your wolves for your twenty-first birthday. I'd suggest that in every conceivable way that matters, witches and wolves are the same. What a delightful irony. I'm sorry, does it hurt to think that you've taken part in the same deplorable customs as Vala?"

"Look you, she's not the same," Amadeus hissed,

snatching his hand away from Mischief and nuzzling closer to *me* instead. Okami brushed silkily down me, tucking himself into my toga, until only his nose poked out. I smiled, as my shadows lapped around Amadeus, buzzing joyfully that he was defending me. "Don't *ever* compare the Charmer to my adopted sister. You've no idea... They're not the same. Crimson had no choice, and I love her brand on me because I *want* to be hers."

When he squirmed around like he was trying to pull down his pants to show off the **WCH** branded on his pale ass, I stilled him, pulling him closer.

"Just so you know, that pleases me a whole witching lot." Amadeus sighed like he'd be feasting on my pleasure for days. "But Mischief is right as well." Mischief arched his brow: he'd be equally insufferable now. "When I arrived back in England, I didn't know what was going on and I allowed myself to be led by Stella. I still chose to go to the Omega Training Center, however, and select Moon like one person can own another. Honestly, I thought because it was tradition, my legacy, and job that made it okay but it freaking didn't. I know that now, and I promise I'll do everything I can to help all of you reclaim your kingdoms or break free from the witch treaties that hold you in collars."

Amadeus burned with a bright beauty as he gazed at me. "Our Wolf Liberator." Then he licked down my neck, and I quivered. "I'll still be yours, even if you free me from my collar." His arms tightened around me. "You'll never lose your Charms."

"Well," Mischief sighed, "that was quite the speech. But witches' promises are cheap, and so are wolves', it'd appear. Unless mongrels are invisible…?"

Amadeus scrambled across me to pin Mischief with surprising strength to the wall of the tunnel. To my shock, Mischief didn't struggle.

"Who's a Mr Sassy God?" Amadeus breathed, teasing down Mischief's chest. "Do you need to see before you'll believe?"

Amadeus' hand hovered over the hardness in Mischief's leather pants, and the god's breath stuttered. Then Amadeus pressed the wall beside Mischief's hip.

A grille clanked open beside my head, and I shuffled to the side. When I peered through the new opening, I gasped.

*Holy hell, I'd thought that only witches stuck wolves in cages…*

Row after row of iron cages lined two sides of a shadowy room without windows. I wrinkled my nose at the musty stench.

*Was this an orphanage or a jail run by dicks?*

I'd have to go with *dicks*.

My throat burned, but I forced myself to look closer.

*Boy, did I wish that I hadn't.*

The kids in the cages didn't even have mattresses or blankets. They shivered as they curled into balls or hugged their knees. Some had green or blue hair, wings, or fangs.

I figured that it was close to dawn now, which meant that I should've been rushing back to the Pleasure Pool but…

I was an asshole who'd thought that I had it tough being the charity case in the elite world of yacht parties and tennis clubs, whilst here kids were caged in a room without windows.

*Here* was the truth behind my second Charm, and I needed to learn it all. How the ever-witching hell had my sweet Amadeus survived growing up like this and how had he managed to persuade us all that he'd been a pampered prince?

I caught the sob in my throat, swinging to Amadeus and cuddling him as epically as Moon ever would. His fingers bit around my waist like he needed the touch as much as me.

"I do not disgrace you as a Charm, now that you know what I am and where I come from?" He mumbled without looking up.

There was no way on earth I was letting him think that I was the type of asshole who cared whether he was a true prince or a pauper.

I pushed him back, gripping his chin so that he was forced to meet my eye. "I love you, and nothing you've suffered makes you a disgrace, right?"

When I glanced at Mischief, he was staring through

at the kids with such fierce distress that I shook. What had happened after Mischief's dad had died? Had Mischief been raised in an orphanage like this or had he been sent to jail?

"But I *am* a disgrace," Amadeus' long eyelashes curved onto his cheek, "because I displeased Vala and now the children's blankets have been taken away, see?"

I blinked. "Hey, I know that you're a prince, but you can't be blamed for every dickish thing, which happens in your entire kingdom."

"He means that Vala uses punishments on the mongrels as a means to control him, do you not?" Mischief's shoulders were stiff. "If you do not obey her, she removes privileges from the children."

*Since when was a blanket a privilege?*

When I let go of Amadeus' chin, he cast a curious glance at Mischief. "Who hurt you?"

Mischief's gaze became carefully blank. "A fanatical tyrant who shall never hurt anyone again because by my hand he rose not into the light but was washed away to his watery doom."

*How did Mischief always manage to make his terrifying pronouncements so hot?*

Except, it was lucky that the fanatic's ass had already been *washed away* or my churning crimson would've broken on his head because he'd been the one to raise Mischief cruelly enough that he looked at those kids in cages and saw himself.

*Holy hell, Amadeus had been one of the kids in cages.*

I clasped Amadeus like he'd break, pulling him into a petal-light kiss. I craved for the sweet taste of him. I needed him to know that he was safe now with *me*.

*Yet look at that... I wasn't safe.*

When I pulled back, it took a moment to realize that his eyes gleamed with tears. My stomach dropped.

"I've done bad things," Amadeus murmured; on each word, his lips caressed mine. Why did he have to choose now to confess to me? *Why did he have to confess at all?* "I've allowed..." His voice shook with anguish. "It's changed me, and my dad would hate what I've become. But on my fangs, I only did all that for the mongrels, see, and I'll never regret it. Even though my dad would be ashamed."

"Your dad would be *proud*." Mischief's eyes blazed.

In this tunnel, there was some serious *daddy issues* going on for all three of us...

But Mischief was right: I bet that both his dad and Amadeus' would've been proud of them.

*What about my dad?*

Would *he* be ashamed that I'd followed in mom's footsteps and taken Charms? Would he have been *afraid* of my crimson shadows or would he be proud that I was trying to put it right and help the wolves, just like he'd tried to protect the Ambassador?

Suddenly, The Cat Empire's "Wolves" exploded into

the Mongrel Pit; the music echoed around our tunnel so loudly that I jumped.

Well, there went my sombre moment of reflection, replaced with a ska beat like a burst of sunshine. That was one way to wake up the kids. If my uncle had tried this, I'd never have been late for school.

My breath caught. *What if the music meant that it was dawn already?*

*Clank* — the cage doors swung open.

The cage furthest from the grille was larger than the other ones. There was a flash of emerald, whir of gold, and then…*a creature*…twirled out of the cage.

When I'd first seen Mischief, I'd thought him the prettiest man that I'd ever seen. Boy, did he now have some competition.

The guy's waves of emerald hair were matched by his huge emerald eyes. He was already dressed like maybe it was the only set of clothes he had (although since I was the loser trussed up in a toga, who was I to rag on him about that?), in a white shirt with slashes at the back and smart black trousers.

Jesus, then there were his burnished gold wings, which he stretched behind him, rolling his shoulders.

*Wing Envy was officially a thing.*

"Who's that?" I breathed, mesmerized.

Amadeus giggled. "A tone-deaf brat who's also a brilliant kisser."

*Okay, that didn't make me squirm with warmth at all...*

I flushed. "I meant—"

Mischief quirked his eyebrow. "We're all quite aware what you meant, witch."

I stroked my fingers through Mischief's feathers and smirked at his efforts to restrain his purr. "So, he's an angel like you...just a kind of Gold Card upgrade?"

The way that Mischief's feathers ruffled in outrage was so worth it. "Nobody is like me."

"Hey, I believe you."

"If it pleases you, the sexy winged one in there is more of a wicked devil." Amadeus licked my cheek. "But until I was chosen as prince, he was my best friend. Since then, I've used these tunnels to visit him. Vala tormented him if I didn't behave...if I hadn't told on you."

My eyes widened. "I know that Ramiel has a crush on Lucifer, but were you holding out on me and—

Amadeus caught his snicker in his palm. "As both you and Ramiel desire kinky roleplay with the ex-king of the Underworld, then I vote Emperor for the part." Amadeus curled his tongue behind his teeth with a teasing wink that crept a blush up my neck. "Jax down there is more of a wolf with a Dark Fae side."

"Well, hello there, Tinker Bell," I breathed.

Jax danced below us in the shadows to the funky drums. He was as fluid as molten gold. His beauty burned me, heating me in crashing waves. His wings beat, as his back arched. I bit my lip at the way that his long legs contorted as he dropped into the splits.

A witch could do a lot with moves like that.

*Naughty, naughty, brain…*

Then Jax grinned, before joining in with the lyrics at the top of his voice…

Mischief, Amadeus, Okami, and I all winced in unison.

*So, fae sucked at singing, who knew?*

Amadeus shrugged. "I asked for this song as a daily reward for the mongrels because I knew Jax would love it. Whenever I could, I taught him."

Mischief sniffed. "Then I know who to spank for his appalling caterwauling."

Amadeus' gaze became half-lidded. "You only had to ask, and I meant his dancing, daft god. I always thought that if only he'd been trained like me, *he'd* have been the one who should've been famous. I wish that I'd been allowed to dance with him." He smiled fondly. "His singing is his own unique gift."

Yet it was the way that Jax's emerald eyes gleamed that enthralled me. It was like caught in that first moment of the day he was alone, happy, and *alive*. For the length of the song *he was free*.

I remembered the way that Amadeus had danced for Emperor in the ballroom. Did Amadeus understand how much earning this song had meant for his friend?

Did Jax think of Amadeus every time that he danced? *Hecate's breath, if it'd been me, I would've done.*

Mischief's eyes narrowed as he glanced at the dancing fae. "What's so exceptional about this spinning fairy that you'd risk everything for him?"

Amadeus' smile lit up in the same way that it had when he'd first seen Moon in Wild Hall. "Please, understand that Jax means happiness and hope." *I was calling a serious case of hero-worship.* "We raised each other as kids here in the Mongrel Pit. Then when I was chosen as prince, he promised to stay behind and always care for the others. But even though I had to obey, he resisted for us both."

*Okay, more like a case of serious hero.* Why was my neck tingling?

When the song shutoff, the kids groaned, crawling out of their cages in uniforms just like Jax's. They ruffled their hands through their messy hair and rubbed at their eyes.

I hadn't been ready to marry (let alone think about having kids yet), but seeing so many orphans in this dank windowless room, when I'd been raised in a billionaires' mansion, made my guts churn. It'd been lonely rattling around in so much space. What would it've been like to have had a new close family like this? But it wasn't as if I could snatch these kids, and my uncle wouldn't be amused to find that his business had been turned into a supernatural orphanage.

*Could my cousins be persuaded to get their asses out here?*

Somehow, nothing had felt entirely real, until I was faced with all these tiny lives because there was no ever-witching way I could leave them here to suffer like Amadeus and his friend had. I knew that I had to fix this myself. Whatever plan Moon and the rest of my Charms had been working on, they'd have to let me in on it. The witches and their Treaty were only part of the picture. There were some wolfie asses that needed kicking, and some that needed saving too.

And some of those asses had added wings or fangs like the toddler with ebony skin and gray wings, who'd flown into Jax's arms: a cute as a button *vampire wolf boy*.

I'd just add that to my list of things I'd never thought that I'd see.

Jax swung the boy around with a dancer's grace, causing him to squeal with glee, before Jax balanced him on his hip in a move that was familiar and practiced. Toads at midnight, he *was* these kids' dad…a *scorching hot* dad, but the only parent who they had in this Dickens style orphanage to look out for them.

*Had all their true parents been murdered the same as mine?*

When the kids flocked around Jax with puppy dog expressions, he grinned.

"Consider me shocked: you little monsters are hungry." Jax's voice was musical and as beautiful as his dancing had been.

When the kids nodded frantically, Amadeus mock-sighed, waltzing to knock on the iron door with a *clank*.

"And what shall I order for young masters today?" When Jax's lip curled back, I saw the sharp point of his fang. "Moonlight, blood, or candies...?"

The kids hopped up and down chanting choruses of *yes, yes, yes*.

Jax cupped his hand to his ear as if he couldn't hear them. "What...? You only want dry toast and water again...? You wish is my command."

He flinched back, however, when the door smashed open and an Alpha stormed into the room.

Amadeus wound closer to me, and Mischief's wings embraced us both.

The Crescents starved the mongrels and their own prince, just as once the Omegas and Betas had been starved, but I couldn't get all judgey because the witches had taught them the trick: to only value the *perfect* and *pretty* and to shut the rest away in the dark. Yet the mongrels had as much right to life, freedom, and love as the rest of the kingdom, and anyone who couldn't look at a fae wolf cradling a toddler vampire wolf and find it beautiful, I was calling out as a dickhead.

Unfortunately, that meant the Crescent backing Jax into the corner was a *dickhead.*

Alpha Dickhead had high cheekbones and silver smeared down her cleavage like the moon had licked her, and *my* Moon would never have touched a wolf like her because her gaze was predatory.

Jax's hold tightened around the boy.

"How about you take the deal today, mongrel?" Alpha Dickhead sneered as she caged Jax in with a pose that would've been seductive if this had been a club and they hadn't been surrounded by silent and fearful kids. "Then I won't have to punish you."

Jax clenched his jaw. "Digby's too young to be chosen." Was the Alpha trying to steal the vampire wolf clutched in his arms, who was now burying his face in Jax's shoulder like if he couldn't see the scary wolf then she couldn't see him? "How about you ask the queen what she thinks? Wait, you don't answer to the queen anymore, do you?"

I'd do anything to protect my new family. I understood Jax's desperation to do the same.

Amadeus gasped. "Now I get why Emperor always speaks of spanking me," he hissed.

Alpha Dickhead's eyes flashed, before she bit out, "Wing."

Jax shuddered, before stretching out his burnished

wing along the wall. *It was glorious.* Then Alpha Dick-head shot out her claws, raking them down Jax's wing.

"Son of a bitch," I snarled.

Instantly, Amadeus wrenched away the grille, drop-ping into the Mongrel Pit and slashing his own claws across the cheek of a startled but now enraged Alpha Dickhead.

Mischief and I exchanged a glance, before breaking our own cover and leaping down on either side of Amadeus, even though Mischief was under Moon Oath to Banan to attack no one within the Kingdom of the Gods, and I risked a tide of blood if I couldn't control my own shadows.

It was dawn, I endangered my family back at the Pleasure Pool, and now to protect Amadeus' people, I threw myself into battle.

## CHAPTER 7

W hen I leaped into battle in the Mongrel Pit, I kind of forgot three things: I'd only ever been in a true battle once before, I wasn't a cross between a graceful dancer and trained assassin like Amadeus, and I sucked at martial arts.

I yelped, falling onto my ass, as my ankle twisted under me.

*Yeah, that was how to make an entrance.*

Mischief sighed, shooting me a glance that was concern veiled by exasperation. At least, that was how I chose to read it, sue me.

I shook the curls out of my eyes, wrinkling my nose against the stench that burned my throat. With a grimace, I snatched my hands away from the sticky floor.

*Yuck, yuck,* and *yuck.*

Had I landed in a dried pool of piss or apple juice? *Please say that they treated these kids with juice cartons...*

The Alpha Dickhead's fangs grew. Her cheek beaded with blood from Amadeus' claws, although it was me who she scrutinized, ignoring Amadeus like he wasn't her prince and weirdly like he hadn't even attacked her.

"Naughty Omega, have you hurt your poor little ankle?" She asked.

*Was she seriously cooing at me?*

I shoved myself up, brushing my palms down my toga and attempting to hide my wince. "Bad Alpha, has someone got a boo-boo on their cheek?"

Like a kid, Alpha Dickhead wiped at the claw-marks, before her eyes narrowed and she caught herself.

When Jax burst out laughing, I jolted with how beautiful his joy was. By the way that Amadeus grinned, I knew that he felt it too. Jax was the most *alive* wolf in this kingdom of the dead. What on earth did it matter that his dad had been a fae?

Unfortunately, Alpha Dickhead's gaze swung sharply back to Jax. Trust me, he didn't want to be the center of her asshole attention because I had the strong sense that he was the only one in this room who she could bully without any consequence, unless you counted the kids, and boy, I didn't want to count them.

Especially the sweet vampire wolf boy who Jax still

clutched to his chest like despite everything, he'd be able to protect him from the Alphas. But then, it looked like Jax had suffered daily to protect him so far. Weirdly, even these kids appeared to be viewed as *worthier* than the guy who'd had the courage to remain locked up with them as their defender.

The wolves' sense of *worthiness* was as screwed as the witches'.

"Moon God, did you wander off your leash?" Alpha Dickhead's false concern as she narrowed her eyes at Mischief, made my body quiver the same as my shadows that swirled around Mischief in a protective mist. His silver rose around him, tingling against my magic. Boy, did I wish that I was touching him *right now,* even if it'd been nothing but our little fingers like when we'd been trapped together in the Lunar Shrine. *I'd even take the feel of his sexy nose…* "Run along back to the shrine, so that we can all *worship* you."

*Powdered mages' balls, that was how to do passive aggression.*

Mischief's eyes flashed, before his wings outstretched, crackling in gilded glory. "I believe it astoundingly unlikely that the queen thinks the mongrels precious enough to be monitored with cameras. Plus, they don't wear collars because I don't imagine that they officially *exist,* until you choose to register them. How interesting your explanations must be to the witches." Alpha Dickhead winced. "Now what was it that I always believed…? Oh yes: A god may be worshiped anywhere. Do you not wish to worship me now?"

Silver disks spun on the palms of his hands like a threat.

*Okay, so Mischief took the passive aggression crown.*

Alpha Dickhead recoiled but then to my surprise, she shrugged. "If you battle me, I'll *worship* you (the Moon God who abandoned us), at the same time as you're sacrificed for breaking your Moon Oath. Come on then, *battle me.*"

When Jax flinched, I wondered how many times she'd taunted him, trying to incite him into a fight that he couldn't win.

Hexes and curses, by the time my pack and I were done with Wolf Kingdom, the Alphas would never look so smug again.

My shadows arose in waves around me, provoked themselves to battle at the Dickhead Alpha's demand. They thirsted to command her, just like she did the mongrels.

*Red, red, red…*

I shook my head, pressing my nails into my palms. I could paint the Kingdom of the Gods crimson. If they were the dead already, what did it matter?

*Wolfie, wolfie, why do you run? Wolfie, wolfie, why do you hide? Wolfie, wolfie, why do you cry? Because of the crimson the girl holds inside…*

My stomach clenched, and I struggled not to hurl as mom's nursery rhyme, which she'd lulled me to sleep with every night, chanted through my mind, chilling me.

I'd been trained even as a kid to hunt and hurt wolves. But I wouldn't be the Charmer that they'd tried to condition me to become.

*I'd be the rebel instead.*

"Witch, control yourself and *control the Crimson Tide*," Mischief hissed. "Was I not clear about the need to halt the cycles of violence and never abuse your power over the wolves, even if their own malice goads you?"

I shuddered, drawing back my crimson with a sharp intake of breath, but they still churned just beneath my skin.

Alpha Dickhead clucked her tongue at me. "There, there, Omega, you mustn't overexcite yourself. I wonder if Omega Witches are prone to hysteria?" I gritted my teeth. *We were prone to shoving our boots up Alpha asses.* Then her gaze hardened, as she sneered at Mischief's disks, "Is your weak magic only for show, Moon God?"

"Don't, *please*," Amadeus begged, before baring his neck to the Alpha Dickhead just for a moment. I still growled. "I was the one who hurt you. I'll take any punishment that you wish."

You'd have thought that Amadeus had just offered Alpha Dickhead his cock and balls wrapped in a bow for Christmas. Perhaps, he *had* by the way that her eyes lit up.

"Vala will be displeased with you, Flame," she chided, before muttering, "Once a mongrel, always a mongrel."

Amadeus winced on the *Flame*, which was the Alphas' assassin style nickname for him because he drew in his targets to love *him* and burn *them*. Except, when I'd been that target, he'd been the one to fall in love and become burned.

Plus, there was no way on earth that my prince would be left to believe *mongrel* was an insult any longer.

"I don't think so," I snarled. "I look around here and I see the most beautiful kids ever." Now it was the kids' turn to look like it was Christmas morning, although I had to swallow hard to hold down the thick feel of tears, because I doubted that they'd ever experienced Christmas. "Fangs and wings are epic extras! Plus, I've always wanted blue hair." The girl with sky blue hair ducked her head, but she was grinning shyly. I pointed at Alpha Dickhead. "You're the asshole who started with the slashing. The cute fae's wing for your ugly face. How about we simply say that we're even, right?"

Jax tilted his head with a wicked grin. "*C*ute, huh?"

I flushed, swallowing. I wanted to slap myself and kiss the grin off his cheeky fae face…possibly not in that order.

Suddenly, Dickhead Alpha backhanded Jax, splitting his plush lip and tumbling him to the side. Even as he dropped to the floor, however, Jax held onto Digby. He banged his own hip and forehead against the concrete but curled into a ball that protected the boy like it was a practiced move.

*Holy hell, I bet that it was.*

"You know better than to speak during a punishment." Dickhead Alpha raised her boot like she was about to stomp on Jax's wing.

Screw controlling the Crimson Tide. My shadows weren't the same dicks who'd belonged to my great-grandmother or mom. *They were mine.* And we could judge together the difference between the wolves who we weren't at war with and those who were about to stomp on a fae's wing.

A *cute* fae…who hadn't even attempted to draw his wing away from Alpha Dickhead's boot.

My shadows exploded from me, at the same time as Mischief's disk hurled from his palm. Yet Mischief screamed, dropping to the floor, as his ankle burned him, and his magic was dragged back inside. The kids flocked around him in comfort, and my guts clenched at the way that he didn't bristle but pulled them closer, as if it was familiar to him.

Mischief might be a god now but he hadn't been raised as one, and the queen's leash had hurt him for trying to protect Jax, in the same way that the Alpha guard had hurt Jax for defending Digby.

This time, I didn't lose myself in the sensation of crimson. Instead, I *was* crimson: it flowed from me, whilst *I* controlled it. My shadows burst over Alpha Dickhead in a wave, just before her boot landed, snatching her with a comical shocked expression and lifting her into the air.

The kids' eyes widened, before they giggled and clapped.

My lips curled into a smile. Then I wound Alpha Dickhead's arms to pin them to her side and spun her towards the cages.

*Slam* — Alpha Dickhead caught her head against the metal.

I winced. That was why I sucked at wolf care. I mean, I fell up stairs for Hecate's sake, unless my shadows had *wanted* to crack her head…?

*Yeah, I was so not thinking about that.*

The kids clapped again like it was all part of the show. I cringed as I lowered Alpha Dickhead to the floor and drew back my shadows who were fluffed up with triumph like they hadn't just…*possibly*…murdered a wolf.

*My shadows were kind of on the scary side.*

Amadeus stared at the felled wolf with the type of shuttered expression and cold eyes that reminded me of his training with Vala and just how deadly he was himself.

It was Mischief who sighed, easing out of the snuggly pile of kids and limping over to Alpha Dickhead. His ankle was seared like it'd been struck by lightning. There were pretty patterns along his pale skin. I hungered to kiss each one and draw away the pain, only that was *his* power and not mine. I was the one with the dickish power to cave in heads.

Mischief examined Alpha Dickhead, before casting a relieved glance over his shoulder at me. "Don't fret. She's only…" He glanced around at the curious gazes of the kids. "…Sleeping."

Digby poked Jax's chest with his small finger. "Sleeping like you."

Jax slid Digby off him, before pushing himself shakily to his feet. "I'm wide awake, little monster."

Digby curled his wings around himself. "Not now, silly," he whispered, "after the guards visit."

Jax froze, before forcing on a wary smile as he edged towards me, which was rude because hey, who'd just saved his way too sexy ass? "Just like that."

Then Amadeus was a blur of weeping incubus as he hurled himself into Jax's arms, knocking him back into the wall with an *oomph*. Jax laughed, musical and joyous again, before wiping the tears away from underneath Amadeus' eyes. Amadeus raised his hand to cup Jax's cheek with such tenderness that I ached.

*Friends* my witchy ass…

Jax might be treating me like I was more dangerous than the guard (maybe he had a point), but the kids flocked around me with excited chants of *Wolf Liberator*.

*Why in the witching heavens was everyone calling me that?*

"What's with the Wolf Liberator?" I demanded.

I didn't miss the way that Amadeus stiffened, before Jax wound his arms around his waist and danced with him, dodging the cages, like they were in the grand ballroom in the House of Silver, rather than the gloom of the Mongrel Pit. I'd never thought that Amadeus could look more seductive than when dancing alone, but held in the arms of the fae who...even I couldn't miss it...*loved* him, they were like sin sprung to life as twins.

*And I wanted both of them.*

What would it be like if they were able to *truly* dance together, as Amadeus desired?

I wet my lips, unable to look away from them or their love. Then Amadeus glanced at me, and I saw the same love blazing for *me* as well, and my heart clenched.

Amadeus was my pack, but Jax had been his before Amadeus had even known me. I'd never take that away from him, but that didn't mean that he loved me any less.

I had a feeling that he loved me *more* because I was

proving that I wasn't the same possessive asshole as Vala.

Then Amadeus yelped, as Jax nipped his neck with his sharp teeth. "Color me surprised: You haven't told her yet...?" He wrapped his wings tighter around Amadeus and danced him towards me. "The Wolf Liberator is a myth. It tells that one day a Charmer would come who wouldn't oppress the wolves but instead, would save them." He rubbed his nose against Amadeus'. "This wayward boy was *obsessed* as a kid."

My shoulders hunched, as I wrapped my arms around my middle. Okami slipped out of my toga, nudging my chin with a whine.

*Had Amadeus only ever cared about me because of his obsession with a myth?*

"Stop," Amadeus ordered with more regal command than I'd yet heard.

Jax snorted, ignoring him.

*So much for Amadeus' attempt to pull princely rank.*

Jax leveled Amadeus with the same glare that Ramiel used on Mischief just before he got smacky. "You're lying to your own Charmer, Ama?"

I couldn't help the growl at Jax's pet nickname.

Mischief raised his eyebrow as he stood, clasping his hands behind his back.

Amadeus pouted, flattening his hands defensively across his ass. When Digby giggled, Amadeus' blush was anything but princely.

"The truth," Amadeus shot an anxious glance at me, "is that I made a pact with the other princes."

My hands shot to my hips in a look so like my uncle in intimidating board room mode that I almost snickered. *Almost.* "Dude, a pact...? Seriously, you don't have to tell me anything, I get that, but *pact* sounds like my wolfies have been hiding something a teeny-weensy bit more important than how you like your eggs in the morning."

"Poached." Amadeus smirked, before yelping, as Jax tightened his wings around him. "Look you, it was a pact to try and save our people," his eyelashes curved onto his cheek as he looked down, "and ourselves. Emperor and Moon knew that they'd be Claimed by the Charmer just the same as me, so we made a pact to make certain that our Charmer would be the Wolf Liberator."

I huffed. "What were you, the three psychics?"

Amadeus raised his ruby eyes to meet mine pleadingly, as if willing me to understand. "I was made to please you, but believe me, I love you because you wish to please *me*. We had to show you the truth and make you our Charmer. Emperor and Moon thought that when a Charmer made us hers, we had to make her *ours*, instead."

When I swayed, Mischief dashed to my side, and I burrowed into the popcorn scented safety of his wings.

I shook, gulping down painful breaths that burned my lungs.

*Take it back...please.*

Why was I shocked? Stella had told me not to be taken in by their angelic eyes and sinful bodies. She'd *begged* me not to allow my Charms to control me.

Even Zetta had warned me in her special way that the princes were tricking me and that I shouldn't trust their beauty.

Yet as Mischief kissed the crown of my head, I realized that it was their *love* that I trusted.

How terrified must the princes have been, spending their lives knowing that they were nothing but their kingdoms' sacrifice for the enemy witch? They were the Tribute to keep the descendant of the monstrous Crimson Terror of the Wolf Wars from slaughtering their people. That their response had been to swear a pact to turn the tables was *epic*. They didn't want to repeat the mistakes of their parents and they wouldn't play the role of the victim Omegas either. Instead, they'd rebel in secret by opening the eyes of their Charmer to the truth of who they were beneath the labels.

My Charms hadn't tricked me. *Instead, they'd been brave enough to allow me to love them.*

Yet Amadeus thought that I'd hate him now that I knew they'd been in charge all along...?

I squirmed out of Mischief's hold, throwing myself

around Amadeus, whilst he was cocooned in Jax's wings, which smelled of cool peppermint like refreshing life amongst this kingdom's death or like peppermint chocolates that I *loved*.

Why had I thought that he'd be any less delicious than Amadeus?

At first, Jax froze like Amadeus was Digby and he needed to protect him from my attack. Then when he realized that I was doing nothing worse than peppering kisses down Amadeus' face and neck, he rolled his eyes.

"This certainly isn't awkward." Jax wriggled, flashing a grin at me that was all fang, "You're into a threesome already?"

I blushed.

"Why wouldn't she want us both?" Amadeus asked with just enough concern that I caught his bottom lip between mine and sucked.

He moaned, before Mischief coughed.

"Little eyes are watching," Mischief said, pointedly.

*Whoops…* Hey, what did I know about kids? Apart from that they pulled *yucky* faces apparently when grownups kissed in front of them.

Jax studied Mischief. "You're uptight but pretty. I like your wings."

Mischief drew his wings more closely around himself. *Shy and uncertain was an adorable look on the royal prick.* "Your wings are assuredly…pretty…as well."

124

Jax nodded like this was a normal opener between a fae wolf and his angelic god (for all I knew, it was). "Is the other angel your mate then?"

My breath hitched. *Ramiel was here?* I drew back, staring around wildly.

The cages were empty.

Mischief paled, before striding to Jax with such a dangerous gleam in his eyes that even I clung harder to my prince and fae cuddle. "Where is he? *Tell me now.*"

Jax swung Amadeus behind him like my second Charm wasn't himself a deadly incubus, before his wings stretched out to mimic Mischief's. "They locked him away because…" His gaze swung to the kids who were circled around Mischief, as if they'd dive on him to defend Jax at any moment. "… He's *sleeping.*"

Mischief bit his lip hard to hold back his cry, as our gazes met.

Where was Ramiel? What in the witching heavens had been done to him? And would we even be able to make him *wake up*…?

## CHAPTER 8

Jax darted to the back of the Mongrel Pit, whilst Mischief and I stumbled after him. Desperation and panic made you graceless, who knew? I skirted the motionless Alpha guard without looking at her, although my shadows did a victory wave over her felled body.

*Honestly, sometimes my shadows could be dicks.*

Amadeus shooed the kids away, although who were we kidding? Perhaps Digby was still young enough to think that Jax was truly left *sleeping* by the beatings, but the rest of the kids' eyes were too knowing for their age. They'd lived as prisoners, watching daily brutalities.

Whatever Jax showed us, these kids had seen worse.

When Jax dropped to a crouch beside a trapdoor, dragging back the iron door with a *clank* to reveal a cage that'd been trapped in the dark beneath, I held back a whimper. But Mischief didn't hold back his. Instead, he dropped to his knees, running his hands across the bars like he was touching Ramiel, who was jammed into the cramped space inside with his wings wrapped around himself.

Ramiel's fairy tale pink hair hung across his pale face that was purpled with bruises, until it matched his pale violet wings, which were streaked with blood.

The asshole Alphas had been playing the Slash a Wing game with Ramiel the same as Jax. Was that some kind of wolf thing or just the cruelest way to hurt an angel whose wings were so sensitive that a kiss there had them jolting like they'd been electrified?

*Holy hell, I craved to kiss Ramiel…*

He was the softest of my guys, even if he was a warrior. The witches had thought that he was a broken Addict Angel, but they'd been wrong.

*How could anyone hurt an angel who was as gentle as Ramiel?*

"Let him out," Mischief's voice was low and dangerous, although his hands shook like he was on the edge of tears, "*now*."

Jax nodded, sliding open the cage. Tenderly, he clasped Ramiel to pull him out. When I dropped to my knees on one side of him and Amadeus on the other to help him, Mischief blinked at us in surprise.

Neither Mischief nor Ramiel were alone anymore. They were both pack, and I'd prove it to them.

The three of us together pulled Ramiel out of the cage. He didn't look any less wrecked lying on the concrete floor. Mischief sat back on his heels, placing Ramiel's head in his lap, before brushing Ramiel's hair out of his eyes.

"The cowards shall die a death worse than every woven nightmare, I swear it," Mischief breathed.

I shivered. *Boy, did he mean that.*

Then Mischief touched his fingers to Ramiel's forehead, and his own breath became harsh.

*He was trying to heal Ramiel by taking his pain.* How much agony had Mischief suffered in his life that he could take others' in silence?

I studied Ramiel's eyes, waiting for them to open and see me. My crimson snaked out, stroking across Ramiel's chest and any inch of skin that hadn't been clawed or bruised...*loving* him.

At last, Mischief slumped back, slamming his fists against his knees with a *smack* that made me wince. "Foul villainy! Am I to become nothing but an impotent toy on a leash with every power denied me?"

When he tore at the cuff on his ankle, it flared up, sizzling. His palms seared.

"*Woah*, enough with the hand barbecuing." I snatched Mischief's burned hands between mine, kissing each one in turn. He shuddered, curling against me. "Okay, so you can't heal Ramiel right now. We'll just have to ask to see Queen Banan and bargain with her to let you off your leash. I learned business tactics from my uncle. Plus, we'll have Emperor with us, and he's epic at diplomacy. If you can keep your death threats to say… once a day…I think that we can demand—"

Jax snorted. "*Demand*, huh? I'm not so sure about your new mates, Ama." He cocked his head. "They give me the crazy vibes."

"And you, fairy with a voice that could slaughter nations, give me the *I need to spank him* vibe," Mischief hissed.

Jax fluttered his peppermint scented wings seductively. "Slow down, sugar wings, you haven't taken me out for dinner yet."

Mischief reddened but before he could answer in spluttered outrage, Amadeus patted his knee.

"No one *requests* to see Queen Banan," Amadeus explained. "If *she* demands to see you, then you should be terrified. I've lived in fear of being asked to dine with her. It'd be a fine thing if she did business or diplomacy like you or the other kingdoms but…" He played with the torn edges of his gloves. "The whole kingdom is her *family*."

"Huh, because all moms keep their kids locked in cages," I growled.

"*Your* mum did." Amadeus' gaze was hard. "She kept *my true prince* in one."

What could I say: *sorry both our moms are dick-heads?* Honestly, maybe I should go with that.

I entwined his fingers with mine. "Our moms are assholes." I ignored the kids' giggles, tightening my hold on Amadeus, even as his eyes widened. "I'll be this Wolf Liberator that you're obsessed with and not because you Charms made me into her but because I'd never have become the same as my mom, just like you'd never have forgotten the mongrels and become a pampered son to *your* mom. Together, we'll help all our pack. But first, we have to awaken Ramiel."

When Amadeus stroked his thumb across the back of my hand, my skin tingled. I sighed, as warmth curled through me.

"Then let me please you," Amadeus murmured.

My gaze shot to the kids who were sitting cross-legged around us like this was a lesson. "Dude, there's a time and a place."

I couldn't help the way that my gaze shot downwards because even the phantom memory of Amadeus licking between my thighs had me squirming.

Amadeus snickered. "There are *other* ways to build my power. Although, maybe not as fun." Then his eyes lit up. "I *am* the criminal prince. We corrupted each other!" Then he whispered, "What do you wish?"

"Command him, witch," Mischief ordered. His fingers slid through my hair, urging me towards Amadeus.

I glanced at Ramiel. "Yeah, seriously not in the mood for…"

Then I caught sight of the ruby sparkle between Amadeus' lips. He was building his incubus power to heal Ramiel. Yet if he did that publicly, he risked revealing something that he'd sworn a Moon Oath never to do.

*Vala would kill him if she found out.*

I drew back, but Amadeus traced his hand down my cheek; his gaze was soft. But black cats, he was as strong as any of my pack and as determined to protect it as an Alpha.

He was far more than simply a *pretty Beta.*

"Sing for me." I loved the way that Amadeus' eyes twinkled at my request; it pleased me, as much as it fulfilled my desire. "You have a voice that could *save* nations."

Amadeus' smile became dazzling at the compliment. He glowed like he was already feasting. I wished to feed him like this every day.

He leaned closer, wrapping his arms around my neck, as if this song was for me alone. When the tip of his nose brushed mine, my breath caught. I was safe in the veil of his midnight hair, and his burning gaze was locked on mine. In the midst of the crowded orphanage, we were alone.

Then Amadeus began to sing, and my red crested around the words, until I was no longer anywhere but in his eyes and song… "The Way You Look Tonight" was being crooned against my lips not by Frank Sinatra but with all the seductive sexiness of an incubus. I was mesmerized.

My lips parted, as I rested my forehead against Amadeus', leaning against him; my skin was hot and tight. A slow smile built inside me, before spreading across my face like light in this darkness. My pulse beat hard and loud in my ears; my heartbeat thundered in my chest.

I shivered, caught in the beauty of my burning incubus' song, until Mischief twisted his hand in my hair, and I snarled.

*Since when did I snarl?*

"It must be morning," Mischief muttered, "and unless our *ruby eyes* here has feasted sufficiently to wake Ramiel, we'll be discovered missing from the Pleasure Pool. I'm already shockingly intimate with Vala's tortures. I'd prefer that you escaped such fun and games."

Amadeus' darted his tongue across my lower lip. "Your pleasure is always delicious."

Then he backed away from me, before hovering over Ramiel like he intended to give him the kiss of life. Instead, his translucent skin glowed, as sparkles whispered from his mouth and into Moon's.

Ramiel's wounds slowly faded. It was like watching one of the paintings in my East Hampton gallery of beaten wolves, bleeding back in reverse, as reds and purples smoothed out into the ivory of the canvas.

Jax booted a cage, sweeping his wings in a furious arc. "I *knew* that your twisted crush on Charmers would get you killed. *Crazy*, yeah?"

*Okay, now I was offended.*

Except, Jax was simply trying to protect the only family that he had: the mongrels. Amadeus had been plucked out of here to be made into a prince, but it didn't stop Jax looking out for him. It appeared that he'd marked me as a threat.

*Yeah, he was a bright…and cute…fae.*

Ramiel awoke with a sigh. Then his eyes fluttered open, and he raised his head to catch Amadeus' lips with his own and deepen the kiss. Amadeus moaned, cradling Ramiel's head.

"Enough hogging the angel. I believe that it's my turn." Mischief wound his hand into Amadeus' hair pulling him away, but I noticed that he didn't let go; he was shaking too hard.

Then Mischief leaned over Ramiel, kissing him with the delicate touch that came from knowing you'd almost lost something more precious than your own life.

*Hocus pocus, I'd spent my entire life knowing how that felt.*

I clambered over Amadeus and Mischief, falling into Ramiel's lap and humming contentedly as his aromatic nutmeg wings wrapped around me. I longed to suck on their tips and show him pleasure to take away the memory of his pain.

"Dude, little eyes," I chided, as the kids watched our contented pile of feathers and cuddles with fascination.

Mischief broke his kiss with a chuckle. "I believe that it's not wrong for them to witness love. They've already been submerged in too much hate. I've removed the stick from my own behind, perhaps you should remove it from your own…?"

Ramiel's lips pinched. "Is this how you've been speaking to our savior in my absence?"

Mischief's eyes widened. He shook his head at me.

How much did I tell Ramiel about the sassiness level of the royal prick? The truth would land Mischief over Ramiel's knee, and the kids seriously didn't need to witness that.

Although, I suspected that both Amadeus and Jax would grab popcorn for the show.

Okami barked, flying out to rub his silky ass in Mischief's face. Hey look, Okami had answered for me.

Ramiel pushed himself up, clasping Mischief's chin; Mischief stiffened.

*Uh oh…*

"You're wearing a toga." Ramiel's hair fell into his eyes, as he tilted his head.

Mischief looked at him blankly. "*Um*, indeed."

Ramiel's brow furrowed, as he examined the cuff around Mischief's ankle. "And bondage gear."

"At least your powers of observation have not been diminished by your ordeal."

Wow, did Mischief like *train* to be a brat...?

To my surprise, Ramiel grinned, pressing his lips once again with affectionate softness to Mischief's. "I'm not diminished because you saved me." He glanced at Amadeus and me. "I shamed Angel World and my Glory, before being declared nothing but an Addict, yet I found family with you all."

When he peeked at me shyly, my stomach lurched with that familiar butterfly excitement. Every time that I saw him, I forgot that he made me as breathless as a teenager with my first crush. He was an ancient and powerful angel, and he was mine like I was his.

I could be a possessive dickhead if it made him feel safe at last, right?

Jax sighed. "What the hell. Do you have room for a *cute* fae?"

What were the chances he was going to forget *that* any time soon?

Jax swooped on top of us, rolling us over into a squirming pile of feathers and outraged snarls. Digby flew over our heads with a giggle, whilst the kids clapped.

*How much did Jax play the clown merely for the kids?*

I panted, staring up into Jax's dancing eyes. His hands rested on my shoulders, and his feathers caressed my neck. When he smiled, his pearly white fangs glinted.

I wasn't thinking about the way that they'd feel grazing my neck...*and I also wasn't lying my witchy ass off either.*

Jax lifted one eyebrow with a smirk like he knew what I was thinking.

*Wait, could fae read minds?* I furrowed my brow in furious thought.

*Amadeus dancing in nothing but a black lace tutu to a ukele rendition of Swan Lake...*

Jax burst out laughing. "I was wrong about your mates, Ama. They're our type of freaky."

Mischief's lips thinned. "I am a god, fairy. And... you're welcome."

Holy hell, Jax *had* read my mind.

*Stop thinking...clear my mind. Aren't you meant to think of a white cat in a dark room or is it a black cat in a white room? Why can I only think of a black and white cat dancing to Swan Lake...?*

Jax nudged me. "Stop scrunching up your face like that or the wind'll change and you'll end up sour like the Alphas."

"It's true," Digby lisped solemnly, "it's why Alphas are mean."

Jax murmured as he rubbed my shoulders reassuringly, "I can only *hear* you when you allow it."

Ramiel glanced between us. "What does he hear?"

*Grrr* – the grumbled growl echoed through the Mongrel Pit.

The kids whimpered, rushing around our huddled group.

*What in the name of Hecate was that?*

"I hear growling, snarling, and yeah, that was a howl." Jax leaped up, wrapping his arms around Digby, who'd flown into Jax's arms, hanging around his neck.

Jax herded the kids to the far wall with his wings outspread like he was ready to fight off the wolves all by himself. I guessed that he'd always been alone, defending the orphans. He stared up at the grille because the noise was coming from inside the secret tunnels and my way out of the Mongrel Pit and back to the Pleasure Pool.

My eyes widened, as my guts churned. "Jesus, it's not the full moon. Your Alphas can't transform in their collars, right? Don't tell me that's another secret you didn't tell me?"

Amadeus shook his head. "Us Charms are the only ones who can transform more than once a month. The witches trapped the rest with the collars."

Ramiel spread his wings as he rose to his feet, dragging Mischief with him. "It matters not what fiends attack. We're at your service, Charmer."

Amadeus slunk to his feet with an outrageous elegance like this was a ball, holding out his hand to me and pulling me up next to him. "What do you wish?"

Mischief's magic thrummed through him. It circled my crimson, which thrashed at the wild howling that echoed through the tunnels.

Mischief's gaze was intent and dark. "Are we here as conquerors to control and be worshiped, or rather as liberators?"

When he glanced at the kids being guarded by Jax, I nodded.

If we fought whoever these wolves were (and wasn't it rude to hunt your honored guests with transformed wolves who weren't even meant to freaking exist?), then we'd risk the mongrels. I didn't care what the asshole Alphas thought. Amadeus was a mongrel, so was Jax and Digby. Every one of the mongrels in this orphanage were now under the protection of Crimson's pack.

*It just sucked that meant I'd probably die.*

I had to lead the wolves away from the mongrels, which meant climbing into the claustrophobic tunnels with my pack and facing my worst fear. If we could lead the wolves away, allowing them to hunt us, but escape back to the Pleasure Pool, then we'd survive.

Yet if the wolves caught me in the narrow spaces inside this kingdom, then just like my parents, I'd finally be devoured by wolves.

# CHAPTER 9

With the way that Emperor kissed me — hungry, savage, and desperate — I'd have thought that he figured on devouring me like the wolves who'd chased me through the secret tunnels.

Wow, I'd *almost* been hunted and caught like my nightmares as a kid.

I shuddered, burrowing closer to Emperor's bare shoulder, as he finally broke the kiss. The sharp scent of liquorice burst through the sweetness of honey that clung to his skin.

"On my fangs, don't ever," Emperor nipped my bottom lip as if in punishment for nearly freaking dying, "leave me behind unable to protect you again."

He pinned me on the circular bed in the room that my pack and I were now locked in. Opulent moon-like doors opposite mirrored the bed, which glowed with an eerie light.

I blinked. Okay, so I was way off base. Emperor wasn't clinging to me like he'd taken up Moon's cuddling rights because I'd risked leading the trans-formed wolves away from the mongrels. It was because I'd *abandoned* him in the Pleasure Pool.

*He'd have been happier if we'd died together.*

How hard was it for Emperor to hide his true Alpha nature and play the Omega?

I gently pressed my lips to his. Emperor had nothing to prove. He'd already spent his life protecting Wolf Kingdom.

*Now I just had to convince him to protect himself.*

Yet when Mischief, Ramiel, Amadeus, and I had clambered back through the grille into the tunnel, whilst my pulse had pounded so loudly that the scrabble of claws and harsh growling had been dimmed by the *thud — thud — thud* of my own heart, I'd been just as prepared to sacrifice myself, as Emperor was.

I could've waited and fought the attackers in the Mongrel Pit but then I'd have been risking the kids.

I might've known more about changing batteries, than changing diapers, but that didn't mean my shadows were dicks. They weren't the same as my great-grand-mother's predators. Instead, they were protectors.

Weirdly, I didn't mind the Wolf Liberator gig.

*Yet were the attackers Alphas? Vala and her Crescent gang…or the Omegas…?*

I'd shaken my head because I hadn't been able to imagine that guys who scampered away at the sight of a tit could be out to savage me. Although, had it been my performance at the Pleasure Pool, which had pissed them off?

Thank every star twinkling in the witching heavens, the wolves still hadn't been close enough for me to make out their fur. But what really had my panties bunched was how they'd transformed in the first place.

The witches thought that they had these wolves tamed. *Boy, were they wrong.*

Mischief had snatched my ass in one hand and Amadeus' in the other, shoving us in front of him, before gently nudging Ramiel after us, leaving himself closest to the wolves. I'd thrown a single glance back at his grim expression.

*Honestly, what was it with my guys and risking themselves to save each other and me?* Yet I was going with *who cared* because it was both hot and tender.

Okami had flattened himself on my head, yapping fiercely.

I'd patted Okami. "Okay, Bravewolf, not helping."

Then Mischief had lifted his eyebrow with an imperious *move, assholes* jerk of his head, and we'd clambered through the tunnels for hours. The wolves had hunted us, and once they'd been so close that I'd turned around and caught a glimpse of their fur.

It hadn't been white or black. Instead, it'd glimmered a silver gray.

I'd gasped: *the wolves hunting us had been Betas.*

Then Mischief had hissed and his magic had whipped out at my crimson, lashing me on. We'd tumbled into the corridor below, just as Mischief yelped at the claws slashing his calf.

Amadeus had snatched my hand, whilst Ramiel had caught Mischief in his wings, then we'd pelted down the corridors past startled Alphas to the Pleasure Pool.

When I'd tumbled through the iron doors, I'd drawn in a shocked breath at the sight of my pack kneeling in front of Vala.

If I'd been the kind of asshole who drew lines, then Vala had just crossed mine. My pack had spent their life being forced to kneel, and now they'd never kneel unwillingly again.

I'd taken a slow breath to calm my shadows, which had raged to dash Vala headfirst into the pool. Then I'd sauntered towards her with Okami scowling at her from the top of my head.

Vala's smirk had faltered.

"Dude, why didn't you tell me that you were visiting your favorite Omega Witch? Then I could've avoided you by not coming back at all." I'd edged past her, yanking each of my guys onto their feet.

Vala's eyes had narrowed. "Yeah, I'm not feeling that excuse. My new *brother*, who my mother demands return to her, played messenger boy."

She'd hauled Moth to her chest, wrapping her arms around him in a way that should've looked protective but instead, had been creepily threatening.

When Moon surged towards Vala with a growl, I'd held him back by his elbow at the same time as Aquilo had.

I'd shot Aquilo a grateful smile.

"My apologies," Mischief had feigned a yawn, "I silenced the cub's tongue. For one with a colossal wit such as myself, he is astoundingly dull."

Moon's growl had been joined by Moth's.

I'd only smothered my own grin because of the practice that I'd had with my cousin's sass at dinner parties.

Vala's fingers had curled into Moon's shoulder, and he'd whimpered. "Naughty Omega, are you going to try the *out for a walk* excuse again? Fur and fangs, you were meant to be cleaning off ready to see my mother, but you're dirtier than before. Queen of Vibrators and now…Togas?"

"Seriously, I slay this look, right?" I'd swished the gauze side to side.

Vala's lips had pinched. "Single skin, you're temping me to slay your behind." When her gaze had swept to Amadeus, she'd snarled. *Why had I forgotten how dangerous she was? Maybe because I'd just escaped being torn apart by freaking Betas...?* "Flame displeased me. Why on the face of the moon is he free of his punishment?"

Amadeus had doubled over like her disapproval had booted him in the balls. My red had stroked over him, whispering how much he *pleased me.*

"Hey, you're the one who sent me to a freaking pool that's drugged with incubus sexy semen," I'd smirked.

"S-semen?" Aquilo had blushed, rubbing at his skin like he'd been marked with invisible come. "Did no one think to point this out to me, *before* I jumped in?"

Emperor had shrugged lazily. "Well, it explains why the water was so tasty."

Aquilo had covered his face with his hands, peeking out at me like I could rescue him. For a sheltered virgin, discovering that you'd bathed in a sperm pool was a shocker, go figure.

"Then my Charm's cock spurted like a chocolate fountain." I'd attempted Amadeus' trick of curling my tongue behind my teeth. I must've pulled it off by the way that Moon had spluttered, pinking all the way down his chest, until he'd matched Aquilo, "So, I had to go taste my *real* incubus. Hey, if you're going to tempt me like that, then it's your fault. You should take it as a compliment. After all, you're the bitch who trained Amadeus."

Vala had looked trapped between preening and

glowering. "And the *Moon God* and the *Addict angel*…?"

*Kudos on turning names into an insult.*

I'd let my smirk widen into a grin. "You know how it is, for the perfect threesome you always need a wolf, an angel, and a god…"

*I'd never thought that I'd have been able to silence Vala.*

Afterward, Vala had led my pack and me in silence to this bedroom, where now Emperor clung to me like a Moon clone. Call me a greedy dick but if I could invent one of those, then maybe my magical tech wasn't all bad.

Okay, I *was* a bad, bad witch.

I was waiting on a summons to Banan and holy hell, was that more terrifying now I knew that she ruled a kingdom with kids in cages and ferocious wolves in secret tunnels. I'd thought that she was a dick when she'd only trapped me in the Lunar Shrine.

Until then, however, I'd allow myself to rest in the arms of my lovers. I was exhausted, hungry, and seriously glad that there were no mirrors to crack with the frizz in my hair alone. Yet I was also surrounded by the mingled warmth and reassuring scents of my pack, rubbing my cheek across feathers, sliding my foot against silky skin, and wriggling my naked ass…

Trust me, squirming out of the toga had been like shedding Vala's tongue licking her ownership all over me, and boy, would I never be able to forget *that* image.

I snuggled further down into bed, allowing my eyes to shut because I was surrounded by my guys, whose bonds and Claims stirred a sense of protection through me like despite everything, I was safe.

Okami must've felt the same because he was curled at the bottom of the bed, snoring in cute little huffs that I knew he'd deny when awake.

Okay, so I wasn't an idiot. Nowhere trapped in the Kingdom of the Gods was safe. But it was only held by the witches' enemies that I felt like I *might* be. Mischief's magic had already blocked the cameras and wormed its way into the collars' monitoring systems. I'd never take simple privacy for granted again.

*What was it like for the wolves to be watched all the time?*

The bedroom's doors pulsed with light, whilst the walls gushed and gurgled with water trapped beneath the surface like a thousand wolves' tears (or since the stench seeped through the opulent room), recycled river water.

I wrinkled my nose, at the same time that Moon nipped it. When I scowled, Emperor only nodded his understanding at Moon.

Did the wolves have a *biting language* too?

The amber of Moon's eyes was bright, as he studied me, brushing the hair from my face. "You're one daft furless if you think that *I'll* be left behind either. I gave up looking to Alphas to protect my hide a long time ago." When Emperor winced, Amadeus soothed his hand down his spine like he was calming a thoroughbred stud. "This is *our* fight, *our* pack, and *our* kingdoms. I didn't sacrifice...we *all* didn't suffer for so long...to not do this together now."

"Well said," Mischief drawled. He was curled in Ramiel's wings along the bottom of the bed as if they were exotic pets, and I'd never known that I even *had* that as a kink before my gorgeous angels. "Yet would you like to elaborate on what *this* happens to be...?"

Moon blanched, shooting a glance at Emperor. Amadeus sank back into the heaped pile of pillows, avoiding their eye.

I'd noticed these secret looks before, but now I understood them. My Charms had been hiding the truth from me, but did it make me messed up that I loved them more for it?

Moon tilted his chin; his curls fell over his eyes. "Cuddle time that you're about to be denied."

Mischief snorted. "An empty threat. Who could deny a god?"

I stroked Moon's cheek, until his gaze met mine: troubled, conflicted, and defiant. "I know about your pact." When he startled, pulling back, I *shushed* him. "Chill out. It's okay."

Emperor twisted to Amadeus, yanking him

sprawling beneath him, whilst his fangs grew. Amadeus panted, blinking away tears at Emperor's scowl.

"It must assuredly is not *okay*," Emperor growled. "I hold a peculiar respect for honor like not whispering secrets that we've held since childhood. How charming that my best friend does not hold the same honor."

Moon pouted. "Aye, choose *him* as your best friend…"

Emperor rolled his eyes. "Yes, because that's what matters, and before you whine, it's possible to hold more than a single best friend. You both mean *everything* to me."

Aquilo bit his lip, as his gaze darted between us. "Why do I have the impression that I missed something wolf related?"

I grinned, pointing at my Charms. "These three drama queens made a pact to manipulate whoever became Charmer into freeing both them and Wolf Kingdom. They've been leading the show from the start."

Moon licked my cheek. "Fur and fangs, you make it sound so simple."

"*Hmm*, maybe because it is…? Look, you need me to become this good version of the Wolf Charmer, and I want to become her, instead of the witch with the dick shadows. So, why don't we work on that together?"

Ramiel waved his elegant hand in the air. "My sword is yours."

"Wow, I was just going for *you have my vote*." I

eyed the rest of my pack. "I mean, we could cuddle all day in this bed together…"

Moon perked up with a hopeful grin.

"…But we're still trapped in this kingdom of death…" Moon deflated, grumbling. "Trust me, I don't like the other choice either. If we risk breaking out, it's not like we'll be greeted by steaming cups of café latte and a selection of donuts. It'll be more like the other wolf kingdoms and witch covens all vying for who can kill us first."

When I sighed dreamily (I could almost taste the coffee and glazed donut), Aquilo snickered.

"How do you manage to look beautiful even whilst drooling?" Aquilo's icy blue eyes crinkled at the edges.

I struggled to focus on the *beautiful* over the *drooling* because could I help it if I lived for the moments when his cold melted for me?

"By my fur, this has never been about *escaping*." Moon smirked. "Did you forget that I got away from you in Wild Hall without any problem to rescue my brother?"

Amadeus squirmed underneath Emperor. "Only because of me."

"He bit my ankle," I shrugged, "and then begged me not to bubble your blood or poison you for leaving me on my freaking wedding night." When Moon cringed, I soothed my shadows through his curls, and he nuzzled into them. "I *let* you have that night of freedom. Call me crazy, but I figure that Banan, the princess, or any of the assholes running Wolf Kingdom aren't going to just give up their power."

Moon's eyes flashed. "That's why we take it from them."

"And what about the Betas who hunted us?" Ramiel asked. "You plan a war against an unknown enemy who's already planning their own battles."

"Betas?" Amadeus whispered, burrowing further into the pillows.

"Their fur looked like yours." I tried to catch Amadeus' eye, but he dragged the sheet over his head like a kid hiding from monsters. What had freaked him out, apart from the whole *pack of terrifying Betas* thing. "It would've been a beautiful sight, if they hadn't been trying to eat us and not, you know, in the sexy way." I nudged Amadeus' foot with mine, accidentally nudging Moon's balls in the tangle of our limbs. Moon shot me an affronted look. "Are your Betas like super soldiers in this kingdom?"

Amadeus shook his head beneath the sheet.

Moon rolled his eyes. "Stop acting like a cub."

"I assure you that it's a shock," Mischief murmured, entwining his fingers with Ramiel's, "to discover that you've been treated in one way, whilst others of your kind have been allowed much greater freedoms."

*Holy hell, that was the voice of bitter experience talking.*

Emperor didn't waste words, however, instead yanking the sheet off Amadeus and hauling him up and onto his lap. Amadeus squawked and struggled; his eyes were red-rimmed.

Huh, he'd been hiding his tears, rather than his fear. It ached that Amadeus still didn't think he could share his pain with me.

Emperor chuckled. "Betas are servants in the Wilds and breeders in the Gods. They're not fighters."

"Keep talking and see how wrong you are," Amadeus snarled.

Emperor raised his eyebrow. "I'm not Moon. If we wrestle, I won't hold back."

Emperor's pupils were blown; he panted. He was so into the whole playfight with a hard-on thing.

*Hey, whatever turned a wolf on.*

Aquilo brushed his fingers across Amadeus' knee. "Crimson isn't the same," he whispered. "She doesn't wish us to smile, during our…" He swallowed. "I may only be a mage and not a wolf, but I understand about being raised as a pretty bauble, and even more about being trained." Amadeus flinched. "I don't believe that either of us need to fear anymore."

When a tear streaked down Amadeus' cheek, Aquilo wiped it away with his thumb.

"See how much *nicer* the Charmer's intended is than you," Amadeus turned his head to nip Emperor's jaw, "Prince Small Dick."

Moon drew in his breath. "Goddess Moon! Why not paint a target on your own dick while you're at it?"

Emperor's fangs and claws grew, and he howled. Then his arms tightened around Amadeus, before he tumbled him off the bed. Amadeus merely shook with laughter, as Emperor caged him underneath him on the floor.

*Uh oh, Alpha prince on the loose…* How did I get Emperor's Omega mask back on?

Okami awoke with a snort, darting off the bed in confusion.

When the moon doors unexpectedly peeled back, however, Emperor and Okami stilled the same as me at the blast of wild guitar and rebellious punky rock, as My Chemical Romance's "House of Wolves" burst from the walls. Then Vala swept into the bedroom like it was her anthem.

Boy, did the bitch like to make an entrance. *Except, hello…irony?*

And yeah, it wasn't as if my witchy ass could've forgotten that I was being held captive as *honored guest* in a wolves' house, just the same as my Charms had once been prisoners in a witch's House. So, maybe more like *karma…*? But Vala didn't need to wear the smug expression of someone who'd pissed on every inch of her kingdom to mark it as hers.

When I didn't hide my smirk at the thought in time, Vala's smugness transformed to rage. Why couldn't I remember that I was meant to be playing the Omega, just like Emperor?

*Wait, Emperor*…who was holding Amadeus down like he was about to savage or screw him, and I didn't know which was worse to Vala.

When Vala's gaze slid to Amadeus and Emperor, before she hugged her arms over her middle, I knew that *screwing* would be worse.

"Wow, every time that I grant you my trust, you disappoint me." She slunk closer with a seductive swing of her hips that reminded me disturbingly of Amadeus. *Had she taught him or had they learned it together?* Amadeus whimpered, but Emperor still didn't move away, shielding Amadeus from his sister. "Since you returned to me, did I tell you to seduce the prince of the Alphas?" She cocked her head. "Because I remember giving you *strict* orders not to touch the other princes."

Emperor clasped his hand over Amadeus' neck; his burning gaze met Vala's challengingly. "Look at that, *I'm* touching *him*."

When Emperor went Alpha, he didn't dick around…

To my surprise, Vala only smiled, slipping her iPhone out her pocket. Perhaps, she was sending a pussy pic to Amadeus? A prank text to the queen? Calling for reinforcement Crescents for another food fight?

Suddenly, a fine silver net fell from the ceiling on top of Amadeus like he was a wild animal to be trapped. Emperor curled over Amadeus to protect him, tucking his face into his shoulder and hissing as the silver burned his shoulders and legs.

"*Son of a bitch...*" I hurled myself off the bed at the same time as my pack of angels, mages, gods and wolves.

Vala only held the phone between us like a gun, hovering her finger over it with a suggestive wiggle, whilst glancing up at the ceiling.

My red surged, wrapping around Vala. She stiffened, but didn't release my Charms. Yet by biting me, she'd weakened my ability to control her.

*Could I even stop her attack?* Her bond with me had been a false one, and my shadows had been flowing stronger every hour but...

If I turned on her with my crimson shadows, the princess would have the justification against my pack, Mischief, and the witches to start a war.

What in the holy hell did I do? All along, Vala had been provoking me to release my Crimson Tide and be the cause of the next massacre.

*I would never be that bitch.*

Vala *craved* blood, war, and death. Me...? I craved the guys who I loved, freedom, and a killer cocktail.

I don't think that there was a meeting of minds.

Okami flew circles around Vala's head, snarling. Although she ignored him like he was no more than a fly, Vala's cheek still twitched.

*Yeah, even if you flush away my magical wolf, asshole, he still comes back to bite your ass.*

"Come on then, you rotten bastard," Moon snarled, shooting out his own fangs (and why had I only been worried about Emperor's protective nature towards Amadeus?). "I'm a prince too, aye, of the savage Wilds as well. You and the Queen of the Gods broke us as kids because we dared to love each other, but we're all grown up now, and if you cage one of us for such love..." He glanced over his shoulder at Emperor who paled, "then by my hide, you'll punish us all together."

I remembered how it'd felt when I'd been taken back in Amadeus' memory: the way that the princes had sworn as kids to protect each other.

What had *broken* them? And why hadn't they suffered it together?

Vala narrowed her eyes. "On fear of silver, if a naughty Omega removes her tentacles, I'll consider your plea."

Moon nodded like he was eager to be punished as well.

I shifted from foot to foot, biting my lip. When Mischief and Ramiel stalked either side of me, the rub of their shoulders against mine gave me strength.

I dragged back my shadows even though they hissed their protest. "Okay, but don't be a jerk about this. You imprisoned us here with nothing to do but wait for your mom's summons. I take it you think that Amadeus should have no friends, and we should've rejected him for being a spy. Trust me, that's not happening. He's saved our lives, fought by our sides, and we *all* love him. If you were any kind of sister, you'd be seriously psyched about that."

Vala's expression became fragile, as her shoulders slumped but only for a moment. Then just as quickly, her gaze became shuttered, before she pointed the phone at Amadeus again.

My hands curled into fists.

*Stop…stop…stop…*

When she swiped the screen, however, the net unwrapped from around Amadeus and Emperor, shooting back into the ceiling like a giant metallic spider.

Okami howled, soaring to wrap himself around Emperor's neck and nibble on his ear in comfort. Amadeus kissed Emperor's seared shoulder, before shooting a look at Vala that simmered with more danger than I'd ever seen in my beautiful incubus.

Vala blanched, before shrugging like she wasn't shaking. "Love, friendship, *blah, blah, blah.* You always were a *whore*, Flame."

The shattered pain in Amadeus' whimper, made me wish that I'd thrust my crimson through Vala to shut her up.

Mischief prowled towards Vala. "It's others who *make* us whores, you insufferable deluded bitch. I shall not have you shame one who's so many times worthier of love and respect than you." His voice was sharper than a blade; he sliced Vala open with each word. "Why, I ask, are you bothering us with your pointless presence? Are you relegated to nothing but queen's messenger? A shadow? Oh dear, are you only now realizing that your attempts at unrest in this kingdom are nothing but desperate grabs for attention because your mother loves your lost brother, as well as both your adopted brothers, more than you…? Or is it simply because she never loved you at all…?"

*Crack* — Vala backhanded Mischief.

I winced, curling my red out to comfort Mischief's silver magic.

But Mischief merely grinned. "I rest my case."

Vala dug her nails into her palms, before twisting on her heel and diving to the doorway. Then she dragged someone after her by their emerald hair (honestly, was that her kink or did she not trust anyone to follow her?), into the bedroom, before tossing them to the floor at Mischief's feet.

I stared at Jax in shock, as he rubbed his sore scalp. His head was ducked, however, whilst his wings were curled around himself. He'd hadn't looked this scared when the Alpha Dickhead had been poking holes in his wing.

Ramiel crouched next to Jax, wrapping his own wings around him. Ramiel's pink hair mingled with the fae's green in the most stunning way that made my breath catch, until Amadeus scrambled up and dashed to Vala. Only then did I notice the tears already streaming down his cheeks.

"You promised..." Amadeus gasped.

Vala studied her fingernails as if she was bored. "Your Charmer has taken you and the mage..." Her gaze glanced with a longing at Aquilo that make him shrink back against me. I caught his hand in mine, stroking my thumb in circles across his knuckles. There was no way on earth that she was ever touching him again. "Why should I be the only Alpha not to have someone pretty to breed?"

"*Please*, you promised," Amadeus repeated brokenly.

Ramiel's wings tightened around Jax, but Jax didn't beg. He'd been brought up as a mongrel knowing that one day an Alpha would choose him. Why would he expect any say now?

"There's such a thing as consent or buried down here did it pass you by?" I growled. "Let's ask the fae if he wants to be snuggle buddies or not, right?"

Vala snorted. "You know, Amadeus told me that you're not like your mother. Now I believe him."

"You swore that you'd take anyone but Jax if I behaved." Amadeus snatched Vala by the shoulders like he intended to shake her.

Her lips became pinched. "Are you behaving? Did you behave by falling in love with the Charmer?"

Amadeus sobbed, resting his head on Vala's shoulder. My crimson soaked the room in tears, desperate to wrench him away from her.

"I'm s-sorry, s-see, I couldn't h-help… But please d-don't… On my fangs, I'll d-do anything…" When he raised his head, his gaze was steely again. "Take me instead."

When I gasped, Emperor and Moon stepped forward at the same time. But it was Jax who spun out of Ramiel's hold with flaming eyes.

"Don't break the rule. I won't allow this, Ama," Jax hissed.

Yet Vala's eyes had already lit up with desperate hope and love because although I wished that it wasn't true, I knew that she loved her adopted brother in a possessive way.

Devastated, my knees buckled. *This had all been a bluff.*

Vala had plotted all along to win Amadeus back, so that she could play out the dark desires that she'd shown him when she'd gone skin to skin in the Lunar Shrine.

Did she figure that in some twisted way she was protecting Amadeus from *us or himself?*

Had she deluded herself that Amadeus truly loved her?

Amadeus allowed Vala to slide her arm around his waist and lead him towards the moon doors.

"Wait, you can't just…take him away… *Freaking stop…*" I hollered.

I'd thought that at least we were finally all together. Yet I was wrong. I should've been able to protect my pack, but Vala was a princess of diplomacy, ruling as an Alpha and using our love against us.

What if Amadeus was already lost?

## CHAPTER 10

I stared at the moon doors that had closed behind Vala and Amadeus, peeling back into place like they'd never opened. Yet they had, and now my pack was missing the sinful beauty of my Prince of the Gods because Vala had led him away with her arm around his middle, as if he was a delicate treasure. I snorted because Amadeus would seriously kick my ass if I treated him as nothing but a pretty Beta to hang on my arm like a trophy husband in the Hamptons.

Yet now *my* Charm belonged to Vala as he had done before I'd Claimed him, and if I came off as dickishly possessive then hey, I could live with that.

*But I couldn't live without Amadeus.*

If I plucked on the strands of Fate that Stella had woven hard enough, could I drag Amadeus back through those doors?

When I clasped Aquilo's hand tighter, his magic flowed through me, and his fingers stroked across my knuckles. *Boy, was he powerful.* Did he even realize just how formidable he could be?

*Hecate, I promise that I'll be the best Charmer who's ever lived...*I won't make jokes about baby dragons in my cauldron, daydream about wolves and their talented tongues (*often*), or even forget my daily meditation...*if you bring Amadeus back to me.*

I scowled at the door that remained stubbornly shut.

*Okay, freaking fine.*

I squared my shoulders. I'd rescue Amadeus and the entire Wolf Kingdom myself. I was Crimson, my pack were epic, and Vala had just used up her last chance to keep on the side of the *good* witch.

My Chemical Romance's "House of Wolves" died out, and the fountain effect of giant tears wept back to life down the walls. In the silence, my ragged breaths and Okami's whines were shockingly loud.

Jax squirmed out of Ramiel's hold with a dancer's grace, shaking out his feathers. "Well, this is awkward."

"Are you mocking us, you golden winged rascal?" Moon growled.

Moon hadn't put away his fangs or claws, and although the look was hot on him, I also didn't like the way that Jax shrank back into the corner. He hadn't raised his gaze yet either like the bedroom itself was giving him the creeps.

Had something bad happened to him here or was being outside the Mongrel Pit too overwhelming for him?

My eyes widened. Was this the first time in his life that Jax had been allowed out of that windowless cell?

I wished that I could reach for Jax's hand and offer him the support that Amadeus would've if he'd been here, but even though my shadows twirled around him like they were desperate to touch his wicked elegance, I still didn't *know* him. At least, not like I knew my guys.

Could I trust Jax simply because Amadeus had?

Jax's grin was all teeth, as he winked at Moon. "Everybody compliments the wings." Emperor chuckled, before covering it with a cough. Emperor had met his match in Jax. *What would happen if I set up one mirror between the two of them?* "And my name's Jax. Amadeus told me that the Prince of the Wilds was…" He fluttered his long lashes at Emperor. "…Less courteous than the Prince of the Alphas."

When Emperor preened, Moon flipped him off.

*Okay, way to prove Jax's point.*

Mischief reached for Ramiel, pulling him to his feet. He assessed Jax. "Believe me, I'm aware that *all* wolves are uncouth. Every day they're discussing some way to compare dicks or…"

"Suck them?" Ramiel suggested in a voice so soft that its innocence in contrast to the *sucking of dicks* made me almost choke on my own tongue.

Jax's laugh was lilting and musical; it thrilled through me. Yet at the same time, I hated how he hunched, as Moon caged him into the corner.

"Why should I remember the name of Vala's spy?" Moon snarled.

"You're just all big, bad wolf, aren't you *Omega*?" Jax's eyes flashed with malevolence.

Moon's breath hitched, and he blanched. *Boy, had that one hit home.*

I'd sworn that no one would call Moon *Omega* again. He was the Moon Child, a prince, and *my* Wolf Bitten. He was no branded Om, Omega, or nameless slave.

I'd never allow him to feel that he was again.

I tugged free of Aquilo's hold, stalking towards Jax who ducked his head.

"I know that you're scared," I hissed. "You've had your ass dragged in here by the princess, before being saved by Amadeus. Except, you only know us as his friends, so why should *you* trust *us*?" I wrapped my shadows around him like warning flames licking across his skin. He shivered. "But you talk about any of my pack like that again and you'll have your cute fae ass handed to you, right?"

Jax bit his lip but he nodded. When he raised his wing with a brave tilt of his head, I blinked in confusion.

"You shall never be harmed in such a way here for

your mistakes," Mischief's voice was low. Ramiel slipped his arm around Mischief's shoulders in understanding. "I once thought that the Charmer was no different to other witches and would trap with pretty lies, punishing with cruel traditions. You need fear neither, I swear."

*Holy hell, Jax had expected me or Moon to slash his wing in revenge or for discipline.*

My guts churned, as Jax still didn't lower his wing. Cool peppermint wound around me like an accusation.

Moon dropped his gaze guiltily, nuzzling onto my shoulder and glancing up at me from underneath his eyelashes as if for reassurance. I nodded, and then together we stroked Jax's wing, before lowering it.

Then I tumbled backwards with an *oomph* in a pile of wolf and fae, as Jax launched himself on me like it was a dance move and I'd been meant to catch him. Well, that was one dramatic way to ask for a cuddle.

When I groaned, Jax straddled me. His eyes twinkled, as his mouth curved into a smile.

"So, I'm still your cute fae, *hmm*?" He ground his ass against me in a way that was all Amadeus. The two must've taught each other moves, and sorry Hecate for breaking my vow already, but that was just begging for a naughty daydream. "You still want me like before? Ama wasn't wrong about that?"

Being locked up, unwanted, and unloved made you terrified of rejection, go figure.

I stroked Jax's cheek but before I could answer, Moon licked down Jax's neck.

"By my fangs, others have both trusted and forgiven me," Moon's gaze was burning and so intense that I shuddered, "when I had no right to expect it. On the furless heavens though, if you betray the place that we grant you in this pack, you won't be getting any more cuddles. Are we clear?"

*Woah, mafia threats Moon style.*

Jax nodded. "Why'd I ever give up these cuddles?"

Aquilo's gaze was frosty. "Surely we don't simply accept that Amadeus has sacrificed himself for this *stranger*? No offense."

Jax's eyes sparked with a magic that I could sense building beneath his skin. *How dangerous were fae?*

Jax's smile was sharp. "Oh, a great deal taken. Don't you think that I've sacrificed? My little monsters are right now locked in their cages. *Alone.* They don't... I mean, they've never been without me..."

When Aquilo rolled his eyes at Jax's distress, it reminded me so painfully of the pretty bully that I'd once thought Aquilo to be, that my chest ached. I knew Aquilo loved our pack, but how hard was it for him to drop his cold act altogether?

"There's not one of us in this room who hasn't sacrificed," Aquilo bit out. "Perhaps, I'm not a wolf, but I'm still the Charmer's intended and I won't lose another prince."

When Aquilo's gaze met mine, my eyes smarted with tears at the gleam of them in his. The true prince of the Gods, the Ambassador, had died to save Aquilo, who'd spent the last decade growing up alongside him.

*Had Aquilo loved the Ambassador?*

I'd lost my family a long time ago, but for Aquilo it was still raw.

When Jax's expression darkened, however, I realized that he didn't know any of that.

"Chill out," I pleaded.

In a gold spray of glitter, Jax transformed into a black butterfly of a fae with wings that glistened, as if polished metal.

*Broomsticks and candle wax…*

"Exquisite," Emperor breathed.

Jax *was* stunning but also like a shadow sprung to life. Hadn't Amadeus said that he was a *Dark* Fae…? Wow, was I glad that he was on our side.

Jax snickered, before fluttering to Moon and nipping his neck. Moon yelped, snapping at him with his fangs.

"No biting," I chided.

Moon pouted, although he retracted both his fangs and claws. "He started it." Then he rubbed at his neck. "Aye, Amadeus would be mates with a Dracula Fae."

Jax squeaked in outrage. Then Okami howled, flying from Emperor's neck to circle Jax and sniff at him. When he flattened out like he was Aladdin's flying carpet, Jax alighted on his back.

I grinned at the grand procession that Okami made of it, as he swooped Jax like a true guest of honor to first Ramiel, who bowed his head, then to Aquilo who smiled icily, and finally to Emperor.

"How fascinating," Emperor murmured, as Okami lowered Jax onto the tattooed butterfly wing that beat over his shoulder. Jax fluttered onto the tattoo: black onto purple.

In a flash of gold, Jax transformed back into his full-size, tumbling Emperor onto the bed. Jax lay on the top of Emperor, grimacing and quivering.

"What dark magic did they put in that tattoo?" Jax's wings curled around both himself and Emperor. "We haven't even kissed, and I'm all tinglie."

Cold rushed through me. What had Jax discovered? He'd sensed the wrongness of the tattoo, which bound Emperor's Alpha scent, hiding his true nature because it'd mean his death if it was revealed. When my shadows had traced the purple butterfly, it'd been stung by the same dark magic.

What had it felt like to be that small on the tattoo?

Emperor ached his brow as he relaxed back on the bed, but I could tell by the way his jaw clenched that he knew the danger of Jax's question.

*What if Jax outed Emperor as an Alpha?*

Ramiel hadn't but then, Ramiel had already been pack and honestly, if he had any more honor in him, it'd burst in rainbows out of his ass. I didn't think that honor rated that highly for Jax. At least, definitely below *pretty wings*, singalongs, and the perfect dance move.

Emperor yawned. "Did you expect any less from a prince?"

Jax patted Emperor's stomach. "It just shows, you should never meet your heroes."

Moon snickered at Emperor's stunned expression.

"Should we not have a plan, rather than waiting on a queen who appears to me no different to my own mother?" Aquilo asked, quietly. "The daughter divides us and steals..." He brushed his snow-white hair back with a frustrated sigh. "How could he have left us with so little fight?" At Aquilo's distress, I clambered to my feet, wishing that he'd allow me to drag him into a cuddle in the same way as Moon would. Instead, I caressed my hand down his stiff arm, and his gaze was tender as it met mine. "I will not stand by as another wolf is harmed."

How much did I wish my witchy ass hadn't thrown that accusation at him in anger?

Jax rolled onto his back, before squirming around in the sheets with an orgasmic sigh that had Emperor tenting his toga. I didn't blame him. Was this the first time that Jax had even lain in a bed rather than a cage? "I thought you said that you were mates of Ama? Look, he plans his moves *decades* ahead. He's the smartest bloke I know. Were you tricked into believing that he was just a pretty arse?" Jax forced himself to raise his head from his nest in the sheets, flashing his sharp teeth. "He's been playing the game with the highest stakes of all the mongrels' lives since we were cubs and after that…" He casually played with Emperor's gold locks. *Wait, Emperor wasn't even bitching about that…?* I waited for Emperor to knock him away, but to my surprise, he allowed his precious hair to be messed up. "My best guess is that our Ama is playing double agent right now. Don't you realize that he plays the submissive but he's really the one with the power? On my wings, the princess *trained* him for the role, and I hope that it bites her on her Alpha arse."

Moon smiled, dragging us both to our feet. "I've changed my mind. We're keeping this one."

Jax's expression became desperate with hope, before he hid it beneath a teasing beat of his wings. "When I have the best feathers in the room, why wouldn't you?"

"Oh, my Ramiel has the best feathers in any room, you puffed up fairy." Mischief raked his fingers across Ramiel's shoulder blades, brushing his wings until he purred. Ramiel pinked but was unable to stop the way that his hips bucked. "I've both known and loved fae before. I know of your power and your danger. I believe that you'll work on our side as long as it benefits your incubus and mongrel family. I assure you, that my pack work to free *all* who are oppressed on either side: witch, wolf, mongrel, Loch Ness Monster…*it matters not*. I am a god and I shall bring down the wall, rip off the collars, and *no one* shall play games that stop me."

Okay, so sometimes I forgot that Mischief was a god, centuries old, and from the Realm of Seraphim. I mean, what other monsters and creatures even lived there with him…who had he loved before me?

*Yet he'd chosen to love my pack now.*

Suddenly, I flushed too because I was surrounded by guys who loved me, as I loved them. Even if we had to take on a crazy queen and her daughter to save Wolf Kingdom and stop the Second Wolf War, I did it with a pack who were equal at my side.

And all I'd thought when I'd returned to America was that I had a wolf waiting for me as a birthday gift.

Jax licked his lips as if it was an invitation. "What a speech! How about you get dressed, *god*? It's not easy to take threats seriously from a bloke in a toga."

Mischief blinked. "My, how droll. Are these my invisible clothes, which the Omegas stole from the Pleasure Pool?"

"I love your sass, violet wings," Jax laughed, tightening his hand in Emperor's hair, "and yeah, those clothes. The princess had them cleaned, so that you'd be ready for the big *meet* with the queen. She was ranting about it, whilst she was dragging me here."

I stared around the room. "Dude, they're not here."

"Omegas are tidy monsters." Jax kicked the bed,

even as Moon growled. "They'll have tucked them under here. I'm good at hidden things."

"I bet you are," I muttered.

Aquilo ducked down, dragging out my dress, which had been cleaned and mended. Emperor rolled off the bed with a howl of joy at the sight of his pristine suit. I snickered, as Aquilo pulled out his own clothes, and finally Moon's.

Hey, the Omegas offered laundry service, which was epic. Except, I guessed not for the Omegas who were press ganged as chastity slaves into working the laundry. I wrinkled my nose at the perfect red-and-black ball gown. Still, at least they were good at it, and why was I even trying to work out their ironing tricks?

Even though Emperor stared longingly at his own suit and robes, first he took the dress from me, and helped me to step into it, doing it up with a tender care that thrummed him with as much pleasure as it did me. When his thumb brushed the back of my neck, I shivered. His hot breath blew my hair to the side, and I melted against him.

"You're beautiful," Emperor whispered, "I hope that we've all told you that with sufficient frequency and fervor?"

"*Hmm*, have I told you enough times that you're gorgeous?" I murmured, as my shadows stroked along *his* neck in teasing retaliation,

Emperor's breath hitched. "You always mention the gorgeous, and it can never be said enough times."

He gave a final stroke to my throat, before placing a small kiss there as if in parting. Then he drew back and sauntered to his own clothes. He traced his hand with the same reverence that he'd just been lavishing on me over his suit.

Jax glanced between us, before burrowing down in the pillows and drawing the sheet up to his ears. Only the tips of his gold wings and his green hair poked out.

"Ama seemed taken with you, Charmer," Jax's voice was muffled but thoughtful, "which was weird because even with the pact he was terrified of the day that you'd Claim him." I flushed. It sucked to be the bad guy. "But he's my best mate and he wouldn't have left me here alone with you if he thought that you'd hurt me or wouldn't want me. At least, you must be better than that bitch princess."

*What kind of a dick would I have to be to reject him now?*

I sauntered to the bed, perching next to him, as my shadows ruffled his hair. He'd done the same to Emperor, so it was only fair. "Wow, high praise."

"Do you think that I praise many witches, Charmer? They're the ones who taught the princess how to control us. She even has a Fallen duke dancing to her tune."

Aquilo hurriedly finished dragging on his velvet top,

before he stormed to the bed, hauling the sheet away from a startled Jax.

"How does Vala control Duke Dual? Tell me." Aquilo straddled Jax in a way that was far too close to how he'd straddled *me* as a kid, holding me down for his bully sister, Lux.

I'd forgotten that Aquilo had sneaked out and become friends with the vampire Dual. Had they been more than friends?

I eased my arms around Aquilo's middle, pulling him against me and away from Jax. Aquilo's breathing was harsh.

*Holy hell, was he going into a panic attack?*

"Just breathe," I murmured.

Aquilo's heart beat too fast through his chest, as I pressed my hand against it. For once, he pressed closer to me, allowing me to ground him with my shadows in a cocoon. His eyes fluttered closed.

How many times could Aquilo be hurt by *both* sides because of an ancient war?

"What happened with Dual?" I asked.

Jax eased himself up in the bed, curling his wings around himself, before he cleared his throat. "Sorry, yeah? I didn't mean to…" He fidgeted with the fraying bottoms of his pants. "The princess stole the duke's son."

When Aquilo curled his hands into fists, leaning even further into me, as he wailed in fury, I understood. That was even more screwed up than I'd thought.

*Why had Dual hidden it from Aquilo?*

Mage's balls, was that what the Kingdom of the Gods held over him and the reason why he hadn't been able to help us against the Alphas in the Justice Chamber? He'd fought by our side with his vampire court against all the covens, but as soon as the wolves appeared, he'd backed down and abandoned us.

He'd said that it was because of something *precious*.

If I'd known that it was to protect his son, then I'd have understood. Too many people's kids had already been killed. Just look at Banan and all the terrible things that she did because of the loss of *her* son.

Ramiel's eyes flashed. "She thinks like a Glory, using a hostage child to make the Fallen court do her bidding. Yet how is the secret kept?"

Jax twirled his fingers in the air and to my shock, golden sparks like embers danced out: Dual and an Alpha. Then he closed his fingers, and the image died.

"The duke has deals with Wolf Kingdom," Jax explained, stroking his fingers through his own feathers as if to soothe them. "Color me surprised that some Alpha *wanted* him. They didn't break any laws there, but I guess that the Alpha was soft because she tried to smuggle the cub out to Dual rather than have him taken to the Mongrel Pit."

Okami whined, flying to settle on Jax's shoulder.

"Pray, tell me that this story ends with a happily ever after?" Mischief leaned closer into Ramiel's embrace.

"It ends with Digby," Jax's gaze raised to mine, when I gasped, "kidnapped from Dual and brought to live with *me*."

The adorable vampire wolf boy who Jax had been protecting from the Alpha Dickhead was Dual's son, a vampire earl...?

"Ama and I battle for all the mongrels and have done so since we were kids. You ask whether I fight for the oppressed and freedom. You've no idea how far I'd go to tear down this kingdom's prisons."

Aquilo turned to Jax. His breathing had settled, and his icy gaze had softened. When he launched himself at Jax, I tried to hold him back, but ended up falling with him on top of Jax. Yet Aquilo only held Jax in a stiff hug. I understood how difficult that was for him with someone new.

"I'm sorry," Aquilo breathed. "Thank you for what you've done for Dual. I may have nothing you want, but I'll find a way to repay you."

Jax smiled easing his wings around Aquilo and me. "This may come as a surprise, pretty mage, but you have *a lot* that I want."

Aquilo's blush spread down his neck, and boy, did I want to lick his flushing skin just to see how far down it went.

Except, if we were all on the same side and trusting

now, we couldn't wait around for the queen's summons. From the moment that we'd entered the Kingdom of the Gods, Vala had been using us as pieces in her war game. She'd recorded us, provoked us into inciting fights, drugged us and even tricked Amadeus into becoming hers.

*The rules had to change.*

Yet the only way that we could force that to happen would be to take a serious risk. Betas had been hunting…or *training*…in the secret tunnels. It wasn't as if I'd been meant to be sneaking around in them. Had they even reported back that they'd seen us or because they'd failed to capture us was that still a secret?

Either way, I had a feeling that the fact they could transform wasn't public knowledge.

I was the Charmer, Wolf Witch, and Wolf Liberator. I was also now an Omega Witch who was protected from the Alphas. In my pack, I had this kingdom's prince and *their god*.

If the princess used her position to control, then we had to use ours to build *influence*. I had to discover wolves who weren't content being buried as the dead. United, *we'd* then have the power to fight for our freedom.

Hey, from gallery owner to Che Guevara within weeks. I deserved a medal but I'd settle for an espresso.

Seriously, what was it with wolves and not having decent coffee?

I poked Jax with my shadows. "Have you ever taken a wander in the secret tunnels?"

Jax huffed. "Who do you think taught them to Ama?"

I glanced around at my guys, before taking a deep breath. "And if I was raising an illegal Beta army that hunts in walls because I was an asshole who wanted to start a war, where would I stash it?"

I ignored the growls behind me (my lovers were scorching hot but that didn't let them off having to *trust* me), whilst Jax furrowed his brows in thought like I'd only asked him what his favorite color was.

*I bet it was green.*

Then his grin became wide. "Why don't I take you sightseeing in the Sacred Crypt, if your balls are big enough, Charmer? That's where I'd hide an illegal army because only royalty can enter."

I narrowed my eyes. "Are you holding out on me? What happens if someone (in this case my witchy ass), enters who's not a royal?"

Jax's laugh was dangerous; it made me shudder. "Don't you see? That's why it's the perfect hiding place. If commoners (and that includes you), enter without permission, then they receive the death sentence."

## CHAPTER 11

In the black, Jax's wingtips flared like beacons, as Jax led my pack and me deeper into the burrow. My chest became heavier at each step, weighed down by the air that stank like it hadn't been breathed in centuries.

I had a feeling that it *hadn't*.

When I shuddered, Mischief's wings that gleamed in the gloom more fairy beautiful than...hey, I could actually say a *real* fairy...swept backwards to brush across me in reassurance.

I should've been freaked out that I was following a Dark Fae who I'd only just met through secret passageways to a Sacred – *forbidden* – crypt.

What if Jax plotted just as many decades ahead as Amadeus and had been waiting for his first chance out of the Mongrel Pit to escape? Was he leading us not to spy on the Beta army but to be devoured by it?

Then Emperor's arm wound around my waist, steadying me, and I could've been marching into battle against the queen herself. It didn't matter because I hadn't left my Charms behind this time, just like I promised that I never would again.

Moon's magic slipped around my hand, before winding up my arm and tangling with my shadows. Moon prowled behind me, but his magic was *in* me, just like mine was *in* him. He was my Wolf Bitten, but the Moon Child would never be anything but my equal and the truth of that thrilled me.

I'd never even thought of leaving either of them behind this time, but they'd bargained to be included like they still thought that I'd tear my respect and love away from them.

"So, let me get this straight," Emperor had shot me a haughty grin that hadn't quite hidden his vulnerability, "only royalty may enter this Sacred Crypt."

Jax had nodded.

I'd lain in Jax's wings on the bed. Aquilo's head had rested on my shoulder.

Emperor's grin had become sharp. "Then that makes it *my* privilege. At last, being a prince pays off."

"Aye," Moon had tilted his chin, exchanging a smug glance with Emperor, "it seems to me that we wolf princes have more right than a *commoner* witch."

*He didn't just go there...commoner?*

Moon had been enjoying this reversal *way* too much.

"Stop your childish crowing, *princes*. What a shock that you'd turn saving even your kingdoms into a competition." Mischief had waved a graceful hand. "Of course, I'm an *archduke* and outrank you all…"

I'd growled.

Emperor, Moon, and especially Mischief had all been in for this *commoner* witch's ass kicking.

Then Mischief had brushed his fingers through Ramiel's wings, dragging him close enough for their noses to touch. "You are *my* ruler," his voice had been hushed with such reverence that I'd shivered, and Ramiel had frozen, "but by name alone you are not royalty."

*Hexes and curses, why did such a dickish thing as titles have to divide us?*

Ramiel had shaken as he'd breathed, "Do not ask me to stay behind as if I'm not an equal warrior."

Mischief had sighed. "I excel at hurting others, when it's rarely my intention. Pray, consider what happens if…quite likely *when*…we're caught on this reckless mission? I shall not have my throat ripped out but…" He'd cupped Ramiel's cheek, curling his wings around him like he could protect him even from the imaginary threat. "How did you feel when I was dying?"

Ramiel's eyes had widened, and his breath had hitched. "Zophia, do not *hurt* me by making me remember."

Mischief's gaze had hardened. "Then do not put me through the same."

Aquilo had squirmed away to the end of the bed. His gaze had been anguished and I'd understood how conflicted he'd been.

After all, he was a posh elitist but he wasn't a royal either.

"When we were children," Aquilo had studied his hands, clasping and unclasping them in his lap, "I cruelly bullied you."

When Moon had snarled, I'd shaken my head. I hadn't needed his protection. Plus, I hadn't wanted him to stop Aquilo because guys like Aquilo didn't say *sorry*. He'd been raised in such a screwed-up way that he shouldn't even *know* that he'd been cruel. Yet he'd grown to be brave and kind in a world that I feared would've turned me as brutal as my mom.

*This was as close as I'd ever get to an apology and I was taking it.*

Aquilo had hunched his shoulders, and his mop of hair had fallen over his eyes. "I never wanted to bully you but I wasn't brave enough to stand up to my sister. Yet once I offered you my hand." Freaking fabulous, he had to bring up the *one time* that I'd fought back. "Quite rightly, you shoved me away," he still hadn't met my eye, "and the rejection hurt worse than anything my sister had ever done to me." My crimson had wound in distressed coils around him. He still hadn't stroked over the blood bracelet that encircled his wrist. "Did you think I'd deny that I deserved it? That rejection changed me." When he'd looked up, his frosty gaze had swept my pack. "Crimson is not in need of our macho posturing, and when she holds both our hearts and lives in her hands, she won't do anything foolish."

Wow, that'd *almost* been sweet.

Ramiel had pulled back from Mischief. "Yet simply because we're not royalty…"

Aquilo had slipped from the bed, marching to Ramiel. "Did I not make it clear? I've let others define my entire life by what I'm *not:* not female, worthy, or marriageable. When I was young, not magical and then, when I was discovered to be a mage, not deserving of freedom, a voice, or life. I refuse now to be anything but what *I am* and never what *I am not*."

He'd pressed his forehead to Ramiel's, and I'd tingled at the beauty of the angel and mage together. Witches had tried to break them both…had thought them *broken*.

*Boy, had they been wrong*.

Ramiel's lips had curved into a smile. "I shall be honored to *choose* to stay with you, Aquilo, because *I am* an angel and you *are* a glorious mage."

"And I shall choose to remain with you, Ramiel," Aquilo replied like the completion of an oath or marriage vows, "because I *am* a mage and you *are* a righteous angel."

Mischief's delighted laugher and the way that Ramiel and Aquilo had hugged had lit me with joy, even though I'd known the danger that I'd been about to face.

I was allowed to imagine my own wedding dress when I walked down the aisle with Aquilo, right? Just a little daydream of the chocolate and raspberry wedding cake...?

Then Okami had barked and tucked himself with a slinky wriggle down Aquilo's top. At least I'd known that Okami also made the choice to stay here, whilst I took the tunnels to the Sacred Crypt.

The tunnels had, in fact, turned out to be passageways like gaps behind the walls of the kingdom with secret doors and peepholes through. This entire kingdom had once belonged to the wolf civilization, which had lived here centuries before, and I thought that they must've been either kinky or a court of vipers who used these to spy.

Honestly, if I never saw another Alpha and mage enthusiastically screwing (and the Crescents had a serious food fetish, which was doing nothing for my gnawing hunger), I'd be a happy Charmer. I'd be even happier if I could just sneak in and lick off some of the whipped cream...

Emperor's arm curled more tightly around my waist, as I trudged through the gloom. Then there was a sudden *whish — crack* and a woman's scream.

Okay, this had just gone *People Under the Stairs*

freaky. There was no way in the witching heavens that was just kinky play alongside the *enthusiastic screwing*, and I hadn't seen an Alpha yet who'd dropped the Dom mask enough to take a spanking.

*Were they hurting a mongrel then?*

When I glanced at Jax, he'd frozen, but his wings quivered in the dark. He turned around with an effort, offering a watery smile that didn't reach his eyes.

*He knew who was being beaten.* Why was he trying to hide it?

When rock guitars screamed out and Black Sabbath's heavy metal "Lady Evil" burst out with its warning about witches from the chamber where the woman was now sobbing, I jumped.

*Now that was just rude.* Who was cursing me out through the medium of song? What was next: a street dancing troop performing a piece about the Crimson Terror? A podcast dedicated to *Reasons to Hate Charmers*?

I bustled to the peephole and peered through. Then I wished that I hadn't.

The chamber beyond was an ancient treasure room like I'd stumbled into Tutankhamen's Tomb, but after a looting had been interrupted. The vases and statues were broken, and gemstone necklaces and jewels were strewn on the floor. The walls were daubed with murals of wolves, but not savage like the witches painted them.

These shifters were peaceful and proud, or gathered in families.

My skin prickled with rage that I'd even for a moment believed the visions that Stella had shown me. What warrior didn't appear fierce in a fight? I mean, I figured that *I* looked terrifying when my eyes glowed silver to a wolf. But here was the truth of a civilization that the witches had decimated.

Yet there was no treasure in that room more precious than the gorgeous woman hanging from a crescent column with her hands chained above her head. She'd been stripped to her waist, and her long midnight hair had been swept forward, so that the whip could strike across her back, which was already silvered with scars.

"Son of a bitch...*Amadeus*," I gasped.

Instantly, Mischief's feathers smothered across my lips like a gag, silencing me. He pressed against my back, soothing me with his magic. He rested his chin on my head.

I blinked back tears. At my side, Emperor held onto Moon as tightly as Mischief held onto me to stop him breaking through to Amadeus, who was in his female form, although Emperor vibrated with intense rage.

How hard was it for Emperor not to protect Amadeus, even though he'd chosen this? Had he known that his sister would punish him?

Holy hell, how hadn't I known from his back that

was mapped in his pain that Vala *would* hurt him in this way?

Vala stalked behind Amadeus, dragging a whip along the floor that was wisps of moon, which solidified into searing lashes, when she struck him again.

I cringed, and Mischief pressed a kiss to the crown of my head.

Amadeus' female form was as beautiful as I remembered, but when he'd transformed before in his dance, it'd been by choice. With Vala, I'd bet my witchy ass that he'd been forced because he'd told me Betas always had to be in their female form for play.

If this was *play*, then the princess needed some serious training herself in sexy times.

It wasn't only the mongrels who needed to be freed. No Beta should ever have the decision of who they were forced on them again. I ached to hold Amadeus as either male or female, but only because *he'd* chosen that form.

He was beautiful, sexy, and *mine*.

Vala paused to stroke her hand down Amadeus shaking arm. "How'd you forget my training, Flame?" Her voice was seductive and smoky. It wound through the chamber, as if possessing it. "How could a *witch* have tricked you into loving her? She was meant to be burned, rather than burning you." When she traced a purpled welt down Amadeus' back, he hissed. "*You're mine*. I offered you everything, and you'd give it up for slavery under our enemy."

"She's not the wolves' enemy," Amadeus rasped.

Vala slapped her hand across Amadeus' back, and he screamed. "*We are the dead*," Vala's eyes blazed, "and Charmers will always be our enemy. Our kingdom owes our ancestors a debt: death to all witches."

Wow, that was some seriously intense trash talk. *Plus, hello the real princess…* I mean, her real face was uglier than the diplomatic one that was still a bitch, but if this was what she truly believed, then I had to stop her war plans, and there was now only a day remaining until the other kingdoms' delegations arrived.

I might've only been an American art gallery owner with a talent for cocktail making (seriously *awesome* talent), but I was also the Wolf Liberator. I could pull off the Die Hard save under pressure…*maybe*.

Yet broken broomsticks, why did I also have to watch whilst the guy that I loved was beaten?

"Bite on my wing if you cannot keep silent," Mischief whispered.

*When had I started crying?* Mischief's cheek was as wet as mine, however, when he leaned closer, to press his feathers more firmly between my teeth. When my teeth pressed down, he winced. When angels' wings were seriously sensitive, that had to hurt. But maybe Mischief needed the pain.

"Why are we…? We can't help," Jax hissed, as his wings fluttered in distress. "Let's just…"

"I'm not leaving him," Moon snarled.

Emperor's glare was enough to make Jax quail, curling against the back of the passageway.

How many times had Jax already witnessed this *training* in the Mongrel Pit…?

Vala trailed her finger down a scar that swept across Amadeus' back. "I'm sorry," she sighed. "Do you remember what I told you when you were little?"

"That I'd hold and break every heart," Amadeus replied.

"If only I hadn't forgotten your incubus blood and whipped you so hard when you were young." She pinched the scar, and Amadeus' gasped. "Still, it's left you sensitive and that's always fun."

*Cool it, Crimson, just…please let her stop now…*

Vala wound the whip suggestively around Amadeus' waist, and his chest rose and fell rapidly in fear. "So beautiful." She coiled a strand of his hair around her finger, just as she'd coiled the whip. Then she yanked on it, and he yelped. "But I can destroy your beauty. Wow, here's a thought: would any of our *enemies* want you, once I've finished marking you? If I *desecrate* you?"

This time, it was Emperor lunging forward, and Jax hurled himself on Emperor's back with a strength that shocked me. Any moment, we'd all go tumbling through into the treasure room and be discovered…

At Amadeus' terrified whimper, my crimson shadows shot out, washing over him. He quietened, despite Vala drawing back and cracking the whip against the ground.

"Okay, let's start with an easy one." Vala rolled her shoulders like she was limbering up for a session at the gym, rather than preparing to whip her brother in earnest. She was seriously throwing out the Gestapo vibe. Jax knocked Emperor to the back wall with a *thump* that the music luckily drowned out, and Mischief tossed his magic like a lasso around them both. They stilled, trapped. "How about you tell me the *Moon God's* secrets?" Contempt dripped from her words like venom. "I don't believe all the worship crap, but that doesn't mean I can't use him. He has power, and I want to know how to twist it to my benefit."

Mischief's expression was carefully blank. I knew that he doubted anyone could love or accept him. What if Amadeus betrayed him now?

I mean, Vala did have a big ass whip. I kind of *did* want Amadeus to say something, rather than let himself be tortured because my guys were too ready to sacrifice themselves for each other. I'd never demand that.

But that wouldn't make it any easier on Mischief.

When Amadeus turned his head, his ruby eyes that were now fanned by even longer lashes than before glittered. "I wish that I could please you, but I don't know any of their secrets. They all just think that I'm a pretty Beta, see, and you're right, they're not like you. They could never love me in the same way."

Vala howled, hurling the whip; it smashed against a statue, before skittering like a moon snake amongst the jewels.

"Think about how to please me better, Flame," Vala snarled, before storming out of the chamber.

Amadeus' face twisted with pain at her displeasure, before he turned to the wall and winked...*at me*.

I pulled my teeth out of Mischief's wing and laughed. The clever...gorgeous...asshole had known that I was there and had been playing his sister.

Amadeus had been in control all along, even if he'd been the one chained.

I glanced at Jax, who straddled Emperor's chest with a smug smile.

Jax had known that Amadeus had been in charge. After all, he'd tried to explain back in the bedroom that I should trust his friend. Amadeus had never forgotten any of his training. How far back had he been plotting? Had he been playing *me* as well as he played his sister?

Witches hats, *it didn't matter*.

Amadeus was throwing me a cheeky grin, rather than sobbing in pain. My lover had a plan, and I'd never make the mistake of forgetting that he was far more than the pretty Beta that he'd been teasing me and the others in the pack about, even if he'd been addressing his sister.

"Our sexy incubus is in for quite the spanking from

*me*," Emperor's voice was tight with tears. "Why did he hide this from us?"

Jax tapped his chin. "Wait, let me think, it couldn't be because you'd have thrown an overprotective fit and I don't know, risked everything for which he's suffered?"

"Aren't you the little puppet of sarcasm?" Mischief eyed Jax, drawing back his magic. "You have my respect. And as to the prince of...*pray, somebody tell me that he's not twerking...?*"

I snickered. "He's twerking."

Amadeus threw another smoldering glance over his shoulder up at where we were hiding.

*Yeah, he was milking it.*

Mischief's lips twitched. "As to our twerking prince, he's this kingdom's hope. The wolves cower before the princess out of fear, but they'll follow him out of love. I assure you that I've witnessed this truth magnificently in other worlds."

Jax tilted his head. "You're right, sugar wings. Ama is brave enough, it's just every other wolf that we need to convince."

I glanced between them. "Why am I getting a Star Wars vibe on this?"

Moon raised his hand to his collar. "Fur and fangs, that's because you are. The witches thought to collar us. It's only fair that we use the tricks they used to dominate us, to free ourselves."

I grinned. "You know that you're all hot when you're rebellious and commanding? Okay, whatever the plan is, I'm in on it. Anything that stops the jerk princess and kicks her up her wolfie ass."

Moon's eyes narrowed. "It's a risk…"

I clasped his hand. "I eat risk for breakfast along with my waffles."

Moon glanced at Emperor and then Mischief, who nodded. Jax waved his hand in the universal sign for *go ahead*.

Moon pulled me to him, licking down my cheek. "It's not enough to spy on these Betas. If they're Vala's army, then we need to turn them into double agents." Did he just say that we had to turn spymaster to the wolves who'd *hunted* us? I quivered, and Moon nuzzled at my neck. "Leave off fussing. Aye, they'll slaughter us if we fail, but when we've all faced death our entire lives. This is it now, either we win them to our side, or they'll fight for Vala against anyone she chooses. This has never been about a single war; it's been about every war."

"And never a single kingdom," Emperor added, quietly, "but our three kingdoms, just as it's also about the witch covens and the human world."

I sucked in my breath. At the end of these passages was the Sacred Crypt with the Betas who'd hunted me, who'd either join us against their own princess or kill us.

## CHAPTER 12

I've done many things that would've shocked me before I'd arrived in England: I'd kissed wolves, fallen in love with them, and even been prepared to die in their name. But *nothing* had shocked me as much as watching a Sacred Crypt filled with sweating Betas either lifting weights or dancing to Britney Spears' "I'm a Slave 4 U".

Hocus pocus, they had the whole panting, licking, and writhing dance routine down.

*Huh, that was some aerobics session.*

I twisted to my pack who'd also pushed through into the crypt. At least they looked as stunned as me.

As Britney's breathy cooing over the hip hop dance track boomed out loudly enough to shake the skulls that lined the cavernous arched crypt, the Betas who were no longer in their wolf form (thank Hecate) and were dressed in nothing but ivory shorts lost themselves in the dance. They flickered between their male and female forms as naturally as breathing. It was stunning.

Wasn't being female outside play forbidden by Royal Decree?

But hey, when these Betas had biceps as large as my head, I wasn't going to be the one to bring it up. The Betas weren't like the willowy beauties of the Kingdoms of the Wilds who'd treated Amadeus as if he was their sultan. Instead, they were like Betas on steroids — super soldiers.

Super soldiers who had some freaking seductive choreography. I was allowed to be envious of the way that they moved their hips, right?

Jax bounced on his toes and flapped his wings like he was only a twirl away from joining in.

I curled into Emperor's arms; his liquorice scent was sharper, barely hidden by the honey. "So, you didn't know…?"

"That Amadeus wasn't the only one who could wiggle his ass like that…?" Emperor's lips curved into a smile against my cheek. "It's an entire shock to me."

"Stop dicking around. I meant the whole Captain America thing that they have going on."

"I don't believe that they're American," Mischief whispered.

Emperor stroked my arm. "I never imagined that Betas would be used as fighters. It's a shock to discover how unenlightened I am, when I've spent my life dreaming that it would no longer matter what nature a wolf was assigned in the womb. No other kingdom would guess that Betas would be trained like this. How delightful that Vala has thought of such a simple but effective weapon."

At the back overlooking the dance like a stage was an MMA style ring, which was looped with barbed wire. When I glanced up, I caught the eye of the youngest but largest Beta who was wearing boxing gloves like Rocky with a braid of silvery gray hair to his ass.

Rocky stiffened and then whistled high and shrill over the music, which cut off.

*Now I'd seriously pissed off the dancing Betas.*

When the Betas prowled towards my pack and me in as close a formation as in their routine, Moon and Emperor circled in front of me, and Jax edged closer. Mischief swooped over their heads; his wings sparked.

"Your Moon God has broken from his shrine, so that you may bask in his light." Hold on, Mischief wasn't trying to pull the god card again…? And since when did he talk about himself in the third person? I hissed, but Mischief only stared down haughtily at the Betas. *Where was Ramiel with the smacky hand when you needed him?* "Why not savor it?"

Rocky leaped from the ring, banging his gloved hands together. "Why not savor my fist in your face, *god*?"

"*Hmm*, my apologies, what?" Mischief spluttered.

Suddenly, the moon leash flared, before yanking Mischief upside down by his ankle. Mischief flailed, beating his wings in outrage, whilst he revolved and his hair hung over his face in a silver waterfall.

*I figured that was one way for the Betas to bask in his light.*

Mischief sniffed. "Well, that was embarrassing."

Moon caught Mischief by his wing to stop his spinning. "By my fur, will you leave off fussing. You're still *my* daft god."

Mischief allowed his wings to hang down, although he crossed his arms over his chest with way more smugness than a guy had any right to, who was strung up his ankles. "Do you see now? *God*."

Rocky snorted, stalking through the other Betas. His russet eyes glowed with menace, and his chest rippled with muscles, as if they'd been airbrushed on. The Betas parted for him like a practiced war machine and hey, wasn't that reassuring?

Rocky snorted. "An *Omega* would fawn over you." Moon's jaw clenched. "But I'm not some nameless worshiper in a shrine…" His gaze darted to Moon, before away dismissively. "…or an Omega prince from another kingdom. I'm Legion and—"

"Let me guess…because you are many?" Emperor drawled.

Legion scowled. "Because the princess didn't see us

only as breeders. On the face of the moon, the Alphas have always taken so much from us, but at least she saw that we could be *fighters*."

"Don't sell yourself short. You could also be backup dancers for *your* prince." Jax's grin was all sharp teeth.

Legion dragged off his boxing gloves, before tossing them to the side. Then his claws extended, as he sank one into Mischief's shoulder blade, before licking up the trail of blood. When Mischief hollered, Moon and Emperor dived forward, only to be blocked by the wall of Betas who moved in a sensuous unison that was as sexy as it was menacing. Yet there was a brutal power that underlaid their every move.

*Could they transform into wolf form at any moment?*

At Mischief's panted pain, my shadows burst out to flood the room. The skulls shook and clattered, painted crimson.

Every single werewolf froze, apart from Legion, who never took his gaze from mine as he burrowed his claw deeper. "Betas are viewed as too *unclean* to even enter your shrine. Does it make us dirty because we're used to breed? To be fathers to our children? Stop our kingdom from dying out? Do you reject us for that?"

"I'm leashed like a dog by *your* queen," Mischief wheezed. "Pray, what choice do you think I have to reject anyone?"

"Good," Legion dragged his claw out of Mischief

with a flourish. "Then you know what it is to be collared. I gave up on you, god, a long time ago."

"It's no matter," Mischief's voice was weary, "I gave up on myself too."

I shook, desperate to pull Mischief to me and pet his wings, until he purred and lost the despair that had him looking so lost. He'd sacrificed to return here with me to help his people, but they believed that he'd rejected them, when in fact, they were the ones who were rejecting *him*.

I wrenched on the skulls with my shadows, and they flew across the Sacred Crypt, shattering on the roof. The Betas cowered in shock.

"Listen up, dick Betas, your Moon God here is a royal prick but he's also epic. He doesn't expect anything from you: your worship or your belief. But he'll give *you* everything now that he's here." I glanced between them, as my crimson wove around me. "Honestly, my pack and me only want to save your asses. You just have to give us a chance to prove it, and believe me, I know that's a tough ask."

Legion stared at me unblinkingly for a long moment. "What are you without your shadows?"

*The dick Beta had a point.*

"*Hmm*, a fabulous cocktail maker and lover of wolf cuddles…?" I ventured.

A curvy Beta who'd been leading the Brittany Spears dance giggled. Hey, I had one fan.

"You're no different to the other Alphas," Legion snarled.

"How astounding that you can't see we're here to offer help." Emperor raised his eyebrow.

Legion flexed his bicep. "Do I look like I need help?"

"Do *I*?" Emperor gritted out. "You're not at all deluded, of course. Just like appearances of strength can never deceive. It doesn't matter how often you work out, if you're tied to the bed or pushed to your knees on behalf of your kingdom."

I winced at the same time as Legion. Emperor had been used by his mother as a pretty bargaining chip in the same way as these Betas were used as their kingdom's breeders to keep their Omegas chaste. They'd better not say that Emperor didn't understand them because boy, did he.

Legion shrugged one powerful shoulder. "Let the Charmer put away her shadows and let's see which of us wins. One weak pretty Beta who supposedly needs your help or a *witch*."

I figured that Emperor hadn't been trying for an MMA smackdown. He shot me an apologetic glance. I sighed, dragging my shadows back in.

Legion looked like he was the type to fight with his claws, fangs, and barbed wire wrapped around his knuckles. I didn't think that cocktail making, wolf cuddling, or basic martial arts would save me. I wouldn't back down, however, because this was about proving a point not just to the Betas but to myself as well.

I'd be prepared to stand without my shadows if that's what their screwed-up sense of honor demanded, even if it meant having my ass kicked.

I could be just Crimson.

*This was going to hurt…*

When I crouched into fighting stance, the Betas fanned out into a ring.

Moon glanced anxiously between Legion and me like he was about to lunge on the Beta in my defense, but I shook my head.

Legion strolled closer, until his breath tickled my cheek. I stiffened, raising my hands in a karate chop.

"You'd truly fight me — a Beta — without your shadows?" He asked with a wonder that I didn't understand.

"Dude, just call me shadowless."

"About that, you'd be better off calling her *Wolf Liberator*." Jax winked at Moon as he writhed in a way too obviously taking the piss out of their "Slave 4 U" routine. When he slipped his fingers over Moon's collar, I stiffened. I didn't think that poisoning Moon with silver on our first day together was ever going to stop haunting me. "Instead of fighting us, how about you listen to your own prince?"

Just as the Alphas could record and monitor the

Omegas through their collars, so by granting Moon his magical power over his collar along with mine, meant that he could manipulate it.

I'd spent years playing with magic and tech and watching Moon playing the same trick in the treasure room had been as hot as anything that Amadeus did with his tongue. Moon had planned a Princess Leia distress call moment, and Amadeus had been the princess.

A life-size hologram of Amadeus shot out of Moon's collar, just as the recording of Moth in the Omega Training Center had once played in the House of Silver. It was close enough to Legion and me that we could've reached out and touched him. Legion shrank back, however, as the other Betas gasped.

When Moon had recorded Amadeus in the treasure room once we'd freed him from his chains, Emperor had tried to cover him in his robes, but Amadeus had squirmed away.

"I earned these stripes," Amadeus had explained. "Please, let my people see the truth for once. I'm no different to them."

"What did you do to our prince?" Legion growled. His hands curled and uncurled, as he studied Amadeus' body, which was purpled with bruises. If the Betas had looked dangerous before, they appeared murderous now. *Mages freaking balls...* "If you show me this to taunt me, I'll taunt you back with my *fists*."

"My mistake, I thought that you were more than the fighters that the princess had created or the breeders of tradition." Mischief rolled his eyes. "If you care so much about your prince's pain, then listen to him."

Amadeus' hologram took a step forward, wincing. "I'm sorry for whatever my pack have said. They're probably tied up or had their sweet behinds kicked." I winced. I'd thought that it'd been funny when Amadeus had first recorded that but now...not so much. "It'd be a fine thing if you heard me out, but I'm not asking as your prince. I know that I'm a mongrel, see, and adopted. I'm no better than any of you. I'm only asking the same as any Beta here because it's my duty (even if I never asked for it), to protect the kingdom as a Beta *and* a mongrel." Despite the fact that he was rejecting being a prince, I'd never heard Amadeus sound so princely. The Betas were watching him with rapt attention; Legion looked thoughtful. Then Amadeus grinned, and his eyes twinkled wickedly. "The Charmer and the rest of my daft pack swore the same. It would please me for you to help them against the princess." He touched his welted shoulder, before swinging around to reveal his scarred back. "She controls me just the same as she does you."

The Betas howled in outrage, as the hologram shut off.

*Amadeus might've overdone the big reveal.*

Legion snatched me by the throat. "Princess Vala marked her own brother?"

Okay, I guessed scars were a big no-no in Wolf Kingdom.

"Indeed." Emperor plucked Legion's fingers off my neck, before shoving him away with a grunt. "How delightful for her that she found in her adopted brother a toy, assassin, and whipping boy. After all, he was nothing but a *Beta*, unlike her precious lost brother. Why not make harsh use of him?"

Emperor knew how to push buttons, which was good, unless you know, the growling Betas now circling us ripped out *our* throats first.

"You'd dare pretend to be better than us, *Omega* prince?" Legion snapped.

Emperor's laugh was hollow. "I'm the last person to pretend that."

Moon rested his hand on Emperor's arm. "You can't mean to still fight us? Did you not listen to your prince and what that rotten bitch has been doing to him and what he's suffered to protect you all?"

The Betas froze and then glanced at Legion. Finally, Legion nodded, crossing his arms.

"Whatever we tell you won't matter. On the light of the moon, the princess runs this kingdom and soon she'll…" He snapped his mouth shut so quickly I was certain that he'd bitten through his lip.

"Soon she'll what?" I demanded.

Legion rocked on his heels, before deflating. "She talks like she wants to battle the witches who buried us in this kingdom but she doesn't…yet." I swallowed. Why wasn't it good news that she didn't want to start a Second Wolf War…*yet?* "Look, the queen has only ever been obsessed with Omegas. But the princess wants to be Chief Alpha. She reckons that it's the only way to keep Wolf Kingdom strong. First, she'll take out the outlaw Wilds and then the craven Kingdom of the Alphas who lick the boots of the witches. She'll rule them all."

Emperor snarled. His nails and teeth extended as golden as his hair. In partial shift he was both terrifying and scorching hot. He stormed towards Legion, who scrambled backward, until he was pinned against the ring. To my surprise, this time none of the other Betas fought to stop Emperor.

"The Princess of the Gods would declare war on the other wolves?" Emperor demanded.

Damn my witchy ass, Emperor was going Alpha and without whipping out my own shadows, there was nothing that I could do to stop him.

Legion's eyes widened. "Well, I'd heard stories about the liberties they allow Omegas in the Kingdom of the Alphas, but you're no *perfect Omega*, are you? When was the last time that you were forced to your knees?"

When Emperor kneed Legion in the balls, I flinched.

So, this wasn't going how I'd hoped, but at least Emperor had dealt out the vengeance that my crimson was wailing for, as it itched beneath my skin.

I'd been so worried about a second war between the wolves and witches that I hadn't thought about *civil war* between the wolves, but then I hadn't known that Amadeus' adopted sister would be such a ruthless dictator.

Or as I liked to call her: *A dictator dick.*

"Don't make me kick your ass." I smirked at the groaning Legion. "But honestly, we're talking about saving *all* our asses here, so how about not being a jerk about your natures, and helping us to find a way to stop the princess who'll truly turn this into the land of the dead."

Legion straightened with difficulty, licking his lips. "The collars don't work on full Betas, only mongrels, when we shift into female form. The witches never stopped to think about our talent when they created them. No one ever remembers us." His voice shook with hurt.

Moon's gaze met mine; its horror reflected my own. "On the furless heavens, if only one kingdom can shift in a battle, it'd be a massacre."

"Trust me, you're going to want to join your prince and my pack and fight against this bitch," I insisted.

Mischief's voice was low, "I've battled in enough

wars to know that the only true way to win is to stop them before they begin."

Legion's gaze hardened. "I don't think so. We can't follow our prince until he rules. Ask us again then."

I hissed in frustration. "Do you think that your princess can beat two other kingdoms *and* the witches? Even if she does, how many will die to prove...what? That she's a bad, bad wolf or worse than *my* ancestors?"

"How about proving that no one can commit genocide on our kind again because *we're* the ones with the power?" When Vala's quiet voice came from the archway, I jumped.

*Holy hell, how long had she been there?*

The Betas cowered back. Kudos to Legion, he at least didn't do more than clench his jaw.

"You mean craziness? Cunning? Seriously over the top villain vibes? Stop me when I'm close." I sauntered towards Vala, and my shadows lashed out as if eager to taste her, even though they were held back by our forced bond.

*Yuck...I so wasn't down with that.*

Vala tilted her chin, but there was a weariness behind her eyes that I hadn't noticed before. "Yeah, you're more than close enough to me, even if you won't admit it." I blanched. *Okay, that one hit home.* "Wow, Moon God, at last you can be useful. You've done nothing to help the people who worship you so far..." When Mischief flinched, my crimson wound around him in soothing coils. "Why don't you prove your love now?"

"How astute," Mischief shook the hair away from his face, as he spun at Vala's command, "that's precisely what I intend to do."

Vala flicked her finger, and Mischief dropped to the ground in a heap of curses and ruffled feathers. "Use your magic to remove all the collars, else I'll have to assume that you don't love us. What do you think I do to those who *hate* us?"

I drew in a breath. *Mischief had the power to free the wolves…?* Rage wound my shadows tighter around him. Then why on all the covens in England, hadn't Mischief freed at least my pack?

*Had he been hiding this from me?*

Mischief scooted closer on his ass, curling his wings around himself. "You mistake me for the all-powerful." His gaze darted to mine with such sadness that my own eyes smarted with tears. "And it appears so does the witch even now. I've been accused of being a *Sly Imp* and a *traitor* for much of my life, and I've been abused for it. Oh yes, ask the impossible and then punish me for failing."

I craved to hold Mischief so that he never felt a failure again, but it'd been my fault that he wore a haunted look now. What did he care whether Vala doubted him? But he did care a freaking hell of a lot if *I* thought that he'd betrayed me.

I didn't give a witch's tit what it looked like or how much he'd bristle, I wouldn't allow Mischief to think that I didn't believe him for a moment longer.

I dived on top of him in a startled ball of feathers, before licking across his nose because it was as much as I knew he'd allow, even though I was desperate to hold him as tightly as I would've done Moon, or as passionately as I would've done Emperor. "I'm sorry. You're my pack, and if I ever think you can do the impossible, it's because you're so freaking epic. I'd never punish you; you know that by now, right?"

Vala huffed. "But I would. This is the Sacred Crypt. I shall have you all executed."

Mischief lay back on his elbows with a smug expression. "Royalty may enter. Mindless creature, I'm an archduke, the wolves are princes…"

"…And your Charmer is a *commoner*," Vala spat, "as is the mongrel."

Moon wrapped his arm protectively around Jax.

Mischief shot me a sheepish look. "Does *sorry* cover it?"

"If you refuse to be of use to me, Moon God, then I'll put your *lovers* to death." Vala examined her claws, before strolling closer to me with a sway of her hips. Her smile was venomous. "Mother has summoned you for an official lunch. Now it can be your last meal before your execution."

## CHAPTER 13

The *screech* of knives over the iron plates made me wince, as I stared down at the burned pheasant that was as dry and dead as everything in the Memorial Dining Room.

*Why didn't I get to choose my last meal?* Where was my burger and fries, followed by a chocolate donut?

Vala had led those of us who were *guilty* of entering the Sacred Crypt (except for Jax because apparently even awaiting execution didn't grant a mongrel family time with her royal assholeness), to a room that appeared to be set out for a grand feast, unless you know, that actually included *feasting*. The walls and floor were riveted iron like we'd been swallowed by a submarine. The black chandelier hummed. It smelled sterile like even the aromas had been sucked away, apart from wafts of overcooked fowl.

Queen Banan had already been seated like a beautiful but aristocratically cold statue at the head of the table. The train of her shimmering dress was so long that it'd wrapped along the length of the table, as if her own shadows had swallowed it, but her crown of crescent moons was crooked.

When Vala had strolled into the dining room with us reluctantly following, Banan hadn't looked up. Instead, she'd continued to coo at Moth, who she'd held on her lap along with her son's security blanket, murmuring a lullaby to him. Moon had stiffened, but it'd been Vala's jaw that had clenched with fury.

*Yeah, there were serious issues in the royal family, and my witchy ass was about to be shot in the crossfire.*

After that, no one had said a word. Honestly, it was harder for me, just like I hadn't taken a bite of dry bird because I was gagged and in the nonkinky way. As soon as Vala had shoved me down in the seat at the end of the table, moon wisps had shot out, tying me to the chair, whilst others had smothered my mouth. I'd choked, until I'd realized that I could breathe but not talk.

Vala had raised her eyebrow at Moon, who'd hesitated with his hand on the back of the chair.

*Holy hell, he hated to be muzzled.*

Moon had only tilted his head defiantly, however, even though I'd known how much it'd cost him, and thrown himself down in the seat next to me.

*My epic rebel...*

I'd winced, waiting for the moon gag to choke him as well, but...*nothing.*

*Huh, so the special treatment was only for me then...?*

I hadn't known whether to be offended or to take it as a compliment. I'd go with...*even my words were so dangerous I had to be silenced.* I'd have to cast an Ego Spell to believe that, but when Vala was attempting an internal coup against her crazy mom, I'd bet she didn't want the queen believing what I had to say.

Banan had leashed her own god and hated the other kingdoms. So, it hadn't been like Mischief or my Charms could tell her anything that'd break her back into reality. Yet Vala had forgotten that I was connected to my guys by more than words. I'd be able to figure out a way past even a gag, right?

At least Omegas in this kingdom hadn't been expected to kneel on the floor, unlike in the Wilds. Emperor had folded into the chair on the other side to me with a practiced elegance. I'd bet that he'd been to more dinner parties than I'd attended in the Hamptons, although I'd never tried it gagged before.

*Had Emperor...?*

Okay, filing that away for fun things to try before I die, which could be *way* too soon.

When Vala had settled halfway along the table like she was claiming it, Mischief had flung himself down opposite her with the smug expression of a royal prick waiting for the perfect moment to strike.

Then Amadeus had sauntered into the room with as much bravado as if *he* was the King.

My breath had caught, whilst Emperor and Moon had both sucked in their breath at the same time. Amadeus been back in male form, wearing a flowing satin top and tights, with long kid skin gloves up to his elbows. He'd looked just like I'd remembered from his dance in Wild Hall before he'd been attacked and his clothes had been torn, only now he'd been *commanding* the room not as a Charm to be Claimed but as a true prince.

*He'd never been sexier.*

Banan's expression had softened as she'd stared at him; her eyes had gleamed with tears. "*My son…*"

My breath had stuttered, even as Amadeus had stumbled, before catching himself because she hadn't been calling for *him*, rather for the *true prince* and first son: The Ambassador.

The Ambassador had been ripped away from his mom and taken to the Omega Training Center where *my mom* had Claimed him. I hadn't been able to think about the way that mom had caged him in the same house, where she'd lovingly cared for me. After mom's death, the Ambassador had been taken in by my aunt, Stella, and the only one to show him friendship had been Aquilo.

Ambassador had died at *Aquilo's* mom's own hand, to save his friend, and the queen mourned the loss of her son to the witches, even though she didn't yet know that he was dead.

*Holy hell, didn't we have to tell her the truth?*

My heart had thudded painfully fast, as Amadeus had stilled like a sculpture. As soon as Vala and Banan had looked away, however, he'd wink at me or wiggle his ass.

*Still…wink…still…wiggle.*

Now, I focused on my pheasant again, as my stomach growled with hunger.

When Moon nudged my knee under the table, my crimson slipped around him in a caress that made him shiver. He licked his lips, pushing his own magic over mine, until I panted into the gag.

*The adorable…distracting…asshole.*

It didn't matter how much danger I was in, that I was tied, silenced, and at a table with my two worst enemies in this kingdom, because I also had my pack with me and I knew that they'd protect me, just the same as I'd protect them.

Emperor's fingers settled on my other knee, even as he pretended to concentrate on his pheasant, drawing comforting but teasing circles. My skin tingled at each pass of his finger, and then the harder press of his thumb. When his laughing eyes caught mine for a moment, I realized that the cocky asshole was paying me back for every time that I'd worked him up and had made Aquilo come in his pants. And all he needed was Moon's love and his finger and thumb edging higher and higher and...

"If you leash a Moon God like a dog, then he's tamed." When Vala leaned across the table, bopping the end of her spoon on Mischief's nose, he froze. *Okay, so here came the acting out for attention.* Vala slid her gaze to her mom who was still feeding slices of buttered bread to Moth. "How many of your lovers must I kill to *break* you?"

If Mischief was Thor, then this would be the part where Vala would be blasted with thunder, but Mischief was the one who should've been gagged because he blasted with *words*.

Mischief's grin was so dark it thrilled me. "Oh, I may appear tame but I've imagined slaughtering you in seven interesting ways merely since we've sat down. Do you wish to hear them?"

Vala blanched, shrinking back.

For the first time, Banan's gaze sharpened, and she appeared to notice that we were even sitting in the dining room. "May the moon shine on you; I welcome you to my table. When I break bread with someone, I hope to make them my friends or discover them enemies. If they're enemies, then on my fangs, they don't live out the night." I shivered. *Now I got why Amadeus and Jax had been terrified of a summons to dine with the psycho queen.* "I hope that my daughter has taught you the truth, see, of my kingdom."

I struggled in my seat, clanking against the table legs.

Why was Banan acting like I wasn't even a prisoner? Didn't she know that her daughter planned to kill me or were her daughter's threats hollow because the queen still held the true power?

Emperor's steely gaze darted to Vala and then Amadeus. "Rest assured, we're no longer blind to the truth."

Amadeus blushed, mid wiggle.

Banan curled one strand of midnight black hair around her finger, scrutinizing me. "Why is your new..." She scrunched up her nose in distaste, "... Omega Witch not eating, daughter?"

Vala smirked. "She's mine, so I choose what she eats, amongst other things." Was that a challenge to her mom, me, or both of us? By her mom's warning growl, I could tell that the power grab hadn't been missed. Plus, was she still weighing up if I'd be executed, just like her mom? I squirmed because being weighed up *twice* sucked. "Anyway, she's watching her figure."

I squawked in outrage through my gag. Oh, that was the last, last... *I didn't even know how many straws there were now but that was the very last straw of them all.*

Vala was in the biggest wolfie ass kicking of them all.

When Banan stroked Moth's cheek, Moth didn't flinch but instead, caught Moons' eye.

*What was he trying to tell him?*

Banan had either become even crazier with grief than since we'd last seen her, or Vala could control these moon wisps like I could my shadows, unseen by her own mom.

If she ran the Beta army in secret, then she hid her power in the same way that my Charms hid theirs. These next generation of Alphas wanted a new world, which I'd have been seriously behind if it'd truly been one of light, life, and freedom. The problem was that it included becoming as dickish as the witches, and that meant that I had to stop them.

Luckily for me, I had the strength of my pack beside me.

Moon rubbed his toes along mine, before stroking up the back of my calf with his foot. I flushed, as my breath quickened. My pulse fluttered in my neck.

*Okay, playing footsie at the same table as the Queen of the Gods wasn't dangerous at all, right?*

Then I yelped as Emperor kicked me in the ankle, even as he kept his gaze on his plate.

*Would these guys make up their mind because I was pretty sure that wasn't how pain and pleasure was meant to work.*

Then I caught Mischief's amused expression from halfway down the table.

Moon's mouth was tight, as he glanced up and caught Emperor's gaze. What were they warning each other about? They'd known each other for centuries and these hidden glance signals to each other were a second language to them.

Unfortunately, I was only a beginner in Furtive Wolf Glances.

Unholy hexes, the tension could be cut with a knife and used to moisten this pheasant (and son of a bitch, had I just used the word *moisten*...?), with what everybody *wasn't* saying. The queen's get togethers were less fun than my uncle's investor dinner parties and I'd *hated* those.

When Banan drained the last of her blood-red wine, waving her glass in the air like a *let battle commence* signal, Mischief, Emperor, and Vala all dived for the crystal wine decanter.

Emperor raised an imperious eyebrow as he stared down at where their hands jointly rested around the crystal like a game of One Potato, Two...

*What I wouldn't give to see Vala play that with Mischief.*

Instead, they stared at each other like this was a How Big Is My Dick Contest (Vala included). I shot my shadows out, tickling under Mischief's wings until he was caught between laughing and beating them in indignation. When his fingers loosened, Amadeus stroked his hands down his hips and cast a seductive look at Vala that even had *me* caught in its thrall. Vala stilled, and her eyes glazed.

Why had I ever thought that Amadeus' didn't have a plan? His power to mesmerize could be deadly, and I was just as certain that Emperor was the one who knew the end game.

With a haughty grin, Emperor wrested the decanter to his chest, before unstopping it and swaggering to Banan. He leaned over her, before pouring her wine.

"Although our visit did not start in the most auspicious way," Emperor murmured in the most sexily diplomatic voice that I'd ever heard and boy, did I now understand why his kingdom had used him as *their* hidden weapon, "I hope that we can come to a better understanding." He paused in his pouring, before he smiled silkily, wiping away an imaginary drip at the end of the decanter. "By my hide, we appreciate your charming hospitality." His glare at Vala was dangerous. "Despite your daughter's threats…"

"Threats?" Banan's eyes narrowed.

Vala's claws lengthened, scratching against the table. "Not now, mother."

"By the furless heavens, indeed *now*." Banan's arms tightened around Moth as if to protect him from Vala.

Emperor finished pouring the queen's wine. "On my

honor, it makes me fear for the safety of my kingdom's delegation tomorrow."

Vala launched herself up with a snarl. "Silence lest you be flayed!"

"You see," Emperor settled the decanter down with the *clunk* of a diplomat who'd played these games as long as Vala; she'd incited us into trouble, and he'd just repaid her with a karmic bite on the ass, *"threats."*

Banan patted Emperor's arm. "On the light of the moon, prince, if I find you my friend, you shall find no terrors here in my kingdom. *No one* shall harm you, or my rage against them shall be terrible." She glowered at Vala, who ducked her head. *That was some queenly scolding.* "The delegation of royal families—"

"My ma and da…?" Moon gasped, reaching for my hand.

I couldn't do more than entwine our fingers, as my wrist was bound by the dick moonbeams, but Moon needed the contact. Emperor's burning gaze met mine.

If my pack and me didn't work out a way to stop Vala, then it wouldn't simply be a civil war sparked between the wolves. It'd mean both Emperor's and Moon's families massacred just like mine had been.

I'd had to live with the aching loss and grief of that for the last decade. It didn't matter that their moms were assholes, I wouldn't let it happen. And what if their dads and sisters were killed too?

The assassination of the royal families would devastate the other kingdoms as much as my Charms. They'd never be able to fight off the Kingdom of the Gods with their leaders lost.

No wonder Vala looked so self-satisfied.

Banan blinked at Moon. "Do you miss them, sweet Omega? I imagine that my son misses me. Perhaps, I was too hasty in my judgment of you." Her expression gentled. Maybe I should've known that it was the vision of a son's love for a mom that would sway her towards us. "It was planned between the three royal houses for us to meet here…the sight of our defeat and loss…on the centennial. Do you know what *I* feared?" She leaned towards me, holding up her wine as if toasting me. "See, the Wolf Charmers never truly defeated us, they only collared us." She hovered her fingers over her own collar. "It's been long whispered that the witches were waiting to wipe us from the earth." I held my breath. How much did she know about Stella and the House of Blood's plan for a Second Wolf War? She did know that *I'd* stopped it, right? "But you've created the turmoil amongst the covens, which means that I shan't need to fear for Wolf Kingdom. An Omega Wolf Witch appearing alongside our Moon God unites and blesses us in every move that we now make." How hadn't I noticed that her smile was as dark as Vala's? "You're both nothing but icons in a shrine, but I may use you as I like."

My guts roiled, and my pulse thudded.

This is what happened when you stumbled out of a plane from America not knowing *a damn thing* about being a Wolf Charmer.

Both Vala and her mom were using Mischief and me but in different ways. Banan wanted to show that the three wolf kingdoms were united and strong, so that they could never be defeated by the witches again. I mean, I didn't like the *use* part of that but I could still get with the plan. On the other hand, Vala intended to use us to show that her war against the other wolves was justified because she had us on her side.

Except, I'd made it all possible by breaking up the covens and taking out the witch who'd kept Vala in line: *Stella.*

Vala had been planning for this centennial for decades, which meant that she'd known I'd be called back on my twenty-first birthday from a non-magical life. She'd guessed that I'd always be different, and she'd trained Amadeus to *use* that.

*Had he...?*

When I caught Amadeus' eye and took in his regal determination and the way that he vibrated with fury at Vala, I knew that he hadn't. I had the sense that he'd been tricked the same as me.

If Vala hadn't been threatening the loved ones and kingdoms of my Charms, I'd have given her kudos for seriously being a smart bitch.

But she was alone, and I had pack.

I flowed my shadows out in waves down the table, tapping Mischief on the head. His lips quirked, before he nodded.

"Oh goodie, I'm now a tamed, leashed, icon in a shrine." Mischief's wingtips pulsed. "Your mother does not perceive me as a danger nor does she fear the Charmer. Why, I wonder, are you so cowardly that you do, princess?"

When Moon snickered, Vala gaped, before fangs elongated. She sprang to me, tracing one claw down my cheek.

*Maybe the piss off the psycho princess ploy had backfired.*

When Vala traced her finger over the gag, it melted away, along with the wisps that'd been tying me down. I sighed, wiping the drool away from my chin because, you know, dribbling wasn't a turn on for me.

Vala leaned over me as she whispered. "*I* rule here. Do you think, naughty Omega, there's anything you can say that'll make a difference?"

*She seriously didn't know me, did she?*

I bit my lip. I'd been the one to go all *Game of Thrones* on the witches, toppling the Oxford Head Coven. Now I had to try the opposite on the wolves and hold them together. Yet the only way to do that was to throw something so unexpected into the mix that Vala couldn't have planned for it.

I glanced between each of my lovers; their gazes

were understanding, and I hoped that I was reading it right, as they each in turn nodded. Amadeus was last but he blazed with such strength that it was awe inspiring.

"Use me anyway you like, Queen Banan, but honestly, the only one at this table who's blind is you." When I sprang up, Vala stumbled back in surprise. "You snuggle Moth but can't you see your own daughter?" Banan's mouth tightened into a thin line, and Vala looked away. "Hey, I get it, you're buried in your grief but you need to wake your queenly ass up because your daughter, who's right in front of you, has been hiding secrets."

"*Lies*," Vala hissed, diving for me. "You're giving me the traitor feels, and my mother kills her enemies."

Moon stalked up, slashing out his claws to block Vala. Vala snarled in shock.

Mischief leaned back in his chair with a grin. "My apologies, did I say that any of us were *tamed*? My mistake."

I shrugged. "Hey, I won't spill your daughter's war plans because why would you believe me? I mean, I *could* show you the recordings from our collars…but then, Vala controls those, and I'm certain that the asshole knows how to wipe or change them. So, no proof, right? Unless, I said…go look in the Sacred Crypt." When Vala howled, Emperor prowled around to her other side, boxing her in. Banan merely watched us with a cold disinterest like nothing we did mattered to her. *I didn't figure that it did, which was the problem.* "But she wouldn't have brought us here bold as anything if she couldn't hide the evidence. So…" When I perched on the edge of the table in front of Banan, the chandelier thrummed dangerously, casting dancing shadows across the walls. I stroked across the Ambassador's security blanket. "I'm sorry, but your first son — the true prince — was never broken by the covens. He stood up to them and fought like a warrior."

Banan trembled, slamming down her wine glass and sloshing the red wine over the rim. "Then why on the moon above are you *sorry*?"

*Come on Crimson, you can do this…*

My pulse pounded through me, as I forced her to meet my intense gaze.

"Because he died like the epic hero he always was," I replied.

For a moment, Banan didn't move; she appeared transformed into a statue for real. It was Vala who screeched, swiping the plates smashing off the table, before diving at Amadeus. When Moon attempted to hold her back, I was surprised to see Amadeus duck across the room and into her arms to comfort her. She clutched him to her chest as she wailed.

I hated that I'd had to use grief against even an asshole like Vala. Yet the Ambassador had loved Aquilo; I didn't think that he'd have wanted more deaths to happen in his name.

I'd expected Banan to sob as openly as her daughter, but instead her eyes were glassy and dead. It chilled me how much the news had shattered her.

If the entire Wolf Kingdom hadn't rested on this move, I'd never have taken it. Maybe that meant I wasn't as ruthless as these other dickheads but I could live with that.

Banan stood with a silent dignity, *screeching* her chair along the floor, as she pushed Moth to his knees. I winced, hopping over the table. Her train snaked around the table like it had a life of its own, whipping around her. When she prowled towards me with a deadly intent that made my eyes widen, Mischief knocked his own chair backwards to twirl me around in his wings and away from her.

"By my fangs, y-you would d-dare lie about this as well? Did I not warn you what h-happened to my enemies?" Even if Banan held her shoulders straight, her lip still trembled.

"How interesting that you are fed lies and yet believe them truth, but when you are at last fed truth, you doubt it as a lie." Mischief curled his wings closer around me.

Banan looked broken. "You promised that you'd be our god. That if…you'd been here against the witches… you'd have protected us. Yet now you stand by a witch…?"

When the moon leash whipped upwards, choking

around Mischief's neck, I scrabbled to pull it free, but it seared my hands.

*Bubbling cauldrons, he couldn't breathe.*

I dropped to my knees next to Mischief, as he fell to the floor.

Then to my shock, the queen had a face full of enraged incubus. "Stop hurting my pack," Amadeus' voice was ice cold and masterful. Had he been taking lessons from Emperor or had he been hiding this side of himself all along? "The true prince was kind, good, and courageous. He chose to die, see, because it pleased him to save someone he loved. Would you take that away from your own son?"

Finally, Banan released the noose from Mischief, who took a wheezy gasp. I wrapped my arms around Mischief. The *in and out* of his breath was the best thing that I'd heard; not even Jeff Buckley could compare, and I freaking loved his music.

Banan cupped Amadeus' cheek. "When did you become cruel?"

Amadeus shrugged. "When did you know anything about me? Plus, wouldn't it have been crueler to not tell you *all of it?*"

For the first time, Banan's gaze swung to Vala and it was clearer than it'd been before and calculating.

Vala licked her lips, before swiping her wet cheeks. Then she strode with affected confidence towards her mom.

"You don't need *him* or *him*," she gestured at Moth and Amadeus in frustration. Then she held out her arms in a way that was so close to the way that Moon asked for hugs that I shuddered. Even an asshole Alpha needed cuddle time, who knew. "My brother's gone. *But I'm still here.*"

In the silence, Banan studied Vala but she didn't move to hold her. "Goddess Moon! Don't you see? That's never mattered. You can't replace my son. I don't want you, and I never will."

I flinched at the raw honesty because boy, was that the truth, and now I understood the driving force behind Vala's bid for power.

Vala let out a wail as she crumpled to the floor.

*So much for not being about to win with words.*

Banan pinned with me such a deadly stare that I knew I'd just jinxed my own witchy ass. "First, I'll hold a funeral for my poor lost son. On the word of the moon, it shall be grander than any held before. And then, you and the Moon God shall be tested, so that I may see whether you're to be trusted once and for all as friend or enemy." Her claws grew, as her hands curled into fists. Her shimmering train swirled behind her. "You've killed my faith, and by my fangs, you might've killed yourself."

CHAPTER 14

W rapped in Emperor's strong arms, I perched on the edge of the burrow's mossy roof. His robes fluttered around me in the breeze like a golden butterfly. Moon and Amadeus huddled either side of me, so closely that their soft hair brushed against my cheek.

Mischief and Ramiel stood with their wings enfolded around each other, as if they were the hottest gargoyles ever; their feathers flared violet in the gloom. Aquilo sprawled indolently at their feet with an ice-cold beauty, whilst Okami rode a whirlwind above his palm with a simple delight that thrilled me.

Mischief had flown me onto the roof, whilst Ramiel had taken Emperor in his wings. Mischief had grinned with dark joy, twisting me around and diving with his wings outspread.

Sometimes you could forget that Mischief was an

angelic god, and sometimes the fact that he was an ancient deity took away my breath.

*This had been one of my breathless with desire moments.*

Okay, so I'd face a trial after the funeral that could lead to my death, but at least if I passed, Banan would finally believe me about her daughter's plans for a coup and war.

Plus, Vala hadn't known that I had other tricks going for me.

*Had any of the wolves truly wanted a war and more death?*

Aquilo had created a wall of wind that'd flown my other guys onto the roof. Okami had howled, chasing his furry tail around, as he spiraled.

Now, I stared out at the river. Honestly, the top of the Kingdom of the Gods looked like a hobbit should be living under it, but the view, as the Thames surged against the building that clung to its side, was *stunning*.

The moon was reborn in its own reflection across the night time waters, as an entire kingdom mourned the death of their firstborn prince. The wolves floated in hundreds of crescent-shaped boats for the symbolic burial of an Omega who the queen had already lost decades before to the Omega Training Center.

My lips thinned, as I tilted my chin. The system that my great-grandmother had put in place with the witches after the Wolf War and that every Wolf Charmer and

Head Coven had upheld since was going to end by my witchy hand.

Wolf Kingdom didn't need another tyrant like Vala, it needed rebels like my pack.

Had a funeral as grand as this been held for *my* parents or the witch equivalent with black candles and the gathered covens?

When my eyes stung with tears because I hadn't been allowed my chance to say goodbye to my parents, Moon nuzzled his head onto my shoulder. His hair still smelled lemony, although it was damp in the warm summer rain that was tearing from the storm clouds.

Amadeus' eyes were also red-rimmed, and his cheeks were wet, although it could've been the rain.

*Nope, there was no way on earth that he wasn't crying for his own lost prince.*

I looped my arm around Amadeus to pull him even closer into our cuddle, and he smiled. Down below, the wolves cast silver waterlily lights onto the river in a wave of gilded grief.

*The Ambassador had been loved by the Alphas.* It didn't matter that he was an Omega, and *that* was the truth.

Suddenly, lightning zigzagged from the clouds.

Once, I'd watched the firework displays on Main Beach with my cousins, and a summer storm had sent us scurrying for cover kind of like the weather was making us dance just as well as I'd once made my cousin's mouse dance ballet.

This time, however, Aquilo's eyes had only narrowed, before he'd swept to his feet. Then he'd blown Okami into Mischief's spluttering face and raised his hands towards the clouds. His flashing blue eyes, along with the way that magic coursed through his body, as he flowed eddies of air across my skin like it was all done in worship of *me,* was both panty melting and awe-inspiring.

Then his magic reached out to *bend* the rain, lightning, and wind away from us, until we were safe and warm beneath a bubble that he'd made and sweet Hecate, Aquilo was powerful enough to control the elements…?

"That's freaking hot," I breathed. Aquilo's lips twitched, even as he blushed. "Your magic is…"

"*Astounding.*" Mischief gripped Aquilo's arm, dragging Aquilo between Ramiel and himself, cocooning him in both their wings. Aquilo held himself stiff only for a moment, before melting into their hold. "I care not how many have tried to trap or bind your magic. They're small-minded fools. You're remarkable, and I shall never allow it to be said that you're not again."

Aquilo glowed with such radiance that the savage part of me wished to hunt Ivy down to punish her for every time she'd forced her son to hide his magic or told him that it was *bad*. She'd even threatened to send Aquilo away to the Rebel Academy like his cousin.

I mean, what had his poor cousin done, apart from being born a mage?

Yet Aquilo's sister was punishing Ivy for threatening her brother and murdering the Ambassador, and that freaked me out even if it meant I didn't have to worry about *justice*. I'd spent my childhood being bullied by Lux, and neither my mom nor Ivy had believed me when I'd told them.

*Yeah, karma was a witch.*

Ramiel twisted Aquilo around in his arms, pressing their lips together at each vow, "*I am* an angel and you *are* a glorious mage."

When Mischief entwined his fingers through Aquilo's hair, holding his head still, whilst he rubbed his wingtips down Aquilo's rapidly rising and falling chest, Ramiel kissed him with such passion that it was as much a Claiming as when I'd sunk my teeth into Moon's throat to Wolf Bite him.

I stroked down Moon's throat, and he whined. Yet he watched the kiss with a desperate longing.

*Why wouldn't Moon kiss me?*

I needed to taste his lush lips…*just once*…to know that he loved me as deeply as I now loved him. My own lips tingled with the phantom sensation of his touch, and I shivered, suddenly too hot.

I grasped Moon's curls, twisting him to me, just as

Mischief held Aquilo. Moon's brow furrowed with confusion, but when my tongue darted out to lick my lips, he leaned closer.

His hot breath gusted against my mouth. On all the blessed witches, *finally*...

Moon's lips brushed mine. "I'm sorry."

Suddenly, I lurched, drawn by his Moon Child magic and the strength of his devastated emotion, *inside his collar.* A silver thread drew me back too fast to see beyond a blur; my shadows fought to pull away because it looked like I didn't do well being the captive, go figure.

Had Moon known that he had this power? Was this another type of mind control? Or had handing him back the control over his collar, also entangled us and our magic in a way that was as incredible as it was terrifying?

Then the blur settled into the recording, which Moon must've been *apologizing* for wanting me to see, which didn't mean that this would be bad, right? After all, he could be showing me all his kissing partners.

Okay, he was a virgin but that didn't mean that he hadn't even *kissed* before.

I glanced around at the gray corridor that stank of chalk. Wait, I recognized this place. It was the same school that I'd seen in Amadeus' memory in the House of Seasons. So, maybe this truly had been a childhood trauma like the first guy I'd kissed had been all tongue kind of like a toad. Then there'd been the one who hadn't even opened his lips, so I'd had to prise them open with *my* tongue. Of course, there'd been the asshole who'd thought that kissing had meant simply lunging...

At least this trip, I wasn't inside Moon's body in the way that I'd been inside Amadeus' because that had been uncomfortable in so many ways.

Laughter and the clatter of footsteps burst out.

*Holy hell, where could I hide?*

Then I flushed: recorded memories couldn't see you, check. To make up for my time travel dumbassery, I leaned against the wall, crossing my arms with the air of someone who did this all the time.

Inside, my pulse was racing, however, and my mouth was dry.

When the three princes dove around the corner, they were older than they'd been in the last memory but were still teenagers, with their arms around each other's shoulders as they jostled and laughed. Emperor was taller than Amadeus and Moon and he hooked his hand into Moon' curls, swinging him against the wall.

I watched their faces in fascination because boy, did they look different.

*What was it?*

Then I bit my lip because I realized what made them look that way: *they were happy.*

I'd seen glimpses of that look in each of them at

different times but here it was in all three of them together and I'd have given up my shadows for my Charms to look like that again.

*What'd happened to rip it away?*

Why had Moon taken so long to accept Emperor's cuddles, when here he was held in his arms like it was the only place that he wanted to be?

When Emperor traced Moon's lips, Moon's pupil's dilated before he surged forward eagerly to kiss Emperor.

*What in the witching heavens...?*

I startled away from the wall, unable to pretend that I was some indifferent observer.

*Moon's first kiss had been with Emperor...?*

Then why in the witching heavens wouldn't he kiss me? My chest ached with a hurt that numbed my shadows; I hadn't known that they could wail with distress but they were now.

"I told you, Countess," a girl's voice crowed from the end of the corridor, "the Omega princes can't be trusted together."

I jolted as much as the princes.

The same bitch Alpha from Amadeus' memory, who'd insisted that Amadeus lick her shoe in order to feed, was smiling smugly at Moon and Emperor, whilst Lyall (who Moon had been promised to as future Bitten), vibrated with fury.

Even young, Lyall looked like a warrior with her

hair held back by black strips of leather and a second strip of leather that hung at her belt, which she now unwound with ominous intent.

Moon's hand curled into Amadeus'. Moon ducked his head.

"I'll flay you!" Lyall hissed. Her hand tightened on the strap. "Om, get your hide here now."

*All this was over a kiss…?*

I hated that every trace of happiness had been chased from the three princes' faces.

Emperor squared his shoulders, before stepping in front of both Amadeus and Moon.

Lyall snorted. "Aye, just like a wolf from the Kingdom of the Alphas. But think about this *prince,* if you don't step aside, then by my fangs, I'll be taking *his* daft self anyway. Do you truly think that I can't? Om's *my* Wolf Bitten." Moon shook, shrinking back against Amadeus. "Then I'll punish him here and now in front of you all or, on the furless heavens, I'll drag him in front of the entire school to make an example out of him. Then I'll tell both your bastard mas exactly *why.*" When Emperor paled, Moon pulled his hand free from Amadeus'. "What do you think the queens will do to your backsides when they discover that you've been *dirty* with another Om? Will they send you to the Omega Training Center, Rebel Academy, or kill you?"

Emperor glanced over at his shoulder at Moon. His gaze was mournful.

"I can't allow her to tell our parents...*your mother.* If there were any other way then..." Emperor reached to cup Moon's cheek, but Moon backed away with a shuttered look that hadn't been there before, but which I recognized.

*No, no, no...*

I gasped because then Emperor *was* stepping aside, and Lyall sauntered forward to grasp Moon by his curls and yank him away down the corridor.

I pressed my nails hard into my palms because I understood why Emperor had made his choice, yet it still hurt like witching hell. He'd tried to save their lives by *not* protecting Moon, and I understood why it'd torn them apart and why it'd taken Moon so long to forgive Emperor.

Lyall twisted Moon, lashing his back with a painful *snap*, and he yelped. He glared at her in a way that made my heart leap at his rebellious bravery but also thud in fear for what it'd mean when she tried to dominate him.

I knew that she'd failed. Nobody had ever succeeded in dominating Moon because he was the Moon Child.

Lyall's eyes blazed. "On my hide, those princes are a bad influence." Just for a moment, her gaze softened. "I care for you, but it was a mistake to allow you to mix with these other kingdoms' Oms like you have a right to clothes, speech, or an education. I won't allow it any longer. You can't think that a Prince of the Alphas would do anything but *use* you?" Then she threw over her shoulder with a smirk, "Oh, and of course I intend to alert *all* your mas to your behavior."

*The two-faced bitch...*

Then I was caught in Moon's magic and dragged through the collar back into the present, where Moon's fragile gaze watched mine like he expected me to shame him, just the same as Lyall had.

Like I was just another asshole who'd blame him for *loving*.

I kissed his cheek, and my shadows stroked down his sides. "Every last jerk word out of Lyall's mouth was wrong. You've already ripped out her throat so, I'd say that what she tried to destroy when you were a kid was much stronger than her. *You're* stronger than her."

Moon shuddered, as he rested his forehead against mine. Lyall had *wrecked* him that day, or perhaps, it'd been the punishments that had followed.

"What did you show her?" Emperor's gaze was wide and fearful.

"What I should always have told her." Moon turned his head to lick down Emperor's neck in reassurance, before catching Amadeus' eye. "What *I did* that ruined everything."

Moon caught the tender flesh of his lower lip between his teeth; he vibrated with a crushing guilt. There was nothing rational about it, but since when had *guilt* been rational...?

Moon had only been a kid when he'd been shamed.

Emperor slid his hand along Moon's shoulder. "How strange that you remember it that way. That was the morning *I* failed to protect *you*."

"*I* enthralled you, see." Amadeus tumbled into my lap, so that he could grasp Moon's cheeks; his eyes glittered. "I couldn't control my power and—"

"Seriously, enough with blaming yourselves." I snuggled Amadeus to my chest, as Emperor held me to his. When Moon nibbled along my neck, I flushed with the intensity of the bond between my Charms and love between all of us. "It wasn't any of your fault, and no one had the right to make you feel that it was. When you rule, Omegas and Betas can kiss who they witching hell please."

"When we rule?" Emperor asked carefully.

I smirked. "Come on, wolfie princes, you made a pact to control the freaking Wolf Charmer, *of course* you intend to take over the rule of your own kingdoms. Now that's out in the open, we just have to make it happen as smoothly as a ballet because that's what you've been doing, right?" I cocked my head. "It's a shame that they put Jax back in the pit because he makes an awesome dancer, schemer, and fighter."

Mischief chuckled. "You didn't imagine that the witch wouldn't have been aware of your plotting…?"

Aquilo snickered, settling more comfortably into Ramiel's feathered hold.

Emperor huffed like a kid caught out in a lie. "I'd

rather thought that I'd made a dashing 007. After all, Daniel Craig pulled off the blond look."

I snorted. "Then imagine that Daniel Craig has been caught by the bad guys and now he's bound, whilst his balls are being tortured with lasers, piranhas, or pliers—"

Emperor squirmed. "You can be rather unsettling with how much thought appears to have gone into that. Let's leave my defenseless balls out of this, for the moment, at least. My father and sister shall never let me hear the end of this."

I blinked. "What have your dad and sister...?"

"You're not displeased with us?" Amadeus asked.

I kissed the tip of his nose. "I'd be disappointed if you *didn't* have a plan worked out. Just show me how to help."

"You already are." Moon gripped my chin, turning me back to him. He wet his lips, which were bleeding from where he'd bitten them too hard. I had to fight the urge to swipe across his mouth and sooth it with my tongue. "By my fur, you've no idea how much I hunger to kiss you or how many times I've thought and dreamed about it. But I'm not ready. Do you understand?"

I shook because it's what I'd needed to hear, even though I desired his touch so much that even the trail of his fingers down my neck made me arch towards him.

"I love you," *boy, were those words becoming easier*

*to say*, "and whenever you're ready, I'm here. Trust me, you're special in so many ways: my Claimed, Wolf Bitten, Moon Child who loves Franz Ferdinand. We're pack, and everyone in this pack meets my needs and each other's in their own freaking epic way. But it's their choice, and it always will be, okay? I love you all..." I glanced around at my guys because sweet Hecate, if I couldn't say it at a funeral of a prince with a reminder of death in every gleaming waterlily on the silent Thames under flashes of lightning, then when could I? "...and that means I fight with you."

*Bang* — I jumped, as a firework exploded above us in the sky.

Bright lights tore out in *whining*, sparkling crescents to form:

**TEST OF THE MOON CHILDREN**

Below, the wolves cheered and howled.

Had it become chilly all of a sudden because I'd come over with the *Hunger Game* vibes.

It didn't settle my nerves that Okami chased wildly between the angels, biting them in random agitation or that Amadeus clasped both Moon's hand and mine like he was terrified of letting us go.

"How droll, the queen is now sending threats via firework," Mischief's affected boredom would've fooled me once but not anymore.

Nor did it fool Ramiel, by the way that he wrapped his wings tighter around both Mischief and Aquilo.

"It means that the test has been extended to all the Moon children: you, the Moon God, *and* the Moon Child," Amadeus murmured.

My eyes widened. "No way. The son of a bitch can't just…"

The problem was that as queen she kind of *could*. Now I understood the urgency of my princes ruling, so that they could remove dick traditions like **Tests of the Moon Children**, which was…*what exactly?*

I was hoping it was multiple-choice because I was good at that.

Amadeus looked down, as tears hung on his lashes. "Criminals can choose it as an alternative to death, see." *Okay, so not sounding like multiple-choice.* "There's a Moon Cave. It was said that it pleased the goddess whether the criminals drowned or not. If they survived, then she favored them and if not, well, they were guilty and deserved to be drowned."

Had I said how much I *hated* traditions?

The only way to prove myself to these moon fanatics was to risk drowning, just like in my worst nightmares.

## CHAPTER 15

When Mischief's gaze met mine in the Moon
Cave, I realized that he was as frightened of
being walled up and drowned as I was.

*Had it been done to him before?*

I figured by his terror and Mischief's rants against
*tyrants* that it both had and he'd kicked the dickhead's
ass who'd hurt him. He didn't need my protection, but
was it kind of weird how tinglie I got at the thought of
his vengeance?

I leaned against the damp wall with my arms around
Moon whose face was pinched and pale, whilst Mischief
paced from one side of the tiny cave to the other. The
only light was the flare of Mischief's blazing wings and
the fairy light trail of my red, as it clung to the walls like
algae.

When it wasn't being threatening, my shadows were beautiful.

I shivered, hugging Moon closer for warmth (yeah, it was nothing to do with needing the feel of him, alive and safe, nuzzling against me or the lemony scent of his curls reminding me of every member of my pack).

Mischief skidded his foot through the water, spraying it against my leg. "Stupendous idea," he muttered. "Tell the crazy werewolf about her dead son that oh, I don't know, *your* relative enslaved, before he died saving *your* fiancé."

"*Hmm*, kind of up there with my mechanical wolves," I bit back.

The cave was dank and freezing. If the water didn't get us then the cold would. You could die by severe goose bump, right? One side of the cave opened up to the river, which stank like a shoal of fish had died in it.

Us three Moon Kids had been stuck in the cave since the firework announcement of our test. At first, we'd snuggled in a tangled pile to keep warm; Mischief's feathers had wrapped around Moon and me like a blanket. But then, water had started to creep through the sides of the wall, and the level of the water in the opening had begun to rise.

*Was someone controlling the sluices? Did anyone pass the test or was the whole point that they couldn't? On the other hand, was the water rising because of the summer storm?*

Sweet Hecate, couldn't you at least stop the rain for me? Okay, so I'd turned my back on the covens and every witch law and tradition but…

Huh, actually there was no *but*. I'd made my choices, and if they meant that I drowned tonight, then at least I drowned as Crimson, rather than just another dick Charmer.

I wouldn't be the Crimson Tide that both the wolves and witches expected me to be. My shadows I were both something new and more primal: I'd sensed it before in the way that they'd surged through me, and in my connection to my Charms. If I survived, I'd be the Wolf Charmer as she'd always meant to be: equal, connected, and as much wolf as witch.

Mischief prowled across the cave. "When *I'm* the Moon God, surely it's my own judgment whether I drown."

With a *gush*, another ton of water sprayed down the walls and Mischief cursed so creatively that I blushed.

*Angels knew some naughty words, who knew?*

Moon cocked his head. "Then can your godly behind please stop these waters rising or are you waiting until it's morning? I've never cared if I die, but my family will be slaughtered on those rotten bastards' fangs, if we don't survive."

Mischief stilled. "Pray, what must I do or say to prove that you *should* care whether you die? You're the Moon Child, Prince of the Wilds and Omegas, and Wolf

Bitten to the best witch who I've met." He arched his brow at me, and boy were those tinglies rushing up and down my spine because from a mage who'd once hated and distrusted every witch with seriously good reason, that was the highest praise. Mischief's gaze darkened. "You're also my pack, *wolf*, and I shan't allow you or the witch to die."

When Mischief stalked towards Moon and I, caging us against the cave wall with an arm either side of us, Moon's eyes widened. My shadows pulsed in time with Mischief's wings, as his magic wound around us, caging us just as securely.

When Moon's magic bowed out, meeting Mischief's in rainbow veneration it was gentle and beautiful and…

*Like a goodbye.*

I gripped Moon's curls. "Hey, this damp has defeated my frizz but it's not defeating me." I cringed at the truth of that. I must look like I'd been rubbing my head on balloons all night. "Drowning in this river has been my recurring dream since I was a kid, and when we were thrown in here, there was this part of me that figured maybe it hadn't been a dream but a divination of my true death or like karmic justice for all the wolves that my ancestors drowned here."

Moon shook his head, but I *hushed* him.

"Trust me, I'm a big girl. I don't need you to pretend and hide the messed-up truth just like my mom and uncle did, or like all you princes did to each other, acting like everything was peachy in your own kingdoms when it wasn't. I know you acted out of love, but between our pack we need honesty now, and *honestly*, I'd get it if I drowned in this river. But you both don't deserve that, so we're kicking this test's ass."

"Single skins are daft." Moon nipped at my neck. "A cave doesn't even have a behind."

"But my beautiful subjects do." Mischief slipped one hand around to cup Moon's ass, whilst tracing circles over mine.

*Well, that was one way to distract us that I was seriously okay with.*

Moon's breath was warm against my neck, as his lips curled into a smile. I pressed my hands against Mischief's hard chest, loving the fast *thud* of his heart and knowing that it was out of desire for Moon and me and no longer out of fear.

"I *am* yours." Mischief's lips were as soft against mine as his chest was hard.

Then he kissed me with a swirl of popcorn scented magic that was passion, magic, and danger. The thrill of his touch spiraled me higher, until my crimson sparkled in a firework show of its own. Moon gasped, and Mischief's grip tightened on both our asses, as his tongue drew mine even deeper into his kiss.

*Holy hell, I was his as well.*

Suddenly, the sluices opened and water flooded on our heads.

Mischief spun Moon and me, shielding us and grunting at the pain of the water, as it broke across his wings. I hollered at the shock; we were pulled under the briny water, and I was dragged away from both my lovers.

What had happened to Mischief and Moon? I'd promised that they wouldn't die. I'd *promised*...

I flailed, as my lungs seared, and I swallowed revolting mouthfuls.

Hocus pocus, this was drowning...? Dark, painful, and *lonely*.

*Please don't let me die alone...*

Then silver hair *thwapped* my face like seaweed and Mischief's arms grabbed onto my shoulders pulling me to a pocket of air next to Moon.

Even as I choked out water, I spluttered with laughter at Moon's affronted look and the curls plastered over his face like a bathed dog. It made me want to dry him off in a fluffy towel. Except, that image was far sexier than should've been possible when we were treading water in the final pocket of air left in the Moon Cave.

My shadows crept over the roof to light us in a crimson glow.

Then Mischief swam around me to appear in the water between Moon and me with the same elegance as if this a swim party in the Hamptons, and his lustrous tail wound around me.

Hold the broomsticks…*tail*…?

"Dude, I love the unicorn look on you, but since when could you change into a freaking *merman*, which is hot, by the way." I shivered, as Mischief slid his tail between my thighs.

Was it as sensitive as his wings? By the way that his eyes became half-lidded, I'd go with *hell, yeah.*

Mischief smirked, lazing onto his back and *splashing* his tail against the water. "Little creatures, I can transform into many things."

Moon growled, clutching Mischief by the neck and towing him closer. "Enough of that. I thought that we'd established I wasn't little…?"

Mischief's smirk faltered. "Indeed, we did."

Moon shook Mischief. "Fur and fangs, if you were able to transform, why didn't you find a way out of here? Why didn't you leave us?"

I bit my lip, swimming closer. "Yeah, like he said."

Mischief's gaze became steely. "I have been working hard to bypass my leash, and it appears that transformation is not controlled as fiercely as my other magics. I'm quite certain, however, that this was a *test*. It's interesting you can't conceive that what matters most is we stand together as pack. We three *are* the Moon Children, and we don't need anyone's faith but our own."

My heart thudded in my chest, just as Moon howled his joy. His silver magic sparkled across the roof at the same time as Mischief's to join my crimson in a miracle that shook me with its glory.

No firework display on Main Beach had ever been as grand.

Then the water level rose again, until the river lapped just below my lips. Mischief wound his tail around my waist and his wings around Moon.

Moon glanced between Mischief and me. "It was a blessing that I met both of you."

A *blessing...?* Wasn't I the Crimson Terror: The monster who he'd spent a childhood terrified of being Claimed by...?

My eyes burned with tears, as Mischief stared up at the gleaming roof.

"I'd hoped to help my people," Mischief said with soft grief, "but they don't want me. I should never have been so deluded that they could love me."

Moon blew a raspberry, which wasn't quite the cuddle that I craved to give Mischief but startled him out of his despair in the same way.

"Stop whining like a cub," Moon commanded. "The Omegas here adore you, and the others *don't know you.* I love you, the daft witch over there loves you..."

"Hey..." I protested.

Moon smiled fondly like he'd just bestowed upon me an adorable pet name. Perhaps, in wolf circles *daft witch* was *cute.*

"And *I* love you…" Emperor drawled from behind me.

I screamed, before swallowing water, and frantically swimming around to stare at Emperor's amused and way too cocky face, as he bobbed in the water like he'd just joined us for a swim.

Except, a pearl-like bubble trapped his head like he'd been swallowed by his own chewing gum. Even his hair wasn't wet, which I'd bet had just made his day when he saw the state of all of ours.

"Sorry," Emperor grinned, (*the smug asshole so wasn't sorry*), "it just sounded like you were having this whole *we're about to die, so let's all express our undying love moment*, and I didn't want to be left out. Tempting as it is to allow you this touching farewell, your hero has arrived."

Emperor looked like the romantic prince, coolly arriving just in time to save us. I craved to kiss him until he didn't even remember that he *was* a prince.

Instead, I strained to look over Emperor's shoulder because sometimes Emperor needed sass, rather than seduction, and Moon snickered. "I can only see a Charm with their head up a bubble's ass."

Emperor raised his finger above the water. "Ah, but what an ass that bubble has…like me. I was the champion swimmer at the Alpha Academy, despite being an Omega." His gaze slid to mine, before he raised his eyebrow. "Of course, it was Aquilo who worked the spell for the bubble and broke through the rock so that I could swim through to you, but I still claim the credit."

Aquilo had planned and spelled this rescue with his magic…? My mage fiancé was as miraculous as my other Charms. I'd never even thought about second dates before arriving in England, but now I shuddered with the need to marry Aquilo and make him mine as firmly as my Wolf Bitten Charms.

"You're my good wolf," I promised, and Emperor shivered like he always did at the praise. He had so many talents: piano playing, singing, diplomacy, swimming… And I had the feeling that I'd only started to learn them. I wanted to know them all like I wanted him to know mine. "Now please tell me that I can clone those bubble thingies with my magic?"

Emperor nodded. "Aquilo said that his magic was connected to yours, so that you could breathe from the life that he gave me." He tilted his head. "It's rather wondrous when you think about it." Then he sighed. "I should warn you, however, that wolves are rather dramatic about their meetings. It's dawn."

"I'm not following."

Moon's voice shook, "Goddess Moon! He means that since it's morning, the delegation has arrived. We're too late."

"I won't let it be too late," I insisted. "We'll break out of here, and then I'm done following either the princess or the queen's rules. The Moon Children survived this test because of their pack. We'll fight and win because of it, and those sons of bitches who'd reduce Wolf Kingdom to a reign of terror once again won't win because we'll stop them."

"*Hooray* for me, I didn't miss the stirring speech." Emperor pressed his lips to mine, and my crimson prickled around the bubble, slipping it over my own head. "Look, Chief Alpha, it's not pretty out there. The battle has already begun."

## CHAPTER 16

Why did no one write about the *noise* of battlefields? The screams, growls, and blasts? But then again, maybe they did, and the fact that I was huddling, shell shocked and stunned on the banks of the Thames by the explosion of noise was my fault for not having read the war poets.

It turned out that Emperor had been all English with his stiffer upper lip use of understatement: *not pretty, my witchy ass.*

*It was a massacre about to happen and for once, it wouldn't be because of a Wolf Charmer.*

The weak dawn sun shone against my neck, as water tears streamed down my neck from my hair. Moon stiffened next to me, and Mischief outstretched his wings like he could cocoon us all safe in his feathers.

Yet it wouldn't work because I had to break free and save Wolf Kingdom.

A crescent-shaped table had been placed beside the rushing waters of the Thames. I figured that the delegates had met around it, before they'd been ambushed because now they used it like a shield.

I spied both the royal family of the Kingdom of the Wilds dressed in leather *and* the Kingdom of the Alphas like exotic butterflies in rainbow robes caught behind it, whilst Vala's gang from the Kingdom of the Gods, the Crescents, attacked them from the front. At the same time, transformed Betas attacked them from behind.

I drew in my breath, as the wave of silvery gray wolves launched themselves in battle lines, which were as beautiful and drilled as their Britney Spears dance had been, over the table towards the delegates. Their amber eyes glowed; they bared their teeth and howled.

I shivered at the eerie sound.

Stella had told me that I'd never seen werewolves in a true fight before and that I'd be terrified if I ever did.

*She'd been right.*

What she hadn't realized was that it also called to my crimson shadows, until I strained forward on my tiptoes, magnetized by both the fight between the wolves and the memory of the war that'd happened a hundred years ago at this site. Zetta had shown it to me in the Discipline Cellar at the House of Silver.

I quivered, struggling to hold back my shadows,

which hummed with eagerness to reach out and pluck the Betas into the sky and then…

*Charm the wolves. Control the Crimson Tide.*

I whispered the manta like a prayer.

I wasn't the same as my great-grandmother or mom. *I wasn't, right?*

Vala stood at one end of the table with her hands on her hips like she could seduce the other royals into defeat by sexiness alone. Amadeus crouched next to her. I'd learned my lesson about doubting him but I still hated to see him by her side.

Aquilo and Ramiel faced them in a way that sang to me, even as I struggled with my shadows, because boy, were they mind-blowingly the definition of *true* sexiness. Aquilo stood tall; his eyes were the coldest ice as he blew back the snarling Betas with blasts of wind. Next to him, Ramiel had grown in size until he was a towering warrior with a rose gold sword. When a Beta pounced for his neck, he swept pink flames from his sword's tip across its haunches. The Beta fell back onto the bank.

*Charm the wolves. Control the Crimson Tide. Charm the Wolves. Control the…*

My eyes fluttered shut. Was this the *tide of blood* that Vala had warned me about? But then, Moon squeezed my hand, and I opened my eyes again.

The battle was real, and my pack needed me without my dick shadows.

*They simply needed Crimson.*

"Fur and fangs, *this* is the plan." Moon's voice was powerful and shook me out of the haze. His silver calmed my red. "It's been centuries of pain and struggle, but *now* we show just who we are and can be. Now we let all the kingdoms *see* us. And *that* was the stirring speech by the way, single skin."

"I'm thrilled that I didn't blink and miss it." Mischief's lips quirked. "Let us Moon Children join the glorious fight for freedom. I warned that foul princess that I'd kill her if she touched my family. We shall teach her just how *untamed* we still are."

The red and silver thrummed under my skin, until it *was* me. Even my palms prickled.

"Show them who we are," I whispered.

*Who in the witching heavens was I?*

The doubt must've shown on my face because Moon clutched my hand more tightly. "You're *our* Wolf Liberator."

Then he tugged me towards the fight, as Mischief swooped above our heads.

Where on earth was Queen Banan? Had she already been slaughtered? Then I caught sight of her on her knees further along the banks of the river, shocked to inaction. She held Moth firmly even though he wriggled to escape.

Banan's Omegas from the shrine had been allowed a

special day out, which had turned into a nightmare, and they trembled in the mud.

When I leaped next to Vala and Amadeus with Moon, whilst Mischief landed next to Ramiel, I'd expected a gasp of shock. Perhaps, some panted terror.

Instead, Vala chanted in triumph, "By the light of the moon, I am dead, we are dead, and shall remain now and always dead."

The Betas circled.

At least we'd drawn their attention. The Crescents still pinned the delegates in on the other side.

Mischief arched his brow. "You'll be happy when I kill you then."

Vala's claws extended. "It's through death that I reign, foolish god. Your blood will birth my new kingdom."

"*My* kingdom," Amadeus' voice was regal, "and your blood is all that I need."

Vala's eyes widened, as she gawked at her brother. I'd bet that Amadeus had never backtalked her like that…or slashed her across the neck with his claw as he shoved her onto her ass.

Vala clutched her neck. "Flame…"

"*Amadeus*," he hissed.

Then Amadeus nodded at Moon, who raised his hands. Silver sparked on Moon's palms.

"Get your daft behind down here, Om. Fur and fangs,

I didn't save you from execution to allow you to die at the hands of the bastard Gods." Princess Morag, Moon's sister, growled. I met her pained gaze, as she battled a Crescent. The green that streaked her pointy face truly did look like war paint now, and her dark hair swung around her shoulders. "This is no place for Oms..."

Moon's gaze darkened into something dangerous, as he glanced between his sister and mom, Queen Rhona, who she protected. "Nay, but it's the *perfect* place for the rebel Moon Child."

At last, Rhona looked up at Moon with a gasp. Her frayed leather dress had been torn, but the fanged necklace around her neck gleamed as brightly still as her skin and the crown of teeth, which balanced on the top of her head. Rhona was as dangerous as Banan (okay, I'd go with *more* dangerous), and to save Wolf Kingdom, Moon had to reveal his secrets.

Silver magic shot from Moon's palm and sparkled into the night sky like it was reaching out to stroke the true moon's face in greeting. Moon arched, revealing the long white curve of his neck; I longed to rest my teeth over the place that I'd Wolf Bitten him and suck, marking him again and joining with his magic.

*Moon Prince. Moon Prince. Moon Prince.*

The Omegas' chant was just as uplifting as it'd been on the day that I'd rescued Moon from re-education. Except, this time I shivered because how long had it been since the Omegas had been allowed to talk? Their words were birds flying for the first time, and their flight was freedom.

The Omegas rose from their knees, backing away from Banan, who froze in shock. Then Moon shone his silver like a blessing over the delegations from the Wilds and the Alphas.

If the Omegas joined the fight or not, then it'd be the first choice that they'd truly made themselves.

*Moon's bravery was so worth it.*

The Omegas wove in and out of the gang of Crescents who were too startled by the wolves who'd been little more than statues for decades coming to life that they stumbled back, frightened of hurting their precious Omegas. Then the Omegas created a shimmering wall in front of the delegates.

"What kind of coward would fight and battle with Omegas?" Vala rasped. "*Unleash your Crimson Tide!*"

Why had I never noticed how lost she was? How desperate for death?

My shadows wove into Moon's silver; the rush was heady. "I already have," I replied. "Every wolf standing here against you is part of that tide, which is Crimson's pack."

"I have a pack too," Vala's eyes flashed with malice, "my Betas will flay the Moon Prince and—"

"Aye, is that so, princess?" Rhona leaped onto the table, stalking towards Vala, who backed away. "You ambush us, breaking your Moon Oath of safety in your kingdom and still swagger around like you may threaten *my* son." Moon's gaze caught his mom's, before her fangs lengthened. *Had she ever stood up for him before?* "You're no royal or Alpha. You were always nothing but a cub afraid of the shadows." When she yanked a fang out of her hair and flung it at Vala's feet, Vala paled. "You're unworthy."

I knew exactly how that felt because Rhona had declared that I was *unworthy* just before she'd hunted me. The ritual had to hurt more to another wolf.

Plus, I didn't figure that Vala would survive an official Hunt when she was already injured.

Vala choked, falling to her knees, as blood seeped through her fingers.

*Had Amadeus already killed her?*

Vala beckoned to Rhona like she wished to whisper into her ear, before the Hunt began.

I stiffened. "*Woah*, she's using villains' tricks for dummies. Seriously, what's she going to tell you? That she's the best lover in Wolf Kingdom? Her secret recipe for the yummiest chocolate pie? Or perhaps, that she's found the missing link between witches and wolves?"

"Pray, consider what the witch says," Mischief warned.

Rhona blinked at me. "Why would I expect a Charmer or mage to understand wolf honor?"

"Dude, that's harsh." I exchanged a glance with my Charms who all nodded, closing in around Vala. "Plus, your asshole *honor* doesn't make much of a toast at your funeral if you're dead."

"*Single skins*," Rhona muttered in disgust, before leaning over Vala.

Vala's gaze met mine. Then her claws sank into Rhona's neck, and she tripped the queen into the Betas below.

"Son of a bitch," I gasped.

The Betas' howled, triumphantly. They savaged the queen in such a frenzy that she was lost beneath them.

When Moon's magic faded in his anguish, Morag bounded up next to him, and Emperor struggled to hold her back from hurling herself into the gray sea after her mom.

Moth's sobs carried on the breeze from the riverbank.

My hands curled into fists, as my chest ached. I knew what it was to witness my parents' murder, and I'd been desperate to save my Charms from suffering the same. But now Moon, Moth, and Morag had.

My shadows burst out, coloring the sky and Thames red in a *Crimson Tide.*

Ramiel and Aquilo rushed forward, catching Moon before he collapsed. Yet when Moon's magic ripped out of him in a tsunami of grief, and holy hell, *here* was the real Crimson Tide, only it was Moon's magic entwined with mine because we were bonded together, it threw me thudding onto my back. My feet drummed on the table, and a coppery tang flooded my mouth.

I quivered, caught between the agonizing waves of Moon's emotion and my seething shadows.

Suddenly, I screamed because *I* was the one transforming. My skin prickled and burned. I panted, as my bones reshaped and my muscles lengthened in a web of shadows. I twisted onto my knees, arching my back. My teeth and nails grew and glittered like rubies.

On the name of every witch who'd ever kissed the covens' altars, what kind of *dick magic* was this?

Then I howled as I changed into a crimson wolf.

## CHAPTER 17

I shook my head and whined. Then I pawed at my wolfie ears with my wolfie paw.

I'd have disappointed mom by not controlling the shifters and my great-grandmother by not slaughtering them, but what in the name of the Hecate would my long line of Charmer ancestors say about me turning *into* a freaking wolf?

I stared down at my beautiful fur, twisting like I could see my ass and whatever that furry thing was, which was wagging.

Okay, so it turned out that I had a majestic *tail*. When I yipped happily, I was glad that wolves couldn't blush.

My ancestors would've flayed me and turned me into a crimson pelt for their bed. After all, I'd had a white Omega one on mine.

When we'd been kids, Lux had once worked magic on me, forcing blood into my mouth to change me into a wolf. Aquilo had sworn that it'd only been a trick. But what if it'd been true blood magic? At the time, I'd thought that becoming a wolf would be worse than dying. In fact, it was like being reborn.

When I shivered, and the breeze swept rain across my snout, sensation exploded through me.

Was this what it felt like in wolf form for all shifters, as if the world was connected in a thousand threads to every sense, and I could come from the lightest of strokes? No wonder Moon had told me that it was a violation to force a shift and demanded so many cuddles.

*What would it feel like for him to suck on my tail?*

I was blaming the bad, bad wolf in me but I couldn't help bouncing up and down, and howling for Moon at the thought of *my* tail in *his* mouth, before my entire pack ran together under the moonlight through the woods, wild and free.

"Settle down." Emperor's hand landed on my head, stroking behind my ear. Okay, who needed to have their tail sucked, when you could have your ear scratched? "You're even more gorgeous than me, but you're not an Omega Witch anymore, you're the Crimson Wolf and Chief Alpha. As much as I respect you… *Snap yourself out of the moon daze, and remember that we're in the middle of a war.*"

Amadeus stroked his fingers down my spine, and my fur stood up like he'd electrified me. "What he said, see, but with an added *please*."

My amber gaze snapped to Moon's. Tears streamed down his cheeks, as he was held by Ramiel and Aquilo. His sister stood stiffly at his side like she was desperate to hug him but didn't know how.

*Somebody had hurt my pack.*

The growl rumbled through me without even thought like thunder. To my shock, the Omegas dropped to their knees, just as the Betas fell on their bellies, submitting before me.

The power of my shadows thrummed through my new form.

Vala hissed in fury. "Crescents, *protect…"*

Yet the Alphas only pulled back, eying me with as much wonder as the other wolves.

Mischief strolled to Vala, catching her under the arms and hauling her up. She struggled but Mischief was strong.

"I once warned you that if you hurt my family, then I'd kill you. I *dared* you to test me." Mischief's words were as deadly as blades. He dragged Vala to the edge of the table, and she shrieked as he held her hanging over by the front of her dress. "*This is what happens when you dare a god.*"

The Betas raised glinting eyes to mine, and I howled my encouragement.

How many last chances had I granted Vala...? Yet still, she'd murdered Moth and Moon's mom.

Mischief's smile was dark and ancient. "I rather think that true death will be less glamorous than you imagine."

Then he dropped Vala, and she fell amongst the swarming Betas, just as Rhona had done. She screamed, as the Betas tore her apart. It was like every nightmare that I'd ever had of being devoured by wolves, and yet when it was Vala, I discovered that I didn't mind so much.

Amadeus burrowed his face in Emperor's robes.

Emperor stroked Amadeus' hair. "Justice, my incubus," he murmured.

Mischief swooped above our heads. "Most certainly *vengeance* but just as sweet."

"My daughter!" Banan shrieked, stumbling up.

"Why, so finally, you see her?" Mischief beat his wings.

Moon caught my eye, nodding to his brother who was now free of Banan's hold.

Moth's look was colder than I'd seen on him before and more grown up. My tail drooped; I hated the way that he'd taken on the role of an adult earlier than he should have had to because he was both Omega and prince. But he'd chosen it when he'd become a spy at Emperor's orders, and whatever happened next, I admired him.

Moth would be formidable when he was older. Frogs legs and toads' eyes, he was freaking formidable *now*.

Moth stalked to the edge of the riverbank, before leaning over.

Banan dashed towards him, as her train swished behind her in the mud. "D-don't s-slip." She clutched for Moth like *he* was the security blanket and not the cloth, which Moth now held between this finger and thumb over the churning waters. "I can't l-lose you as well, son…"

"I'm not your son," Moth replied coolly, even though he was shaking, "and your daughter murdered my true ma. Don't you have faith that your Goddess Moon will save you if she favors you?"

Then he opened his fingers, and the Ambassador's security blanket fluttered on the breeze as if held there on Banan's wail, before it disappeared into the river's dark waters and was carried away by the currents.

Banan didn't even hesitate and weirdly, I didn't expect her to. She fell into the river like she'd been waiting for this moment for decades and had only needed permission to let go. She disappeared into the water, as if her kingdom had held a joint funeral the night before for both mother and son.

For a long moment, there was a deep silence. Then the Moon Leash around Mischief's ankle fizzled and died, releasing him from its control. His magic sizzled out in a wave. He hollered, struggling not to unleash its power after so long bound, before dragging it back inside his wings.

Morag leaped off the table and tore towards Amadeus. I turned to tear after her, but Moon placed his hand on my shoulder to stop me, and instead, followed his sister.

Moth had walked to meet his sister and brother with a mechanical stiffness that I knew meant he was hiding his fear and grief. Moon wasn't the only rebel in his family. Moth should've been *cleansed* into obedience in the Omega Training Center but instead, he'd just talked back to an Alpha.

*And oh yeah, kind of killed her.*

When Morag snatched her brother by the neck, I winced, but instead of backhanding him or any of the other typically dickish Alpha moves, she clasped him just like I'd hoped she'd hold Moon, then as soon as Moon had dived into range, she cuddled him as well.

"Fur and fangs, I'm proud of you," Morag's voice rang out with a commanding certainty that was for the benefit of the other Alphas as much as it was for Moth. "You're worthy like an Alpha."

"Worthy like an *Omega*," Emperor drawled, examining his nails, "because I count three Omegas, a Beta, a mage, an angel, a god, and a…" He waved at me, "… Well, she outranks *you*. But the rest of us acquitted ourselves rather admirably in battle for not being Alphas, wouldn't you say, princess?"

"That's wouldn't you say, *Queen Morag*," she spat back but she hugged her brothers more tightly.

Moon peered up from underneath his eyelashes. His face was radiant with joy.

*Had he wanted to be held like this by his sister his entire life?*

Yet Moon still made himself insist, "Don't forget that it wasn't just Moth and me who risked our hides tonight, sister, it was every Omega in this kingdom." Startled, Morag glanced at the naked ranks of Omegas who still shielded the other delegates and stared back at her shyly. "We're more than perfect toys for either witches or wolves. You're queen now and…" He shuddered, and I forced myself not to look down where his mom's body still lay amongst the wolves. "You said once that you'd shut the Re-education Centers if you could. You know how much I feared them, and the rumors about the cruelties that are done there are true."

Morag blanched. "Lyall didn't…?"

"Crimson saved me," Moon reassured, "but not before…" He swallowed. "She couldn't save the others who are still imprisoned there, however, and you can. Are you still nothing but the witches' puppet? That rotten bastard Stella from the Head Coven was the one with the deal for the Omegas and with the Omega Training Centers."

Morag sighed. "Aye, and what happens when she

poisons every wolf through the collars for stopping her supply?"

Moon blinked. "Either I'll be crazy or she'll be a zombie. I tore out her throat myself."

Morag took a step back, staring between her two brothers like she'd never seen them before but then, she never had. All she'd known had been the two Omegas with Om branded on their chests.

"*Free the Omegas*," Moon insisted, "bring them home."

*How long had Moon been planning this?*

At last Morag nodded, and the Omegas cheered; it was more life and light than I'd felt in all my days trapped inside the Kingdom of the Gods.

Amadeus *whooped*, clinging around my neck, as Emperor caught Aquilo like a startled kitten and waltzed with him.

Ramiel crouched in front of me. His sword melted away, and he returned to his normal size.

"A crimson wolf — a genuine wolf witch — is the rarest of magical creatures." Ramiel drew the pad of one of his fingers all the way down from my head to the tip of my snout, and I shivered. "You're magnificent and a wonder. Return to me, my savior."

How was it that only a few words in Ramiel's soft voice was more of a turn-on than a whole night's dirty talk with anyone else?

Ramiel's intent violet gaze made me feel like there

was no one on this battlefield but us, and nobody that he'd quite need in the same way as he needed me. That called me back, snapping the shadows inside me, until in a spray on ruby, I transformed into my witchy form once again.

I stared down at myself to check that my tits and ass weren't on display because my guys managed to change with their clothes on, but I was new to this whole wolf business. It'd be just like me to be spread out naked before all three kingdoms.

Mischief smirked and landed next to Ramiel. "Welcome back, witch. Do you still retain the urge to sniff asses?"

Wow, that was one way to get cursed out by a hundred wolves at once. Mischief cringed, before grinning, unrepentant.

"Well, that was quite the party." Queen Aurora from the Kingdom of the Alphas, rested her elbows on the table like she was waiting for a cocktail (I did make an epic cocktail). Her hair hung to the waist of her billowing yellow robes and the golden band nestled on her head, as if she'd not even been in a fight. But then, she'd been clever enough to allow others to protect her, hadn't she? "I traveled all the way to this wretched kingdom and now there's not even a queen to sort out the mess." She rapped her short cane that was tipped with silver on the table, before pointing it at Emperor. "Far be it from me to criticize, but my son hardly appears to have behaved as I'd hoped when he was Claimed."

When Emperor paled, it was Amadeus who stepped protectively in front of him.

*Had Amadeus ever done that before?*

"The queens made the mess, see, and now it's down to me — *the King* — to sort it out." Amadeus puffed out his chest.

"You, little bastard? Why, you're nothing but a mongrel." Aurora laughed but it was laced with malice.

Then I remembered how the three princes had been discovered together as kids by Lyall. Had Aurora hated them since then or had it been because she'd hoped that her daughter, Princess Hope, would Wolf Bite the Ambassador as she'd once said, and resented that his place as prince had been taken by Amadeus?

I didn't care, as long as she didn't hurt my pack.

"Trash talk, I get it. You've just had your over-entitled Alpha ass saved by Omegas and Betas. I figure that you're questioning every dickish prejudice right now. Also, there aren't many wolves left alive who've called Amadeus *mongrel*, you know I'm just saying…"

Aurora's jaw clenched, and she glanced around the Alphas of the Kingdom of the Gods. "You're so weak that you'd be led by this…"

"*King*," Amadeus roared, as his teeth grew, and the Betas watched him with awe, "who saved you from civil war today. Let none of the three kingdoms forget who stopped the Second Wolf War." He glanced around at our pack. "It pleased every one of those standing here to battle as equals." I didn't miss the Alphas' shocked gasps. My shadows reached out to wrap around Amadeus to soak in his thrilling power. "I'm King of Mongrels too, see, since my Deputy will be one, and my first decree is that *the mongrels are freed.*"

Amadeus quivered with tension. He'd dreamed, suffered, schemed, and sacrificed for this moment his entire life.

My mouth ached with grinning, as Ramiel and Mischief swept me around in their wings. Their mouths kissed at each corner of my smile: popcorn and nutmeg magic.

Then Jax led the mongrels towards the table out of the building like a procession. His burnished wings beat proudly, and his emerald eyes sparked, although I didn't miss the way that he quivered. He held Dual's son, Digby, on his hip. Dual laughed and flapped his wings, gazing at the moon like it was a feast...*which it was.*

*Had these mongrels ever been allowed out before?*

My heart soared at the thought that Dual would finally be reunited with his son again.

Amadeus' lip trembled, as he forced himself to keep his chin regally up and not to break down, but I knew how much it cost him. This was everything to him, just as the freeing of the Omegas was to Moon.

Digby squirmed free of Jax, flying into the night sky

and giggling as he spun. Mischief snatched Ramiel's hand and dived upwards, chasing the squealing toddler like he'd played the game before.

Jax jumped onto the table with a dancer's grace and cupped Amadeus' cheek. "Thank you for saving my little monsters and me." Then to my shock, he twirled and wrapped his wings around me, shivering. "And thank you for trusting Amadeus and wanting me."

"How nauseatingly familiar you are with mongrels," Aurora sighed. "Still, it appears that the bastard Beta has taught you little better, and my son has been even worse an influence. By the moon, it's fascinating that you're a genuine Wolf Witch! If I do owe you a debt of gratitude, why not visit my Kingdom of the Alphas, and I shall endeavor to repay it with a better education. After all, these other kingdoms are hardly civilized."

*Elitist asshole...*

I stroked my fingers through Jax's feathers. "*Hmm*, that'd be no way on my witchy wolf ass."

When Emperor flinched, my brow furrowed.

Then Aurora cracked her cane against the table, and I jumped. "Please, your defiance may work on others but not on me. Do you see other royals here from my kingdom?"

I shook my head.

Moon's dad wasn't here, but then I'd figured that they'd decided not to bring him as an Omega. Where was Emperor's dad and sister? And why was Aurora so relaxed?

"The Kingdom of the Alphas has long survived on strategy and diplomacy. Did you think that we were blind to Vala's ambitions?" Aurora mocked. "So, either your Charms and you come with me now and ensure that this *peace* you love so much isn't broken, or threaten me as I'm certain you plan to, and my daughter shall start a war of her own."

"You were always a bitch, Aurora," Morag snarled.

Aurora straightened her robes. "Guilty as charged. Although, I don't intend to keep you prisoner, Charmer. I'm not a fool like Queen Banan."

Mischief casually spun silver discs on his palms. "Or I could simply kill you. Three dead queens has such a satisfying ring to it."

Aurora stiffened. "I wouldn't wish to take away your enjoyment, but if you murder me, then your Wolf Witch shall never meet her brother."

Aquilo's concerned gaze trapped mine.

"I don't have a brother," I insisted.

Aurora's mouth twitched, before she examined Aquilo. "Only, you *did*, didn't you?"

I shook. Stella had told me that my parents had lost a child before me. *What had she meant?*

I shook my head, but Aurora *tsked*, "Well, witches never do appear to love their families. Forgive me if I find all your talk of *pack* amusing…" Again, her gaze drifted to Aquilo. "As the Alpha speaks, remain here and condemn your brother, or return with me and save him. If you're the Chief Alpha, his life is yours. Will you leave with me now for the Kingdom of the Alphas or see your brother slaughtered?"

## CHAPTER 18

I sprawled in the middle of a golden four-poster bed, snuggling under purple velvet sheets in a nest of feathers and wolfie cuddles. My shadows lapped around me in contented ripples. If the Kingdom of the Alphas was a prison, then it was a gilded cage.

I stared out of the Penthouse Bedroom's wall, which was glass floor to ceiling, over the Wilds' woods below, the Gods' by the river Thames and in the distance, Oxford's spires and domes. My hands clenched at the thought of both the covens and the human world. The sun glinted through like woven gold, painting us in light. It was no wonder that the Alphas thought they were better than everybody else, since they literally looked down on them from their glass tower. My witch aunt, Stella, had done the same from her House of Seasons.

From here, the silver wall that encircled Wolf Kingdom, before reaching into a latticed dome to trap it below was starkly obvious.

Huh, the Kingdom of the Alphas would never be able to glance out of their windows and forget that the witches were keeping them prisoner.

The far wall fluttered with the vast wings of a purple butterfly. Instantly, I remembered Emperor's tattoo that bound his Alpha nature. Hadn't he said that the Emperor butterfly was the Kingdom of the Alpha's national emblem?

Amadeus had left Jax in charge of the Kingdom of the Alphas. By the way that Jax's eyes had sparkled, I'd wondered whether *he'd* been the one plotting all along. The Alpha Dickhead guard who'd hurt him for decades would be in for a witch load of karma.

The Betas and Crescents, along with their mage lovers, had all sworn Moon Oaths of loyalty to both Amadeus and Jax.

There'd never been either a Beta or a mongrel on a wolf throne before. *This was true revolution.*

It'd taken a cauldron's worth of persuasion, but Moth had stayed behind with Morag to represent Moon in the Kingdom of the Wilds. I hadn't thought that Morag would ever let go of her brother's hand now that she had him returned to her again. In the end, Moth agreed because his sister swore that he could start freeing the Omegas. I'd never seen such joy and pain in

Moon's face warring at the same time. But Moth wasn't his kid brother anymore, and Moon trusted him.

Once my pack and I had arrived in the Kingdom of Alphas, we'd been hustled to the top of the tower like something out of a fairy tale and urged to rest. I'd demanded to see my brother, but it turned out that even a Wolf Witch and Liberator had to play diplomacy.

If I wanted my brother to survive, and *mage's balls*, I'd never even known that I had an older brother who was alive, but now that I did, I couldn't lose him.

Okami curled on the end of the bed like a silver patch, snoring. I burrowed my nose into Ramiel's wing, breathing in his nutmeg scent, until I was heady. When Ramiel purred, I licked out my tongue, and he arched. Mischief snickered, holding Ramiel down.

Then Emperor leaned over me on his elbow. "Well, as much as I wish that we could rest here with you like you were our Queen…"

Mischief snorted. "I assure you that Americans do not believe in royalty."

"I'm not in America now," I protested (and boy did I know that). "Say it again. Honestly, it was hot. Plus, your kingdom is freaking beautiful. How did you cope underground in the dark?"

If the Kingdom of the Gods had been all about the moon, then this kingdom basked in the sun. It was no wonder that Emperor had to be their Prince Charming.

Emperor adjusted a crease in his robes. "I'm aware

that *I'm* hot. In fact, I'm not blind to the beauty of my kingdom. How curious that a Charmer can't tell that it's the most beautiful creatures that are the deadliest." When he straddled me, I *eeped*. His gaze blazed. "Of course, how did I forget, that's been our only advantage against witches."

When his lips brushed against mine, I smirked. "*Uh-huh*? Your angelic eyes and sinful bodies, right?"

Amadeus stretched, sliding his hand down himself. "Did *mine* please you, Charmer?" His gaze was half-lidded.

"Holy hell, you never stop pleasing me but not because of how you look. You make me proud because of what you achieve. You were incredible in the battle. You're *my* King." I grinned, as Amadeus' eyes fluttered shut; my pleasure fed him, until he moaned.

Moon casually carded his fingers through Aquilo's hair. "What about the rotten queen, who hates me like I'm a Charmer dipped in silver?"

When all the wolves grimaced, I raised my hand. "Is that like a standard insult around here? I mean, you should see me in this silver dress that I wore for New Year…"

"I dream about dipping you in *my* silver." Mischief flushed. "I assure you, that sounded sexier in my head."

I snickered. "Dip me in silver, baby."

Ramiel *thwapped* his wing against my nose, and I spluttered against the feathers.

Mischief sniffed. "Oh, how delightful, the mawkish pet names have started."

Emperor brushed Ramiel's wing away, before his intent gaze met mine. "I'm petitioning that mine shall be *gorgeous*, but only after my sister and father…talk with us. I've been waiting a long time to return home with my Charmer."

*His* Charmer, huh?

I couldn't help the way that my skin tingled at Emperor's possessiveness. It hadn't taken him long to slip into Alpha dickery, and could someone please tell my shadows that they shouldn't be curling around him in delight?

I tapped the end of Emperor's nose. "Your sister and dad, huh? You mentioned them before. Unless they're going to bring me a soy latte with donuts, why should I care?"

Emperor's haughty mask cracked, as he gaped at me. "You don't wish to meet my family without the Claiming shadowing us?"

I reddened. *Okay, Emperor wasn't the dick, I was.*

"Trust me, I'd love to meet them," my expression gentled, "as long as they don't want to tear out my throat, bind my powers, or drown me because honestly, that's been happening to me way too much over the last couple of weeks."

Emperor's lips quirked. "Well, if you expect them to be perfect…" Then he became serious. "Moon is correct that my mother hates him almost as much as *I* love him. But then, my mother has always been the scheming for revenge sort." He bit his lip. "Oh, and the savage you directly type as well. Perhaps, I should simply have issued a simple queen-sized warning?"

"Jesus, as if I don't already know that the queens are bitches," I sighed.

Amadeus giggled. "Look how badass our Charmer is. She just called the prince a *son of a bitch*!"

My eyes widened. "Hey, I didn't mean…"

Emperor growled, but it was at Amadeus. Then he gripped Amadeus by his hair, wrenching him next to me on the bed.

Amadeus squirmed, pouting. "Look you, I'm a *king* now."

Emperor froze, before his pupils dilated in a way that made his desire as obvious as the hard-on that pressed against my thigh. I panted myself because the bad, bad wolf was sexier than when he played the good wolf, and sweet Hecate, he was *bad* right now.

"And this," Emperor snarled, "is *my kingdom*. I shall protect you all here because I'm…"

*Holy hell, he'd been about to say an Alpha.* Were we being monitored?

I slammed my lips against Emperor's to swallow the word in a kiss. Emperor's gaze met mine in shock, as I tried to silently get him to understand how close he was to revealing his secret by the stroke of my tongue alone.

*Hey, you worked with what you had.*

When he pushed me down with greater urgency, I knew that Kiss Language was almost as good as telepathy.

"Neither Crimson nor I need your macho posturing, remember?" Aquilo's frosty drawl cut across the passion, cooling it.

Reluctantly, Emperor drew back.

"Emperor on the other hand, clearly needs to reassert his position in our pack after such a battle." Ramiel's voice was soft, but his glare at Aquilo wasn't. Aquilo shrank back into Moon's hold. Why did Mischief ever risk getting on the wrong side of an angel like Ramiel? My *clever angel* who always saw what we needed and knew that Emperor was an Alpha. "Who would deny him?"

"I'd take it back if I were you, mage," Mischief muttered to Aquilo, "I'm shockingly intimate with that look and it's usually followed by the brat smacking hand."

Aquilo's gaze hardened. "I'm not a brat. Why should I?"

*Nope, he wasn't asking for it at all…*

When Emperor's gaze met Moon's, I didn't miss the sparkle of amusement that passed between them, before Emperor crawled towards Aquilo. Just for a moment, my guts roiled because Aquilo was still so new to these games, and I didn't want him to think that he didn't have a choice, in the same way that Vala had treated him.

He wasn't property; he was the guy who I loved.

Emperor smirked. "If you would deny me, then I shall *deny* you. I hope that you enjoy watching, whilst your lovers have wild, dirty, mind-blowing sex." My pulse fluttered in my neck, and my breath hitched. I couldn't even wait another moment, how was Aquilo not meant to touch or join in? "Hold onto the headboard. Bad cubs don't get to play."

Aquilo flushed, frozen.

Moon licked down Aquilo's cheek. "Fur and fangs, you'll miss out on the fun now."

Aquilo cast me an uncertain glance, but then he grinned. "Didn't you hear? I don't follow orders. *I'm a rebel.*"

I winced. Testing Emperor whilst he was in Alpha mood was like lighting a firework and not letting go.

Unexpectedly, Emperor burst into laughter, however, feathering kisses along a startled Aquilo's cheeks and nose, as Moon banded his arms tighter around him.

Mischief rolled his eyes, before resting his head on Ramiel's shoulder. "How astonishingly mushy. Why is it that you never halt *my* punishments?"

Ramiel smiled fondly. "Because unlike Aquilo, you truly *are* a brat."

Moon and Emperor dragged Aquilo closer to me, and I loved the way that he relaxed against my shoulder.

I gazed at my guys. I was allowed a moment of tenderness before the mind-blowing sexy times, right? Weirdly, lying here together was more intimate than anything that we'd done together. It felt like…commitment.

*And I'd spent my life being scared of that.*

Mischief pushed Ramiel onto his back, sucking and kissing his way down one wing, before moving onto his next with a reverence that was *worship*.

I played with a strand of Aquilo's hair, just like Moon earlier had. *Why was this so hard to say?* "Do you think that it'd be like this if we were all married?"

Aquilo edged towards my neck, and his hot breath gusted against my skin on each word. "You mean, cuddling in bed, whilst Moon wanks me off…?"

I raised my head to see that Moon had opened Aquilo's pants and slipped his hand down to stroke his dick.

When I caught Moon's gaze, he grinned and shrugged his shoulders. "Goddess Moon! I helped to get your intended all worked up, so now I'm giving him a helping hand."

Aquilo's lips curved into a smile on my neck. "Such a gentleman wolf."

Moon nipped Aquilo's stomach in retaliation.

I huffed. "I didn't mean like that…"

"Nay, you meant some daft single skin tradition, as if scrawling our names on a piece of paper would make us any more bonded." Moon bared his neck. "You bit my throat."

Amadeus twirled onto his stomach way too cheerily, before snatching my hand to press to his ass. "And you stamped property of **WCH** on my sweet behind."

Emperor raised my hand to trace my fingers over the brand on his chest that had seared over his **OM** mark. "And you freed me."

I shivered. I didn't care if it'd sound bad to my cousins, uncle, or friends back in America. It was the hottest thing that my shadows and I had heard and made us both shudder with joy.

Then Aquilo sucked hard on my neck, as if he was trying to mark *me*, before he murmured, "But I'm only your *intended*, am I not? I have nothing but this blood bracelet." He anxiously pressed across the band of blood around his wrist. "We're engaged, but at a word, you may slay me. What am I thinking? Merely allow the month to go by without marrying me, and I'll die anyway."

I paled. I couldn't allow Aquilo to continue with that death sentence hanging over him any longer. I'd have a bad attitude too, if I knew that the other lovers were secure, but I was the one who could be killed with a word.

"No more talk of dying. You're mine and whether you like it or not, this entire pack will protect you." Aquilo appeared caught between delight and surprise, at the nods and muttered agreement of my Charms and angels. "We'll ask the queen to marry us tonight."

I couldn't miss Aquilo's shocked intake of breath. When he stared up at me, his eyes gleamed with tears and this time, it wasn't out of grief. Then his expression settled back into one of smug haughtiness, as he glanced at Emperor.

"This *bad cub* shall be playing tonight on my Honeymoon it appears. Although," his jaw clenched, "any marriage that removes a blood bracelet needs the Head of the Covens to officiate. And that would be... who again?"

"Your snarky mage asks an interesting question. He's bright. I'd snap him right up." The Alpha's voice was cold but with a punky edge to it; I jumped, examining the Alpha who was leaning in the doorway. "Well, I'd heard that Charmers were minxes..."

It was the same Alpha who'd brought Emperor to me with his mom to be Claimed. She wore silky imperial purple robes with matching butterfly clips in her hair, and appeared a couple of years older than me.

Emperor smirked. "Let me introduce my sister, Princess Hope."

Okami awoke with a snort, as if sensing danger. He fluffed up his fur, darting off the bed to circle Hope's head, whipping his tail across her forehead on each pass.

Hope stilled, but she didn't back away. When she dragged her cool gaze over me, I blinked. Then I realized three things: one of my hands was still clutching Amadeus' ass, whilst the other was pressed to Emperor's chest, Moon's hand was still down Aquilo's pants, and Mischief was sucking Ramiel's wing.

*Awkward.*

I snatched my hands back to myself, but it surprised me when Moon actually *increased* the speed that his hand slid up and down Aquilo's dick, until Aquilo bucked against him. Moon's gaze met Hope's like a challenge.

Mischief lazily raised his head from Ramiel's wing to assess Hope.

Hope scrunched her nose, which was decorated with a gold ring. "Well, aren't I glad that I offered to…wake you." Her gaze darted to Emperor. "Using your time wisely then, brother…?"

Moon's growl shocked me. "Like you'd care or even know what he's been through for your kingdom. Do you mean, has he been a *perfect Om…?* On my fangs, I won't let you touch his hide."

"I'm a king now, see, and I didn't battle my own sister to allow you to hurt *your* brother," Amadeus hissed.

"As we're having a *Three Musketeer* moment here," I raised my hand, "then I'm in on this protect Emperor stand."

"Aren't we all," Mischief scrutinized Hope, "but I rather think that this Alpha had no intention of threatening our Golden Boy." I hadn't expected the way that Hope smothered her snicker, or exchanged a secret smile with her brother. *Was Hope different to the other Alphas?* "Please tell me that you're not a deplorable tyrant. You don't have a whip hidden in your robes?"

The way that Hope raised a haughty eyebrow reminded me so strongly of Emperor that I could almost believe she wasn't an asshole. *Almost.* "Glittery, sarcastic, and perceptive. Brother, I approve of your mates."

"You forgot his tight ass," I added. "But what's with the BFF routine?"

Hope stalked to the bed and boy, was she *not* looking like my BFF right now. "What's with *my* routine? What about yours? You take my brother away, monster, and I don't even get to check on him…?"

"Hope," Emperor said, softly, climbing off the bed, before drawing Hope to him, "you may bore me by checking for injuries later. This Charmer is quaintly decent because those American non-magicals didn't teach her witch laws or traditions. I promise, it wasn't as we feared."

I gawked at them because the way that they were speaking was like equals. *And why did that feel so unnatural?* I'd been stuck in the wolf and witch worlds too long. No wonder the power of the Alphas had soon become accepted.

Hope shot me a final glare, before clutching her brother to her chest.

Then she rubbed her thumb over the back of his hand. "I've been busy here on our…project." *What wasn't she saying? What was their project?* "It's ready for you, brother. If someone here hadn't caused instability in the witch world…"

"Hey, you're welcome," I crossed my arms.

Okami howled, rubbing his ass across Hope's face. I stiffened, but Hope only chuckled, plucking him by the ear.

"Yours, I believe?" Then she sighed. "There's little holding back my mother as it is, and then that bitch who's Head of the Covens is killed…"

I scowled. "Again, you're welcome."

"…That leaves both witch and wolf kingdoms open to my mother's control."

"And you're just a snuggly Alpha, right?" I arched my brow to mirror hers.

Hope flicked Okami on the ass, and he yelped as he flew back into my arms. I stroked over his head, as he wrapped around my neck with a sniffle.

Hope smoothed down her robe. "I wouldn't say *snuggly*." Her smile was all fangs. *Well done, piss off the wolf princess who already blamed me for stealing her brother.* "Do you believe that every Alpha dreams of nothing but oppressing and dominating?"

"*Umm*, yeah?"

She *tutted*. "So, you reckon that all Alphas are bastards?"

"Again, with the *hell, yeah*."

Hope straightened her brother's waistcoat as if checking out a soldier's uniform. Was she about to assess the shine of his shoes? "Okay, then all witches are bitches then? After all, it rhymes."

Mischief snickered. "Well, it must certainly be true then."

Hope met my gaze. "Some Alphas have always been trying to change things, and some Omegas…" She glanced between the princes. "…have always been in charge."

*Okay, mind officially blown…*

All of a sudden, the purple butterfly on the wall beat its wings with a resounding *clanging* against the glass. I startled, and Moon finally stopped stroking Aquilo's dick. Aquilo hissed in frustration at being *denied*, after all.

Hope's expression became tight. "Mother summons Emperor, you, and me to the Emperor Suite."

I perked up, grinning at Emperor. "Dude, they named a set of rooms after you! No wonder you've got such a big head."

Emperor exchanged a glance with his sister. "Not quite."

Hope wet her lips. "You know what I said about Alphas…? Forget all that with my mother. Dominating and oppressing are her happiest daydreams, and she's never *snuggled* in her life."

When Hope shuddered, hugging Emperor like she was making up for her mom, I reluctantly slipped off the bed.

Queen Aurora could tell me the secrets about the Wolf Witch, show me my brother, and find a way for me to marry Aquilo. Yet she could also *deny* all of that and prove to be the deadliest queen.

## CHAPTER 19

The glass roof of the Emperor Suite swarmed with butterflies like it'd been swallowed by a purple cloud. I gawked at the fluttering above my head because *broken wands*, now I understood that this room hadn't been named after my Charm but the butterflies that cocooned it.

Why had I thought that the queen would honor her *Cursed* son?

The Kingdom of the Alphas was smothered in its worship of transformation, as much as the Gods had been buried in its worship of the Moon. I hadn't understood just how much it must hurt them only to change into wolf form once a month. Moon had called it *magical chastity*, and having experienced the thrill of becoming a wolf myself, boy had he been right.

To a kingdom who saw themselves as the beautiful

butterflies of their people, being denied the right to transform must be a type of death.

When an aroma like rum and danger wrapped around me, I finally looked down, only to meet the amused...*and snootily insolent*...gaze of an Omega. He was dressed in a tiger orange suit and robes, which were embroidered in flashy patterns like wings. His golden hair was styled with even more care than Emperor's... *and snap my broomstick and call me a mage*...this had to be Emperor's dad, even though he was shorter than him.

*Bad, bad Crimson, I hadn't even bothered to find out my father-in-law's name...?*

This Omega prejudice was catching.

I glanced at Emperor, but he was buried in an intense conversation with his mom. His head was ducked, and I'd never seen him act so submissive before, as they stood by a wall of glass that ran down the middle of the room. Butterflies were trapped inside the glass, and their wings beat in patterns of fear, unable to escape, against it.

I wished that I was still tangled in the arms of my lovers back in the penthouse or at least, that they were all with me now. Okami would've wound himself reassuringly around my neck at least or bitten the snooty queen on the ass.

I'd enjoy that.

Flustered, I stared down at the crystal tumbler of

martini that the King of the Alphas was holding out to me.

He shook the glass and the ice *clinked*. "I promise, it's not poisoned."

"Said the poisoner." I arched my brow.

When Emperor's dad shot me a dashing grin, I forced my knees not to buckle because honestly, if his charisma could be bottled, then I'd be wealthier than my uncle.

"My son would kill me if I hurt you," he whispered conspiratorially, edging closer and wrapping my fingers around the drink. "He's been screaming *I licked her and now she's mine* ever since he stalked in here through his Alpha scent, of course." My eyes widened. *But I'd thought that I wasn't supposed to know…?* "And if you're wondering who the startlingly handsome Omega is who can also mix the best martini you've ever tasted…"

When he stared at me expectantly, I rolled my eyes but still sipped the martini. I moaned way too indecently but hey, it was the best thing that'd passed my lips, apart from the chocolate taste of Moon's dick. And I wasn't going to tell Emperor's dad *that*.

"It's like magic in my mouth." I took another sip. "And every coven's been invited."

Emperor's dad pulled a face. "It took decades of practice to pull off that drink, and you destroy it with one revolting image."

*So, the king was a drama queen.*

I smirked. "The witches are waltzing to the taste, there's black cats waggling their fluffy tails to "Witchy Woman", and my shadows are twerking."

*So sue me, my crimson loved to get down.*

I hadn't expected the way that he flinched back, however, at the mention of my shadows.

I blanched. Emperor had been there on the day that my great-grandmother, the Crimson Terror, had defeated and massacred the wolves, as the royal families had been forced to kneel and watch. Then she'd chosen the Omegas for her Charms, before murdering the rest.

*Emperor's dad must've witnessed it as well.* He'd have been paralyzed by the shadows and helpless to save his people. Had he been one of the Omegas forced to kneel, terrified that he'd be chosen by my great-grandmother?

When I shivered, Emperor's dad's look was shrewd.

"Drink up," he murmured, "it's always better to be a little drunk around the queen, I've found."

*Okay, so that wasn't reassuring at all.*

I downed the drink, enjoying its warm buzz.

Emperor's dad took my empty glass with an exaggerated bow, before placing it down on a coffee table, which was in front of a pair of purple silk sofas. Then he clasped his hands smartly behind his back and waited kind of like a servant.

*In fact, exactly like a servant.*

I swaggered over to Emperor and his mom because hey, I was a badass Wolf Charmer, Witch, and Liberator with my shadows slapping against the glass walls and bleeding them to red, but this was still the Alpha who could threaten my family and pack.

I wouldn't become like my ancestors or mom, ruling by force. My shadows churned inside, urging me to wind around Aurora and make her my puppet. Mischief and my Charms had taught me more about the dangers of power in the last couple of weeks, however, than I'd ever known before, and now I wouldn't allow myself to give in to the Charmer side of my nature alone.

My princes had planned for decades to free the Omegas, Betas, and mongrels, as well as to transform both the Kingdoms of the Wilds and Gods. I knew that Emperor had a plan for his own kingdom. I just had to make sure that I worked by his side and didn't screw it up because I was a dick.

Sometimes, I struggled not to be a dick when I was surrounded by assholes. If there wasn't an official syndrome name for that, then there should be.

"As the Alpha speaks, has Pumpkin attended to you properly?" Aurora leaned on her silver tipped cane.

I needn't have bothered to swagger; this was Aurora's kingdom, and she was in charge here. She might as well have had the message pinned in dead butterflies' wings to the walls.

*Wait, Pumpkin…?*

The moment that I spluttered with laughter, I regretted it. Emperor's dad — *Pumpkin* — stiffened, and Emperor shot me a reproving glare that made my stomach flip.

I wrinkled my nose at the waft of sharp liquorice that told me Emperor was all Alpha right now.

"I didn't choose my name," Pumpkin's lips thinned, but his eyes twinkled, "but don't you think it suits me...? After all, I'm so adorable."

"Adorable asshole," I muttered, before catching Aurora's darkening expression and the ominous way that she was tightening the hold on her cane. I hadn't forgotten how she'd pressed the silver tip onto Emperor's hand. *Did she punish her Wolf Bitten in the same way?* "Pumpkin was the perfect gentleman."

Aurora snorted. "Now I've heard it all. My Bitten is *anything* but a gentleman."

"I'll drink to that." Pumpkin grinned, glancing around him for the alcohol, but Aurora rapped her cane on the floor, and he flinched.

"You've done more than enough of that already today, and *you* only believe that pitiable creature adorable, perfect, or a gentleman because he plied you with one of his special drinks."

"*Oi*, objection," Pumpkin called.

Pumpkin was a hell of a feisty Omega. I'd bet that Moon and he would become best rebel buddies, even if their asses were kicked royally by Aurora.

"*Father*," Emperor hissed in warning, "please, behave…"

"Like you?" Pumpkin's voice was gentler than I'd been expecting. "Such a perfect Omega you are now. Was it the Charmer who showed you your place?"

I'd been about to tell Pumpkin that Emperor's place was by my side like all my guys, when Emperor shot me a glance that was just as warning as the one that he'd sent his dad.

So, he *didn't* want me defending him?

Since Emperor and I had stepped in here with his mom, Emperor had been playing the perfect Omega. Except, I knew that it *was* only playing, and that Emperor must have a plan.

If he wanted me to act the big bad Charmer, then I could do some witch badassery.

I smirked. "*Aw*, aren't you pleased that your son is now such a good wolf?"

"Your Charm's wretched father has no idea how to be good." I didn't miss the flash of hurt across both Pumpkin's and Emperor's faces, before they both hid it. "It's lucky for him that he was the prettiest Omega of his generation." Now *that* I could believe, especially since I might've ragged Emperor about his obsession with his looks, but there was no doubting that it was true. "Now, *sit*."

At the *rap* of Aurora's cane on the glass wall, the

butterflies fluttered in fear, at the same time as Pumpkin dropped to the floor on his ass.

Although Emperor managed to stifle his growl, I didn't.

Aurora scrutinized me. "How fascinating that the most powerful of the witches is now so much wolf." She sauntered to the sofa, before perching on it. Then she patted the seat next to her like we were about to have a friendly mom to daughter chat, although I'd rather jump on my own bonfire than cozy up with an Alpha who treated her Omega like a dog (and no witch jokes about being burned at the stake). "It appears that my son's schooling was more than worth it. He's shown outstanding diplomacy with you." Emperor looked like he'd been slapped. *Had his mom ever praised him before?* "Well, sit down." She gestured impatiently at the sofa.

"I take it that you want him to kneel?" I sighed, as I settled next to her on the sofa.

The fresh scent of sunflowers wafted from Aurora, but with something sharp underneath that promised of hidden brambles.

Aurora patted my hand. "You're still on the *kneeling* power trip, are you? I'm not the one who ever asked that of him." I pinked. When Emperor had first been brought to me to Claim in the House of Seasons, I'd made a lame assed joke about kneeling, which had led to Emperor being seared with silver. I'd learned my lesson about thinking it was sexy for anybody to be on their knees unwillingly. "On the moon, that's his best suit and the knees get so dusty that way."

I jerked my head at Pumpkin. "His suit looks pretty snazzy too."

Pumpkin puffed up, as Emperor settled on the edge of the sofa.

"I'm overjoyed that I have your agreement that he should be punished for ruining it then. The ritual is that discipline for poor appearance is performed before bed. I'd say, ten strokes." Aurora adjusted the band of gold in her hair.

Pumpkin deflated, scowling at the cane.

*Witches tit, I'd flown my broomstick straight into that one.*

Was that why Emperor was so obsessed with his suit and robes: his mother's obsession with their appearance and punishment if they weren't neat and *perfect*? I itched to check that my own fingers weren't covered with paint and that my hair hadn't frizzed because my own mom had always scolded me about both.

I'd never been good enough for her either. Yeah, I got how they felt, only I hadn't been caned when I fell short.

"How about bed without milk and cookies and we call it even?" I offered.

"I don't get cookies anyway," Pumpkin grumbled. "Plus, a wolf could die of bloody thirst around here."

"*You* couldn't," Aurora muttered. Then she leaned closer like we were back to our friendly chat, "Did you know that we Alphas are more enlightened than the other kingdoms? We don't keep our Omegas stripped of clothes, speech, or education. I've long bargained and bartered with the Head Coven, so that our Omegas don't have to attend the Omega Training Centers but can be schooled at home. Only the most rebellious and disobedient are used as Training Omegas at our Alpha Academy."

My gaze darted to Emperor, and I craved to kiss him, until he returned to the cocky asshole who I loved and lost the anguish that trembled through him.

As we were sitting right in front of his parents, however, I settled for demanding, "Let me guess, you signed up the prince to this Asshole Academy?"

"*Alpha* Academy," Aurora corrected patronizingly like I'd simply misheard.

I cocked my head. "Like I said, *Asshole* Academy."

Pumpkin guffawed and didn't even attempt to smother it.

"Twelve," Aurora hissed, pointing the cane at him, before studying me with sudden respect. *Woah, that was unsettling.* "Omegas are prized and useful, but if they're not restrained, then they can be *toxic*, rather like you, I'd imagine."

My shadows burst out in hurt fury, stinging her skin.

She froze in shock, dropping the cane, which rolled across the floor with a *clatter*.

"I've had a couple of messed up weeks." I knew that Emperor was tugging at my sleeve, but I vibrated with the shadows that licked through me. "Now I'm here with a psychopathic queen and a drunk off his ass king, and you honestly don't want to see how toxic I can be if you push me."

To my shock, Aurora ginned, and there was the *psychopath* that I was talking about. "You shall make an outstanding Wolf Witch! I hardly believed it when I heard that you were the cause of the vile creature who ran the coven's death, but now I see you like this and... well, it's harder to imagine you *not* savaging throats."

I swallowed. "That vile creature was my aunt."

Aurora waved her hand dismissively. "I've known her for longer than you, silly child...*knew* her. How delightful to be able to talk about her in the past tense. But this is why you'll do so well in the Alpha Academy. I was certain that my son would be able to win you over to our side, after all, he's had enough experience in such diplomatic enticing, just like his father."

Both dad and son winced. I knew exactly the type of *enticing* she meant: the sort that started with being tied naked to someone's bed, as Emperor had been to mine.

*She allowed her own Bitten to be used like that as well...?*

I figured that was one definition of Omegas being

*useful*, just like my boot was *useful* for kicking this dickhead's ass.

When I snarled and launched towards Aurora, Emperor banded his arms around me and hauled me onto his lap, disguising the move by kissing down my neck. I couldn't help the way that I relaxed into the familiar strength of his arms, so I wouldn't tease him about the way that he couldn't help poking my ass with his hard dick.

"Fur and fangs, I don't require a demonstration." Aurora laughed indulgently like we'd shown her our engagement ring and then snogged. "I believed that my son was ruined by that atrocious little heathen from the Wilds." When Emperor stiffened, I stroked his arm in reassurance with my shadows. "But here you are. That it'd be my son who'd control a Charmer, so she'd turn her shadows on her own side and kill the Head of the Covens...!" I pressed closer to Emperor. *Was that what'd happened?* Had I been controlled or only freed to make my own choices? "You don't even know what you've done yet, do you?" Her eyes blazed. "It takes the most educated of the kingdoms to realize the simplest of things, but it'll free us all." When Pumpkin stared at her in shock, she shook her head. "My, you're eager all of a sudden."

"I haven't forgotten, my dear," Pumpkin murmured, "what it is to be free."

Aurora's expression softened. Then she pushed

herself up, before brushing off imaginary lint from the shoulders of her robes. "You and your Charms shall attend the Alpha Academy. By my hide, you'll be a shining example as the first witch who's eager to join."

"Like a mascot." I clasped Emperor's hand, and he played with my fingers. "I kind of wouldn't say *eager…*"

Aurora swept towards the door. "It's settled."

"Nope, unless, you know, *it's not.*" I leapt up. "You forced me here with a threat to my brother and then, hello, *no brother*. So, if you want me as Poster Witch for this academy, then I need to see him."

My pulse thundered in my ears, as Aurora's claws grew.

Then she snarled, "Your pathetic brother is of no concern to me. He works for the principal of the academy, Dame Break, who was once Emperor's tutor. Go see him, if the moon so moves you."

I didn't miss the way that Emperor flinched and paled. *Okay, someone was getting a wolfie ass kicking for making him look that way.*

"I need your help with a mage." I narrowed my eyes. "I'm engaged by Blood Bond and unless, you know, we're married then—"

"He dies and oodles of other stuff that I don't care about," Aurora drawled. "My, aren't you the angsty one. Attend the academy and I'll consider it."

She swept out of the Emperor Suite, trailing her robes like the rays of the sun, and I stared after her.

What the ever-witching hell had just happened? Had I just been signed up for an academy, even though the thought of returning to any sort of schooling was terrifying, otherwise I wouldn't be able to marry Aquilo?

"Well, Aurora was as bracing as always." Pumpkin bounded up, before strutting to the glass wall and leaning against it, as he traced across a fluttering butterfly.

Where was the half-drunk, half-dashing rake out of an English romance novel? Pumpkin was clear eyed all of a sudden and more sober than me.

I pointed at him. "Did you just pull a *Bruce Wayne stunt to hide your alter ego Batman* on my ass?"

The corners of Pumpkin's mouth twitched. "I prefer to see myself as a Scarlet Pimpernel. Plus, surely I tricked more than your ass, perky as it is?"

"Are you flirting with my Charmed?" Emperor demanded.

"*Pfft.* I flirt with everyone, apart from your mother." Pumpkin shuddered.

I stared at him. "But doesn't she know…? Aren't you monitored?"

Emperor sprawled on the sofa with his arms behind his head. "How sweet that you still believe most Alphas truly *see* Omegas. They create illusions, and so it's staggeringly easy to feed them back their own lies. Plus, these are the royal rooms and so private. This isn't the Kingdom of the Gods with its obsessional paranoia."

"Don't forget the dab of rum behind my ears each morning," Pumpkin added. "When in fact I haven't touched a drink in..." Emperor raised his eyebrow at his dad, and Pumpkin shrugged his shoulders sheepishly. "Well, tell me that you wouldn't drink if you had to—"

"*La-la*, can't hear you," Emperor scrunched his nose in disgust.

"I can *smell* you though." Pumpkin shot me a knowing look, and Emperor startled. "The Charmer guessed on your first night that you're an Alpha, come on, we have a bet riding on this."

*The sneaky...gorgeous...assholes.*

I'd thought that Emperor could be tricky to handle, but his dad was more complex than any of my guys and had made a bet with his own son on whether the fact that he was a male Alpha (which could mean his execution), would be discovered on his first night with the Charmer.

I was tempted to tell him that I'd never known Emperor was anything but a perfect Omega, but I'd never be able to pull it off. Emperor had looked more like he'd hungered for me to be on *my* knees, even whilst I'd been Claiming him.

When I nodded, Emperor groaned.

Pumpkin smiled wickedly. "You sing me a song of my choice, at a time of my choosing."

I stared at them blankly. "That's what you dicks bet on?"

Pumpkin blinked at me. "Like we have money or, I don't know, anything else that belongs to us but our *pride*. Emperor and I have been playing this game since he was a kid. The key is how to get away with it."

"Or not," Emperor growled.

Pumpkin winced. "The trick to a long con is to allow yourself to get caught sometimes but only for small offenses." He swept his hand through his golden hair, and boy, did he remind me of Emperor. "On my fangs, I'll do anything to distract the queen from our son."

When he tapped the trapped butterflies, they startled and flew in spirals. Pumpkin glanced at Emperor as if asking his permission. Emperor hesitated, before finally nodding.

"This screen opens, you know." Pumpkin pressed his finger on the glass as if he wished that he could break it, even though his words were soft. "When Emperor was a cub and he behaved in any way that was more *dominant* than his sister, he'd have to pull it back and trap another butterfly inside." Why hadn't I noticed that Emperor was unable to look at the glass wall? He'd become motionless now, but then, so had I. I struggled to pull in each breath because *hexes and curses*, I was transfixed by Pumpkin's intensity. My shadows coiled around me in distress, however, at what horror he'd say next. "At the end of the week, his mother would force him to count the butterflies and for each one, he'd receive a stroke of the cane with his hands pressed like this…" He braced himself against the wall like the ghost of his son, and Emperor closed his eyes with a whine. "Every night, his sister and I would take turns sneaking in to set as many butterflies free as we could because on my fur, *we couldn't bear for him to be punished for his own nature."* His breathing was so ragged that it was as if he'd been punished himself. He rested his forehead on the glass, just like his son must've as a kid. "When he was no longer a cub, however, and couldn't control his Alpha urges, the screen became so full of butterflies that they'd crush each other and the thrashings…"

I dived for the sofa, kneeling and hugging Emperor, as if I could wipe away his mom's cruelty. Moon had been trapped in the Training Center, just as Amadeus had been forced to play the part of pretty prince for the Gods. But Emperor had spent his life hiding his entire identity.

*And that sucked.*

I'd only hidden my magic from the non-magicals in America, ashamed of my abilities because my uncle had feared them. I understood now why a man raised by the covens would've thought that I'd turn out just like any other Charmer unless he raised me differently.

Had Emperor's mom *feared* her Alpha born son in the same way?

"You're not worried about your knees getting

dusty?" Emperor murmured into my shoulder, before kissing my neck with a tenderness that made me shiver.

When I drew back, he wiped the tears from my cheeks. *Wait, I'd been crying?*

Yet Emperor was smiling, and so was his dad.

Pumpkin shook his head ruefully. "I admit it: You win."

My eyes narrowed, and I nudged Emperor with my elbow. "Don't tell me. You had a bet on whether you could force me to make an ass out of myself by feeding me a fake sob story?"

*Why did that hurt so much?*

Emperor wrapped his hand around my hair and wrenched me closer. "You're making quite the ass out of yourself, and maybe we *are* con wolves," he exchanged a glance with Pumpkin who looked stricken, "but we'd never lie about…something like that."

*Okay, now I wished that they had because it meant that the butterfly story was true.*

"On the night before he was taken for his Claiming," Pumpkin crossed his arms and for the first time, I truly realized that he was both a king and intimidating as witching hell, "I raged that no *monster* would take my son." *Harsh but fair.* "Then he told me about the pact that he'd sworn with the other princes, and we in turn made a bet, which he won."

Emperor smirked. "A song of *my* choice, which you'll sing at a time of *my* choosing."

Pumpkin grinned. "You're on, son of mine, and I've never been so relived to lose a bet." When I raised my eyebrow, his expression gentled. "He swore that he'd not only persuade you to treat him as an equal but that when he returned to this kingdom, he'd be *happy*." When Emperor's gaze met mine, my breath stuttered. Holy hell, he was both scorching hot and everything that I'd ever dreamed I wanted in a guy but all that mattered was the *joy* dancing in his eyes because I'd been the one to place it there. "That look right there…it's been a long time since I've seen it on my son. By my Moon Oath, I don't care if you're a wolf, witch, or blow up doll…"

"*Father*," Emperor hissed, blushing.

Pumpkin winked at him. "What? I'm just saying that I wouldn't judge. I don't know what cubs are into these days, although I read such things…"

"*Enough*," Emperor growled with enough Alpha force even to make me jump.

"Spoilsport." Pumpkin strolled over, settling himself on the arm of the sofa. "Take your Charmer to see her brother. He'll be helping the principal in her rooms right now."

Hey, I was down with any plan that meant I'd get to see my long-lost brother.

Emperor paled, and his scent bled to sweet honey. "I-I'd rather not."

My brows furrowed. Hadn't we just been trying to convince Aurora to let me see him?

"I know," Pumpkin replied, gently. "I never thought that I'd see you look... I don't know what it feels like to be in love but...well, you certainly both appear to be and with that comes trust. Sweet witch, you need to see why my son was never happy before. To discover your brother, you'll have to take my son back to his worst fear."

Emperor shook, and I cocooned him in my shadows. What would Emperor show me?

I dreaded that to save my brother, I needed Emperor to face the Kingdom of the Alphas' terrors.

CHAPTER 20

I n the penthouse, I'd thought that the Kingdom of the Alphas had been all about the sun, but in the basement of the glass tower there was nothing but dark.

I squinted through the gloom of the corridor, wrinkling my nose against the stench. I hunched my shoulders, uncomfortable under the roof that was gilded silver.

What in the witching heavens was this place? It gave off the same vibes as the **DISCIPLINE CELLAR** in the House of Silver, which considering this was the palace of the witches' ancient enemies was ironic, right?

Why would a wolf gild anything silver? Who were they trying to discipline or ward against?

When Emperor's shoulder brushed against mine, I glanced at him. He was struggling to hide his shallow breathing behind a snooty mask that would've conned me once. But now, I knew that this place freaked him out, and my shadows shuddered with the urge to protect him, even if the terror was in his past. I hooked my arm around his waist, and the corner of his mouth turned up into a smile.

"It's your choice if you come with me down this *The Shining* corridor. I love you; you're pack. I don't need you to tell me anything that you're not ready to because you think that I won't trust you if you don't. Although, if you do stay, then you can walk at the back, where the spooks usually snatch the first victim."

Emperor chuckled. "I thought that the maiden was normally killed first…?"

I pinched his ass, and he yelped. "Lucky that there's no maiden here, only me."

Emperor rubbed his ass. "We are indeed blessed." Then he marched down the corridor, before glancing back over his shoulder at me. "Don't you want to see if your brother has the same insane mane of red curls as you do?"

"Hey," I jogged after Emperor, "was that an insult or a compliment?"

Emperor merely smirked.

*Okay, so he was back to the same hot but haughty asshole as usual then.*

I skirted my hand along the wall. "What in the name of Hecate is this dungeon?"

"This is the delightful prison where I — *the*

*Cursed Prince* — was locked away from birth." When I gasped, Emperor's amused gaze met mine. "Did you imagine that my mother allowed me in the light with the other Omegas?" He pointed to the end of the corridor, although his hand shook. "My tutor, Dame Break, who is now the principal of the Alpha Academy, has her rooms there, so that she might always oversee me."

Emperor's gaze slid, however, to a low door to the side, which gleamed silver as well and had no doorknob. It must've burned him every time that he pushed it to enter. Plus, if he'd been shut inside, there'd have been no way for him to escape. He didn't even attempt to hide the way that he struggled for breath now, and since this was the place that he most feared, go figure.

Yet he was facing it for my sake, and that meant he was both courageous and a seriously loyal lover.

When I shoved on the door, I couldn't help holding my arm across my face to block out the dank air. The room (cat's whiskers, it was a *cell*), was nothing like the glass, gold, and silky purple that I'd seen so far in the kingdom. Well-thumbed books were ranked around the walls, and a thin mattress was pushed against the far wall with a single horse plushie that looked seriously well loved placed in its center. I'd have called that blackmail material. Except, it was the only toy in the room that (small mercies) at least had concrete rather than silver walls and floors.

Had Emperor ever possessed more than a *pink* horse with only one eye?

"Home sweet home." Emperor's jaw clenched. "Only my sister's campaigning enabled me to leave here during the day for schooling. You're honored. I've never shown anyone my bedroom before."

The smirk didn't reach his eyes.

"Have you shown anyone My Little Pink Pony before? He's so cute." When I reached to pick up the plushie, however, Emperor barged past me, swooping into his bedroom.

I gaped at him, as he snatched up his plushie, cradling the horse in his arms. "His name is *Combat,* and he's a war horse."

"*Aw*, is someone protective of their pink…?" *Only childhood toy…?* I flushed. "Does he transform into a werehorse?"

Mollified, Emperor allowed me to stroke Combat's mane. "His teeth can rip out a tutor's throat, and he can kick her behind with his hooves."

"He's talented."

"Indeed," Emperor sighed, "and I believe that he was one of my sister's many toys, before she gave him to me."

That explained the pink, which meant that Emperor had never been truly given a gift before. I'd bitched about being the orphan and charity case, but my uncle had lavished me with presents every Christmas and birthday. Emperor was a prince with two parents, and the only gift that he still loved with such fierceness, was a hand-me-down from his sister.

I wound my arms around Emperor's neck, whilst my red nudged him from behind, tumbling us both onto the mattress. Combat was soft between us, as I captured Emperor's mouth with mine. I sucked on his lower lip, until he moaned, and then darted my tongue inside.

"Do you also love unicorns as well?" I teased. "Mischief would allow you to pet him."

Emperor forced his knee between my legs, urging them to part, before pushing up beneath the skirt of my dress. "I'd prefer to ride him or his horn."

Warmth coiled through me, as Emperor's fingers copied the way that his knee circled but this time across my aching nubs.

*Harder, please, harder…*

He teased my peaking nipples, before breaking the kiss to lower his mouth towards my tit. Holy hell, I needed to feel his hot mouth sucking on me, until I was caught in that place of *too much*, and *don't you dare stop, wolfie…*

Emperor appeared to have caught my thought because he grinned teasingly, before he licked over the fabric of the dress above my nub. Then his fingers edged beneath my dress.

All of a sudden, he yelped,

"Scuttling thing with an embarrassment of legs that

shall have no name," he gasped, clutching Combat harder.

*Did he even know that he was doing that?*

"Honestly, even a werehorse isn't going to protect you from a spider." *Would it be okay if I just grabbed Emperor's hair and directed him back to my tit?* "Weren't we about to do something a lot more exciting than...?"

Then I noticed how pale Emperor was, and the way that his lips were pinched. I'd known that he hated spiders, but was it more like I feared water?

My shadows streamed out to caress his cheek. "Let me show you something..."

My other power, as well as being a Wolf Charmer, was the ability to control animals. I didn't like to use it now that I understood just how control could be abused, but if it helped Emperor over his phobia then it'd be worth it.

I spun a web of red around the spider that'd been lurking behind the mattress, and it danced out.

Emperor let out a harsh gasp, but then the spider raised its spindly legs and bowed. When I started to hum *Swan Lake*, Emperor narrowed his eyes at me suspiciously. Then the spider began to dance like he was Amadeus in the ballet, playing the role of the black swan.

*Wow, I'd never known that someone's jaw could literally drop open in shock.*

When the dance finished, the spider bowed again and scuttled off.

Emperor cleared his throat. "Well, that was unexpected."

"Beautiful though," I said. "You should see my flea circus."

Emperor laughed. "You remind me of him. He always tried to distract me from the fear with jokes and tricks."

"Who?"

Emperor clasped his hands in his lap. "Didn't I warn you that beautiful things can also be the deadliest? It was Dame Break's thoughtful addition to my schooling: *Fear Training*. Apparently, I didn't allow myself to be dominated." His cocky pride was matched only by my own. He'd been brought up in a dungeon but he'd still defied the Alpha assholes. "So, she had the cunning idea to break me with fear. Hence, tying me down and things that crawl."

*Now that wasn't an image that'd go away anytime soon.*

"But you just let me…with the whole dancing…and she made you…" I spluttered.

"It was different. I have you with me now." When Emperor's raw gaze met mine, I shivered because *that* was trust.

*My witchy ass had better never let him down.*

"And Combat." I stroked the socket where the

horse's eye had once been. "*Hmm*, how was he blinded?"

"Honorable war wound," Emperor boasted, "against a witch. It was this whole epic battle…"

"*Uh-huh*?" I pushed Combat onto the mattress, before capturing Emperor's wrists between mine. "It looks like this witch has won. What should I do with my war spoils?"

Emperor arched his brow. "Are you certain about that? This is deep in the bad wolf's lair. Maybe I dragged you here to ravish you."

I shivered, and Emperor's pupils dilated. Okay, ravishing sounded hot, and like Emperor's mouth would get back to sucking my tits.

*Yeah, I could get with the whole ravishing roleplay.*

At least, until a shrill voice called from the doorway, "Ah, my two new students." Then spat out as if the Alpha was tasting something nasty, rather than being nasty, "*The witch and her bitch.*"

Wow, when this asshole went for the insults, she put her whole heart into it.

Instantly, I dropped Emperor's wrists, and he straightened.

The Alpha was tall in sickly yellow robes with a severe bun. She was the Alpha who'd twisted Emperor's arms behind his back when I'd known him as nothing but the aristocratic Omega who'd tried to help Amadeus in Wild Hall during the attack.

"Dame Break, I presume?" I smiled at the Alpha who was scowling in the doorway; I'd *always* wanted to say that.

"The Wolf Charmer and her boy, I presume," she mocked back.

*She didn't do banter then.*

*Clatter* — a pile of folders spilled into the doorway behind Dame Break, followed by a mop of shiny red hair that ducked down and started frantically collecting them.

"Sorry," the guy muttered who was dressed in a gray suit without a robe, "clumsy me."

Break *tsked*. "Idiot mage. How many times must I break your fingers, before you learn not to drop my things?"

My breath caught. *Could he be my brother who was also a mage? Had my parents thrown him to the wolves simply because he'd had magic?*

Then the mage raised his head and his silver eyes met mine.

Silver eyes were the mark of the *House of Silver.* I let out a cry because witches above, I only knew at that moment that a part of me had always been missing and it'd been *my brother.*

His eyes gleamed with the same grief, before he composed himself. I'd imagine that my brother had a lot of practice at that, working for a freak who broke fingers for being clumsy, especially if he was anything like me.

*Was it weird that I hoped he was?*

"How dare a mage stare at his betters," Dame Break snarled, snatching my brother by his curls and wrenching up his head.

I grimaced because I knew what that felt like and at the same time, my shadows acted on instinct. My brother was *my* blood, and no one would hurt him. They shot out, bouncing Break against the door. She squawked, as she was seared, before I twisted her and flung her against the far wall, pinning her like she was a butterfly. When she screamed her protest, I gagged her with crimson.

My brother straightened, studying me in shock.

Yeah, that was an epic way to introduce myself like I was a monster in the *The Witcher*. Who knows what stories these wolves had taught him about the terrifying Wolf Charmer?

At last, he smiled. "You defended me?"

Was this what Moon felt like with Moth? Now I understood the brothers' devotion and obsession with sacrifice.

I nodded.

He appeared to think about this like it was an alien concept. *I'd bet that it was.* "I love your magic."

"Just wait, Sterling, that was just a taster." Emperor bounded up, swinging his arms around my brother —

*Sterling* — and dragging him out into the corridor. Why was Emperor so familiar with him like they were…? I didn't know, but then, why hadn't Emperor told me that I had a brother? "Come on, witch, your *bitch* wants to talk away from the academy's principal."

When Sterling huffed with laughter, I couldn't help the jealousy that he wasn't in my arms and directing that joy at me.

It wasn't fair but neither was being parted from my own freaking brother for my entire life. The witches had murdered Kolby merely because he was a mage, and they'd threatened Aquilo that he'd be thrown to the wolves, just like my brother had been. My family and the covens had erased my own brother like he'd never existed, and yet all the time he'd been living here in the Kingdom of the Alphas.

I trailed after them into the corridor and then slammed shut Emperor's bedroom door to silence Break's muffled curses.

When I turned, Emperor clutched Sterling like he'd cradled Combat. My eyes widened.

*A whole witching universes of no… Were they lovers?* Did Emperor only love me because he already loved my brother?

When I let out a choked sound, Emperor glanced over Sterling's shoulder at me.

Emperor must've caught my thought because his gaze became steely, before he winked and said huskily,

"What can I say? I have this twisted *thing* for screwing my enemies like the heirs of the House of Silver…"

Sterling shoved Emperor away, smacking his arm with a reproving look, as if Emperor wasn't a wolf prince and *he* wasn't a mage at his mercy. "Play nice, Per. Do you always tease my sister?"

Emperor grinned. "She enjoys being teased."

"And that's more than I need to know." Sterling turned to me.

I scrutinized his face, fascinated by the way that he scrutinized me back. He was handsome and so like me, despite the shadows under his eyes that spoke of over-work and lack of sleep, as well as the bruise on his cheekbone that I figured had been put there by Break. But then, I doubted that I looked the type of presentable that mom would've been happy with. Considering that mom had thrown my brother to the wolves, however, I no longer cared about that, go figure.

"So, you're not…?" I made a kissy face.

Sterling lifted his brow in a way that reminded me of Mischief. "Either five years old or lovers…? Nope, Per's like my older brother, and he's always tried to protect me. Dad was the same. Please believe that dad always tried to protect me from mum, before she sent me here."

Emperor clasped his hand on the back of Sterling's neck, reassuringly. It hurt that I'd never had a relation-ship with Sterling, but I couldn't wish that Emperor and he hadn't had each other in these dark rooms at the bottom of the tower.

Despite his own suffering, Emperor had still been kind to his tutor's mage assistant, and if it was possible to love him more, then I seriously did now.

Alphas ranted about protection, but this was what it truly meant.

My mouth was dry, but I forced myself to demand, "Why didn't you tell me about him? We could've—"

"Stormed my kingdom with your Crimson Tide to rescue him?" Emperor growled. "I'm entirely unclear at what point you wouldn't have been *distracted* by this piece of news. We've been rather busy surviving over the last couple of weeks, and all that I knew with certainty was that your parents had betrayed their own son, just in the same way as Aquilo's hurt him. Sterling is my *family* and *pack* as much as you are, and I knew that I'd return here with you as soon as…"

"I could be trusted?" I demanded.

"I'd be able to free us all," Emperor whispered.

"Time out." Sterling shrugged away from Emperor. When he slipped his arms around me, it felt like coming home. "Please, give Per a break. He and his sister saved my life." His cheeks pinked on sister. *Interesting, so my brother had a crush on Hope?* "They're brave, and if I didn't trust them, I'd be dead." Then he fixed me with a glare that made me wonder if I looked just as terrifying sometimes. "You'd better be treating Per as if he's a good wolf because I promised that any sister of mine would."

I traced my finger across Sterling's lips, until his frown melted away at the unexpected touch. "He *is* a good wolf, and I love him."

Emperor preened. "What did I say? I'm irresistible."

Sterling snorted. "You're an irresistible bighead."

"Still."

When I entwined Sterling's hand with mine, he glanced between our hands like he was so unused to the gesture that he wanted to check that it was real.

I battled to stop my tears from falling as I forced myself to ask, "Why did mom...? I mean, how old were you when...?"

Sterling's fingers tightened around mine. "I was eight, and mum was pregnant with you. I'd never seen her so happy because this time..." He ducked his head, and his voice was soft, "she'd been told that this baby would be a girl. But I was happy too because I was excited to have a little sister to care for." My heart clenched. What must it've felt like for Sterling to be the unwanted boy? Yet Sterling had still been *happy* because he wouldn't be the only kid anymore. "It was at breakfast, and I was listening to mum chatting about baby stuff. I was excited, but sitting quietly because I'd already been told off for not sitting straight, and you didn't get told more than once before... Then these silver sparks started to dance on the tips of my fingers.

They were beautiful. I laughed and danced them right down the middle of the tablecloth. When mum screamed, dad started to plead with her, before she slapped him. I cried then because I hated it when she hit him and…" He broke off; his eyes were silver pools. I shuddered because I knew that dining room where his magic had come in; I'd eaten my breakfast every day trying to sit straight just like him. Had I even sat in his chair…the son who'd been *vanished* for having magic? "Mum snatched my arm, everything went dark, and then I woke up in the Kingdom of the Alphas."

"I wish that you'd been my big brother," I murmured, "you'd have been epic."

Sterling's face lit up. Then he asked shyly, "I could apply for the position now?"

"You're hired." I crushed him in a hug that knocked the air out of him.

Emperor chuckled. "Does that mean I get to boss you both around?"

"*No*," Sterling and I barked in unison.

"The Terrible Two," Emperor sassed, disgruntled, "and I thought that you were both difficult enough individually."

"You mean lovable, right?" I fluttered my lashes.

Emperor rolled his eyes. "Always."

"I listened out for stories about you." Sterling pushed me back enough to meet my gaze. "Although, I didn't believe half of them. Wolves aren't the most reli-able witnesses when it comes to witches."

"Or witches when it comes to wolves," Emperor added.

Sterling bit his lip. "I don't imagine that you heard about me...? Did mum cut me out of pictures? I thought that maybe dad would be able to keep some. There was this amazing portrait that mum had commissioned on my fifth birthday above the staircase, was it...?"

I froze. Holy hell, how did I tell him that every trace he'd ever existed had been removed from the House of Silver before I'd been born or that my parents had never even told me that I'd had a brother? Only my aunt had admitted that they'd had a kid before me, but she'd implied that he'd *died*.

I must've hesitated too long because his expression became one of crushing sadness, before he forced himself to shrug. "I'm a mage born to witches. Our parents only followed tradition. I don't deserve any better."

"Hey, enough of that bullshit." I gripped Sterling's chin, and he stared at me in shock. "I know two mages, and they're pains in my ass, but their magic *is* beautiful, they're kind of awesome, and I love them both. I don't care that mages are meant to be the witches' enemies, the way that witches treat men is messed up, and don't even ask me about jerk tradition. The only reason that we're playing along with the dickhead who's tied up in my shadows right now is because I'm trying to marry a mage."

Sterling's eyes widened. "Marry a…?" Then he tapped his foot in big brother mode. "Congratulations, but also, don't you think that you should *untie* your shadows if your marriage depends upon it?"

*Okay, he had a point.*

I pushed open the door to Emperor's bedroom, squinting into the gloom. Perhaps, Break had calmed down? Well, if I was making wishes: I'd like Mischief with chocolate coated wings, I wasn't greedy.

*Okay, so no candy Mischief and still an Alpha asshole cursing me out.*

I sighed, yanking my shadows out of Break. She collapsed onto the floor, panting.

Then she fixed me with a furious glower, as her claws scratched along the concrete like she was imagining my throat. "I'll flay you! You'll fight me in the academy's arena tonight. If the queen wants you schooled, then by my fangs, you will be."

Tonight, I'd face the Alpha who'd been a heartless tutor to Emperor and raised my brother even more brutally. Even though she was the principal of the Academy, and I'd have to battle her, I still smiled because at last, I'd be able to take revenge for their pain, even if it killed me.

CHAPTER 21

The moon shone between classical arches that had been sprayed with graffiti in the savage image of wolves breaking free from chains: the emblem of the Alpha Academy. I shivered, wrapping my shadows around myself as if they were the red cape that had once been my mom's.

Fascinated, I studied the silver wall that trapped us beneath the dome, which witches had erected to imprison the entire Wolf Kingdom away from the non-magical world at the end of the Wolf War. The arena in the academy was at the edge of the kingdom, skirting the wall; it stank of sweat and the wall's dark magic. My crimson coiled around me more tightly to escape its sting.

Here was the witches' gilded dickery. The *wolves' dickery* was in their *Gladiator* style posturing. Break could've just given me a detention, instead of turning Fight Club on me.

Alphas from the academy circled on the opposite side of the arena like bursts of rainbow if the rainbow had been seriously pissed off rather than beaming over the world. The Alphas' glares could've torn out my throat. Break marched between them, muttering orders.

Yet weirdly, there were also some Alphas on *my* side of the arena around Hope, who waved and offered reassuring thumbs up.

Were they Hope's gang? Did that mean they *didn't* want to see me slaughtered?

My guys had been allowed into the arena, and I hadn't realized just how much I couldn't freaking breathe without them all beside me, until they were there again, together. Then my shadows had reached out, stroking over each of them at once, and the sensation had been mind-blowing. By the blissed-out sighs from my guys, I'd guessed that it'd been good for them too.

Okami had flown to perch on my shoulder, nipping my ear in greeting.

I rubbed his silky head. "I missed you too, wolfie."

Yet it was Emperor who the Alphas from Hope's gang petted like he was their favorite kid brother. I had to hide my grin in my cupped palm, when they cooed, passing him between them like mothering hens.

Aquilo snickered, as a tall Alpha ruffled Emperor's

hair. *Emperor must be desperate to adjust his hair right now.*

Yet Emperor clenched his jaw, politely allowing the attention, as if he was visiting relatives. Except, it was *exactly* like they were relatives who believed that he was *precious*, rather than Cursed.

I sneaked a glance at Break who was scowling even more fiercely now at Emperor.

Hope had told me that not all Alphas were assholes, and it turned out that she had a point. But unfortunately, I wasn't fighting the cooing sweethearts, but the wolf with *asshole* stamped on her forehead, who'd broken my brother's fingers just because he had the same clumsiness gene as me, and who thought that arachnophobia was a useful teaching tool.

Sterling hovered next to me. "Pan's balls, Dame Break chose this arena to school you because you can't win. She doesn't allow the use of magic or weapons."

"What am I meant to fight her with, my sass and charm?"

"Why, if it were on sass alone, then you surely *would* win." Mischief stalked to the edge of the arena. "May I request that you tell me how you landed yourself fighting a werewolf on your first night?"

"It wasn't her fault," Sterling insisted, stepping in front of me. I glowed because boy, did it feel good to have a big brother to protect me, even if he didn't realize that Mischief was all sarcasm and no bite…for me, at least. "She was saving me."

Mischief arched his brow. "And you are…?"

Sterling puffed up with pride. "Her brother."

Ramiel gasped, before twirling Sterling around in his wings, as Amadeus grasped one of his hands, and Aquilo the other.

I frowned, however, at the way that Aquilo grimaced like he was in pain. Had he been hurt?

Sterling caught my gaze, bewildered. Had anyone shown him kindness apart from Emperor?

"You'll get used to them," Emperor called over, "like those annoying songs that you can't get out of your head."

Then Emperor yelped, as his sister swiped his ass.

*I liked Hope.*

"On my hide, I'm pleased for you," Moon murmured. He nuzzled against my neck, and I breathed in the lemony scent of his curls. "Moth is a rascal but I love him, and I'd give my life for him. When we were apart, it was like being dead. Your brother is now pack, and it'll be an honor to know him."

I could tell that Sterling had heard by the way that his breath hitched.

Moon deserved another cuddle for making my brother feel welcome. My arms encircled Moon, and he licked down my neck.

Then Mischief's eyes narrowed, and he waved

Emperor over. Emperor disentangled himself from an Alpha who was patting him on the head and strolled to join us.

"Are you done being stroked?" Mischief demanded.

"Jealousy is an ugly thing." Emperor flashed a cocky grin.

"Your hair looks like you've been dragged through a hedge backwards," Moon said with a pretend innocence that wasn't fooling anyone.

Emperor shuddered, smoothing his hand through his locks. "Is the fight starting?"

"It would appear that for some, it already has." Mischief nodded towards a huddle of Alphas who had **L** scratched on their foreheads; blood dribbled into their eyes from the gouges. "May I hazard a guess what insufferable bitch marks even her own if they fail?"

"*Insufferable bitch*, rather gave it away," Emperor drawled, although his dark gaze didn't leave Break.

"What does the **L** stand for?" *How did I know that I wouldn't want to know the answer?*

"Loser," Emperor relied.

"Childish," Mischief sniffed.

"Literally," Emperor gritted out. "The good-natured tradition is that the loser of each bout has to wear their shame, until it heals.

*Now something that I wanted to know the answer to even less...*

"How many times has Bitch Break worn **L** on her head?"

Emperor tapped his chin as if in thought. "*Hmm*...never."

*Freaking fabulous.*

Moon gave my neck one final lick, before stepping back. When his gaze met mine, it was determined and brave, filling me with the same courage.

When Break slipped out of her robes and prowled to the center of the arena, her Alphas fell silent. I stretched out as if the exercises that I'd been taught in gym class were going to intimidate an Alpha warrior. I could try out my martial arts again, right? I'd only made Mischief and Ramiel laugh last time I'd tried but without my shadows, what other moves did I have?

I hadn't trained as a warrior; I was an artist. My strength was in my magic and my pack, and Break had stolen both of those from me.

"Sorry, but you need to sit this one out." When I tapped Okami's nose, he howled, and bit into my dress like if he didn't let go with his silky teeth, I'd have to take him into the arena with me. "I want you by my side as well, but the rules say no magic."

Okami had been my friend since I'd created him as a kid; he'd been as much my comfort as Combat had been Emperor's. Was Combat as real for Emperor? I hated to reject Okami, but this was one battle that I needed to face without magic.

When Okami whined, I winced.

Then Ramiel held out his wing. "I too wish to fight for my savior but can't. There'll be other battles, and then we shall show them what true warriors we are."

Okami gave my shoulder a final bite, before darting to Ramiel and flattening against his wing like a silver patch on the violet.

I strolled out to meet Break, hiding my fear, whilst both Hope's Alphas and the rest of the Academy circled the arena.

When Break's nails shot out, and her fangs extended, until she'd almost partially shifted, I tilted my chin with false bravado, even if my knees felt like they'd been melted to jello.

*Come on Crimson, find your inner wolf...or think wild and wolfie thoughts...like how sexy my tail felt...*

I hissed in frustration. It would've been useful if my Wolf Liberator side had decided to change me into a Crimson Wolf but apparently that was only to save kingdoms and not my own ass.

I don't know why. My ass was epic.

At Break's growl, I realized that I hadn't been paying attention to my imminent ass kicking, which was considered bad form.

I raised my eyebrow. "So, no weapons, but you're allowed claws and fangs. I'm calling serious unfair advantage."

Break snarled through her fangs, "And I'm calling the start of our fight."

"*Wait*," I hollered. When Break blinked at me in confusion, I hesitated because I hadn't expected her to listen to me, but if fangs and claws were allowed, then I *did* have them in my Charms. "A Charmer doesn't fight alone, and neither does a Wolf Witch."

When I turned and nodded at Moon, his eyes lit up like I'd just offered him the best gift that he'd ever received. Perhaps, I had. His radiant smile with its warm respect was the one that I was now definitely addicted to, just like I'd known would happen when I'd chosen him in the Omega Training Center.

Amadeus *whooped*. "It pleases the Charmer to have our sexy behinds by her side."

Emperor's claws and fangs extended, and his eyes glowed dangerously.

When my three Charms stalked to stand by my side, I'd never felt stronger, and I hadn't wrapped them in my red, but drawn them to me by their free will alone.

*They weren't puppets but powerful princes.*

If I'd been Break, I'd have been whimpering. Instead, she reddened with outrage.

"How dare you risk Omegas in a battle?" She spluttered.

"Be silent," Moon commanded with such nobility that Break's mouth snapped shut. "We're Charms, princes and kings, *and we've chosen to risk ourselves*."

Break's expression hardened. "Then I'll scratch **L** on your pretty heads, just the same as your idiot witch's."

My guts clenched. I'd never let Break touch my Charms.

Yet just as she readied to pounce, I glimpsed Aquilo clutch his wrist, before he staggered to his knees.

*The blood bracelet was hurting him.*

Bats and broomsticks, how long had Aquilo been in pain and hiding it? How urgent was this wedding, and yet because of the conditioning by his family that he was *invisible* and worth nothing, Aquilo hadn't pushed his own needs, prioritizing the rest of the pack, instead.

*Was that why he'd been acting off for the last week?*

"Jesus, there's something wrong with Aquilo. We need to get back to him," I hissed to my Charms.

Moon's eyes widened, whilst Amadeus' gaze focused on Break with a wicked glint.

Emperor nodded. "Then it will my honor and pleasure to make this quick."

Break squawked in shock when my three Charms prowled towards her like death, war, and vengeance wrapped up in sexy packages. She spun around, swiping at them, but she'd become the prey.

My Charms moved like they'd always been meant to hunt together.

*Like they were pack.*

Holy hell, a rebel, an assassin, and a Cursed

Alpha…and when they fought together because they'd chosen to defend me, they were both deadly and scorching hot.

"Lie down," Emperor growled. The Alphas on both sides of the circle watched in intent silence. Emperor glanced up to meet Sterling's eye. "Didn't you enjoy this fun game, when you were playing it with your assistant and me? Lie down and don't move, whilst we *play*."

Break scanned the Alphas, as if they'd protect her. Instead, they gawked at the sight of *Omegas — and their Omega prince —* threatening the principal of the Academy, who'd terrorized him for decades.

Break slashed at Amadeus, but he leapt back with a dancer's speed. He dodged behind Break, before snatching her arm and twisting it behind her back. She hollered, but then Moon grabbed her other arm and forced her to lie on the ground. Her eyes were wide with shock at his strength.

It must've sucked for her to realize that Omegas and Betas weren't weak after all.

Break thrashed and snarled, as Emperor leaned over her. "Three against one: *I'm calling unfair advantage*."

When I sauntered closer, she flinched. "Do you feel powerless, helpless, and shamed?" I glanced at the wolves with **L**'s carved on their heads, who were avidly watching. "Honestly, I thought you built this arena to teach the Alphas to feel that way. How else would you keep them under your power? But they can choose to break free like we did." Half my audience didn't look swayed, but the other half looked ready to break the chains as surely as their emblem on the wall. I leaned closer to Break. "Plus, wasn't it why you were such an asshole to this kingdom's prince and my brother? But despite that, who's the loser now?"

Emperor dropped to his knee next to Break. When he hovered his nail over her forehead like he was about to mark her with an **L**, Hope's gang burst into laughter.

Emperor glanced over his shoulder at his sister, whose gaze was understanding. Emperor shuddered, but then retracted his claw.

"I shan't ever be like you, Dame Break." He stood, dusting off his knees. "You're a loser, and everyone in the academy can see it. I don't need to lower myself to your methods to prove it."

Moon patted Emperor's shoulder. "Aye, the Alphas can all see us...*and her*...for what we are now."

My heart ached with joy, and my shadows entangled with Moon's silver magic. Amadeus wound himself around Emperor, kissing him to vanish his somber scowl.

When Aquilo gasped with pain, however, I dashed across the arena on a wave of my shadows, crouching by his side. My eyes smarted with tears.

I hated that Aquilo had felt he had to hide his hurt

from me. Could I get in just one good shake of my *too brave for his own good* fiancé?

Aquilo brushed his sweaty bangs out of his eyes (*did he have a fever too?*), before wetting his dry lips. "I'm not—"

"I don't think so." When I pressed my hand to his forehead, he shivered. *Witches above, he was burning up.* "I'm done with your dicking around. Was I meant to notice that something was wrong with my psychic powers? Or did you think it wouldn't matter to me that you're... What in sweet Hecate's name *is* wrong?"

Aquilo tilted his head, assessing me, even as he allowed me to card my fingers through his hair. "What do you wish me to answer first?" When I raised my eyebrow, he sighed. "All right, I'm only a male, property, and bound to you though magical engagement. Didn't you know that there'd be repercussions if we didn't marry quickly? The bracelet took the delay to be hesitation and displeasure with me on your behalf. In such cases, the male is punished in the hopes of encouraging the marriage or..." His gaze slid away from mine. "...Hastening a decision on the breaking of the engagement."

"And killing *you*, right?"

His smile was fragile. "I am the property."

"You're the freaking man who I love. You'll never be property." I wrapped my hands around the blood bracelet, staring at it in shock.

The bracelet throbbed scarlet and was hot to the touch. When I pushed up Aquilo's sleeve, however, I hissed in shock. The scarlet had bled out like an infection in his blood into tendrils that trailed up his arm.

"Eventually, they shall reach my heart." Aquilo's eyes were crushed ice; his voice was carefully cold. "It shall stop my heart because you haven't married me."

I drew away my hands like the bracelet had burned me. I fought to control my ragged breathing.

I could've murdered Aquilo, and he'd had the method of his own execution creeping up from his wrist the whole time.

I clasped my hand around Aquilo's neck, pulling him until my lips rested against his. "Trust me, I'll never allow that to happen. I'm sorry that your mom put that nightmare on you because of me but I'm not sorry that I asked you to marry me. Do you still want to get married?"

Aquilo's lips caressed mine, as he smiled. "More than anything that I've ever dreamed." *I'd take that.* But then, he frowned. "Only the Head of the Coven can marry us, and your Charm devoured her."

"Oh, I'm aware that I kicked my aunt's ass and then left the witch world in a mess. I'm going to sort that out now, which is why we both need to pay your sister a visit."

Aquilo stiffened, drawing back from me. "Lux is too dangerous."

"I'm the Wolf Charmer who killed the last Head of the Coven. She should be scared of me."

Aquilo snorted. "Good luck with that."

Aquilo knew his sister better than anyone, and the House of Blood had been the site of my childhood torment. I had no choice but to risk stepping back into the witches' world, however, and facing Lux.

Otherwise, Aquilo would be poisoned through his own blood, until his heart stopped beating.

## CHAPTER 22

The House of Blood was just as opulent a witches' house as I remembered, and creeping into it under the rays of the moon was just as frightening. Only, this time I wasn't investigating a mage's murder but requesting to marry one.

*Why did the two things feel the same?*

Perhaps because Aquilo would die if I couldn't convince his older sister that being married to me would be better for him than death...? I mean, it wasn't like I was the kid who she'd despised and bullied our entire childhoods... *Okay, it was exactly like that.*

When I sighed, Okami whined and settled more comfortably around my neck. He was the only one of my guys who Aurora had agreed could accompany me along with Aquilo out of Wolf Kingdom.

*Hello, trust issues...?*

Moon had assured me that he'd *hunt me and then bite my behind* if I didn't come back, at the same time as Mischief had backed Aquilo into a corner with one hot but intimidating sweep of his wings and told him the same thing, just with longer words.

Was it weird that I was starting to understand wolf romance? Mischief was simply the godly version.

I clasped Aquilo's hand, which was damp from fever, just as his hair was plastered to his burning forehead. He forced himself to smile at me. His expression was tight, and considering that he'd grown up here, only to have his magic painfully bound once he'd became a mage, go figure. I knew that he'd loved his family, despite how they'd treated him.

*He'd lost them to help my pack and me.*

When Aquilo and I had squelched along the bank of the stinking Thames, he'd been quiet and withdrawn. He'd stumbled, shivering with the chills and agony of the blood bracelet's corruption but too proud to ask for my help, even though my shadows had supported him anyway.

In the shadow of House of Blood's towering gates, he'd placed his hands over the carved orbiting planets, and spun eddies of air into the wards to deactivate them. The last time that I'd broken into the coven, I'd been stalked by stone wolves and covered in blood because I'd set off the alarm.

*At least I wouldn't have to face Lux dripping in blood this time...*

"Do we have to sneak in the back way as if we're servants?" Aquilo had asked as he'd pressed his hands to the gate.

"*Hmm*, we could knock and allow Lux the chance to, I don't know, hex our asses," I'd scoffed. "Why don't we give her time to set a trap or ambush us because no witch has *ever* done *that* to me before or—"

Aquilo had snorted. "I'll take that as a yes." Then his eyes had sparkled. "If we're servants, I could always play the maid."

When I'd let out a choked sound, Aquilo had laughed.

*Okay, that wasn't an image I'd forget...ever...*

Now, Aquilo and I crept through the upper floor of the House of Blood towards Lux's bedroom. The shadowed corridor echoed to the emotional R & B ballad "I'll Make Love to You," which bled from Lux's bedroom.

I wrinkled my nose. "Boyz II Men, seriously?"

Aquilo rolled his eyes. "My sister had this whole *phase*: posters on her wall and these dolls of the band who she'd kiss and…" He shuddered.

I hadn't thought that anything could be scarier than Lux in her severe black dress and corset with her sadist vibe, but the thought of her snuggled in bed, listening to the crooning of Boyz II Men, whilst smooching their dolls was a cauldron full of scary.

Except, what if she was smooching someone who wasn't a doll…? Was that better or worse?

When I pressed my shoulder to the door but hesitated, Aquilo caught my eye.

"Do you imagine that this is easier for me?" He hissed. "My sister wasn't expected to remain as innocent as me." He flushed, and in turn, so did I because the way that the blush stained from his neck to his chest made me want to lick every inch of his skin. "Plus, her tastes have always veered towards the kinky. She's a member of Witches Who Swing."

I blinked at him. "That's a thing?"

Aquilo caged me against the door. Only, he was also shaking, and more in the way that made me wish to tuck him up in bed with medicine and a blanket, than rip off his clothes. "Why would a witch need their services who already has the love of a mage, god, angel, and wolves?"

*Well, put like that…?*

I kissed him, slow and gentle because even now he needed the reassurance. "I don't."

Aquilo nodded, then he added his shoulder to the door as well, and we pushed at the same time.

I gritted my teeth against the sugary music, as well as the coppery tang of blood. The walls of the bedroom were hung with the white wolf pelts of murdered

Omegas. When I marched further into the room, I grimaced as my feet sank into a wolf fur rug. I'd forgotten just how much I hated being in a witch world that saw the death of wolves as decoration.

Lux sat up on the bed; her eyes blazed with outrage. It was weird to see her dressed in a loose black t-shirt that skirted her ass. I'd expected a lace nightgown at least. She was Aquilo's twin but also his opposite: her hair was as black as her t-shirt. Then she shifted to the side, and I noticed the...*naked guy*...stretched out next to her with his arms above his head.

Aquilo squeaked, turning around on his heel to face the wall. Huh, I hadn't realized that he could blush any redder. That was seriously cute.

Okami flew off my shoulder to wrap around Aquilo's eyes like a blindfold.

Lux scrutinized me. "What an unusual Charmer you are." I forced myself not to shudder, even as her voice slipped over me like oil. "Did I forget that I'd invited you both into my bedroom?"

"Oh, you so didn't and please, don't ever put it like that again." When I stepped closer, I couldn't help the glance at the guy in her bed because boy, was his muscled ebony body stunning.

Then the silk sheets fell away, and I gasped. The guy's large gray wings spread out.

*Lux was screwing a vampire?* But they were the

350

witches' enemies. I knew that because it was one of the first rules that you learned in the House of Silver.

There was only one vampire who'd fought on my side, until the Kingdom of the Gods had forced him to back down because they held his son, Digby, prisoner.

All of a sudden, my breath hitched, and my heart raced.

*Witches dancing in the moonlight, could it be Duke Dual...? And why did it fill me with such intense longing like he was one of my lovers?*

I stumbled backwards, clutching Aquilo to jerk him around, just as Okami whipped away from his eyes to hover over the bed.

"I have no wish to see a stranger's dick, especially one who's sleeping with my sister..." Aquilo muttered.

It wasn't his dick, however, that Aquilo and I stared at, however, but the sexy softness of Dual's eyes.

Aquilo and I both stepped forward at the same time, but it was Aquilo who demanded, "Are you insane? I escape to your court, but you'd willingly do...*this*...with my sister?"

"*Ow*, the blue-eyed slayer." Dual grinned. "And as much as I'm into kinky, I wouldn't say *willing*."

When Dual attempted to lower his arms, chains *clanked.* He couldn't raise from the bed or change his position because of shackles that'd been hidden by the pillows. Then he hissed, as the metal seared him as punishment for his escape attempt.

"Stop hurting him," I hollered. "What kind of dick-head are you that you need to chain a guy to your bed to screw him or snog a doll because no one else wants your scrawny ass?"

Lux slid off the bed and stalked towards me; my shadows vibrated around me in fury. "What little you think of me."

"She has this obsession with consent, permission, and choice." Aquilo studied his sister. "I know that it's unusual amongst witches."

Lux's eyes narrowed. "Not all and not now. I wouldn't touch the duke in that way because it'd be like two tigers fighting for dominance."

"But you'd chain him to your bed, right?" I raised my eyebrow.

Lux looked at me like *I* was the dummy. "Well, of course. If he chooses to break in…"

I shot my shadows across Dual, who squirmed uncomfortably under my hard gaze. "Dude, sniffing around a witches' house again…? Is this like a fetish for you?"

When Dual arched his back and chuckled, the rainbow beads threaded through his hair *clicked*. "Perhaps, I have a thing about sniffing witches."

I prowled closer to the edge of the bed, encircling my fingers over the still warm shackle that'd burned his wrist. "Perhaps, you have a thing about being captured."

His gaze was intense, and his voice low; I shivered. "Only if you rescue me."

"I apologize, am I interrupting?" Lux sneered. "It's just that I'm about to choke on the sexual tension."

When Aquilo snickered, Lux stared at him like his laugh was a sound that she'd rarely heard and ached to. Then her arms were around him and she was hugging him hard enough to make him squirm.

"Is he ill? Why have you not been caring for him properly, Charmer? Why is he so hot?" She pressed her hand to his head, as he wriggled to escape, before crushing him to her again like he was a precious lost doll who'd been returned. "I imagined that you'd never wish to see me again," she whispered.

Aquilo blinked. "You called me the wind. You told me that I should never be seen or heard. You said that it would've been better if I'd never been born."

Reluctantly, Lux drew back. "I was wrong. I knew it as soon as our mother magically engaged you to *her*…" The look that she threw me was venomous. "…and then after, when she tried to kill you. If I hadn't been able to save you, then I'd rather that we'd both died."

Aquilo's gaze became icy. "The Ambassador saved me: An *Omega*. Do you not see that the wolves are no longer our enemy? I shan't ever see you again if you torture or kill a single other wolf."

Holy hell, that was some ultimatum for the asshole

353

who'd spent a lifetime in the House of Blood, which prided itself on training and flaying Omegas.

Would Lux truly choose her mage brother over her legacy? But then, I'd chosen my new family over my own past.

Lux froze, before her finger stroked Aquilo's cheek. He flinched like he expected a smack.

"Well, you've grown a tongue on you," Lux pondered.

"I'd say balls," Dual offered.

Lux's lips pinched. "Why should I worry about his balls? After all, his fiancée controls those."

"Dude, enough." My shadows painted the white pelts crimson. "My blokes don't need controlling, and I get it, you don't like me, but suck it up because this marriage needs to happen or your little brother is dead." Dual flinched as much as Lux. *Did he love Aquilo as well?* "Honestly, you should be most worried about other witches like your mom. Where is she?"

Lux's eyes flashed with a dark viciousness. "We played Hide and Seek." Then she grinned, and I knew what true darkness looked like. "And I found her."

My mouth was suddenly too dry, and I swallowed with difficulty. Okay, I so wasn't going to ask anything more about that.

"I'm serious about marrying Aquilo," I insisted. "But the blood bracelet is killing him, and we need it to be now. Show her your arm."

Aquilo rolled up his sleeve, and Lux gasped. She traced her finger over the throbbing scarlet that wound up from his wrist. Then her eyes narrowed at me.

"So, it's not a trick?" She cocked her head. "You don't intend to kill my twin to get back at me for everything that I did to you when we were children? You do love him?"

I startled. Mage's dick on a stick, that's what she'd thought all this time? That'd I'd hold her brother's life over her as revenge? *Had Aquilo thought that too, no matter what I'd told him?*

By the way that he shuffled his feet, even as he sought out my gaze, I'd go with *holy hell, yeah.*

Yet even so, he'd fought by my side and risked his life. He might be a prickly elitist on the outside, but he was one brave mage.

"I love him, I want to marry him, and he's pack." I glanced between brother and sister. "I was never tricking either of you." The relief on both of their faces made me remember just how twisted they'd been raised. At least I'd had the last decade in America amongst non-magicals and only now did I understand how lucky I'd truly been. "Let's start with taking away the chains that are around Dual because tied up isn't a good look amongst friends, unless, you know, it's all negotiated and in fun."

Lux stalked to the bed and ran her hand over the shackles, which vanished. "The Fallen are not friends."

"He's *my* friend." Aquilo tilted his chin defiantly.

Dual grinned, pushing himself up and stretching his wings. "You tell her, Blue Eyes."

I wrenched Dual's head back by his hair, and he moaned as his eyes became half-lidded. "Seriously, why are you here?"

Dual pulled out of my hold, spinning me on the bed to pin me down. Warmth curled inside me at his touch, and I dragged him closer by my shadows. I smiled, as his lips pressed to mine. When his fang caught my lower lip, he groaned at the taste of my blood.

*Witching hell*, that shouldn't have made me tingle like I'd been caressed all over.

Finally, Dual drew back, and I was aware that we both had an audience, as Okami flew between both twins, flattening against their eyes like blindfolds. I laughed.

"I heard a rumor about the Kingdom of the Gods," Dual murmured. His grip on my arms tightened. "It'd appear that a certain incubus of yours now sits on the throne…a mongrel."

I stiffened. *Well, that was one way to chase away the tinglies.* "Don't call Amadeus that."

Dual licked along the broken skin of my lower lip, sucking. Then his dark gaze met mine again with fragile honesty. "How can I see it as an insult, when my son is one?" Dual's face lit up with hope. "Did you meet Digby?"

I nodded, but how could I tell Dual that his son had been kept in a cage, and had only been saved by Jax's sacrifice?

"Digby's just as cute as you." I nipped the end of Dual's nose.

Dual flapped his wings, until we were covered in their dark and hidden from the others. "I'm never cute; I'm a vampire duke with my own court. My son is an earl. I'm certain that he was dignified and…"

Dual stared at me bewildered, when I snickered. "But he's safe…?"

"Yeah, like all the mongrels now."

Dual rested his fangs against my neck but didn't break the skin. Then he said, "The wolves held what was most precious to me, and so I didn't dare to fight with you. Now I'll battle, tear down the wolves' world, and then claim my sexy princes and mage, of course."

"I can hear you…and so can my sister," Aquilo's embarrassed voice called.

"Excellent to know that your hearing hasn't been damaged by the atrocious music that your sister plays." Dual waggled his ass.

"I can hear you too," Lux reminded, coolly, "and am willing to smack that rude arse."

Dual's eyes sparked. "I know that, witch." Then he whispered, "I intend not only for my son to join our family, but I'm generous enough to have room for that glittery god and his angel. They'd fit well on my lap."

I spluttered with laughter, twisting Dual, until he was splayed out on the bed next to me.

Ramiel and Mischief both perched on Dual's lap was way up on the list of things that were never going to happen, but I wasn't so cruel that I wouldn't let Dual dream.

"So, what can we do about the bracelet?" I gestured at Aquilo's arm.

At last, Okami flew back to me with a satisfied huff.

Lux studied me. "You can marry him. But to do that, you need the Head of the Coven, and you killed *her*."

I took a deep breath. "What's to stop me making *myself* Head?"

Dual clapped his hands. "Spoken just like a Fallen. You snatch that power, witch."

"Wolf Charmers can't be Head." When Lux sauntered towards me, I noticed that the walls were tinged with scarlet, and it wasn't my shadows but *her* blood magic.

*Witching heavens, did she mean to fight me for the position?*

"Let me guess: because it's tradition, right? Look, I'm not making a power grab," I promised. "I only care about saving Aquilo."

"Then make *me* Head of the Oxford Covens. The House of Blood has long been the most powerful House." Lux's eyes blazed with the same ambition as her mom's. *What the holy hell had I done?* This was my childhood bully and the sadist who'd hurt Omegas for years. Could I make her Head, even to save Aquilo? When I hesitated, she insisted, "With your backing, I can stop the chaos that's threatening to tear apart Oxford. I know that you were raised in ignorance but believe me when I tell you that uncontrolled covens are much more dangerous than *controlled* ones."

Aquilo met my gaze. "I trust her."

When Lux's eyes gleamed with tears, that was answer enough for me. Our gazes met, and with it an understanding of *both* our love for Aquilo.

"Firstly, you won't harm any more wolves because we're renegotiating the Treaty that was created after the Wolf War, and secondly, I don't give a witch's tit about tradition, the way that witches treat non-magical men and mages is messed-up. You'll help me change it."

Lux held her out her hand. "Agreed."

It wasn't as difficult as I'd thought it'd be to stroll to her and take the hand of my greatest bully as my new ally.

"It'll take me a day to ensure everyone falls into line," Lux's grin was fiendish (*okay, it helped not to think about her methods*), "and tonight, I'll marry you to my brother."

When Aquilo pulled *me* into a hug for once, my shadows wrapped around him with surprised joy. He shook, clutching me as hard as his sister had clasped him, like he'd never let go and as if he at least believed that I truly would marry him.

*Witching hell, tomorrow night I'd marry Aquilo.*

I kissed his neck, burrowing even closer. Yet to save Aquilo, I had to trust both the witch and wolf world to his violent sister.

# CHAPTER 23

Q ueen Aurora smashed me against the glass
wall in the Emperor Suite with a *clank*, which
rang through my ears and throbbing head.
The butterflies inside trembled. Perhaps, I should've
been worried more about Emperor's wolf mom, than
Aquilo's witch sister.

On the other hand, perhaps there wasn't that much
difference between the two. Except, Lux loved her
brother and didn't want him to die, whereas Aurora,
Queen of Assholes, had wanted to savage her son at
birth because he was Cursed, and the way that her fangs
grazed my throat told me that she hadn't changed her
neck savaging ways, you know?

The dawn light had been breaking over the dome
and winking against the tower by the time that I'd stumbled back into the Kingdom of the Alphas, struggling to

drag Aquilo with me, who'd given up the pretense of not needing my help to walk. Dual had supported him on the other side, and Okami had lain himself as a silk cloth over Aquilo's forehead to cool him. Then a gang of apologetic Alphas (who I guessed had to be Hope's gang), had dragged Aquilo to the side.

Dual had shot out his claws about to defend Aquilo, but I'd shaken my head. Then Dual had allowed himself to be manhandled next to Aquilo, clasping him in his wings.

The lead Alpha had told me that I'd been summoned — *alone* — to Aurora.

Yet Aurora had left me alone, waiting for her, all day until evening. The moon had been shining through the windows, when she'd finally marched into the suite.

*Clank* — Aurora slammed my head against the glass again, and I groaned.

My shadows tore out of me, painting the suite crimson, as if the sun had aged.

"I know what you did," Aurora snarled.

"Last summer…?" I smirked.

Hope lounged on the sofa, but there were shadows under her eyes like she was exhausted or in pain.

*Who'd hurt her?*

I didn't expect the harshness of her glare. *Didn't she like pop culture jokes?*

When Aurora raised her fangs from my neck, leaning her hands either side of my head, her aroma of sunflowers choked me; the sharpness beneath was stronger than before.

"Don't you imagine that every wolf in all three kingdoms sensed it, even your Charms? It's agonizing to be poisoned with silver. But then, Charmers have always loved these collars and the wall, which the witches linked with their fiendish magic." Aurora's hand hovered over her own collar like she was desperate to claw it away from her throat and was only stopped by the fact that it'd poison her again if she touched it.

My Charms had been tortured by their collars? *Every wolf had been?* Well, that explained Hope's pained look.

I fought the urge to shoot my shadows through Aurora and toss her to one side so that I could race to my pack and check that they were safe.

Instead, I insisted, "I'd never poison any wolf with silver. I hate those jerk collars and I'd remove them if I could."

Aurora's eyes narrowed. "By my hide, I wonder if any wretched witch can understand what it means to be free of the prisons that we're forced to wear every day." She sighed. "It wasn't you, I know that. It's automatic on the election of a new Head of the Covens to assert their authority. Tell me, you wouldn't have done something so foolish…?"

When I glanced at Hope she was looking just as grave as her mom.

I licked my lips. "You know that *instability in the witch world* that you kicked my ass over? It's solved, and you're welcome."

Hope rolled her eyes, at the same time as Aurora slammed her hand against the glass. I hated that I was standing where Emperor had been forced to brace himself for punishment.

"*All this over a mage's dick,*" Aurora hissed.

I shrugged. "Yeah, but you should see his dick."

*Dumb mouth…*

Aurora's eyes flashed, as she raised her claw to my neck, but then Hope laughed.

Aurora's gaze shot to Hope. "I forget: My daughter has a thing for mages too."

I froze. *What did the crafty edge to Aurora's voice mean (and why did I have a feeling that it'd bite me in the ass)?*

Hope shoved herself up with too much urgency for her casual tone to be anything but an attempt to cover up the truth, "Guilty."

*Son of a bitch*, Hope was…*something*…with my brother?

The surge of sudden protectiveness hit me like my brother and I had never been parted. My shadows surged towards Hope, even as she scrambled backwards, pinning her to the sofa.

"Your loser ass had better not be hurting Sterling…" My eyes flashed silver.

"Did I say that *he* has a thing for hot wolf princesses as well?" Hope panted.

"Sickeningly, it's true." Aurora eyed me, before shoving away and hauling Hope to her feet, as I dragged back my shadows, which coiled around me in angry swirls. "As is the simple fact that you appear to have chosen the only House who's hated more than your own to become Head." I winced. The Kingdom of the Alphas were diplomats, and holy hell, if anyone knew both our legacies, it was Aurora. "By the furless heavens, your pitiable peacekeeping attempts don't concern me. My kingdom shall always be the strongest, and my academy has trained an army for centuries. If you've granted the House of Blood power, then you've ensured the Second Wolf War."

I stared at her, ashen. I'd battled to save both the wolves and witches, but was I as bad as my ancestors? Was it impossible to escape my Wolf Charmer legacy?

*Despite everything, would a Second Wolf War still be my fault?*

I shook my head. "If you choose to fight, *you're* the one who'll be condemning the innocents again. You *watched* the massacres last time. You were there with your kids." Hope was paler than me and couldn't meet my eye. "How could you put them through that again?"

Aurora lifted up her chin. "Who says that this time *we* won't be the ones doing the massacring?"

My breath caught. *Yeah, because that was better.* "Please, stop being an asshole and—"

Aurora strode to the far wall, gazing down on her kingdom. "Such ingratitude, especially when I've just bought you a gift." The way that her mouth twitched slyly on the *gift*, had my fists clenching because somehow, I knew that it wouldn't be an espresso machine. She waved towards the glass corridor that led through to my Penthouse Bedroom. "The Om Prince of the Wilds is guarding it." She smacked her lips like even Moon's name was toxic. "Your other wolves and angels have been taken on a tour of the kingdom by Pumpkin. He was most insistent and when he's in those moods, I admit that I indulge the sweetheart."

I narrowed my eyes. *What was Pumpkin plotting?* "Why was Moon left behind?"

Aurora glanced over her shoulder at me; her eyes glittered maliciously. "The Om was worn out from Dame Break's demonstrations on him in the academy."

I growled, surging towards her. Why had I trusted that my pack would be safe here? I would tear this empire down, just like Dual had promised.

Aurora merely sighed. "Don't you want to see your gift? I'm certain that Om has had time to study your creations and understand what type of witch you truly are beneath the soft words and lies."

*No, no, no... Jesus, she hadn't...*

"What in witching hell did you do?" I demanded.

"Did you know that Stella told your uncle and cousins in America that you'd died?" Aurora smiled, as I doubled over. *So, that was what it felt like to be gut punched.* My uncle and cousins must be grieving, just like I'd grieved for my parents. I was going to hurl. "Interesting how single skins think. I believe that she wanted to ensure you couldn't return to your non-magical life. Your gallery was closed. How strange for a Charmer to paint, as if she needed an escape from real life. Is this one not exciting enough for you?"

*My aunt had taken everything from me.* But I'd taken back the control, creating my own pack and legacy. I wouldn't allow anyone to destroy that now.

Aurora flinched, when I stared her down. "I don't paint to escape life; I paint to set myself free."

Aurora's smile was creepy assed; my skin crawled. "I wonder if your Charm will be set free by it. I bought as many of your belongings and the paintings, before they could be sold off, and had them shipped here. They arrived this morning; they're in the penthouse. No thanks necessary."

Holy hell, *she'd left Moon alone with my paintings.*

Aurora's grin was wide and cruel, although Hope's head was ducked.

*How much did the queen hate Moon?*

I slammed my red into Aurora on instinct, *clanking* her head against the glass, as I darted down the corridor towards Moon. But would it be too late? As soon as he saw my paintings, which I'd drawn as part of my therapy ever since my parent's murder, *he'd* hate *me…*

I shuddered because I no longer recognized the witch who I'd been: the one who blamed every wolf for the massacre in the House of Silver, where my parents had been murdered.

My breath caught in desperate sobs. I shoved against the heavy door, stumbling through into the penthouse. The far wall fluttered with its purple butterfly wings, and the golden bed was empty. The floor, however, was a mess of canvases, which were reflected endlessly in the glass.

My shadows howled at the sight of the painted werewolves in agony under the moonlight.

I've never wanted to take something back so much, but that's not the way life worked because it sucked.

Instead, the wolf who I loved and desired to kiss and never kill was kneeling surrounded by my canvases of werewolves in agony. I'd painted my hate, and I couldn't bear that now he saw it displayed raw like this. What made it any different to the murals in the House of Seasons that boasted of the witches' massacres in the Wolf War?

I'd been the *monster* that Moon had always feared he'd be Claimed by, but I'd changed.

*Please, please, please let my Moon Child believe me…*

Moon studied a painting intently, before bending to

trace over a white wolf — *an Omega* — who was crying.

When Jeff Buckley's haunting "Hallelujah" stuck up from my iPod speakers, which Aurora must've shipped over along with the other things that'd been left behind in my studio where I'd worked, I shivered. Every hair stood up on the back of my neck because it was like the ghost of my past blowing down my neck.

I'd sat on my stool at the studio in East Hampton, whilst the beauty of "Hallelujah"'s guitars and soaring vocal had spun its web around me, and created death.

*Sweet Hecate, please don't let Moon hate me...*

Moon startled at my choked off cry, as I threw myself into the penthouse, which was flooded with moonbeams. I leaned down, spinning the canvas that was he was touching away from him. I didn't want my past...like his own...to poison him, just like Mischief had once warned that all witches did. Then I stamped on the canvas with a *crack* that echoed through the penthouse.

Moon cried out, and the butterfly wings on the wall quivered.

My shadows flooded out of me in my grief and guilt, as I stamped on the canvases — *crack, crack, crack* — but when I leaned down and snatched one up to shred it with my freaking nails if I had to, Moon stood up and gently took it from me.

*When had my hands started shaking?*

Moon tossed the canvas onto the bed without looking at it. Instead, his gaze was focused on me, and for a moment, I was terrified to meet it, in case it no longer held the love and respect that I'd become so addicted to.

*It wasn't like I deserved it.*

Yet Moon shook his head, pulling me closer, until his curls brushed my cheek. "Goddess Moon! Enough of that. Did you forget that we were enemies once? But now you're my Charmer, and I'm you're Wolf Bitten. Don't you think that I need to see you too?"

"How can you love…?"

Moon growled in frustration, silencing me by pressing his lush lips to mine in a kiss that was a claiming and a surrender.

My eyes widened, and my body tingled down to my curling toes because *Moon was kissing me at last.*

I wound my arms around his neck, stroking his curls, as his tongue played across mine, and I moaned. The kiss was everything that I'd dreamed and longed for all these weeks but it was also something more: *it was trust.*

Moon had seen the worst of me, and he'd chosen still to make himself vulnerable in the most intimate way.

Aurora's hate had pushed us closer together, rather than driven us apart.

Moon panted, deepening the kiss, until I panted too.

His lips were soft, but his passion was as fiery as Amadeus'. Then as Jeff Buckley with grace and sacrifice sang Moon and I to heaven, Moon growled and broke the kiss, only to kiss my neck and all the way down my body until he paused between my thighs. Then he shoved me backwards, catching me as we fell and twisted amongst the broken paintings.

Moon pushed up the skirt of my dress. His eyes dilated with desire, and his hard-on rubbed against my thigh.

I shook, desperate for Moon's touch, as he pulled aside my panties to kiss me, before glancing at me from underneath his eyelashes.

*Holy hell, I needed him inside me now.*

My shadows caressed down Moon's shoulders and ass, tugging at him, before tweaking his nipples into peaks.

Moon's eyes twinkled at me, as he slid up me in retaliation, nipping my stomach, rubbing his thumbs across my tits, before licking my neck. I slipped my hand along the hem of his pants, teasing his dick through the leather. He arched and whined.

Then I guided his hips towards mine because he was my first Charm, *and he'd freaking kissed me at last.* I never wanted him to stop kissing me. Our magic wound out; silver and red entangled to cocoon us. I shuddered as Moon's stroked over mine, just as my shadows stroked his. Around us, the canvases quaked in the grip of our power.

I gripped Moon's chin, and he smiled, before lowering his mouth to mine like it was now the most natural thing in the world (*kissing therapy: I could get behind that*).

All of a sudden, the music shut off. Instead, screams exploded from the iPod.

*What in the ever-witching hell...?*

That was one way to kill the mood. Why did the screams sound so familiar? There was no way on earth that this death track was on my playlist.

*Please, no... death track...? Was this a recording from my parents' massacre in the House of Silver?*

When I cowered, shaking, Moon sheltered me in his arms. His expression was fierce, but he was paler than I was almost like the screams had thrown him back into the same memory as me.

"As the Alpha speaks, this Om has always poisoned everything with a kiss." When Aurora's voice boomed over the noise, I could've stamped on her like I had the canvases because Moon tried to pull back from me like he believed her.

Moon's kisses were epic, however, and I wouldn't let her steal them away from him again.

"You're the asshole who poisons," I snarled. "It won't work, you know. There's nothing that you can say or do that would make us hate each other."

Moon sighed like I was a dummy for having jinxed us.

Aurora's voice was smug, "You can't mean to say that you don't recognize this soundtrack? After all, you lived through it."

My hands clenched, and I closed my eyes, struggling to breathe.

Holy hell, I wished that I didn't but of course I did when I'd been so traumatized by the night of my mom and dad's murder in the ruby ballroom that I'd spent the next decade taking it out on painted werewolves.

"What is this?" I whispered. "A pop quiz."

Aurora *tutted*. "I always imagined that you'd wish revenge on your mom's killer, but you've been tamed by the tricks of our sweet Oms, haven't you?"

My eyes snapped open, as my red yanked back from Moon in hissing fury. "What?"

Aurora's voice echoed through the penthouse, "This recording is taken from the collar of an Om who was present at the murder of your parents. I wonder how many witches he killed. After all, his mother murdered *yours*. Tell me, did you enjoy kissing the wolf who you promised to hunt and slaughter?"

I recoiled from Moon, staring at him in shock, but he merely ducked his head, before nodding.

I'd planned my revenge on my family's killers for a decade and finally, I knew that Moon was guilty.

## CHAPTER 24

Moon scrambled away from me, until his back hit the bed in the penthouse. His thumb caught in a destroyed canvas, tearing through it with a *rip* that was shockingly loud in the silence. Even though Moon's shoulders were tight and his jaw clenched in fear, he still tilted his chin in defiance.

"Fur and fangs, just do it then." Moon's voice was raspy with tears, but he didn't drop his gaze. "Don't you remember what you told me on my first day in the House of Silver? You said that if you ever found out who the wolves were who killed your ma, *you'd kill all of them*." His smile was sad. "I didn't doubt you then, Charmer, and I don't doubt you now."

*Come on Crimson, just breathe…breathe…breathe…*

My chest was too tight, and my lungs burned. I pressed my nails into my palms because I'd ignored

Zetta and Stella, trusting the wolves over the witches, but Moon had been there on the night of the massacre all along.

*Who knew that betrayal tasted of shadows and blood?*

My crimson shot out in a tide of grief and fury, banging Moon against the bed and holding him paralyzed. He gasped, as red wound tighter around him.

An ache bloomed in my chest at Moon's resigned look like he'd only been waiting for the moment that my shadows would act against him, rather than out of love…*for when I'd turn into a Wolf Charmer just the same as mom.*

I shuddered, and my eyes screwed shut. The memory of the night that my mom and dad had been murdered flooded through me. Images of a ballroom waltzed through my mind: ruby floors, crystal chandeliers, and my parents dancing between their guests. Then they were chased away by the *clacking* of claws, the *growl* of wolves, the *screams* and *red, red, red…*

Yet in the midst of the carnage was a *white wolf*, dragging me up the staircase and then pushing me into my parents' wardrobe. Outside, the wolves howled and fought over me.

Had that white wolf been guarding me?

*Holy hell, had that white wolf who'd saved my life been Moon?*

When my eyes snapped open, I stared at Moon. He

didn't even attempt to reach out through his magic or plead for his life.

*Black candle hexes*, Moon had spent every moment in my witches' House and by my side, hiding that he was the son of the one wolf who I'd sworn to kill out of revenge and knowing that I'd kill *him* as well if I discovered the truth.

It was no wonder that he'd always tried to sacrifice himself because it must've been like living on Death Row. It was kind of no different to how he'd been trapped in the **REJECT** cell, waiting to be executed.

*He'd only wanted to save the other Omegas before he died.*

Just like that, the anger blazing through my shadows calmed to embers, and I swallowed. I crawled to Moon, tucking one of his curls behind his ear and hating that he flinched. I released him from the hold of my shadows, which stroked him comfortingly.

Moon blinked at me in confusion. "Single skins have a daft way of starting their executions."

"Stop playing the freaking martyr. Does it suck so much to imagine living with me, rather than dying?" I straddled Moon, gripping his cheeks, as I was enveloped in his warmth and citrus scent. Sweet Hecate, if I'd followed the desire for vengeance that'd driven me to paint the wolves' pain for the last decade, then I'd have destroyed this beautiful life beneath me with a snap of my red. I shuddered at the thought, wriggling closer to Moon and tugging at his magic; I needed the feel of it, as it coiled around me. "You were the white wolf that night, right? You saved me."

Moon bit his lip, before nuzzling against his favorite spot on my neck. I held him there for a long moment, desperate for the connection as much as he was.

Then he drew back, and his eyes were anguished. "I wish that I could lie because you've no idea how much it doesn't *suck* to imagine a life with you. I was the white wolf, but…I'm not perfect, pretty, or a protector. I was your enemy, and you were too quick to forget it. Fur and fangs, if you only knew…"

I tugged on Moon's curls. "Whatever you did, it happened a decade ago. I don't expect you to be any of the asshole things that the other Alphas do. Did I ever demand that you had to be *perfect*? And this may come as a huge witchy surprise, but I didn't just roll over for any of you Charms. Forgiving isn't the same as forgetting, but trust me, I've learned my lesson about the cycles of violence."

Moon hunched his shoulders, shifting from side to side. "I was meant to be the *savage* who killed you." When I couldn't stop my gasp, his pained gaze met mine. "My ma wished it to be her son who had the honor of striking down the last in the Charmer line, just as *she* killed your ma. If I did, then I'd be permanently freed from the Omega Training Center and if I didn't… then my brother would also be sent there as punishment."

*Woah*, they'd offered him his *freedom* for killing me: The enemy who'd otherwise grow up to enslave him through a Claim…? I knew how much Moon loved his younger brother as well.

*Then why in the witching heavens hadn't he torn out my throat? Why had he failed and let both himself and Moth suffer for a witch?*

When my red prodded Moon impatiently in the stomach, the corners of Moon's mouth twitched. "I should've known that you'd be keen to know why I chose you."

I startled. Hey, put like that, Moon had *chosen* me, before I'd ever chosen him in the Omega Training Center.

I was Moon's, as much as he was mine, and I was seriously okay with that.

I twined my fingers with Moon's, just as our magic entangled above our heads. "Whatever. You're my hero, and I don't care if that makes your wolfie ass squirm because you thought that you were the villain."

Moon's eyes widened, then he kissed me like he was making up for every time that he'd held back…as if he could devour me. At last, he drew back, panting.

"By my hide, I saw you that night," he whispered, "and you weren't a monster, you were just a cub. Plus, I could sense your magic, curling inside and singing to mine. I wouldn't become the *beast, savage,* or *killer* that the witches thought wolves were. You were crying, and I knew what it was like to lose someone you love. I couldn't become what my ma wanted, even to save myself or my brother. By my fur, do you see why I had to break Moth out of the Center though?"

My brow furrowed. "Who did you lose? Your parents were still alive then."

Moon snorted. "Right, like I'd have meant them. I told you once about my cousin, who was a fierce woman who never cared that I was an Omega. She risked gifting me the nickname Moon, even though Omegas by right aren't allowed names."

I nodded. How could I forget Moon laid out naked on the lawns of the House of Silver, gleaming under the moonlight, whilst he'd told me the creation myth of the wolf shifters and how his cousin had tucked him in each night with a kiss to the end of his nose and a stroke to his curls, before saying *Goodnight Moon*?

Now that I knew Moon had been involved with my parents' murder and had been waiting for the moment that I slaughtered him for it, I knew he'd risked even more by sharing such an intimate memory. That was the night I'd first used his true name, realized that were-wolves were more than beasts, and started to fall in love with him.

Moon's fingers squeezed my hand more tightly.

"One night, that rotten bastard Lyall overheard my cousin and how she called me by name and schooled me to rule like I was an Alpha princess, equal to my sister. My ma punished my cousin in the Hunt, murdering her just the same as she murdered your parents." His eyes blazed. "Except, I'm the one to blame that she died."

"Hey, you can't blame yourself…"

"Didn't you for *your* parents' deaths?" Moon demanded.

I winced. *Okay, he was going there.* "I was wrong."

Moon's gaze softened. "You were, but my cousin's murder drives me to endure for my people because she taught me that *anything* was worth sacrificing to be equal. Was *I* wrong?"

Broken broomsticks, Moon's rebelliousness made sense now like why he'd refused to be dominated in the Wilds or was so driven to save all the Omegas.

He'd make an epic leader…*he already did.*

I tipped up Moon's chin. "You're freaking right. We're going to make sure that every wolf has equality throughout the kingdoms by the time that we've kicked Alpha ass."

"Can I get in on the ass kicking or is it a private session?" Emperor's voice drawled.

I jumped, glancing over my shoulder.

Emperor leaned in a doorway that hadn't been there before. The wall with the butterfly wings had drawn back to reveal a passageway. Emperor looked immaculate in his suit and robes: A gleaming ruler of the sun. His hair was slicked into waves; I figured that he'd been messing around with it in front of a mirror for ages, whilst Amadeus had rolled his eyes at him.

*He was panties on fire hot and he seriously knew it.*

Emperor gave a haughty grin. Moon and I exchanged a glance, before hauling each other up and fussing at each other's curls to smooth them down and straighten our clothing.

*Nope, it didn't help.*

Moon and I looked like we'd trashed a room, had wild sexy times, and then...*almost*...killed each other, after being dragged through the emotional wringer, whereas Emperor looked like he was about to conquer the world.

Emperor arched his brow at the trampled paintings. "I like how you've chosen to display your art."

I narrowed my eyes. "It's called *Bad Wolf Gets a Spanking for Being a Cocky Dick*."

Moon snickered.

Emperor only smirked. "Promises, promises." Then he pointed into the passageway. "My father and sister have a fun gathering on the roof if you're quite finished with..." His lips quirked. "...whatever *this* is. How do you feel about a Welcome Home party, where we break the Kingdom of the Alphas from its chains?"

Moon's eyes sparkled, as he bounced on his toes and launched himself at Emperor. He cuddled him, until Emperor choked, but Emperor didn't push Moon away.

"*At last*," Moon whispered, whilst his voice was tear tinged, "at last, at last…"

Finally, Emperor pulled Moon's arms away from his neck. Then he smiled, as he stroked his thumb along the line of Moon's jaw. "I swore in our pact and I swear it now. When I return home, we shall have our freedom, and so shall our people."

"From me?" I hugged my arms around myself, and my shadows shook in pain at the thought of my Charms' rejection.

Emperor held his arm out to me, and I rushed into his hold, desperate for the feel of both him and Moon united. "I shan't ever wish to be free of you. I'm sorry, but you're stuck with my gorgeous self…forever."

"Right, make it sound like a curse," Moon grumbled.

I laughed at Emperor's outraged spluttering. "Then what will you be free of?"

Emperor's gaze became steely. "The queen and the academy, as well as the shackles of our natures." He hesitated. "I'll show you."

He clasped both Moon's hands and mine, dragging us after him into the dark of the passageway. My feet sank into the floor like it was cushioned with silk. I tripped on the steps that led upwards in the black, but

Emperor steadied me. Then suddenly, we burst out onto the roof.

The moon in the velvet sky cooled the glass of the tall tower in its beams. Sleeping butterflies perched along its corners with their wings closed like they were the crenelations.

Far beneath us, the three wolf kingdoms were spread out, as if they were no more than the map, which my aunt had shown me in the House of Seasons and boy, did that now feel like a long time ago, even if it'd been less than a month. The river wound through the Kingdom of the Gods, and the ancient woods were a dark stain beyond for the Kingdom of the Wilds. Over us all, was the great silver wall and its latticed dome. This close, its dark magic smarted mine.

In the far distance, the non-magical world of Oxford and the witches, slept like the butterflies.

All of a sudden, I had an armful of alabaster skin and midnight hair, as Amadeus launched himself onto me in sexy koala mode. He pressed his chocolate scented mouth to mine, and I moaned at the sensation of all three of my Charms — friends and rulers — united once again.

Amadeus smiled against my mouth. "I missed you, see, and now our Charmer is here to fight with us. I never let myself dream that my wish would come true but then, I'm already a king. You're our Wolf Liberator, but it'll be a fine thing to liberate Emperor's people together."

"*Hmm*, fight…?" I asked.

Amadeus released me, gripping my hand instead, and pulling me around with a twirl to face the back of the tower.

My eyes widened.

*Jesus, my whole pack was here, and it'd appear, Emperor's too.*

I hurriedly glanced at Aquilo who was even paler than he'd been when I'd last seen him. Dual and Moth held him up on either side, but all three flashed me grins like this was Christmas, I was Santa, and my shadows were particularly naughty elves. Mischief and Ramiel flew above them, wing to wing with such protective fierceness that my heart ached.

I sucked in my breath, however, when I saw that it was Emperor's dad at the front of my pack. He looked even more dashing than he had before, and his orange suit and robes were equally as immaculate as Emperor's golden ones. I flushed when Pumpkin winked at me (why was I surprised that he was flirting?), but he was also like Batman once he'd removed his mask, which was freaky as Princess Hope stood at his side, along with her gang of Alphas.

Did that mean Pumpkin had revealed his true self to the Alphas? Except, it felt more like he *ruled* the Alphas as their king, and *they* submitted to *him*.

*Had Pumpkin ruled these Alphas as an Omega in the shadows for the last century?*

Then I noticed Sterling with his arm slung around Hope's shoulders. He met my gaze and smiled without the pinched expression that haunted him around Break. I threw as much of the *if you hurt my brother, then I'll kick your ass* into my glare at Hope as I could, and she rested her head on Sterling's shoulder as she nodded with understanding.

It was comforting that Sterling had Hope as well as Emperor to look out for him and love, even though she was an Alpha. I figured that if these Alphas weren't the kind of assholes who judged Omegas and Betas, then I had no right to judge them either, and that included Hope's gang that'd definitely grown in numbers since the defeat of Break in the academy.

Yet it was still weird to see so many Alphas casually standing behind an Omega king, whilst a princess stood at his side with her mage lover. When I'd been on my knees with Aquilo in the naughty corner of the Crescent Base, watching the all-female Alphas with their screwed-up ideas of protecting Omegas by controlling them, I'd thought that Alphas had been **ONLY PROTECTORS**.

*Boy, had I been wrong.*

The new generation of Alphas who'd been kids during the first Wolf War and who'd petted Emperor like he'd been precious in the Alpha Academy, stood ready to side with *my* pack as equals: Omegas, Betas, mages, an Addict angel, god, vampire...*and witch*.

The role of protectors had oppressed these Alphas as much as the demand for Omegas to be perfect, or Betas to be pretty. Emperor had promised that tonight the shifters fought to free themselves.

Honestly, with the way that my shadows weaved around me and I rocked with restless energy at the sight of my pack together, I'd never been so ready not simply to become the Wolf Liberator again but to step back, and allow the wolves to liberate themselves.

I understood now that true heroes didn't need the cheer of crowds or some dick telling them that they were *worthy*. They were brave enough to give those they loved the space and choice to fight for themselves.

Emperor nudged my shoulder, before strolling towards Pumpkin. Moon dashed after him as fired up as me. Amadeus grinned, before pulling me after him.

Emperor was flushed with pride as he announced, "Let me introduce you to my father and sister."

"Dude, I've met them before."

Emperor's expression hardened. "You've met puppets. We've spent our lives..." His gaze darted to Amadeus and Moon. "...*all of us* have, hiding who we are. My father and sister happen to be the leaders of the resistance."

Pumpkin arched his brow. "There's no need for dramatics. I'd say that I was rather the *true king* or the secret Omega in charge. Which do you think has the best ring to it?"

"Rebel," Moon said, softly, "we're all the rebels."

Pumpkin nodded; his gaze became sharp as it assessed Moon. *Please don't let him hate Moon like his wife had...* "Well, isn't the wolf who first stole my son's heart smart? You both have good taste and my blessing, although Goddess Moon knows, Emperor has never bothered about that before."

Emperor hissed, "*Father...*"

I snorted with laughter.

Pumpkin blinked with pretend innocence. "Am I embarrassing you? Don't worry, I'm sure you cubs are getting up to all sorts of kinky—"

Hope elbowed Pumpkin. "The rebellion...?"

Pumpkin smoothed down his robes. "It's an honor to finally lead you against the queen and then to rule as your new king."

Jesus, that would make him the first ever Omega King. Yet the Alphas were as radiant with joy as Moon. *They wanted this, and okay, I respected them for changing the system, even if it'd favored them.*

"I wish my da could see this..." Moon breathed.

Emperor's voice was tight like he was holding back tears, and I didn't blame him because so was I. "He will, just as soon as my father seizes the throne. Yet we've already fought in so many ways for our king-doms, wearing masks. This time," his gaze met Moon's, before flicking to mine. "I wish to emerge from my cocoon."

I stiffened, and my shadows coiled around Amadeus, who'd edged closer in surprise.

*On the face of all the witching heavens, did Emperor truly mean to reveal that he was an Alpha...?*

Emperor tore off his robes with jerky movements, followed by his suit jacket, waistcoat, and shirt (although, he didn't go entirely crazy because he shook them out and folded them so that they didn't crease, of course).

I stared at Emperor's muscled chest and the purple butterfly that was inked on it. The butterfly's wings beat across Emperor's heart and over his shoulder. My shadows reached out to trace over its outline.

Half-naked and standing beneath the moonlight, Emperor looked commanding and dangerous. He didn't need fancy clothes to look like a prince.

*Like this, he was even more regal.*

"You'd plan a strip tease and not invite me...?" Amadeus pouted. "Why would you want to miss out on this fine behind?"

When Amadeus spun away from me, pointing his ass at Emperor (and it *was* fine), Pumpkin chuckled.

"You've convinced me, King Amadeus. But I intend to bare something other than my son's behind."

When Pumpkin nodded at Hope, she kissed my brother, before striding forward and tenderly placing her hands over the tattoo that magically bound Emperor. I flinched at the same time as Emperor because its dark magic nipped my shadows in retaliation.

The scent of liquorice wound around me. Moon's shocked intake of breath told me that I wasn't the only one who noticed it.

Pumpkin twisted to face the Alphas who were staring at Emperor in shock, as Hope drew out the tattoo that'd repressed and masked his Alpha nature since he'd been a kid. "I'm proud to announce that my son is an *Alpha*. Such status is denounced as Cursed only out of *fear*, but you all know that there are other male cubs who are born Alpha and murdered. Such atrocities shall never happen in my kingdom again. Every cub shall be celebrated and free."

My shadows fell away in shock, as the purple butterfly tattoo burst free of Emperor's chest and flew into the night sky. Emperor's chest was now flawless, apart from the branding, and I wished that I could regret that but it tied us in such an intimate way that I couldn't.

When Emperor's gaze met mine, it was filled with the type of happiness, which I'd seen in his memory and been desperate for him to rediscover. I'd known how much it'd hurt him to be bound by the tattoo. But his joy also burned with a deadly determination because freeing his kingdom was just as important to him.

"Beautiful," Mischief breathed, swooping closer to

Ramiel who clasped his hand. "I swear on my feathers, your kingdom shall be unbound as well."

Then Moon and Amadeus stalked either side of Emperor sniffing and licking up his neck.

I bit my lip. What on earth would happen now that they knew he'd been an Alpha prince, hiding amongst them all along?

Moon took another sniff of the sharp liquorice scent before shrugging. "Aye, it figures."

*Okay, seriously...what?*

Emperor gripped Moon's curls to tip back his head. "Is that your quaint idea of a joke?"

Moon settled his arms around Emperor's shoulders. "At least now I don't have to hide my need for a cuddle."

Amadeus' ruby eyes glittered. "It explains why you're so bossy."

Emperor huffed. "And you're *never* bossy, of course, your Majesty."

Amadeus smiled like it'd been a compliment. "Please call me *your Majesty* again; it sent a shiver right down my dick."

Then Emperor kissed Moon's head and winced. "How much trouble am I in for hiding this from you?"

"Fur and fangs, more than you can imagine," Moon replied with a dangerous glint that even had my own ass clenching in sympathy. "But right now, we have your rotten ma to dethrone."

I turned to see Aurora marching towards my pack and me across the roof with Break scurrying at her heels. Aurora *thwacked* her cane against the glass on each furious step.

My shadows whipped around me at the same time as Dual swaggered closer, shooting out his claws.

Dual grinned around his fangs. "It's time to tear out this world's throat."

## CHAPTER 25

Aurora's dress whipped around like the furious sun's rays, and her eyes glowed. She prowled towards Pumpkin, cracking her cane against the roof on each step.

I winced. If she thought that she'd be caning anyone, then she was one deluded soon-to-be-ex-queen.

The wolves didn't need to be controlled. They deserved to be free.

"Naughty Pumpkin," Aurora scolded as if the king was a kid, shooting him a withering look. "I indulged you and allowed you to lead a tour of the tower. I don't believe that included…whatever *this* is…on the roof, do you?"

"I don't know," Pumpkin sauntered closer to Aurora with Emperor at his side, "I'd say that the kingdom has needed *this* for a long time."

"Silly me, you've been drinking again, haven't you?" Aurora mocked. She tapped her cane against her hand like a threat. "That's ten strokes tonight for the drinking and ten for this *gathering*. There's being a hedonist, and then there's being a degenerate. It looks like you need a lesson on the difference again, my darling Pumpkin."

My hands curled into fists. *Seriously, I needed to start the ass kicking.*

When Break barked with cruel laughter, Pumpkin flushed.

*It didn't make me a wicked witch that my shadows thrilled that the **L** was still visible on Break's forehead, right?*

"That's not my name," Pumpkin said.

Aurora sighed. "You truly are drunk, aren't you? It's pitiable how you feel the need to escape into the bottle to the extent that you can't even remember your own name."

Pumpkin's eyes flashed with such rage that when he stepped towards Aurora, she recoiled. "*Alphas* gave me that name, and soon, every Omega shall have the right to take their own name."

"What nonsense," Aurora scoffed. "You're lucky even to *have* a name. Alphas make the decisions, and you've just added another ten strokes…"

Pumpkin growled, smacking the cane out of Aurora's hand. The cane rolled to the edge of the tower and tumbled over the edge.

Aurora stared at Pumpkin in shock. When Break launched herself towards Pumpkin, Emperor blocked her path, and she cringed back.

*It looked like she hadn't forgotten her defeat in the academy.*

"*I* am now making the decisions because Alphas no longer have an automatic right to rule." Pumpkin straightened his shoulders; he was as commanding as I'd ever seen Emperor be. "All shall be equal, and my name is *Sol.*"

Aurora hid her shock under scorn. "As the Alpha speaks, what an appalling attempt to make your Omega self sound wise and statesmanlike. You can't change what you are. Would you pretend that your pathetic behind is now a serious figure in our wolf world?"

"I'm a Cursed Alpha, and my father is the first true Omega King. Why do we need to be serious?" Emperor grinned at Sol, who I'd never think of as *Pumpkin* again (thank Hecate for that). "Remember that lost bet…? You have to sing a song at a time of my choosing…"

Just for a moment, Sol looked uncertain, but then his grin became as mischievous as Emperor's. "*Ah-hah!* But you lost as well. So, a song of my choice…" Emperor groaned. *This would be good.* "You know the one I sang accompanied by Hope and you on piano as entertainment at that feast, until your mother," he glanced at Aurora, "dragged me away and banned me from choosing the playlist ever again…?"

"Tell me you're not serious," Emperor deadpanned.

"Deadly," Sol smirked.

Emperor nodded, before bowing to the watching Alphas and our pack and then at Aurora and Break mockingly. Then Sol and Emperor broke into a rousing anthem of Billy Idol's "Rebel Yell".

I blinked. *Woah*, dad and son were both freaking fabulous singers, and under the moonlight, knowing that they were rocking out to punk because for the first time ever, they could be themselves in public, it made me shiver with delight, as my red streaked up into the black sky and painted it scarlet.

Dual laughed, retracting his fangs and claws. He slipped his arm around my waist and pulled me close to his warm body. My skin tingled, as he waltzed me around. Amadeus *whooped*, pirouetting with a grace that was spun out of his newfound bliss. It was as if he'd grown wings on the inside, which were shown in his dance.

Hope looped her arms around Sterling's neck, brushing his curls back, as she kissed him. He smiled against his lips, swaying to the song.

Aquilo wasn't dancing. Instead, he slumped to the floor with Moth by his side, and Okami wrapped around the arm, which Aquilo held to his chest like it was broken.

*The blood bracelet must be hurting him.*

Dual arched his brow at me, as I laid my hand on his arm to pause our dance. Moon marched across the roof to crouch by his brother and rested his hand on Aquilo's forehead. Then Moon turned to me with an anguished expression, and I understood.

Aquilo was burning up with a fever. *Would Lux keep her promise to marry us?* I had to finish Aurora's reign to save Aquilo.

All around me, Alphas chanted the song's chorus, jumping up and down to the call for rebellion and *laughing* like they were in on their new royalty's prank.

Aurora reddened, shaking. "What in the name of the furless heavens are you doing? Stop this singing. Why are you laughing?" She stamped her foot like she was a toddler who was acting out. Anger or aggression she could've coped with but wild *joy* she didn't understand. Who'd have thought that the way to defeat a conceited Queen of the Alphas was to treat her like an irrelevance? "Silence lest you be flayed!"

Mischief and Ramiel dived to land next to me. There was no way to miss that they were both ancient and powerful angels now, and I couldn't wait for some alone time with them to kiss along their feathers to their sensitive wing tips to show them how much they were loved.

Mischief eyed Dual. "May I cut in on this dance?"

Dual winked at him. "You minx, I knew that all your bluster was just to hide how much you wanted my arse."

Mischief flushed with outrage. "I rather think that it is *my* arse that *you* want."

Dual shrugged, although I didn't miss the hopeful glint in his eye. "If you come to my court, then I'm open to negotiation."

Mischief stroked down my cheek. "It's the witch who I wish to dance with and never stop." My breath caught, and my pulse fluttered in my neck. Dual released me to Mischief, who spun me to Ramiel, until I was caught between both angels. Safe in the wings of two angels was a heavenly place to be, who knew? "I berated you when we first met for who I thought you were, and later for my fears of who you'd become," Mischief whispered; his lips grazed mine, just as Ramiel traced patterns on my hands with his long fingers that made me tingle all over. "I'm proud of the woman you are now: *Our Crimson.* You've given me a new home, people, and family. At last, I perceive that a witch can keep her promises to a mage." When he kissed me, his popcorn scented magic wove around me with blinding intensity. I moaned, and missed him the moment that he pulled back. Then his whisper was so soft that I almost missed it, "I perceive that I can be loved."

I kissed him again, desperate to make certain that he believed it. I kissed him for all the times that I'd craved to cuddle him like I would've done Moon but had known that he couldn't accept it. I hated everyone who'd ever made him doubt it, and I knew that my pack would ensure that he never doubted it again.

I sucked on Mischief's lower lip, and he sighed, pulling back to feather kisses along my jaw.

"I'm honored to be your pack," Ramiel murmured.

I stroked through Ramiel's hair. "I love you too."

"Now we have that mawkishness out of the way," Mischief lifted one elegant finger, "why don't we free all of your Charms from their cocoons and transform them? I'd rather like to bring down the wall and remove the collars from my people as well." He glanced at Aquilo. "After all, we have all night for singalongs. Excuse me, what am I thinking, *of course we don't.* Tell me, am I the only mage who you love?"

*Ow, that was a serious dick punch...if I had one.*

I frowned. "Jesus, you know that I love Aquilo as well."

Ramiel traced his wing between my tits, and I shivered. "Then take that fire and use it to save him, our savior."

"Let your Charms deal with their enemies," Mischief nodded at Aurora and Break, "and our magic shall attack the wall."

"What's that got to do with the collars?" I asked.

Ramiel and Mischief wrapped their arms around me and then swooped up into the sky. I *eeped*, as they rose above the tower, hanging over the wall and almost touching the dome.

"When we were investigating Kolby's murder in the library of the House of Silver, we also sought out information on the Treaty after the first Wolf War," Ramiel murmured.

I shivered, shifting in his grip.

"Pray, what do you think we discovered about the wall?" Mischief demanded.

"It was built by the House of Silver…?" Holy hell, I understood now. My ancestors hadn't merely led the massacres that'd ended the war but they'd also designed the tech that'd oppressed the wolves afterward. I'd inherited their design skills after all, right? I paled, but what did it mean? I'd tried to take off Moon's collar but I hadn't been able to, although I had managed to manipulate it. "Aurora told me that the wall and collars are connected with the same magic."

"If you take down the wall, then you'll remove all the collars," Ramiel confirmed.

*Mage's balls, could I free every shifter?* "How?"

Mischief's magic thrummed, reaching out to mine. "Have you forgotten that after your aunt's death you're the last of your line here in Oxford? It's interesting that you still do not fathom how potent your magic is. If you wish to pull down this wall, then you can."

My eyes widened, and my breath became ragged. I stared out at the city of Oxford beyond the wall. My shadows surged towards the silver, licking around its edges. Yet should I take down the one thing that was stopping the werewolves from attacking the witches and non-magicals?

Mischief's gaze hardened. "Don't you trust the shifters or perhaps, you trust that you know what's best for others better than they know themselves? There's a name for that and it's *tyranny*. I've fought against those who'd imprison and curtail freedom my entire life because they won't *trust*. Oh, here's an idea, how about being different?"

Finally, I grinned. "*Hmm*, then here's to being different."

A crimson tide flooded from me over the wall and then in waves over the dome that spread across the kingdom, until it was no longer silver but swelling red.

I clenched my jaw against the sting of dark magic. My House had built this prison, and I could undo it, one flowing thread at a time. When I tugged, the wall wavered, yet it didn't break.

"I should've savaged you at birth. Why couldn't you have been born a girl?" Aurora howled over the song.

I glanced away from the wall, as Aurora prowled towards Emperor.

Moon glanced up, catching my eye.

Emperor had never been allowed to run as a werewolf free under the moonlight because he was a male Alpha. It was seriously time that his asshole mom saw how amazing her son truly was.

When Moon nodded, I took that for all the permission I needed, and slipped my shadows from the wall to my Charms' collars, instead. Moon's magic wove out as well, into his own collar, then Amadeus', and finally Emperors'. They were joined in silver rainbows.

Sol stopped singing in shock, and my pack and the Alphas stilled to watch.

All three Charms arched and howled, transforming in sprays of silver into their wolf forms: white, gray, and *black.*

Emperor threw back his head and howled. His midnight fur was long and glimmered; his eyes glowed. He was large with a powerful tail. He was everything that I'd once feared, but now he was all that I loved.

*He was freaking magnificent.*

I pressed my lips together to stop myself from bursting into tears or laughter because at long last, *Emperor had emerged from his cocoon.*

Then Aurora slow clapped, even as she stalked towards Emperor. "Congratulations, my Cursed cub. Now everyone can see how *ugly* you are."

*The dick…*

I growled, and my heart ached for Emperor.

Okami snarled, darting to bite Aurora's nose. Aurora yelped, batting at him, as he savaged her in full on warrior mode. My three Charms, shoulder to shoulder, prowled after her, pinning her to the edge of the tower. When Break attempted to slash at them, Sterling bit his lip, before steeling himself and shooting sparks into her.

Break stared at him in shock like she'd never expected that a beaten dog could bite back, but right now, he was biting her ass.

Break staggered next to Aurora. "Goddess Moon! Do your duty," she snarled at the Alphas, "protect your ruler."

Sol's face was hard. "They are."

My eyes fluttered, as I whispered my red into the butterflies, gently waking them. I could use my power to control animals, but this time, I only *freed* them from Aurora, who'd held them to this tower. The Emperor butterflies rose up in a purple cloud that was both stunning and deadly.

*If you screwed with nature, it screwed with you. I'd learned that.*

Aurora wailed, as she was lifted flailing into the air next to Break above the tower that she'd reigned over. Below, my Charms stood proudly next to Sol. Then the swarm of butterflies parted like the beating of giant wings, and dropped the two asshole Alphas off the tower.

I shuddered at their screams as they fell.

"I believe that you can break Wolf Kingdom free," Ramiel urged. "Please believe in yourself now."

That was just a fancy way to say that I could *wreck impossible's ass,* right?

"I am a god," Mischief whispered, and I shivered at his heat and desire that coursed through me like the vibrations of his magic. "The witches imagined that they could trap the power of my Gateways, but I share them only with those who've earned the right...and who I love. Would you like to feel what it's like to topple worlds?"

Mischief's magic zinged through mine with an electric burst that took away my breath. My shadows tinged to silver before they broke against the wall like water against a dam. The wall groaned its death throes. Then it began to melt. Yet as it did, my eyes widened because what if the dome crashed down on the wolves below, just like Zetta had tried to drown my Charms in silver in the **DISCPLINE CELLAR**?

My family's motto ran through my head:

*Charm the wolves. Control the crimson tide.*

What if I'd always been meant to be the Wolf Charmer who didn't free the werewolves but finished the job started by my great-grandmother to exterminate them? Was it my destiny as the last of the Wolf Charmers to end the wolves as well?

Screw destiny, legacy, and tradition. I was Crimson and the Wolf Liberator.

If this wall thought that it could trick me into harming my wolves, then it didn't know just how determined my witchy ass could be.

I called out to Aquilo, "Time to show your newly grown balls."

*Okay, that had come out wrong.*

Mischief gave a delighted laugh, but Aquilo nodded, raising to his knees.

Holy hell, either he'd wriggle out of his pants and show everyone his gorgeous dick and balls, or…

Moth and Dual supported Aquilo, as he leaned on them, before raising his shaking hand. A whirlwind built on his palm, before twirling out and catching the silver as it melted.

I shuddered as I was caught in the thrill of Mischief's magic, the tumbling silver rain, and the gusting wind that trapped it.

*Around, and around, and around…*

The wall and dome across the entire Wolf Kingdom had melted to silver. It was held in Aquilo's thrall. My pack and the Alphas on the roof watched in awe.

I seriously hoped that Aquilo understood how powerful he was now. His hair whipped back, and his eyes flashed. Did I look the same combination of hot and masterful when I wove *my* magic?

When I nodded towards the Thames, Aquilo's face lit with understanding. He dashed the silver into the river, just as once my Charmer ancestors had drowned the wolves in the same waters, until it became nothing but a silvery tongue beneath the moonlight.

Then every wolves' collar opened and fell to the ground.

Euphoria washed through me, and my eyes gleamed with tears.

The shifters were free. Black cats and cauldrons, *my pack were free.*

The Alphas *whooped* and cheered, dancing around Sol and Hope. They rubbed their necks with wonder.

Holy hell, they'd never been able to touch their throats before. What would it feel like to have your body ruled like that? Yet now, they'd been freed, and I wouldn't be a tyrant. I knew that what happened next wouldn't be easy. But I couldn't make those choices for them.

In the silence, Mischief and Ramiel flew me back to the roof, lightly landing. My Charms bounded over to me, rubbing against me. I grinned, hugging them and stroking through their fur. They fell over each other in a snuggle fest of joy.

Then they started to lick.

"Hey, wolfie cuddles are okay," I giggled, "but what is it with the licking?"

Sterling wound his arms around Hope, before winking at me. "I'd get used to that, sister, it's a wolf thing."

Then Aquilo groaned and doubled over, clutching his arm.

"Why did you trust your sister after all that's she done to you?" Dual brushed Aquilo's hair out of his eyes, kneeling next to him. He rested his hand on the back of Aquilo's neck in a gesture that was both possessive and tender. "She'll never marry you to our witch, Blue Eyes."

*Our witch?*

It was as possessive as Dual's hand on Aquilo's neck, and I was so not analyzing why it sent warmth curling through me.

I rushed to Aquilo with my Charms at my side who whined in distress. Okami howled, biting my curls to hitch a ride like he was my silky bridal veil.

*Please…please…let Lux not break her word.*

But then, she was a dickhead.

I dropped to my knees next to Aquilo like we were kneeling before an altar. Except, one with three wolves snuggling their furry asses around us.

I stroked Aquilo's pale cheek. "Dude, you were epic."

He tried to smile, but it was forced through his pain. The blood bracelet pulsed scarlet; tendrils wound up his forearm.

"It's your Charms and the resistance fighters who deserve your admiration." *How had I once missed the kindness behind Aquilo's cold mask?* "I've dreamed of the day that the wolves would be free, and when I wouldn't have to hurt them. Yet the mages are still trapped in so many ways. Did I not attempt to help them? Yet it's not enough." Aquilo's voice hitched, and he gritted his teeth against a wave of pain. "My cousin, Fox, was a mage who was funny, kind…and helped me to understand why I should help the wolves." His gaze darkened. "Yet he's been sent to terrible punishment at the Rebel Academy. I'd give anything to save him. Without this bond, even if it kills me, *that would've been me*. I can't regret that you asked me to marry you. I never shall."

I stiffened because Aquilo would rather die under his magical engagement, than have been sent away to this Rebel Academy with his cousin.

My shadows seethed. I'd already torn down one world; I could tear down this academy.

"I promise," I murmured, "we'll rescue your cousin. But first, I'm not losing you. We're getting married, so suck it up."

"My, such a romantic," Lux's cool voice wound out of the darkness.

Then with a whiff of coppery blood magic, Lux appeared in front of Aquilo and me. Her black dress was grander than before, like it'd been dipped in crushed obsidian, and I could sense the raw power flowing through her.

She was dicking around with proving that she was now Head of the Covens.

"How romantic are my shadows up your ass?" *Okay, even my shadows cringed at how that sounded.* I flushed. "Vows, followed by drunk guests and our Honeymoon… I seriously don't give a witch's tit, as long as Aquilo stops shivering in agony."

"Agreed without the crudity and with far more class." Lux clicked her fingers and black candles materialized in the air, hovering around us.

Huh, they were beautiful in a dark witch kind of way. Why did I get the feeling that confetti and cake weren't going to feature in my wedding?

When Take That's earnest pop song "How Deep Is Your Love" struck up, I rolled my eyes.

"Was this one of Lux's phases as well?" I muttered.

Aquilo grinned. "She snogged her Gary Barlow doll every night. You should've heard her squeal when Take That broke up and—"

"Do you wish to marry tonight, brother?" Lux snapped.

Aquilo edged closer to me. "With all my heart."

Lux's expression gentled, before she snatched both our wrists.

"*Woah*, don't we need..." I flailed, as Mischief and Ramiel strolled behind to watch. "...I mean, we haven't even got rings or..."

Lux's eyes darkened. "How did one who knows so little of witch tradition best the other covens?"

"She has an astounding arse," Dual offered, "and sometimes you need to be the outsider to create change."

Lux sighed, then she pointed at the watching wolves. "*Witnesses*," she sneered, before waving at Dual, "a *daddy* to give Aquilo away."

"Hey," Dual protested, before grinning. "Actually, I retract my protest."

Then Lux waved at Mischief and Ramiel. "And your two pretty bridesmaids."

Mischief flapped his wings in outrage. "My protest most certainly stands."

Lux rubbed her fingers together and spun a black thread that sparkled when the light hit it. The magic charmed into the thread was powerful; I could feel it warming across my skin but in a way that made my shadows reach for it.

Then she ordered, "Cross your arms and then hold hands."

I turned to Aquilo and matched him, crossing my arms and clasping his cold hands. *Woah, that looked like the infinity symbol.* I figured that was the point.

My crimson slipped down Aquilo's arms, aching to be joined with him as well.

"With this thread I bind you: two as one. Let it never break." When Lux wove the thread three times around our wrists, the blood bracelet and the painful tendrils up Aquilo's arms faded, as our new marriage bond settled into place, instead.

I'd expected the black thread to disappear, but it etched itself into my wrist like a tattoo.

Aquilo glanced at me warily as if he thought that I'd be upset about the ink, but I snatched him and kissed him because I wasn't missing out on my wedding kiss, right?

My pack cheered, before my Charms tumbled us over, howling and licking down my neck. Aquilo chuckled, before Dual demanded *his* marriage kiss as well, and then there was a flurry of feathers and my angels joined us.

Holy hell, what would my Honeymoon be like? I wasn't a demanding witch but I was putting in my order for Champagne and chocolate sauce now…

Aquilo's bright gaze caught mine, as he giggled under the cuddle attack of my Charms. "Control your wolves, *Mrs* Charmer."

I shivered like we were on Honeymoon, and he'd just thrust into me for the first time (and boy, I was excited about that). "I'm sorry, *Mr* Charmer, but no one controls my wolves anymore."

Aquilo shivered like hearing *Mr Charmer* had fast-forwarded him to the same moment on our wedding night.

He grinned. "Did I not make it clear? When I married you, I also married your wolves, angels, and god. We're pack, and I love you all."

Less than a month ago, I'd returned to England to be gifted my Charms, but *they'd* gifted *me* a new future, love, and family.

I'd chosen to be bound to Crimson's pack and I'd never stop loving and protecting them, just as they'd never stop loving me. Our Honeymoon would be epic, but after that we still had the mages to rescue from the Rebel Academy and the witch and wolf worlds to bring into the dawn.

Tonight, I'd love my pack who I'd once thought were nothing but beasts with beautiful faces. Tomorrow, I'd help teach the witch world the truth.

When my Charms howled to the moon, I howled with them.

THE END...FOR NOW

Continue the adventures of Aquilo's mage cousin, Fox, in **REBEL ACADEMY: CRAVE** in Book One of the Wickedly Charmed Series **NOW**
https://rosemaryajohns.com

Thanks for reading **Only Protector Alphas**! If you enjoyed reading this book, **please consider leaving a review on Amazon.** Your support is really important to us authors. Plus, I love hearing from my readers! Thanks, you're awesome!

**Rebel Werewolves** with its sinful shifters has been a series that I've planned for five years. I'm so excited that you've shared this journey with me!

The idea of the coven-run college for supernatural bad boys — **Rebel Academy** — has been with me for almost as long.

At the heart of the paranormal prison is the wickedest witch of them all. It's a twist on academies like you've never seen before. I can't wait for you to discover the ghost witch who haunts Oxford's secret college and her delicious immortals (including Loki's son).

You're total stars for your recommendations, word of mouth, and reviews because it's how my books reach new readers. I'm truly grateful to you. Even a single line review raises the series' visibility.

Thanks, you're awesome - my Rebel family :)

Rebel here, yeah?

Rosemary A Johns

# BECOME A REBEL

Sign up to Rosemary A Johns' Rebel Newsletter for two FREE novellas. Also, these special perks: promotions, discounts, and news of hot releases before anyone else. **Become a Rebel today by joining Rosemary's Rebels Group on Facebook!**

REBEL ACADEMY

## DISCOVER THE SECRETS OF THE REBEL ACADEMY TODAY!

**Nothing is more deadly than secrets…**

…and mine could bring this mysterious academy to its knees.

Many have forgotten my name. Magenta: the wicked witch whose dark magic created the Rebel Academy — a magic paranormal prison for supernatural bad boys. But now I'm back and eager to claim the love and life that was stolen from me, even if first I have to survive the start of term.

My enemies trapped me as a ghost on the very cursed grounds that I helped to create. Yet thanks to three deliciously tempting immortals, I've been awakened. One is a beautiful incubus who hungers for pleasure. The next a gorgeous shifter-mage who always senses the truth but enjoys his lies far more. Oh, and who could ever forget Loki's hot trickster son?

Why choose between these sexy delinquents when having them all is such sinful fun?

The immortals risked everything to free me, and I'll stop at nothing to protect them from the elitist princes who rule the reform school. Will my bond with the magical students and new friendships be enough to battle the dangerous rivalries, as well as the cruel professors' schemes?

Or will I be forced back into the darkness…

…and left to fade away?

**DISCOVER THE SECRETS OF THE REBEL ACADEMY…**

The vampire's fangs shot out, and I shuddered, as he grazed them along my neck.

"I love you, Violet." Ash's pupils were blown, and his gaze was desperate. "I know that you don't want my protection." He kissed my neck; his large hands stroked up my spine. "But just once…pretend. I'm not a hero but I could be—"

"I don't need to pretend." I caressed Ash's bare chest, and his wings fluttered.

When my fingers moved towards the waistband of Ash's jeans, however, his breath hitched.

"How can you touch me?" He rested his head on my shoulder. "When you know what I am?"

"You're mine." If Lucifer killed us tonight, at least we died claimed and together. "You're family and the Brigadier. No one can take that away."

I'd show Ash just how much I craved to touch.

I pushed open the button on his jeans, and although his breathing became harsh, he didn't stop me this time.

I slid my hand lower again…

Binge-read the addictive **REBEL ANGELS: THE COMPLETE SERIES** by the USA Today bestselling author Rosemary A Johns TODAY for FREE with Kindle Unlimited.

**Grab this magical, dark, and sizzling hot vampire and angel Romance now!**

# APPENDIX ONE: OXFORD WITCH COVENS

## House of Silver

Crimson Tide, the Wolf Charmer

Zetta and Daniel, Crimson's parents

Crimson's legendary great-grandmother

Sterling, Crimson's brother

## House of Seasons

Stella, Crimson's aunt and leader of Oxford's covens

## House of Blood

Ivy, the Blood Witch, mother to the twins

Lux, twins with Aquilo

Aquilo, a mage

## WOLF SHIFTERS

Ambassador, Stella's wolf

Okami, magical wolf created by Crimson

## SUPERNATURALS

Mischief, (god, mage, angel name 'Zophia', from the Realm of the Seraphim)

Ramiel, Addict angel

'Zetta', magical essence of past Wolf Charmers, ward in House of Silver

Dual, Duke of Oxford's vampire court and Fallen angel

Digby, Dual's son

Jax, Dark Fae and 'mongrel'.

## ACADEMIES

**Rebel Academy**, where 'bad' supernaturals are sent

Alpha Academy, where Alphas are schooled

Omega Training Center, where Omegas are trained

Re-education Center, where rebellious Omegas are 'corrected'

# APPENDIX THREE: WOLF KINGDOMS

## Kingdom of the Wilds

Omega Prince Moon (Moon Child) – First Charm

Omega Moth, Moon's brother

Queen Rhona

Princess Morag

Countess Lyall

## Kingdom of the Gods

Beta Prince Amadeus (half incubus) - Second Charm

Queen Banan

Princess Vala

## Kingdom of the Alphas

Alpha Prince Emperor ('Cursed Alpha') – Third Charm

Omega Pumpkin/Sol, Emperor's father

Queen Aurora
Princess Hope
Dame Break

## ABOUT THE AUTHOR

ROSEMARY A JOHNS is a USA Today bestselling and award-winning fantasy author, music fanatic, and paranormal anti-hero addict. She writes sexy angels and werewolves, savage vampires, and epic battles.

Winner of the Silver Award in the National Wishing Shelf Book Awards. Finalist in the IAN Book of the Year Awards. Runner-up in the Best Fantasy Book of the Year, Reality Bites Book Awards. Honorable Mention in the Readers' Favorite Book Awards.
    Shortlisted in the International Rubery Book Awards.

Rosemary is also a traditionally published short story writer. She studied history at Oxford University and ran her own theater company. She's always been a rebel…

Want to read more and stay up to date on Rosemary's newest releases? Sign up for her *VIP* Rebel Newsletter and grab two FREE novellas!

**Have you read all the series in the Rebel Verse by Rosemary A Johns?**

Rebel Angels
Rebel Academy
Rebel Legends
Rebel Vampires
Rebel Werewolves

**Read More from Rosemary A Johns**
Website: https://rosemaryajohns.com
BookBub: https://www.bookbub.com/authors/rosemary-a-johns
Facebook: https://www.facebook.com/RosemaryAnnJohns
Twitter: @RosemaryAJohns
**Become a Rebel today by joining Rosemary's Rebels Group on Facebook!**

Printed in Great Britain
by Amazon